*Martine Bailey*

# An Appetite for Violets

HODDER

First published in Great Britain in 2014 by Hodder & Stoughton
An Hachette UK company

First published in paperback in 2015

1

Typeset by Hewer Text UK Ltd, Edinburgh
Printed and bound by Clays Ltd, St Ives plc

Hodder & Stoughton policy is to use papers that are natural, renewable
and recyclable products and made from wood grown in sustainable
forests. The logging and manufacturing processes are expected to
conform to the environmental regulations of the country of origin.

Hodder & Stoughton Ltd
338 Euston Road
London NW1 3BH

www.hodder.co.uk

*Praise for* AN APPETITE FOR VIOLETS

'Martine Bailey writes with such easy, compelling grace, and in a fascinating new genre - best described as culinary gothic. I was hooked and enraptured.'
*Fay Weldon*

'An absolutely delicious novel; I savoured every page.'
*Imogen Robertson, author of Instruments of Darkness*

'I adored this novel.'
*Maria McCann, bestselling author of The Wilding*

'A tour de force . . . full of twists and turns with marvellous moments of drama and some super revelations I never saw coming! I'd recommend this novel to anyone wanting an insight into the period and a jolly good read with satisfying and very real depths.'
*Rebecca Mascull, author of The Visitors*

'It's not often that I read a book as voraciously as this . . . I just had to know how this story of deception, intrigue and passion ended.'
*S D Sykes, author of Plague Land*

'The recipes, the voices, the places, the atmosphere and tension – it was all so high-coloured and vivid I felt it was playing out in front of my eyes.'
*Lucy Dillon, author of A Hundred Pieces of Me*

'A hugely evocative novel that transported me right back to 18th Century Europe. *An Appetite for Violets* is filled with sensuous food writing and Biddy has such a distinctive voice.'
*Sarah Vaughan, author of The Art of Baking Blind*

*To my two great-grandmothers,*
*Ada Hilton, famed for her wedding cakes,*
*and Gertrude Hill,*
*remembered for her fine pies and a tea kettle*
*forever boiling on the fire.*

# I

## Villa Ombrosa

*Tuscany, Italy*
*Low Sunday, April 1773*

As Kitt tramped on alone towards the villa, unease clung to him like the rancid sweat that soaked his shirt. He was weak-headed, sure enough, after five days of throwing up over the boat rail. At Leghorn, his port of arrival in Italy, he had disdained the other disembarking English passengers. They had jostled and jawed in gaudy Paris costumes, their ruddy faces peering into Mr Nugent's *Grand Tour*. While they dawdled over vast portmanteaus, he had pushed past them with only a saddlebag slapping his hips. He was no mere tourist, Kitt told himself. He was here to hunt down Carinna, not follow some vulgar Itinerary.

Yet, at eighteen years old, Italy was entirely unknown to him. Uncertainly, he had hired the first unshaven ruffian who grasped his sleeve and offered himself as a guide. Soon he regretted that attempt at swagger: at Lucca, the rogue had urged him to enter a squalid inn to meet his purported *bellissima* sister. By then Kitt understood he was very far from his usual Covent Garden haunts. No doubt a gang of sharpers, or even cut-throats, waited inside. The coin of dismissal he had tossed at the scoundrel lost him use of the horse, but later he blessed Lady Fortune for that.

There had been no news from Carinna since her last letter, the letter he kept tucked against his ribs. He knew the words by heart and worried them afresh, squinting at the bleached ribbon of road she had ridden more than six weeks before him:

> *7th March 1773*
> *Villa Ombrosa*

*My Dearest Kitt,*
> *I have at last arrived and am mighty glad to have the key to our uncle's villa. Trust your sister, for all will turn out well in time.*

3

*Forgive my evasions – if only clocks would run faster we might soon be together again and all our troubles over. I can say no more, for I cannot trust the truth to a post that may be tampered with.*

    *Your sister,*

    *Carinna*

When he had first read her letter he had felt only mild alarm. What was this truth she concealed, and who did she imagine would open her post? He had persuaded himself he could do nothing, suffering as he was from his usual lack of funds. Then, when his letters begging for news had remained unanswered for four, then five weeks, his agitation had heightened to a sort of madness, and he had pawned his best coat and set off without a word to any other soul. He had written to her from Marseilles, assuring her he would arrive on Easter Sunday. But that damned boat had first been delayed by the weather and then blown about like a cork on the heaving ocean. All had been against him. Yet – how had it taken him six weeks?

The iron gates of the villa yielded with a rusty squawk and Kitt glimpsed the white bulk of the building through the avenue of lime trees. The sun was sinking, and bands of honeyed light fell between the trees as his boots crunched loudly across the gravel. A sudden gust rose and lifted the branches with a hiss like a hidden torrent. Even the evening breeze was as warm as an animal's breath.

It was a decent property, this retreat of their uncle's. Though the devil only knew what vice Uncle Quentin had purchased it for, so far from English eyes. He would certainly stay awhile, Kitt mused, as the broad house with its leprous statues, terrace and lawns came into view. Whatever Carinna was running from, this was a comfortable bolthole. He revived to picture her at first overjoyed to see him, then sympathetic as she heard the account of his damnable journey. They must still be at siesta, he thought. A clever notion that, however foreign. Later he would rest on a cool pillow to ease his throbbing head. Before supper he would bathe, have the servants clean his clothes, and drift away from all his burden of cares in luxurious sleep.

'Carinna?' He called her name into the stillness, but only a shower of paper-dry leaves sighed in reply. Mounting the terrace he found inviting chairs and cushions bleached by many seasons of sunshine. The door stood ajar.

He entered the hall's deep shadow. 'Carinna,' he demanded, blinking in the murky coolness. 'Carinna? I am here.'

He was answered by silence. Ah, not quite. The jingle of a silvery bell reached him from the rear of the house. Someone was at home. Opening his mouth to call again, he found his tongue was suddenly too dry to speak. There was a new sound that was oddly irregular and – inhuman. A *clink*, and claw-like tapping. And then that tinkling of a doll-like bell. With silent care he pushed the door open and passed into the first room. It was empty. There were shabby furnishings: a sofa, gilded mirror, and ticking clock. Standing on the hearthrug Kitt listened acutely, all the time watching the gaping door that led to the back of the house. Now he could hear no sound save a low irregular buzzing. It was only then, as he inhaled sharply, that he noticed the stench: a gross, high stink that recollected the putrid bowels of the ship from which he had just escaped. He gagged and buried his mouth in his linen. In the act of dropping his head, he had only one moment to comprehend a small demonic being rushing across the floor towards him. With a cry he kicked out hard with his riding boot. The creature screeched with pain and then retreated, whimpering backwards against the sofa.

'Bengo!'

By Christ, it was Carinna's little pug, a dog no larger than a rat, with tinder-stick legs and doe eyes. Around his neck was a silver collar hung with a tiny bell.

Crouching, he whispered the dog's name and stretched out his hand to pet its trembling back. 'Where is she, little fellow?'

The dog's eyes flickered with suspicion, his worm's tail twitched. Crusty yellow vomit hung from his snout.

Holding his kerchief to his mouth, Kitt hesitated. He would have wagered that death lay in this house. He steeled himself to go into the back room and confront what he had travelled so far to find.

Before him stretched a table laden for a feast. Yet no guests sat on the velvet chairs. No bodies slumped across the cloth. A vast lump of meat had place of honour, rippling as if alive with a swarm of steel-blue flies. The tarts standing on gilded china were blotched grey with powdered mould; the bread sprouted puffy hairs of creeping fungus. A pyramid of sweetmeats had collapsed. Grapes had wrinkled into puckered raisins. Groping backwards, he saw a decanter of wine on the sideboard and reached out instinctively for a restorative gulp. Yet as his hand clutched the glass, a bulbous fly crawled over the rim and buzzed towards his face. Slapping it away, he saw the scene with greater clarity: pearly maggots wriggled amongst dishes of mould. The white cloth was smeared with trails of hardened dog excrement. On the instant he fled back to the hall and the gaping entrance door, where he gasped fresh air in greedy mouthfuls.

The air revived Kitt a little, though it brought no peace to his racketing head. Sweat broke out on his face. Where the devil were the servants? As furtive as a snake, Bengo slinked between his boots and bolted for the undergrowth. That dog had the right notion, Kitt decided. Carinna was not here. Something had happened. His youthful loathing of petty laws and officials made him keen to run away, too. Pretend you were never here, his instincts whispered. Rapidly he reviewed his route: he had kept his destination secret. He could be far from here by midnight. Yet, if he left now, he would never know Carinna's fate. She might be upstairs. She might have left a message. Christ be damned, he would have to go back inside.

Turning on his heels he made a rapid tour of the lower rooms. He found a fussy sitting room with signs of occupation by a housekeeper or other damned hireling. Then, a kitchen still in disarray from preparations for the meal. Broken cakes on the table cast up a nauseous fragrance. The scent fleetingly recollected lilies at a funeral. All the downstairs were deserted. He had to pause at the gaping front door once again to refresh his lungs. If she is here, he thought, alive or dead, I must go upstairs and find her.

The stairs groaned as he climbed. He could give no name to what he feared. For which untimely guests was that sickening banquet laid out? And why would Carinna abandon Bengo? Reaching the first floor he entered the lesser rooms and found them all empty. Then he found a dressing room with water growing putrid in a ewer. Finally, he faced a closed door with a brass handle. He guessed it was the finest room, the one with broad windows above the villa's entrance. He grasped the handle and swung it open.

'Carinna!' For an instant he believed he had found her. She stood with her back to him in a ruffled gown of rosy silk, quite motionless in the centre of the room. Approaching, his sight cleared: the gown was hanging on a wooden dressing stand, the face a globe of wood on which Carinna's hat was hung, the whole display a cruel masquerade. He strode up to the figure and gaped at it in bafflement. Carinna's familiar scent of violets rose from the gown, tantalising him with her presence. In frustration, he hit out at the mocking skeleton of wood and sent the head crashing to the ground. That it was a jest intended to torment himself he knew for certain when he saw his own letter tucked deep in the gown's bodice. It bore the imprint of his broken seal. He had himself written it from Marseilles, barely a week past. He felt like a lunatic; brain-choked and baffled.

Yet in dislodging the letter something else had clattered out onto the floor – the Mawton Rose. It was the ruby belonging to that old fumbler Sir Geoffrey, a jewel so famed for its fierce scarlet fire that it was valued at more than one thousand pounds. So she *had* taken it, the clever puss. Greedily, he pocketed the Rose and his own crumpled letter. Finally, his mind lurched to the only possible conclusion. Carinna might have left Bengo behind if she were ill or crazed or forced by a pistol. But to abandon a jewel worth a fortune? He knew in his blood that Carinna was dead.

He could not bear another moment in that mocking house. In a tumbling descent he fled down the stairs, through the trees and gates and back to the lonely road. Should he find some authority, he wondered? Make a report? No, no. He had the Rose – why surrender that to some buffoon of a magistrate? His need was greater than theirs. Besides, if Carinna was dead he was her closest living family. And he needed cash so badly. It was providence. Oh, but Carinna was gone. He sensed he was only a few desperate days too late.

Behind him a twig snapped loudly. Crying out in anguish, Kitt swivelled as he ran, half stumbling but fearing to halt and investigate. Deep shadows loomed about him now; the undergrowth on each side of the track rose like the walls of a labyrinth, far taller than he remembered. Footsteps rustled behind him. Had they seen him? God damn that he had lingered! He ran faster, his fingers clutching at sharp briars, his boots stumbling. Why had he come here? It was almost dark; he would be hunted through the night.

Then the jingle of a silver bell unmasked his pursuer. It was only that squashed-snout lapdog Bengo, fearful of being left behind.

'Be off, damn you,' he shouted at the pale smudge of conscience that followed him. Yet still it trailed behind him over each wearisome furlong. Every few minutes he believed he had outrun the dog, only to hear, once again, its patter and jingle. Then at last he saw the huddled rooftops of a village and heard the tolling of an evening bell. Finally, a wagon crossed his path drawn by a plodding donkey. In desperate tones Kitt hailed the driver. '*Taverna. Presto,*' he urged, shoving a coin at the startled man. Inside the tented cart a gaggle of dark faces peered at him in inquisitive silence.

He ached for the hot sting of spirits against his throat. Cards, a fine bottle, the baize table; that was his realm. Fingering the Rose inside his pocket he traced its cold angles and wondered how quickly he might turn it into cash. He needed to find a town where a bed and brandy were cheap, and questions were few. Rocked by the wagon, he felt suddenly as vacant as air, as if the uncertain attempt at manhood that was Kitt Tyrone had vanished from the earth along with his sister. Until that day he had smouldered with fury at his life's injustices, but now only fitful ashes of fear fluttered at his core.

He dropped his eyes into his grimy fists. He could not rub from his inner eye that final image of the dog. It haunted him again – indeed, it continued to patter at his heels all his life. Especially when fatigued, when alone, or most horribly, when passing from waking to sleep, he heard that whimpering and those scurrying short steps. Even when he had finally given up hope of finding her and wanted only the oblivion of an empty bottle, it still followed him. Long after all the *lire* from pawning the Rose had disappeared into quick Italian fingers, that pale shadow hobbled after him through the darkness. To his desperate end he could not stop himself from picturing that dog's jingling journey, backwards down the white road, once again to face the gaping gates and that mouldering feast.

*A half year earlier*

# II

## The Kitchen, Mawton Hall

*Being the day before Souling Night, 1772*
*Biddy Leigh, her journal*

## ~ My Best Receipt for Taffety Tart ~

Lay down a peck of flour and work it up with six pound of
butter and four eggs and salt and cold water. Roll and fill
with pippins and quinces and sweet spice and lemon peel as
much as delights. Sweet spice is cloves, mace, nutmeg, cinnamon, sugar & salt. Close the pie and strew with sugar. Bake
till well enough.

*Martha Garland her best receipt writ*
*on a scrap of parcel paper, 1751*

Every cook knows it's a rare day when you have all the parts of the perfect dish. But that day back at Mawton I had everything I needed: white fleshed pippins, pink quince, and a cinnamon stick that smelled like a breeze from the Indies. My flour was clean, my butter as yellow as a buttercup. It's not enough, mind you, to have only the makings of a dish. There's the receipt honed through the ages, written down in precious ink. And beyond that is the cook, for only she can judge how much stirring is enough, or have the light fingers to rub a pastry well. It's no common event, that gathering of all the parts that make the perfect dish.

It makes me think that's how it is for us servants. No one pays you much heed; mostly you're invisible as furniture. Yet you overhear a conversation here, and add a little gossip there. A writing desk lies open and you cannot help but read a paper. Then you find something, something you should not have found. It's not so very often, with your servants' broken view, that you can draw all the ingredients together. And it's a rare day when all the parts combine in one story, and the chief of those parts is you.

So that is where I'll start this tale, on that October baking day. I was making taffety tarts that afternoon in the kitchen at Mawton, as the sunlight flittered across the whitewashed walls and the last roses nodded at the window. I'll begin with a confession, mind. I'd crept into Mrs Garland's room when she wasn't there and secretly copied out her best receipt. It's no wonder our old cook used to say I was as crafty as a jackdaw. 'Your quick eyes miss nothing, Biddy Leigh,' she always said, shaking her head, but laughing. I'd kept my scrap of paper secret all year long and often pondered how to better it. That baking day was the third day Mrs G had shut herself away in the stillroom, dosing herself with medicinal waters. As I rolled the pastry I lived out a fancy I had nourished since the first apple blossom pinked in May – the making of the perfect dish.

Next day was All Hallows Eve, or Souling Night as we called it, and all our neighbours would gather for Old Ned's cider and Mrs Garland's Soul Cakes. After the stablemen acted out the Souling play, the unmarried maids would have a lark, guessing their husband's name from apple parings thrown over their shoulders. So what better night, I thought, for Jem to announce our wedding? At the ripe age of twenty-two years, the uncertainties of maidenhood were soon to pass me by. Crimping my tarts, I passed into that forgetfulness that is a most delightful way of being. My fingers scattered flour and my elbows spun the rolling pin along the slab. Unrolling before my eyes were scenes of triumph: of me and Jem leading a cheery procession to the chapel, posies of flowers in my hand and pinned to Jem's blue jacket. In my head I turned over the makings of my Bride Cake that sat in secret in the larder – ah, wouldn't that be the richest, most hotly spiced delight?

And all the bitter maidens who put it underneath their pillows would be sorrowing to think that Jem was finally taken, bound and married off to me.

The only sour note that struck was the sudden bang-slapping of a bird against the windowpane. It was a robin redbreast pecking at the glass, his wings beating in a frenzy.

'Scarper,' I shouted, flapping my hands about. What was it he warned me of, that he stared so hard and tapped all in a frenzy?

'Is it a robin?' Teg had crept in from the scullery and the fear I felt was echoed in her gawping tones. 'He be a messenger. 'Tis a famous omen. Death be coming here.'

'That's enough of your claptrap,' I snapped back. Risking breaking the glass, I lifted a ladle and knocked it against the pane so hard that the bird flew off on the instant.

'You see. He were only a fledgling tricked by the glass. If you've finished the apples there are fowls to pluck.'

Teg cast me a poisonous glance and swore she had not finished half her chores. I'm not daft, I knew our scullery maid would be off to tell her gossips what a Miss Toity that Biddy Leigh was and how this omen must herald my bad end. She wishes it true, I thought, as I checked the oven's heat with a sizzle of spit. She is jealous and rankles under every command I give her. But it was only a gormless fledgling. No person who knew their ABC would give a farthing for such a sign.

The tarts were scarcely in the oven when the noise startled me. A right how-row it was: hollering grooms, clattering gates, dogs yelping and barking. Then a fancy hired carriage rolled right inside our yard, the team of horses snorting, the heavy harnesses creaking and jingling. My first thought was, what on earth was I to feed any company with? We had a good stock of provender for the servants, but nowt for the likes of Sir Geoffrey if he'd come up all the way from London.

Off I scarpered to the back door to see who it was. What with the stable boys jostling and a stray pig upsetting the cider pots, at first I could barely glimpse her. Then I pushed my way through and saw a young woman climb down, no more than my own age, only she was as pale as a flour bag, with rosebud lips pressed tight together, and two spots of rouge high on her cheeks. She stared at the rabble, her eyes narrowing. She weren't afeared of us, no not one whit. She lifted her chin and said in a throaty London drawl, 'Mr Pars. Fetch him at once.' Like magic the scene changed: three or four fellows legged it indoors and those staying behind hung back a bit, fidgeting before this girl that might have dropped from the moon for all we'd ever seen such a being in our yard. What drew my eye was her apricot-coloured gown that shone like a diamond. I drank in all her marks of fashion: the peachy ribbon holding the little dog she clutched to her bosom, her powdered curls, but most of all it was her shoes I fixed on. They were made of shiny silver stuff, and in spite of the prettiest heels you ever saw, were already squelched in Mawton mud. It were a crime to ruin those shoes, but there were no denying it, she'd landed in a right old pigsty.

I knew she had to be Sir Geoffrey's new wife, this so-called Lady Carinna we had jawed about since they got married some three weeks ago down in London. One of the grooms had told us she was near to forty years younger than Sir Geoffrey, and hadn't that set our tongues wagging? While the men made lewd jests, we women asked, what was she thinking, to let herself be married to our master?

Next, another woman tottered from the carriage, a scrannil-looking creature with a chinless, turtle head. She was waving a big lace handkerchief before her nose as if she might waft us all away like a bad smell. Her mistress never even gave her a glance, only lifted the little dog and made daft kisses at it, like we weren't even there at all. It were quite a performance, I can tell you.

Thank the stars our steward Mr Pars came bustling out just then and yelled at the boys like a sergeant to get back to work.

'Lady Carinna,' he said, bowing stiffly. 'What brings you here, My Lady?'

She never even gave him an answer, so I wondered at first if she knew he was our steward, trusted with the charge of everything while the master was away. He seemed suddenly shrunk beside her, with his greasy riding coat and tousled hair.

'My quarters,' she said at last, avoiding his eye.

He made a half bow; his face were liver-purple. Then she followed him down the back corridor. The show were over, and I scurried back into the kitchen.

'Get them fowls spitted,' I yelled to my cook maid Sukey. 'And a barrel of cabbage chopped right this minute,' I said to scowling Teg. Then I stood awhile, hands on hips, and pondered what on earth a woman like that would ever eat.

\*    \*    \*

We were nearly shipshape when Jem's knock shook the door. Even with hands still claggy with flour I couldn't get to him fast enough, my heart fluttering like a pigeon in a basket. Then there was Jem leaning on the door frame with the afternoon sun gilding him; I am tall for a woman, but his golden hair near touched the lintel.

'Did you see 'er?' His hazel-gold eyes glinted. 'Under all them frills she ain't nowt but a girl. Dirty old goat, he is, to take such a bantling to his bed.'

'She may be fine-looking but she don't look frisky to me.' I'd seen her youth, sure enough, but also something tight-knotted in that pretty face. 'Not like some,' I said with a prod at his chest.

He made a grab for my hand, grinning all the while. 'Yer got flour on yer face,' he laughed and smeared it so I must have looked worse. 'Are them pies I can smell?' He craned forward, stretching the thick tendons of his neck. 'Give us a taste then,' he said, so low and slow my belly fizzed. That boy could make me melt like butter.

'You rogue, you'll have me out the door with no wages,' I protested, pulling back away from him behind the threshold. We could never forget the rules all we female servants lived under: no husband, no followers, not even a wink. Even Mrs Garland only held her title from tradition, for every cook was Missus, though almost all were spinsters. 'No callers' was the rule set by every respectable master. It was the curse of my life, to choose to cook or to choose to marry.

'Now you won't forget about tomorrow night's Souling?' I chided. 'You will tell Mr Pars we're to wed?'

'I'll do it, love. Then we can start up our alehouse and you can get cooking. I don't half fancy being a landlord.'

'Aye, but we need the means to start it up first. We need the capital, Jem.'

It was the grand future we dreamed of. If ever we won a bonus or were remembered by a generous master, we would turn the old ruin at Pars Fold into a tavern. It was in a most fortunate place, right by the new highway. With all the new money rattling around from turnpikes and trade, I'd heard travellers would rather eat beefsteak for a shilling than bread and cheese for tuppence. But sometimes I wished I'd never told Jem my notion, for now he talked of little else.

'The time will come, my love,' I added, then reached to touch his cheek.

'One kiss,' he croaked. 'Look, I fetched some Fat Hen for you.' Jem offered me a bunch of wilting greens.

I reached for the plants, rubbed the leaves with a snap of my finger and thumb and sniffed. They were as fresh as spinach but not so peppery and warm. And wasn't that a faint whiff of cat's piss? Mrs G always said I could sniff a drop of honey in a pail of milk. I used my nose then and saved us all from a night of gripes.

'That's not Fat Hen, you noddle. That's Dog's Mercury. Once I knew a band of tinkers that made a soup of it and near died. If I serve that up to the new mistress I could be hanged for murder.'

'God help us. Give it back here. It's ill-omened.' He hurled the plants towards the hogs' trough. 'I'll fetch you whatever you want from the glasshouse.'

'I have fruit by the barrel-load,' I laughed. 'Get along now. I've Her Ladyship's supper to see to.'

'Wait, I near forgot my news.' He held me back with his calloused hand. 'This footman fellow of hers just come from town. A brown-skinned fellow he is, a right chimney chops, wearing one of them gold footman's coats. He'd got a letter from London. Billy saw it in his hand. So maybe the master is coming home after all. Sir Geoffrey might put his hand in his pocket when we wed.'

'Maybe, maybe not, Jem. When he was younger, perhaps. His bride coming up here on her own, that don't bode well.'

Just then a waft of bitter smoke reached me from the kitchen. 'My damned pies!' I cried and turned back inside.

Jem caught my wrist as I turned. 'Where's my kiss then?'

'They're ruined,' I snapped. 'Teg must find you a morsel.' I am sure that's what I said that day, that I confused his victuals with his kisses.

When I rescued the pies they were greasy brown and tasted of cinders. 'You stupid distracted numkin,' I cursed to myself as I stared at my ruined handiwork.

But before I could tip them in the trough I felt a shadow at my back. Turning about, I found Teg twitching like a puppet on a string.

'Biddy, come quick. There's a lady in the kitchen asking for the cook, but I just run off dumb.'

# III

Loveday dropped down to squat outside his mistress's door. He didn't like those chairs that left his legs dangling, and to stand all day made his old wound ache. Squatting on his haunches, as he had always sat with the other men of Lamahona around the fire, he could think. His velvet breeches pulled at his knees, and his gold-trimmed coat dragged in the dust, but his muscles stretched taut. Behind the door Lady Carinna was weeping and shouting, spitting fire like an angry mountain. He puzzled over the words of the letter he had half an hour earlier secretly opened and read:

> *Devereaux Court*
> *London*
> *27th October 1772*
>
> *Dearest Sis,*
> *I received your letter this morning and must confess to my absolute confusion. Why the devil have you journeyed alone all the way up to rustic Cheshire? Puss, what schemes are hatching in that clever head of yours? If you had but invited me, we might have travelled in style together, but instead you abandon me alone here, subject to the ranting of our uncle. He is not happy, sis, that you have left your husband*

*so soon – but then what did he ever know of the feelings of others? As for me, I at least comprehend that you cannot abide another moment in that old man's disgusting company. Bravo sister, for reclaiming your freedom!*

*You ask for news of Town, so here is what little I have. In short, the gaming table has not favoured me, but I believe one may win as easily as lose, it is all in the turn of a card. My losses are nothing beside Lord Ridley's; the rumour mongers report it at £10,000, and he has departed for the Continent to escape the consequences. Our uncle laughed to hear Ridley will pass by his old villa in Italy, claiming he will be harried by another stinging plague of mosquitoes.*

*Other gossip is that I saw frowsty Sarah Digby about town with your old admirer Napier, who has certainly shown his true colours, as I predicted he would. The story is that they were married last week at the Fleet, all on account of her £30,000. Jane Salcombe is also making a fool of herself, and danced all evening with Col Connaught (only a measly £2000) which is desperate measures indeed.*

*I am certain that since our uncle has made a match for you, he plots the same for me. My only saving grace is that he thinks me too much of an idle drone to snare some vulgar heiress, and thank the devil for that. He is still as tight as ever, but did give me £50 to parade myself at the pleasure gardens last week, but instead I went alone to Mr Garrick's Jubilee at Drury Lane and savoured each word spoken by the divine Prince of Denmark.*

*As for the rest of the cash, I am now the possessor of a black velvet coat that I am sure you will like me in well, but with only a modicum of gold, the rest I lost quite heroically at the tables.*

*So tell me, is your husband's estate worth the journeying? Our uncle boasts it is a fine place that brings a steady income. I expect you have splendid horses up there, and judging from your husband's scarlet Malmsey nose, a fair cellar. P'raps you could invite me to more closely inspect his property while the master continues away? What a jest would that be?*

*How soon do you return, sis? If not within the week, might you also send a little ready cash, and kiss it for luck to help me turn our fortunes?*
*I Remain Your Ever Affectionate Brother,*
*Kitt Tyrone*

The letter was from his mistress's brother, whom his mistress indulged like a child. Yet the meaning was hard to understand. Ridley, Sarah, Napier, Col: they were names of no meaning to him.

His letter-reading was a secret, the gift of kindly Father Cornelius from the mission on Flores. Only a white priest would have paid the high price of a Portuguese dollar for Loveday, broken as he had been after living as a slave of the Damong clan. In return for shelter and schooling he had learned to be a good houseboy and pray on his knees before the big stone Mary. But all that Bible chanting and sitting on hard benches could not make him forget who he was. He was Keraf, father of Barut, a hunter of the Lama Tuka clan. He could read and speak some English, but he still secretly honoured the skulls of his ancestors. And when he prayed he did not chant mumbling words as the Catholic fathers did, but let his mind drift on the tides of time, just as his mother, the daughter of a Spirit Man, had always done, and her ancestors before her.

Behind the door the sounds of shouting and Bengo's excited yapping quieted. Loveday stared past the flower-decorated papers that lined the corridor and began to still his mind. Since falling out of his old life into this chilly underworld, his habit was to sink into reveries when alone. He recollected his life on Lamahona, summoning his wife, Bulan, and his little son Barut. Was Bulan still as lovely as the moon after which she was named? He wondered if her dark lips still smiled and twitched in her sleep as the baby sucked at her breast. No, Barut must be tall now, he must be sailing his father's *prahu* out across the bay. Or so he prayed. Or were Bulan and Barut also slaves? For all the pleasure his visions gave him, their pain pierced Loveday as sharply as the iron harpoon that had once been his greatest treasure. Shifting on his haunches, he set his wits to tackle his problem. How could he return to his own world, to Lamahona and his precious wife and son?

Willing his breathing to slow, he let his mind slip like a sea serpent, away from the quayside of this cold world. He conjured the beach on Lamahona; heard the hiss and tumble of the waves. Crossing the sugar-white sand, he waded into water that shone like blue glass and was as warm as mother's milk. Flipping onto his back, he floated like a sea cow in the twinkling, bobbing sunlight. The salt on his upper lip tasted good. Ideas bubbled and popped around him. When he was still like this, alone and untroubled, he could fish for the future as well as any Spirit Man. For a long time he drifted, seeing once again his wedding feast, his son's birth, his parents' pride.

He was lost. This alarmed him, as he knew the ocean as well as any man knows the landmarks of his own country. But as he swam amongst the islands, each scene was unfamiliar. The conical peak of a mountain loomed towards him where he expected to find a jagging reef. Here was another unfamiliar island, and then another. In frustration Loveday searched the horizon, peering through narrowed eyes. Then, glancing down into the darkening ocean, he started back to see a strange boat directly beneath him. It was not a Lamahonan boat at all, but a ship as big as a whale, with pearly sails and pale-skinned men wandering the deck. Loveday peered down, so close that the brine stung his widening eyes. If he could hold his breath like a pearl fisher and explore that magic ship, he would find his journey's end. He reached down deep into the water and felt the wisp of the ship's pennant pass between his fingers like a ribbon of seaweed.

Loveday felt a blow to his side that sent him headlong against the hard floor.

'What's this, you idle heathen? Asleep at your post?'

He had been kicked by a vast leather boot that stood by his blinking eye. With a lurch he scrambled up and tried to stand poker-straight to attention. The old man Mr Pars stood over him, his face as grim as a time-worn boulder. This man was Number One over all the servants, he knew that much. Loveday rapidly grasped that his work as Lady Carinna's footman was an easy post that he must strive to keep, for it promised days of idleness, free of beatings.

'Only one instant my eyes close, good sir,' he said, his head bobbing like an oar in a storm. 'On my life, it is the first time.'

'Your mistress has three letters waiting for you,' the big man said. 'And I've got my eye on you, you cheating ape. Do you understand the King's English?'

'Yes, sir. I always listen good, sir.'

'Then understand I will have you kicked out on the streets if I find you asleep again. Understand?'

'Yes, sir.'

Loveday scuttled off to his mistress's door. As he entered, he wiped all expression from his face, so that Lady Carinna would have no reason to shout at him. He held out the silver tray so they need not touch as she dropped a neat new letter. His mistress's red cheeks still looked feverish.

'Jesmire has left one, too,' she snapped. He picked up a second, neatly copper-plated letter.

'Mr Pars, he say three letter, My Lady.'

She stared at the crumpled balls of scribbled paper. 'The other is impossible to write. Take those.'

Back outside, he puffed his cheeks out in relief to see that Mr Pars had disappeared. He raced up the stairs two by two, singing under his breath in celebration of the hour of freedom a journey to the post house would earn. He hesitated by the gallery fire, unsure whether to open the letters or not. That fellow Mr Pars had stared at him like a devil man. But his instincts told him that his survival depended on understanding the private thinkings of those around him. Picking up a lighted tallow stump he headed for his garret. Once he was alone in his gloomy room beneath the eaves, he sliced at the seal with his razor and read the first letter.

*30th October 1772*
*Mawton Hall*
*Cheshire*

*Dearest Uncle*

*I have arrived at my husband's estate and found it to be a moulder-ing ruin on the far edge of nowhere. Is this the reward for my suffering? As for the bitter cold and damp, (not to mention the strain to my nerves), it is all most dreadfully injurious to my health. Sir Geoffrey refuses to write or to see me and has sailed away (the arrant coward!) to his estate in Ireland. I am quite ill from it all and wretched, truly wretched.*

*I know that you would say I should gather my wits and play on. I must puzzle it all out myself I suppose, and play my hand the best I can. I expect the immediate business here to take some short while, after which I shall write again, so I beg you prepare my old chamber at Devereaux Court for my return.*

*We may speak freely then,*
*Your devoted niece,*
*Carinna*

Loveday shook his head and bit down the urge to smile. 'Turn back London,' he muttered, as he wet the seal with a drop of stolen wax. Whatever tide he was riding, it was turning rapidly, after all.

The second letter was in Miss Jesmire's curly hand. The message was less veiled and he understood every single word. So the old woman was eager to escape as well:

*The Editor*
*The Lady's Magazine*
*30th October 1772*

*Messrs GGJ & J Robinson*
*No 25, Pater-noster's Row*
*London*

*My Dear Sirs,*
*I should be grateful if you would post the following Notice in an*

attractive and prominent position in your Advertisements for Employment, within the pages of your soonest edition. I enclose 2 shillings secured within a twist of paper in payment for your services.

*NOTICE*
*A Lady of Age & Most Estimable Experience, most genteel, the daughter of a much admired late Suffolk clergyman, who understands the business of making up clothes and linen, is dextrous with a needle, dresses hair admirably, & possesses the benefits of a genteel private education, would wait upon a respectable Lady and make herself useful in any Capacity such as Maid, Nurse or Companion. Most eager to take up a suitable position without the slightest delay. Please reply in the strictest confidence to Miss J at Mrs Wardle, Haberdashers, The Strand.*

# IV

## The Kitchen, Mawton Hall

*Being the day before Souling Night, October 1772*
*Biddy Leigh, her journal*

# ~ To Make A Fricassee of Chicken ~

Take your chickens fresh killed and cut in pieces and brown them quick in butter. Have some strong gravy, a shallot or two, some spice, a glass of claret, a little anchovy liquor, thicken your sauce with butter rolled in flour. Garnish with balls of forced-meat, cockscombs and toast cut in triangles all around.

*A dish given to me by a Tavern Cook at Preston as being in the great court style, Martha Garland, 1743*

That Jesmire creature was indeed in my kitchen, peering at the row of spoiled tarts. She was dabbing a handkerchief to the tip of her pink nose.

'What in heaven's name are those?'

'A small accident,' I said shortly. 'So what can I do for you?'

'Lady Carinna requires some chicken cooked nicely,' she announced, pursing her vinegar lips. 'But you will have to do better than this. These will never do.'

Oh, I was right ashamed she'd even seen them.

'Of course I'll do me best for her, ma'am.'

With a snort my visitor began to peer about the kitchen.

'So, the chicken. Dress it as well as you are able. The diner is – a true gourmand.' A nasty twitch played at the corners of her lips.

I'd been looking her up and down and decided she was nowt but a servant like me. Her fancy green gown was plainly a hand-me-down too large for her frame – she were a pilchard dressed as cream, as Mrs Garland would say.

I stopped nodding and glared. 'So are you fetching it up then?'

You would have thought I'd told her to mop the floor.

'Me? Why, I have never lifted a plate in my life. Loveday, my lady's footman, will come down for it. I am taking the carriage directly. Well, get to it, girl.'

Sauce-box! I racked my head to remember the fine old dishes that Mrs Garland used to make for Lady Maria. Fricassee, I settled on, for it had a fancy French sound to it. I browned the chicken in my pan and dressed it up with the proper garnishes.

No one came. That footman of hers – was he also too tip-top to fetch and carry? With a curse I sent the hall boy upstairs. Moments later his sleepy head reappeared.

'There in't no one there, Biddy.'

With a cuff to his head I decided to take it up myself. There were no backstairs at Mawton to keep us servants out of sight, though I reckoned little then how unmannered that must seem to the Londoners. Since my first day's hiring I had loved Mawton's castlements and crumbling towers, the black panelled halls and creaking stairs. It was built in the pattern of great houses hundreds of years past, with new parts clustered about a chilly keep tower from the days of the Conqueror. To pass above stairs was a rare treat for me, like visiting a palace of wonders, a chance to feel soft Turkey carpets beneath my boots and gaze at the shining pewter chandeliers.

On the stairs the pictures slowed my pace. Above me in a golden frame, Sir Geoffrey looked lordly in his ermine gown, and much more personable aged forty than he did now he was more than sixty. Yet even then his gaunt cheeks and thin lips foretold his coming ruin. What in God's own name did his young bride make of her new husband? I remembered the first time I'd seen him in this very same place. Not long after I'd arrived at Mawton I'd been summoned upstairs to help choose herbs for the linen. Afterwards, I'd fancied myself alone, and loitered to admire these same paintings. At the sound of a tapping cane growing ever closer, I'd frozen stock-still. It was too late to hurry off downstairs, so I drew back against the wall as Sir Geoffrey himself appeared above me. I saw him for only a moment, but his countenance was one I would never forget. Unlike his portrait he was a wreck of a man, his white hair hanging in greasy tails, and his back bent beneath a faded velvet coat. Two pale eyes lifted from his florid face, meeting mine for an instant and narrowing in annoyance. His eye rims, both upper and lower, were unnaturally scarlet.

Mrs Garland's instructions suddenly rang in my ears. 'Biddy, if you should ever meet the master, turn to the wall.' I swiftly turned about, dropping my head and praying with eyes screwed up tight that he might not speak to me. He lumbered closer, his cane thudding on the floor as he dragged himself behind it. As I held my breath he passed me like a frost creeping through the night. Long ago he'd been good-tempered, by all account. 'When he married Lady Maria he treated the whole village to a roasted ox,' Mrs Garland had told me. Yet all I'd ever known of him were tales of drunkenness and vicious harangues at any who crossed him. I pitied the young mistress, fleeing up here and fretting for his return.

Beside his portrait was a dainty picture of his first wife, Lady Maria, her timid face as pale as a pearl. Every inch of her was bedizened with jewels and lace, and at the picture's heart her thin fingers dandled the ruby called the Mawton Rose. For hundreds of years it had been kept at Mawton, after being ripped from a saint's grave by one of Sir Geoffrey's ancestors. It had been painted very finely, every sparkle tricked as if it stood before your eyes. The foolish tale was that the jewel had leached away Lady Maria's strength, so all of her babes miscarried, and she herself was dead at less than five and twenty.

Mrs Garland had known her, when first she came to Mawton. A fine confectioner she called her, and said it was true that the poor mistress had worn the jewel night and day, till Sir Geoffrey had finally plucked it away as she lay cold in her coffin. She was long dead, of course, with no remembrance at all save by us, who made free with the ruins of her precious old stillroom.

No footman waited at Lady Carinna's door. So there was nowt for it but to knock. No one answered, so I knocked again. Finally, I heard a weak voice. Inside, I found only Lady Carinna all alone. God's tripes, I swore under my breath. I was not at all used to serving gentlefolk.

'Me Lady,' I racked my brain-box for polite words. 'I've fetched you your dinner.'

She was propped up on the vast four-postered bed, almost hidden by its twisted pillars and blue brocade. The room was so thrown about with cloths and chests that I had to be mighty careful with the tray as I made my way towards her.

She flicked a limp finger towards the table at her bedside. I set down the tray and took a quick look about me. She was lounging on the bed in a gaping lilac gown, and showed a pair of white stockings with dirty grey soles. Scattered on the quilt were the remains of a cake, and a greasy rind of ham. Honestly, I wanted to spit, I was that offended at her fetching her own dinner.

She was staring at a letter, a frown between her painted brows. There were signs of tears, too, in the pink rings about her eyes. I was so busy gawping I almost cried out when one of the heaps of silk suddenly shifted and moved. An ugly little face pushed out from beneath the bedclothes. It was that poxy dog.

My mistress sniffed at the plate and pulled a face. 'Scrape that stuff off,' she said, pointing at my stately garnish of toast and cockscombs. Some people just don't know fine food when it's put in front of them.

'Cut it up,' she demanded, as I curtseyed in readiness to leave. So I set about cutting it, wondering that a lady such as she could not even master her own knife. With another small curl of her finger she bid me come closer with the dish. And then I had to stand as still as a sentry with the plate held before me for a full ten minutes as she fed the dog my perfectly fricasseed chicken. What had that old toady said? 'The diner is a gourmand.'

Oh my stars, she would pay for that one day.

Whenever the dog distracted his mistress I looked about myself. She had set down the letter she had been so mighty interested in and folded it over so I could make nothing of it. That she had been trying to answer it I could see from the balls of crumpled paper thrown around. I did my best to spy them out and found I could read a little of one of her crumpled fragments. It had been crossed out so hard that the paper was torn right through. Ink blots smeared much of it but I did my best to cipher it:

*dear love, it pains ~~~~~~~~~~~~~~~~~~~~~*
*~~~~~~~~~ most terrible letter I ~~~~~~~ write. My*
*~~~~~~~~~~~~~~~~~~~~~~~~~~~~~~~~~~~~~~~~~~~~~~~*
*~~~~~~~ my life's blight for happiness ~~~~~~~~~~~*
*~~~~~~~~~~~~~~~~~~~~~~~~~~~~~~~~~~~~~~ reckless*
*taint will not go ~~~~~~~~~~~~~~~~~~~~~~~~~~~~~~~*
*~~~~~~~~~~~~~~ fire's heat that in truth*

It made no sense to me at all, for only gibberish words were left. Yet even I could comprehend her unhappiness. What was Sir Geoffrey thinking to grieve the girl so? It was a tragic case indeed.

Finally the lapdog turned his head aside with a yap of temper. Lady Carinna fell back on her bolsters, all exhausted. Staring absently into space, she nibbled at nails that were bloodied to the quick. I suppose her looks passed for beauty in London, for her complexion was as smooth as a boiled egg. Yet her rosebud lips were cracked beneath the carmine, and her hair, half-down to her shoulders, had little powders of scurf. Then I remembered she was an abandoned bride and to be pitied.

'Me Lady. Is there nowt else I can fetch you?'

She didn't even look at me, only shook her head while lifting the letter to read it again. I retreated to the door.

'Wait. Can you fetch me these?' She picked up a ribbon-festooned box of sweetmeats. 'Jesmire,' she said, as if the word tasted like a sour lemon, 'has gone to look for some, but I doubt she will succeed.'

'Can I see?' I hesitated and then at her nod, came forward and peered into the paper-layered depths. A fragrance rose from the wooden box of fine sugar and a pulsing scent that one moment delighted and the next disgusted, like charred treacle.

'Violet pastilles?' I ventured.

I took her silence for agreement.

'You won't find them in these parts,' I explained. 'Yet I could have a go at making them.' My blood was still up, from the offence I'd taken over my fricassee. 'Well,' I shrugged, 'I could make summat like 'em. I pride myself I can cook almost any article I taste.'

I pride myself. Puff-headed words.

'What did you say? Damn it, girl, I can barely comprehend your foxed speech. You could make them?' From her grimace you would have thought I had told her to pin them in her hair. 'Why, these are from *The Cocoa-Nut Tree* at Covent Garden. You have heard of that establishment?'

No doubt she expected me to scratch my head like a right country numkin.

'*The Cocoa-Nut Tree* at Covent Garden? Why it's the finest confectioner in the capital and sells bonbons, macaroons, candied fruits, and ices,' I said in my proper reading voice. I had long studied their advertisement in Mr Pars' *London Gazette* after he'd left it by the kitchen fire. It was a beautiful advertisement, with little drawings of sugar cones, ice pots, and tiny men attending wondrous stoves.

'Why, you are quite the monkey mimic, aren't you?' I felt her scrutiny like something crawling on my skin. Beneath her slummocky ways she had wits aplenty.

'Yet I reckon,' I added quickly, 'I would need one to copy.'

'What's to lose,' she sighed, falling back upon the pillow. 'Take one. Your name?'

'Biddy Leigh, Me Lady.' I curtseyed deep.

'Take one,' she repeated. 'But if you cannot make a perfect copy, Biddy Leigh, you must send to London for a whole box, all from your wages. Do you understand?' I felt a quickening of alarm. A fancy box like that might cost me a quarter year's wages.

'You do understand? A perfect copy. Not just – what was it you said? "Summat laak um".'

She laughed at her aping of my speech, a hoarse chuckle that I did not like at all. Did I truly sound like a witless beast?

'Aye, Me Lady.' I bobbed deep and slipped the sweetmeat in my pocket. As I turned to leave I saw her grasp the ratty dog and begin a new game. She made it dance on its hind-legs while she dandled one of the precious violet sweetmeats, till with a gobble the pastille disappeared.

# V

## The Stillroom, Mawton Hall

*Being the day before Souling Night, October 1772*
*Biddy Leigh, her journal*

## ~ To Make Violet Pastilles ~

Take your Essence of Violets and put into a Sugar Syrup, so much as will stain a good colour, boil them till you see it turn to Candy Height, then work it with some Gum Dragon steeped in Rosewater and so make into whatever shape you please, pour it upon a wet trencher, and when it is cold cut it into Lozenges.

Lady Maria Grice, given to her by her grandmother the Countess of Tilsworth, from a receipt well favoured in the days of Good Queen Bess

Later that evening I marched to my dear Mrs Garland for help, leaving the servants singing over their cider, and the kitchen scrubbed clean. To Lady Carinna I'd sent what I could conjure from the larder: white soup, a little hock of ham, jugged hare, medlar jelly, and the speedy whipping of a plum fool. Still, I felt wretched as I trod the sodden paths through the Old Plantation with my lantern held high. Tonight I had finally to choose between life as a cook with Mrs Garland or as Jem's sworn wife. To prick my guilt further I knew my old cook was ailing, and feared she would not bless our union. As the dusk gathered and the ravens' mournful cries split the air, I shivered to think of her all alone, for the still-room was no place for an invalid. In the time of old King Charles it had been a fine brick-built distilling house, with twin pillars at the door and glass panes in the metalled windows. But it was now many years since Lady Maria had made her fashionable cordials there. Some of the more foolish maidservants avoided that dark avenue and talked of glimpsing a thin white lady in the twilight. Her ill-luck was a warning, they said, against meddling in herblore. Mr Pars called them empty-headed minxes, for he still came by and helped himself to bundles of herbs to ease his lungs. For myself, I saw no ghostly shade in the dark trees. As for Lady Maria's uneasy rest, I now wonder if that wronged lady was indeed stirring in her barren grave.

Inside the stillroom I tiptoed between teetering rows of bottles and flasks, and skirted around chests heaped harum-scarum with spices. Dipping my head, I knocked against bunches of herbs that scattered powdered dust. It was a worse mess than I remembered.

It was here that Mrs G had given me my education, in this kingdom of smells and flavours. Now apparatus stood furred with mould
on the tiled floor. The air was sour with mildew.

It pains me to think how I found my dear old friend asleep on
the couch, her breath wheezing, and the grey fuzz of her hair escaping its cap. It is cruel to see what a life of hard labour can bring: I'd
seen her knees, back, and hands failing day by day.

Then her eyes opened and I saw joy in them. 'Biddy dear,' she
sighed.

For a while we chattered on about the kitchen and Her Ladyship's
arrival. Then I made an effort to revive her in the best way I knew
– by challenging her clever wits.

'I wonder, did you ever make these?' I dropped the violet sweetmeat into her swollen fingers. She pressed it, squeezed it, sniffed it.
Finally, she nibbled the edge and licked her dry lips.

'Lady Maria made many such sweetmeats. Long ago.'

'But what is that to us now?' I said. 'For she is not here to show us.'

My friend stayed silent, which was strange. I met her eyes and
the shine in them was aguey, I thought.

'I have found something, Biddy. But first, you must swear not to
tell.'

'On God's blood.'

'It's a book,' she burst out. 'I saw a mouse run out from a loose
brick, or I should never have found it. It was hidden, Biddy. By
Lady Maria herself.'

And there it was, tucked away beneath her bolster. As she pulled
it out, I saw it was leather-bound, and bore on its cover the words:
*The Cook's Jewel, being the Household Book of Lady Maria Grice, given
to her by her mother Lady Margaret Grice, being a Treasury of the whole
Art of the noble Grice Family of York.* I craned to see inside it and
turned a handful of pages. There were close scribbled sheets on
every sort of fruit, fowl, and fish, all the pages copied in different
long-stemmed scripts. On a sudden I, too, began to grasp our good
fortune. It was a marvel.

'It is *her* book,' I said in wonder. 'Is it everything she made?'

'It is more,' she said, her eyes flashing bright. 'Her own mother's art, their housekeeper's, and friends'. Perhaps a hundred years of women's stuff, all written clear as day.'

'Hidden away. Of course it would be here.' I reached and stroked its dusty cover.

I didn't truly understand, yet, what it was. As well as Lady Maria's receipts, I glimpsed Remedies and Physick for Diverse Ailments and parts copied out on many interesting matters: The Art of Dining Genteely, The Right Behaviour of a Gentlewoman, How to Judge a Proposal of Marriage, and many more.

'You have started adding your own receipts? You are not so ill, then?' I noticed my old cook's box of scraps standing at her bedside, and felt a spark of hope. If she was not so ill, I was not so great a traitor.

'It is because I am ill I write.' She sighed. 'It is time to preserve my work here. You don't think it too high-handed to add my own stuff, Biddy? A plain old cook like me?'

I stroked her soft cheek, sprinkled with moles like furry velvet.

'It's the right thing to do. Your receipts may not be noble, but are the best I ever tasted. But are there violet pastilles?' Slowly she licked her finger and began to turn the pages. They were all in a jumble, written on whatever day the dish appeared in Lady Maria's life.

'Violets,' I insisted, and grappled to turn the pages faster. 'Ah, there it is,' I squealed, reading upside-down. It was an old receipt in the elegant hand of Lady Maria herself. 'How to distill violets, to preserve, to candy and – here, to make violet pastilles.'

Mrs G gave me the list of items and we found we had all the makings about us. As for the news of my marriage to Jem, that would just have to wait. First I set out rows of tallow flickering along the shelves, till the room glowed like a fire-lit cave. Then I set a flame beneath a trivet, that soon danced as crimson as the devil's smithy.

Mrs G had risen from her couch and sat quietly with the book on her lap, tracing the writing with her finger and slowly nodding her white-capped head.

'First, take one pound of gum dragon and steep it in rosewater,' she began. I found a jar of hard gum and tried my best to rid it of twigs and dust. Next, I made a sugar syrup and added violet essence till it was rich purple. All looked well, we agreed.

'It must be boiled to Candy Height,' she said.

Soon the sugar frothed and pulled away from the pan's sides. It was a rare skill of Mrs Garland's, this transformation of sugar. In her box of scraps lay all The Six Tests for Sugar, from making syrup to forging hard crack toffee.

'Yet now I would give all my knowledge to have but one sweetmeat,' she said. 'I read in this book today of the Manus Christi, a sweetmeat like Jesus's own hand made of sugar, gold and pearls. No better cure is known for any ailment.'

Then, remembering the mixture, she called out, 'Try the test for Thread.' I lifted a drop of purple syrup on my thumb nail. When I pulled it apart with my forefinger the tiny thread of sugar soon broke.

She shuffled forward to watch and announced, 'It is now one "Our Father" till it is done.' And so we recited the Lord's Prayer together until at our shared Amen I tried again and the thread stretched a full span from finger to thumb without breaking.

Rapidly, I added the gum dragon to the syrup. It was too hard. So I began again and fearing the gum dragon was too old, made another mixture with hartsfoot, but that turned brittle. Finally I added lemon juice and kept the mix much cooler. Maybe it was the late hour or maybe it truly was a better confection, but this last mixture had to do.

Only when it was all pressed into wooden moulds, like rows of violet buttons, did I slump down and stretch my aching legs.

'You have the touch, Biddy,' my old friend smiled. 'It steadies me, to think you will stay on here at Mawton when my old bones fail.'

The heat rose in my face despite the cooling fire. 'Do not say that. You will soon be banging about again.'

Her face was as serene as the moon. 'Next year I'll ask Mr Pars to give you better wages. With you beside me, I can last another year.'

There could be no more of this. Tomorrow was Souling Night and my wedding would be announced to everyone. So at last I told her my news, that I would marry Jem, and could not stay.

My dear friend's mouth sagged and her blue eyes glazed with bewilderment. Then, when I'd finished, some spark of the old kitchen tyrant awoke. Her chin lifted and she called me a fool.

'A fool?' I answered. 'Do I not have a right,' I said, with my voice suddenly trembling, 'to have a natural woman's life?'

By now she had recovered her strength. 'You have God-given talents. To marry Jem Burdett would be the saddest fall I ever heard tell of. You would be naught but – oh, poor cottagers at best. Poor cottagers with a brood of wailing babies. You would be right back where you came from.'

Shame sent anger rushing through my veins.

'A sad fall?' I mocked. 'Why, all the maids yearn for Jem. Would you yourself not have married given any chance? Why should I always be alone? Why should I wear myself out for ungrateful masters the whole of my life? At least *I* will have children to keep me when I'm worked to death.'

The flush of surprise on her face was as dark as if I'd slapped her with my own hand. I buried my face in my hands and prayed time might turn backwards, that I might eat my cruel words.

'Biddy.' Her voice was knife-sharp. 'I cannot bear you by me.' She stared past me, as if at a terrible vision; with a wave of her marbled arms she dismissed me.

# VI

## The Blue Chamber, Mawton Hall

*Being this day Souling Night, October 1772*
*Biddy Leigh, her journal*

## ~ A Plum Fool ~

Take a pint of plums and scald them till tender, strain through a hair sieve leaving the skins. Add to the pulp orange-flower water and five ounces of fine sugar. When cold, mix it with a little cream till it is smooth, then add thick cream, mix it well, and send it to table.

*Given to me, Martha Garland by my granny Anne Garland of Tarvin who had it from her Granny Haggitt before her*

Next morning the pastilles were as hard as rocks. I tried one and had to spit it back into my palm. There was no disguising that they were shocking poor copies of the originals. Yet I determined to deliver them myself, for to me the worst humiliation was to be thought a coward.

'Name and business?' a strange voice said.

In my temper I almost barged past Lady Carinna's footman. I snapped my name back at him, wishing only to have the whole ordeal over and done with.

'Your business, Biddy Leigh?'

I shook my head with impatience. 'Her Ladyship was after me making some sweets. Yesterday, when you scarpered off and disappeared.' The footman looked surprised and a little frightened.

'You come here yesterday?'

I nodded. He was a pretty creature close up: a slender youth with smooth caramel skin, a flat nose, and the sloe-black eyes of a Chinaman.

'I sorry Miss Biddy. I should a' been here. It first time ever—'

'Oh, don't fret yourself. I won't tell on you.'

'You not tell?'

'Course I won't. I don't know about you Londoners, but up here we stick together – against them.' I gestured towards Lady Carinna's door with a tilt of my head. I could see he was trying to catch my meaning. 'We're loyal. Friendly-like,' I explained. 'To each other.' Well, I had used to think that true before I broke Mrs Garland's heart.

Finally he got my meaning. 'That very kind, Miss Biddy. You good woman.'

'I don't know about that. I'm a banging idiot to tell the truth. Look at these.'

I held up the dish of sweetmeats and groaned. 'I was trying me hardest to please Her Ladyship, but they're nowt like they should be. Don't!' I snapped as he reached out to sample one. 'You won't look so fancy with those teeth of yours all broke into splinters.'

He laughed out loud.

'Aye, you may laugh, for it's not you who's going to lose a quarter year's wages.'

'For making Her Ladyship's pastilles too hard?'

Ashamed, I nodded miserably.

'You could have stayed away,' he said kindly. 'Perhaps she forget?'

'I could never do that,' I protested. 'It would be like I was afeared of her.'

'Or maybe you clever woman. The mistress want everything jus' such a way, yes sir.' He shook his head. 'Listen,' he whispered conspiratorially. 'Miss Jesmire fetch many those same pastilles last night. She give guinea-piece to lady from Bath city. How say I go pinch handful for you? No one see.'

'You would do that?'

He gave me another grin and a nod of his white-wigged head.

'Like you says, we friend.'

He knocked at Her Ladyship's door, and I heard him mumble something about changing the cloths. In a few moments he returned with an armful of linen hiding a dozen plump little gems of violet and sugar. I stuffed the old ones in my pockets and arranged the Bath-bought beauties in their place. I could have kissed that footman. Instead I asked his name and smiled at its aptness.

'Mr Loveday, you are a godsend. I promise I'll pay you back one day.'

He hushed me and ushered me inside.

Today her chamber was an even worse mess. The chamber walls were all hung about with gowns of red, green, yellow, and blue; it looked like a haberdasher's shop spun by a gale. On the floor were bundles of lace, single shoes, and mismatched gloves. A feather with a broken spine was being chased by that ratty dog. Lady Carinna herself was up and out of bed, sitting at a writing desk, scratching away at the far end of the room. Not dressed, though. A loose morning gown of silk lay open at her white breast. Her copper-coloured hair showed through her powder like beefsteak seeping through a dredge of flour. I tiptoed around the mess and held out the tray of sweets.

'Me Lady.' I curtseyed.

'Ah, Biddy Leigh.' Her spirit was up today, glittering behind bright eyes. The thin fingers with their red-bitten quicks stole out of her lace to take a pastille. She chewed it thoughtfully. The recollection that she might have chewed one of those jaw-crackers made my mouth turn dry.

'And last night's supper was edible too. A passable plum fool. We enjoyed it, didn't we Bengo, my baby?' She scooped up the vile dog and clapped its front paws together. It glared at me with the popping eyes of a frog. I bowed my head a little and curtseyed.

'Thank you, Ladyship,' I mumbled.

'I am sorting my gowns,' she announced, after staring so long into my face that I wondered if I wore a smudge of oven grease. 'And it pleases me to be generous to persons I like.' Her eyes swept over her bounty of costumes. 'I believe you deserve a reward, Biddy Leigh.'

'Not me, Ladyship,' I muttered, bobbing low while edging backwards. 'I only done my duty.' I had rescued my wages and wished never to see that strange woman again. She twisted sideways in her chair and pointed. 'Now that dress, the rose silk. What is your estimate of that one?'

I did not have the eye of a town girl, to know my *Française* from my *Indienne*, but I could tell a fine stitch when I saw one. It was a beautiful dress, like a great blossoming bouquet of ruffled silk.

'It is—' I stopped and swallowed hard. The dark rose taffeta bodice was worked with tiny frills and bows that must have taken a seamstress many weeks of blood-pricking work.

'Try it on.'

'I could not.' I backed away like it might strike me. She truly was the most peculiar mistress I had ever known.

'I am commanding you. I want to see you in that dress.'

'Me Lady,' I protested. 'I cannot—'

'Do it!' Her face was pinched with annoyance; the dark brows fierce. With eyes cast down I approached the dress and lifted it off its hook. It felt satin-cushioned, and as warm as newly risen dough. The skirts trailed the floor and I prayed I might not damage the precious fabric.

'Over there, girl.' With a waft of her wrist she directed me into a darker corner where a table stood littered with all the fine items of a lady's toilet.

By the time I had heaved off my old woollen bodice I was hot with shame. My shift was brown with sweat and kitchen grease. The skirt I had so proudly stitched from a length of woollen drab now looked coarser than a horse blanket. A cloud of perfume was freed as I stepped into a fine pink petticoat that danced about my legs like whipped froth. As I eased into the narrow bodice it strained at my shoulders. Hard work changes a woman's body, I knew that. For a moment I glanced up at my mistress and envied her the narrow shoulders and thin arms of those who can barely lift their own soup plates.

'Aha. You look quite changed.' She was laughing again; leaning back to release a husky chuckle. Then she walked towards me and stared so intently I blushed.

'Look at yourself,' my mistress commanded, taking my arm and leading me to a great glass on a frame. Have courage, I scolded myself, it is only a dress. I felt like a beggar shamming in a queen's robes. As I reached the mirror I expected to look as foolish as a gimcrack doll and for my mistress to scoff at me.

So I was mightily surprised to see my reflection. I saw a fine woman gaze back from the glass. Tall and straight, with chestnut hair freed from her kitchen cap. A pale face with cheeks flushed like pippins fresh from the tree. A lively astonishment shone in eyes the colour of greengage wine. And the gown – why, it suited me better than many a merchant's wife traipsing in lace along the Chester Rows. I stared at a delightful stranger who was straight, elegant, and pleasing to any eye.

'Will they ever heal?' Lady Carinna stood frowning beside me. I followed her gaze and lifted my forearms so the lace frills fell back. Bands of puckered flesh ran from fingertip to elbow – some were old silvered scars and others new and scarlet.

'Never,' I answered, 'so long as I cook.'

She was beside me in the mirror, and for a moment we both gazed at our twin reflections. I was half aware that my mistress watched me, but was too entranced by my own reflection to look at her. With red roses in my hair I would be the bonniest bride our village had ever seen. Why, I would make Jem a fine coat from old brocade to match. We would be the finest couple who ever married from Mawton. Afterwards, of course, I would sell it. A gown like that would be worth five whole pounds at a second-hand clothes stall.

'Take it,' she announced suddenly.

I could not stop myself arching around in the mirror to see the elegant back falling like a pleated cloak down to the hem. 'Thank you, mistress,' I gabbled, 'for letting me try it. But I cannot take it. It's too fine for me.'

Her eyes narrowed in the looking glass.

'Do not be a dunderhead, girl.' She was walking away. 'I could not wear it now you have touched it. I'll think on how you pay me back. Go now. Take it. I must write a letter.'

I slipped it off as she returned to her desk. My head was addled to think that the dress was mine. As I pulled on my own worsted skirt it prickled like woven thistles. I picked up the scarlet gown in a great fat bundle that felt as heavy as a child.

'Thank you, Me Lady,' I repeated, frog-throated with gratitude. She waved me away without even lifting her head from her papers, so rapidly did she scribble. I would never have guessed that what inspired her was the scene she had just witnessed in her looking glass. For while I had stared starry-eyed into that mirror and seen me and Jem kissing at the church gate in all our finery, my mistress had seen an entirely different future for her pathetically grateful under-cook.

It's said that dead souls walk on All Souls' Night, bringing mischief to the world. That the Souling sets spirits free to play cruel tricks, bringing portents in mirrors, and messages glimpsed in moonlit wells. But that night no ghostly message came to me. Yet as for mischief coming my way, Lord, there was plenty of that brewing.

The servants' hall was stuffed with that many revellers we could scarcely carry the food through them. A fiddle and pipe were screeching out songs and Old Ned warbled along, tankard sloshing in his hand. The young folk were whooping and dancing, with Teg cackling in their midst, her bubbies bouncing. I only half watched, for my new gown burned in my head like a rick-fire. By rights, my lady's cast-offs were Jesmire's, and I had only Lady Carinna's word that I had got it honestly. If someone found it and she gave back-word, I might be hanged.

Our steward Mr Pars arrived; the crowd made a path for him and touched their caps, though he paid no heed to them at all. He stood apart, eating venison pie with pickle and cheese. A pettifogger some called him, and tonight he looked especially sour, his grizzled head hanging low and his jowls sagging. One parlour maid said she'd heard the new mistress hollering at him behind the door, but that sounded like hogwash to me. But anyone could see he were troubled. He was chewing as if his supper were sawdust, with his gaze on some other distant scene that would not leave him be.

Jem meanwhile was lurching with his cronies, swigging back pots of ale. I had a sudden pang of misgiving as I watched him. The addlehead had been drinking all day long. He can at least stand, I sighed inwardly. I must be patient and let the ale drop to his boots.

Once me and Sukey had cleared the few scraps of food left over, I could at last watch the Souling play. Our coachman George Stapleforth was King George in a red-crossed tabard. It was a treat to see him pricked on the end of a wooden sword. The Quack Doctor was trying to raise dead King George with his potion when I noticed Mr Loveday standing all alone by the side of the stage. No one had befriended him; all day the lads had found sport hollering 'Hey, Tarbrush!' and 'Chimney Chops!' as he went about his business. I swore I would return his kindness in some way, even if it meant some bouncing from the others.

As I watched him, Mr Loveday's sad eyes turned around to a spot behind me, and he stiffened like a sentry. Mr Pars looked up and also gave a start. Turning around I found the object of their interest. Right near me, at the back of the hall, stood Lady Carinna, splendid in a blue gown that shone like an angel's glory.

It was a battle for Mr Pars to reach her; his blood was up for he knocked a few loiterers out of his path.

He was stiffly correct by the time he bowed before her. 'Lady Carinna. If you had but rung—'

'Rung? Damn you, Pars. If there is no answer to my ringing?' Her voice carried loudly and those close by began to turn and stare. Then the play halted too, for old George had missed his cue. For a moment there was a hubbub, till silence fell and Lady Carinna noticed us all agog.

'Mr Pars,' she hissed, as loud as a swishing whip, 'I must discuss our departure at once.' Then she turned with a rapid shimmer of blue silk and our steward trotted after her.

After a moment's silence all the company burst into curious chatter.

'Where she be off to then?' asked fat Nell the laundress who stood close by me. 'Back to London, you fancy?'

'I hope so,' I said, puzzled and uneasy. 'For I reckon she brings only trouble here.'

# VII

## Mawton Lodge

*The Correspondence of Mr Humphrey Pars*
*All Souls' Day, 1st November 1772*

*North Lodge*
*Mawton*
*1st November 1772*

*Mr Ozias Pars*
*Marsh Cottage*
*Saltford*

*Ozias,*
*Brother, I have no time for courtesies, for the news here at Mawton is so prodigious I must share it at once. Two days ago, Sir Geoffrey's bride arrived here without news or notice. And this close on word that Sir Geoffrey himself has retreated to his Irish estate, after no more than ten days' dalliance with his bride in London. Oh, the folly of old men!*

*As for the girl, she had not been here a single day before I knew her to be as tainted and shallow as a puddle. However, she does not lack a vixen's cunning, as you will learn. Last night she confided to me that by the month's end she will leave for France and onwards to Italy, where her uncle owns a property. I asked if her husband would join her. 'No, no, he is too liverish to travel at this time of year,' says she. 'But he insists I must go for my health that declines in this northern chill. And I should like you to lead my little expedition, Pars, for I do so need a man of good sense to make my arrangements. Indeed, he writes to me of his absolute trust,' she said, 'that you will appoint a sound deputy while you are absent.'*

*Now letters had arrived, I knew that, but from her insistence on always sending her own man for the post box I had lost my usual intelligence. I left her with assurances I would think on the matter.*

*I have been considering the situation with great thoroughness of mind. I have sought assurances from young John Strutt that he will do his best to oversee my land agent's duties, the farm and household. Then, last night on Souling Night my lady brought all to a head, interrupting the revels to tell me she wished urgently to gather the funds for her travel. No sooner was Sir Geoffrey's dresser open than she rifled through it, as quick as a dealer of cards at the Assembly Rooms. Soon there was close upon £1,400 upon the table.*

*'This is not sufficient,' she said. 'Look here, I bring with me a letter of credit signed by Sir Geoffrey himself. You must visit Sir Geoffrey's banker in Chester tomorrow and draw a further £1,000 for the journey.' I perused her letter and found it most properly drawn up, with Sir Geoffrey's own seal and signature – a little shaky for sure, but I would swear in a court of law it was his own hand. Brother, you see how these Town Madams may run through a Fortune?*

*'Speed is all,' she entreated, 'for we must leave for London and reach Dover before the winter storms.'*

*She then told me who should make up the party, the splendour of her equipage and so forth.*

*'And I am to choose what jewels I like,' she said, 'for I must not embarrass Sir Geoffrey's good name.'*

*Then she commanded me to give her Lady Maria's jewel, the Mawton Rose. Oh, with what reluctance did I hand her that precious stone. If I were a man of fancy, I should say the gem cast a baleful glow on its new mistress's greedy face. She pressed me to hang it about her neck, and as my fingers fumbled with the clasp I was dreadfully tormented by the memory of sweet Lady Maria.*

*Only as I left the room did she ask, 'So you will join my little adventure?' I looked at the bonds and the jewel and her cunning narrow face and replied, 'I will indeed, My Lady.'*

*To my advantage, I believe she thinks me some sort of witless drudge, but I will watch and wait and bide my time.*

*E'en so, brother, my heart beats as quick as a soldier's tattoo at such a rapid change in my affairs. I have maps to obtain, strongboxes to be commanded, horses to inspect, and sailing times to negotiate. I will go Ozias, and I will protect my master's interests. On my oath I will do all in my means to protect the Mawton fortune, should I travel from here to Italy or around the world and back again. I shall write when I may from the road and by that means I shall instruct you as,*

*Your zealous brother,*
*Humphrey Pars*

# VIII

## *Mawton Hall*

*Being All Hallows to Martinmas, November 1772*
*Biddy Leigh, her journal*

# ~ A Portable Soup for Travellers ~

*Take three legs of veal, one of venison, two pig's feet or whatsoever other good meats are at hand. Lay in a boiler with butter, four ounces of anchovies, two ounces of mace, five or six celery, three carrots, a faggot of herbs, put water in to cover it close and set it on the fire for four hours. Strain it through a hair sieve and set it on the fire another day to boil till it be thick like glue. Pour it on flat earthen dishes and let it stand till the next day. Cut it out like a crown piece and set out in the sun. Put them in a tin box with writing paper betwixt every cake. This is a very useful soup for travellers for by adding boiling water it will make a good basin of broth or mix readily with pottages, stews or gravies.*

*Martha Garland, 1750, a most useful receipt
given me by Mistress Salter of Chester*

On Souling Night I kept looking out for Mr Pars, so I could send Jem over with news of our wedding. But when at last he did come back he clambered quickly onto the Mummers' stage.

'It is with deep regret I must address you,' he said, raising his hands to quiet the crowd. 'For I have just learned that neither our master nor mistress will be home next year. Consequently, the estate will not require such a great number of you to be employed. Firstly, there are those persons who might remain at Mawton on reduced pay. These are the stablemen and others needed to tend the stock.' This met with cries that they must all have full wages to live. 'The second list,' he boomed above the racket, 'are those persons to be laid off at the month's end.'

'So it's the poorhouse for us,' wailed a shrill voice, to a chorus of jeers. I looked over to Jem, but he still had his head in a pot. 'Finally, there is the list of those who are to accompany Her Ladyship to the continent.' At that, silence. 'And that list being so short, I can instantly give it,' he said.

'Firstly, myself. I will be travelling to Europe as Lady Carinna's guide and protector.'

So that is it, I thought. He is all puffed up at being chosen to travel abroad.

'And Miss Jesmire, of course, being Her Ladyship's personal maid. And also Loveday, Her Ladyship's footman.' I glanced at my new friend, who nodded his head slowly. 'Next, so far as to Dover with His Lordship's carriage, George Stapleforth.' That caused a roar, for old George had never been outside the county.

Then Mr Pars looked into the crowd, and to my surprise, his gaze lit on me.

'And lastly, so we need not eat these foreign kickshaws, Her Ladyship will take Biddy Leigh.'

It was all too outlandish. I was no London servant able to smooth the way of a lady in foreign parts. 'No, sir!' I cried out without thinking. 'I in't going nowhere.'

'You shall go, miss,' Mr Pars commanded. 'And show proper gratitude to your generous mistress.'

To my own astonishment I answered back, before the whole company.

'I will not go, sir, begging your pardon. For I am to marry Jem Burdett and cannot and will not go.'

That left all the company jabbering like geese. A great hubbub broke out, for this was news even to my kitchen maids, who shrieked to hear I had ensnared their favourite. Jem attempted to stand, though nearly legless with ale, but did agree that 'Biddy will have me for a husband and I durst not refuse.' I could have brained the lummocks, and all those who roared with laughter.

'Both of you come to my office. Eight o'clock,' Mr Pars commanded.

Next morning we stood uneasily in Mr Pars' office, as our steward sat at his desk beneath costly maps and leather books. Jem was still lushy and held a cloth to his mouth.

'So, are you forced to marry?' Mr Pars began, then blew a plume of blue pipe smoke towards the ceiling. 'If so, the rules state you must both lose your positions.' Not receiving a reply for I was too amazed, he demanded of me, 'Have you been playing the wanton with this young fellow?'

Jem spluttered into his kerchief. I had caught my breath at last. 'That is not true at all, sir. Such talk is slander.'

'Slander is the ruling of a judge,' Mr Pars mocked, 'and not the whim of a kitchen maid.'

'I never granted Jem that freedom, I do swear it,' I said earnestly. 'Mr Pars, sir. Do hear me when I say I cannot go, sir.'

Setting down his pipe he clasped his hands across his round stomach. 'Now listen, my dear. Consider. It would be a shame to put a newly married man out of work.'

'Oh, you would not,' I wailed.

He shrugged. 'He is an outdoor man and may not be needed.'

'Then we will leave together and find other work.' I grasped Jem's hand and made to get up.

'Hold! I have not finished.'

Reluctantly, we bumped back together like skittles.

'There is your bonus of five guineas to consider.'

At this Jem finally seemed to wake. 'Five guineas, Mr Pars, sir?'

'Aye, lad. I will pay your betrothed her full wage and another five guineas bonus on condition she takes her year abroad. What better foundation could there be for your marriage, lad?'

He pulled out a golden coin from his strongbox and set it standing on the mantel. How Jem gawped at King George's fat face, which beamed like a great lardy woman. Then my sweetheart tugged his cap and said, 'Thank'ee, Mr Pars, sir. Say thank'ee, Biddy.'

'We could find other work, Jem,' I begged, but I knew Mr Pars had won. For five guineas that lad would send me away with less sorrow than a pet pig to slaughter.

I hate boiling bones. Day after day I made Portable Soup, throwing dead creatures into the cauldron, till the mass of boiled sinew smelled like a renderer's yard. To add to my misery, it seemed that Mrs Garland was punishing me, as well she might, for she knew that butchery was the one branch of cookery I hated.

As I stirred the cauldron I recalled a day when the master and his hunting cronies had galloped into our yard, the horses steaming and blowing from a dawn hunt. The stablemen ran to them, but whilst the others dismounted, Sir Geoffrey sat victorious on his jittering mount, downing a tankard of liquor. With raw satisfaction he watched the gamekeepers unload his bounty. Then his eye fixed on me where I stood at the door.

'You, kitchen maid! Do I pay you to stand idle?' he shouted like a deaf man. 'That doe that was brought to bay by the thicket, I'll have her liver for breakfast.'

I looked about myself – there was no one else watching but me.

I waited at a distance as the men unloaded the creature, and Sir Geoffrey dismounted to slap the doe's haunch with all the pride of a conqueror. I saw then that all his skin was plaguey, even his crooked fingers looked scalded. There was something of the slaughterman about the master, especially in his way of measuring antlers and hooves. As I recollected that his lordship was the true centre of all the bustle and carry-on of Mawton, suddenly everything seemed tainted, even its wondrous mullions and towers.

Reluctantly, I followed a pair of gamekeepers, who lugged the beast down to our cold larder. But either the hunt or the liquor had left them in a harum scarum mood.

'Get along then, Biddy Leigh,' said the chief of them. 'We was up riding hard, afore you even thought of rising. You can gut the quarry for a change. His Lordship's waiting for his breakfast mind.' And off they went, leaving me to it.

I looked at the poor creature slung on a hook, her head lolling, her china-eyes staring, her wounds still red and claggy. I was keen to learn and give it a try, though I'd only watched the bloody business once before. As I made ready to butcher the creature, her warm fur stank of terror and half-stomached grass. It took me a while to decide where to make the first rip with my knife. Then with a few tugs I got the front of her parted, like two grisly doors opening up from throat to tail. The stinking guts had just dropped steaming to the floor when my eye was caught by an odd little thing.

At first I thought it was a twisted gut or raddled spleen. I peered more closely and found a long-snouted face the size of my thumbnail. What I saw near had me fainting to the ground. A perfect tiny fawn lay curled in the sack of its mother's womb. I reached out to tug it away and suddenly, through the womb-sack, it kicked at me with its tiny cloven hoof. Lord, I screamed all the way to the yard until the stablemen came and sorted it. I knew it couldn't live, poor baby, all slimy and soft with the cord from its mother sliced off like a squirting purple pipe. But long after I'd sent the master his liver fried in butter, I wept for the blind waxy-legged creature that twitched and then mercifully stiffened on the larder floor. Since that day I'd always left the butchery to those who have a stomach for it.

Of those last dark weeks at Mawton only two memories shine to me now. One is of my dear Mrs Garland. We had stayed on poor terms, and then two days before my leaving, she called me to the stillroom. Pacing through the murk of a winter's afternoon I picked up a switch and hit out at the spiky brambles that crowded the path. Everything about me was dying. The golden year, my wedding hopes, all my familiar ways. I had a mighty strong wish to hit some-one hard with my fist.

There my old cook sat by the fire, much as she had done the night we attempted those violet pastilles. And she said to me, 'Biddy, I cannot let you go without making my peace.'

For a moment I heard only the fire crack, then a whimper broke from my lips and we grasped each other's hands. Tears fell down my cheeks and I wiped them away fast.

'I cannot forgive myself. You have treated me better than my own mother. And you will be left here all alone.'

She shook her head and sighed. 'God willing, me and Teg will make do till you get back safely.'

Then she sat up straight and passed me a clean rag to wipe my face, and said some words I will never forget.

'Now listen to me, Biddy. If you only listen once, do it now. I've been puzzling, and it seems to me you have two ways ahead of you.' Her eyes shone as bright as a young girl's as they met mine. 'You can suffer all this as a trial and waste a whole year complaining.' I lifted my head sharpish at that, but she would not be interrupted. 'Or you can learn to be more than a plain cook like me. Learn how to make those fancy French bomboons and dishes à la mode. What a chance, girl,' she said, shaking my captive hand. 'I have seen advertisements for cooks with the French Style and do you know what they offer? Twenty guineas a year. You shall be a cook to nobility.'

'But I am marrying Jem when I get back.' I spoke it like an article of faith that only I believed in. She sighed, her solid bosom heaving.

'Then cook at this alehouse Jem boasts of. I've heard there are taverns that sell spanking fine food in London. Oh, if I had my youth again I should dearly love to try what they offer. And as for Paris! This could be the making of you, with the talents God has given you. You shall taste food I never even dreamed of.'

'I think not.' I was quite fixed on being miserable. 'I am only the pan-tosser, taken along so Her Ladyship needn't eat foreign stuff. Maybe I'll only be cooking for that rat-dog of hers.'

I did not tell her that the previous day I had been summoned by Lady Carinna for a few chilly moments. She told me to pack a chest with linen, glass and plate, and store cold victuals in the well of the coach. But before she dismissed me, she said, 'And you will bring the rose gown.' My heart thumped to hear her words. Why, I wondered, did that dress make me so uneasy?

Mrs Garland's voice interrupted my worries. 'But you will go marketing in all these foreign parts?' she insisted.

'Aye. Perhaps,' I said wearily. 'Though to hear Old Ned, we'll be eating only frogs and snakes. Just this morning I told him I'd been practising the frogs' legs and had put one in his pottage. You should've seen his face. And I will do it too, if he doesn't shut his trap.'

Mrs Garland's lips fell open and then gathered in a hoot of laughter.

'Oh, that is more like the old Biddy,' she wheezed. She squeezed my hand tight and I returned her smile. 'But do mind that tongue of yours. I'm thinking of Lady Carinna. She's a queer one, but she is your mistress. My advice is to do her bidding as quick as you can and then stay well away. Jesmire too—'

'Lord, I cannot abide her.'

'You need not abide her. Only be quick and quiet about her.'

Reluctantly, I nodded.

'And if you have any troubles, Mr Pars is a good sort of Christian gentleman under all his grim manner. Well lettered he is, and well trusted by the master. If you look to anyone for help, have a word with Mr Pars.'

If only she knew what a conniver he is, I thought. Yet what she said was true, that my life would be easier if I did not rile him.

'Enough of all this,' she said. 'I want to give you something.'

She offered me the silver knife that she always kept at her waist on a chain. It had been Lady Maria's, till my old friend found it blackened and blunt behind an old chest.

'It's the finest knife I've ever used. I should like to think of it chopping all those garlics and fruits of paradise.'

'And skinning them frogs?' I teased.

'Aye, even those. For Lady Maria's sake.'

I took it, and it did fit sweetly in my palm.

Then she sat back and folded her arms, giving me a long stare.

'Now you may reckon me an old maid, but I have seen more years of life than you, Biddy, so take heed of what I say next. First, I'm right pleased you've kept your virtue. Now don't look at me like that. I know you've let Jem court you, but all the house is repeating what you told Mr Pars – that you never granted him that freedom.'

Lord! I buried my face in my hands to think of all those tongues wagging over my private concerns. 'Stop it. You're shaming me to death,' I said, peeping through my fingers.

'All I'm saying, girl, is when you're in these inns, sleeping by these tapsters and grooms and suchlike fellows, you must keep your prize safe beneath your skirts.'

I couldn't help but laugh out loud. 'My prize?'

'You know what I'm saying. Your greatest treasure – worth nowt once you've spent it.'

'Of course I'll take care. I'm not daft.' I might have said I'd kept it safe long enough from Jem all that fevered summer, so I wasn't going to waste it on some snake-tongued tapster.

'And lastly, what I ask is this. Write it all down for your old friend, Biddy. Tell me what you see, who you meet, and mostly – what you eat. Write careful descriptions and copy the receipts if you can. If I were but twenty years younger I should fight you for this chance. So do not disappoint me. Watch, learn and taste for me, girl. It's time the book had new dishes.'

And so my dear Mrs Garland gave me this book, *The Cook's Jewel*, written in so many hands: Lady Maria's, her friends', cooks' and neighbours'. My guides from the past, who had cooked and perfected and written down their finest inventions. And she had sewn in new white pages to bear the dishes I was yet to discover.

That evening I walked with Jem to Reade Cottage. Or I should say, he took my arm and led me there, for I was faint with misery. When we reached the tumbledown building, just the sight of our ruined hopes set me weeping. Pars Fold was the lushest valley in those parts, near the new turnpike road but sheltered by a copse of birch trees. Some said it had been in Mr Pars' family since no one could remember, but Sir Geoffrey had bought it from Old Mr Pars and had it parcelled into the Mawton estate. Our steward never spoke of it, but at least had the pleasure of overseeing it as Mawton's steward. It was our dream to be tenants, to rebuild Reade Cottage as a thriving tavern, and live and prosper there.

''Tis only a year, sweetheart,' Jem said, paying little heed to my sorrow. 'T'will soon be passed. Think on it, we're set up for life. I shall have my tavern, yet,' he said, clenching his fists with joy. I thought of Mrs Garland calling him unworthy, and shook my head. Then he kissed my lips, and his tongue, all wheat and sweet flesh, burrowed inside my mouth. Yet all I felt was pain, I was so afeared of losing him. The spell I held over Jem needed daily attention. I could not feed him from across the water. I could not send him a bowl of kisses.

'We must run off,' I begged, grasping his hands. I told him we might get married and go to some large town to find work. 'I could never be parted from you, Jem. I cannot go.'

But he could barely keep the grin from his lips. He was a man with golden guineas blinding his eyes. And Mr Pars had promised him easy work too, for the long year of my journeying.

They say it is night and its desolate fancies that drags a heart to despair, and once dawn arrives it brings new hopes. So it seemed to me on that last Mawton morning. I woke in the kitchen corner to the racket of the stablemen. Cold water, fresh linen, and a glass of steadying ale set me nearly right. I peered in a shard of mirror and found that my face was not quite so destroyed as when I fell crying to sleep.

Around me shone the kitchen I'd worked in each day: the copper pans hung neatly, the scratched wooden table and neat blue plates set in rows on the dresser. I got up to rake out the cinders and suddenly clutched at the black stone of the hearth. How long was it since as a new girl I'd first spiked a fowl and set it to roast on that fire? What great sides of beef had we roasted on the smoke-jack, while bacon dangled on hooks, and meat juices basted puddings as light as eggy clouds? Never, in all my ten years at Mawton, had I let that fire die out. Every dawn, in winter or summer, I'd riddled the dying embers and set new kindling on the top. I touched the rough stone and let my cheek press on its everlasting warmth, wishing I could take that loyal fire with me. Foolish, I know, but a fire is a cook's truest friend. It was a good fire at Mawton: blackened with hundreds of years of smoking hot dinners.

I think no heathen ever worshipped fire like a cook. So I kissed the smutty hearth wall and packed instead my little tinderbox, to light new fires I knew not where.

# IX

## *Mawton to Nantwich*

*Being Martinmas, November 1772*
*Biddy Leigh, her journal*

## ~ A Brandy Posset ~

*Take a bowl by the fire and break in nine eggs mingled with half a bottle of brandy, one whole cinnamon, three blades of mace. Now grate in nutmeg for half a minute and place near the fire taking care not to curdle. Heat a quart of cream with a basin of sugar and watch with care till it almost boils and frizzles at the edges. Lift it and pour from a height into the wine and eggs. Let it sit still by the fire till it is settled then strew upon it fine sugar.*

> *How it was given at the Star Inn, Nantwich, served in a posset pot of blue stuff and was as good as was ever made, Biddy Leigh, 1772*

We should have left at nine on the bell that morning. Mr Pars fumed like a boiling kettle, fretting over the horses that stamped and jangled in their harness. I stood with my bundle tied up at my side, jittering like I'd swallowed a flock of live birds. It was miserable weather too, for it never got properly light at all and the clouds were as heavy as grey, lumpy porridge.

Three dreary hours later Jesmire approached, flapping along behind Mr Loveday, who carried her box. She bustled inside the carriage, then when she stepped down I heard her say to Mr Pars, 'You are not suggesting that my lady would share the carriage with a – cook maid!'

My cheeks burned as hot as grill-irons. But there was nowt I could do. Just you wait, Miss Toady, I repeated silently, until the day I dress your dinner.

Then I heard a swish of silk and there was Her Ladyship, quite splendid in a grey cloak trimmed with swansdown, watching from the doorway.

'What is going on?'

Mr Pars stood forward like a bull.

'Miss Jesmire informs me it is not genteel for Biddy Leigh to travel inside. So we must make room for her with the driver.'

My mistress turned to stare at me and I bobbed low.

'No. Biddy must travel inside. Pars, you are directing this expedition. Don't you comprehend the hour? Get my bags on, and for heaven's sake let's be off. Jesmire, hold your tongue.'

I shot a skewering glance at Jesmire, who made a face like she'd just drunk bitter aloes. So, my mistress did care for me, I crowed, and that old shrew must like it or lump it. At last I climbed into the soft nest of the carriage and rested my feet. It was gloomy and stuffy inside, but perfectly dry. Then the wheels lurched and we were away. Once the horses got trotting it was a thousand times more comfortable than an open cart.

That parting from Mawton was a terrible heartache for me. I sat facing backwards, and had to watch the road dwindle to a ribbon behind us. As we passed through the park I saw a gang clearing hedges across the fields, and a fair head amongst them. I sprang up from my seat and murmured 'Jem!' at the rain-blistered window before I could stop myself.

'For pity's sake, shut up,' my mistress barked. 'It is bad enough that I bear this rocking motion. Sit down.'

'When I was a girl,' Jesmire said airily, 'a creature like that would not have dared make a sound in my presence.'

I remembered my promise to Mrs Garland then, that I should mind my tongue and have nothing to do with either of them. Thank my stars, within the hour they had both dozed off, so I alone marked our way. We passed a long train of packmen halted on a hill, and I saw the rain-sleek horses resting in their harnesses like solemn statues. Later, we jolted past two hunched travellers dragging bundles through the mud of a vast forsaken moor. Those two travellers might have been me and Jem, lugging our worldly goods to a parlous future together. If only Jem and I had run off to marry, I wailed silently. I pulled down my cap and wept, like a bag of whey that drips without end.

When I woke the copper glow of sunset filled the carriage. Jesmire was still asleep, her chin hanging slack towards her bony chest. But my lady was awake all right. I could just see her in the reddish gloom, watching me with her eyes shining.

'So, Biddy,' she said, 'where is it you are from?'

'Me, miss? I mean, Me Ladyship.' I was fair startled at her talking to me. 'Nowhere special.'

Her face was just a creamy oval, but those glassy eyes stayed bright.

'You must be from somewhere, I should think.'

'A place called Scarth, Me Lady. There ain't nowt there.'

She huffed very loudly. 'There is nothing of note, is how you might say it.'

'There ain't nothin' of nowt, as you might say it.'

She laughed at me then, but I wasn't sure it was a nice laugh.

'You must have a family? Tell me about them.'

This time I did more than rack my brain, I positively scoured it.

'Well, there ain't much to tell, miss – Me Lady. Jus' me old ma, that's me mother, and me sister Charity.'

'Charity is a very peculiar name.'

'Aye, Me Lady. Me father had strange notions when it come to names.'

'Biddy. That is Bridget?'

Oh Lord, here we go, I thought. 'Obedience,' I mumbled too soft for her to hear.

'What's that?'

'Obedience, Me Lady.' And she laughed that husky laugh and said, 'Very apt, I am sure. Obedience, you have a very small family. What of your father?'

'He calls himself a cow leech. Mends cattle. But he rambles off as he likes, Me Lady.'

She was quiet for a minute and I was glad, because I never liked to tell of my old da. It was him who named me after his Bible-bawling mother. He fancied himself a roaring dissenter, but all I ever saw him dissent from was a hard day's work. He'd come home and sponge off my ma, leave another baby on the way, and then get back on the road. A lady like Carinna wouldn't have a notion of such a tosspot.

'And brothers?' she asked suddenly.

'I did have once. They're all gone now.' I counted on my fingers to check the number. 'Brothers and sisters. Seven gone to God.'

'Death casts a long shadow, does it not?' she said. 'I have a brother. On my mother's deathbed I promised her I'd love and provide for him all my life.' She fell silent then, and all I could see was the blurry bobbing of her face in the twilight.

'So you can count,' she said suddenly. 'And can you read at all?'

How could I make a dinner for thirty if I couldn't count? Or read, come to that. Where to begin? I told her of the Widow Trotter, who had lived in the fine end cottage at Scarth. From a young scrap of a child I'd carried her bundle the four miles to market each week in return for a few hot mouthfuls. The first time I tasted her herb-stewed rabbit I near swooned away with pleasure. After that, I traipsed to her cottage every day to help her scrub and cook and brew. My ma said I plotted to steal the widow's hidden money, but her son would chase me off.

'And did you not make eyes at the son?' my mistress suddenly interrupted.

'Why, I was nowt but a clod of a child,' I said. And why should I want to betray the good widow? I nearly added. For a husband was not what I was after at all. Most afternoons, once the pewter was shining and the son's dinner simmered on the fire, Widow Trotter would draw out her book of letters.

'What wage could better that? The chance to read,' I said, and my mistress was quiet again.

'And what was it you read?' my mistress asked.

'I read *Goody Two Shoes*.'

'Oh, that ghastly morality. What was your opinion?'

'Well, I thought Margery Meanwell a right crafty minx.' Then I stole a quick glance at my mistress but couldn't see her expression.

'Indeed. She certainly had the good sense to find a rich husband to raise her up from the gutter. And what other treasures did this noble widow possess?'

'Well I read *Robinson Crusoe* – now that is a tale. And *Pamela*, too.'

'And your favourite?'

'Well, Mrs Haywood is my favourite lady writer. *Fantomina*,' I said in a low voice.

Her Ladyship chuckled. 'Is she not the lady who pursues Mr Beauplaisir in a variety of intrigues?'

'It is, Me Lady.' We shared a sudden smile of knowingness, for it is a right saucy tale. 'But best of all I like Mrs Haywood's *Present for a Servant-Maid*. It has some excellent advice on all the ways of dressing foodstuffs. It is a marvel what that lady knows.'

Then my mistress laughed, but it was not so cruel-sounding as before. 'You are well formed for your rank in life, Obedience. But why did you leave the estimable widow?'

I told her how Widow Trotter's son had married and how she wanted to move to the town and let him have her cottage – and how I grew downcast, for at twelve years old I had dodged joining my ma and Charity picking coal for a living for long enough. It was like the answer to a fairy wish when Widow Trotter said they needed a girl at Mawton Hall.

'So I got away from the coal fields and my family,' I said at the end, coming finally to my senses and remembering how I had meant to keep my tongue still.

'To find yourself at that rotting old pile?' she snorted.

I made no answer to that, for I didn't agree, not one whit. When first I saw that jumble of towers and mullioned windows it looked to me like the happy end of a storybook. Only now, as I spoke out loud of all my learning and pushing myself forward, what I'd done with my life so far seemed a trifling thing. My mistress was much the same age as me, yet she had all those gowns and London manners besides. And, like *Goody Two Shoes*, she'd trapped a rich old man. The nub of it was, I was nowt beside her. But *Goody Two Shoes* she was not. Of that I was already very sure.

Voices woke us. Lamps glimmered at the windows, ostlers saw to the horses, and servants gathered to carry our trunks. 'Come along inside, good people,' harried the innkeeper, and all in a bustle we were led to the roaring fire where tankards of hot ale steamed for all but me and the other low servants.

That night my mistress said I must wait at table in the private parlour. I was all fingers and thumbs while my stomach growled from smelling the lamb, brisket, and duck. No sooner had my lady, Jesmire and Mr Pars gone away, than me and Mr Loveday attacked the broken food. The leavings were even tastier for being half-cold; the lamb was sweet and pink and studded with salty capers.

'Where is it you are coming from, Mr Loveday?' I asked between mouthfuls. 'China or Africa?'

He licked his gleaming teeth. 'You never travel, Miss Biddy, that for sure. I come from island past Batavia, white people got no name my place. Island of fire.'

Later, when he was sharing out the last of the cheese, he looked at me all sheepish. 'Miss Biddy, you say we servant be friends?'

I told him that was true.

'I go back home one day,' he said, raising his sloe-black eyes. 'I go back my wife and son.'

'You must take care what you say,' I said in a hushed tone, 'for Lady Carinna owns you now.'

'She own me,' he said, looking truly miserable. 'But maybe she lose me, Miss Biddy? You think a man ever get lost and be forgot?'

'Maybe. But it would be a crime to purposely lose yourself. It would be stealing valuable property. You could be hung for it.'

'What that mean?'

So I told the poor lad of the gallows, and how the crowds flock to see a body twitch and die. He looked so afeared to hear of it, I squeezed his arm.

'You take care now, Mr Loveday,' I said, 'and confide your notions to me before you carry out any daft nonsense.'

He nodded and we left it at that, for Mr Loveday was my only friend now, and we had to look out for each other.

\*   \*   \*

Later, I saw an old waiter make a brandy posset by the parlour fire and made a memory of the whole receipt, for Her Ladyship said she liked it. I tasted a little of the dregs by offering to carry the posset pot back to the kitchen. It was light and sweet and warmed the body as a brass pan warms a chilly bed. And so, having no other duties that night, I went to my closet and unknotted my bundle and took some sad pleasure in looking over my goods. Not being sure yet what I should write down I began with this list of all I had in the world:

*A comb*
*A petticoat*
*A flannel gown*
*My nightcap and another day cap*
*One shift*
*A pink ribbon given me by Jem at Chester Fair*
*Lady Maria's silver knife on a chain*
*A Prayer book inscribed by Widow Trotter*
*A picture cut from a newspaper that recollects my mother's face*
*The Household Book called The Cook's Jewel wrapped in a fustian*
  *piece*
*Quills and ink a gift from Mrs Garland*
*My sewing bag containing precious locks of hair wrapped in a linen*
  *cloth*
*Stockings and strings*
*One pound, three shillings and threepence halfpenny*
*The Red Silk Gown and petticoat given me by Lady Carinna*

Next I wrote the making of the Brandy Posset down. Then, laying down I thought of Jem so far away back down the benighted road and wished sorely I had left him on better terms. But in a few blinks of an eye I slept as sound as a dormouse.

# X

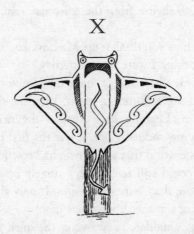

Loveday blinked and then closed his eyes, feeling water stream down his cheeks like unstoppable tears. He was perched on the back footboard of the carriage, shaken by every rut and rock in the broken road. The rain was dripping inside his collar, chafing his old wound so it ached without end. This was the coldest place he had ever known. Sometimes he was sure he would die soon, but his bones did not fail, nor his hair turn white. For some strange purpose his ancestors were keeping him alive in this terrible place.

He had already been soaked while he waited, standing to attention by the carriage door while the others fussed around. His only moments of warmth were with Biddy. She didn't call him names but talked to him eye to eye like a friend or cousin. True, her eyes were horribly pale, but they did not, as he had once believed, have the power to penetrate his skull with dangerous spirits. And she laughed with him, teasing him when he talked about home.

'In my country the rain is warm as tea,' he confided, as they huddled beneath the overhang of a roof, waiting for their mistress.

'You are having me on there, Mr Loveday. How can rain be warm?'

He told her how he would pick a tray-sized lontar leaf to carry above his head, to shelter from the tea-warm rain. She shook her head again.

'I don't know how you think it up, Mr Loveday. Sheltering under a leaf. You must think I were born yesterday.'

*Mr* Loveday. He liked that. It made him feel for a moment like a solid man and not a fluttering ghost. Then she reached out and touched his arm. Leaning back against the dripping carriage Loveday's eyes grew suddenly hot. It was the first time since passing to this strange world that any person had reached out to him in friendship. He could still feel Biddy's fingers on his arm, and it warmed him more than a thousand fires. If only she knew him as he once had been; a hunter, a warrior, a man!

As the carriage shuddered and swung, the spirit that lived inside him, his *manger*, felt like a bird caught in a net. Commanding his limbs to balance on the narrow board, he released his spirit to go where it chose. Soon, somewhere else there was rain, pain, and misery – here in the limpid turquoise water the waves sucked and broke, with the rhythmic sound of the ocean's heartbeat.

He was hunting with his clan; standing high on the harpoon platform, a warm rush of air refreshing his body each time the boat crested a wave. They were skimming just behind a vast *bĕlelā*, a black ripple-edged devil ray speeding beneath the water. Fear and excitement mixed in his veins. It was a monster, the length of three tall men, its wingspan even wider. It was an easy strike – he raised his right arm and drove the harpoon down deep into the creature's back. The harpoon stuck firm and hard in the black shining flesh.

'Stick another hook in. Quick, quick,' he cried in triumph as he held the bucking rope. But from the corner of his eye he saw his younger brother, Surti, leap down from the platform onto the creature's back, gaff in hand. Very fast, before he could form words of warning, the creature made its move. The vast *bĕlelā* raised its two great wings and wrapped them tightly around Surti's body, knocking him flat and trapping him like an oyster in a shell. The boy gave a gasping scream, and Loveday watched as his terrified face was knocked flat against the creature's night-black skin. Then, with a shudder of farewell, the *bělelā* tugged with all its might and vanished below the water.

Loveday looked about himself, amazed. The crew was crowding at his back, gaping at the white foam where the *bělelā* had plunged, carrying the boy wrapped inside its wings. Someone had to do something. The discarded rope at his feet was unravelling faster than a snake darting into the bush. Grasping a second harpoon, Loveday ran to the front of the platform and dived after the disappearing rope. In a gushing eruption of spray he found the harpoon line and grasped it tightly. It pulled him crazily down into the water, dragged by the monstrous *bělelā* that strained and plunged at the other end of the rope. Surely the harpoon will loosen, he thought. Yet it stuck firm. He was descending fast from the sun-warmed shallows to the frozen indigo deeps. I must die, he told himself, rather than lose my little brother. I will never let this rope go.

Yet he needed air. His chest rasped with pain and his head felt as fat as a watermelon. Time wore on, like a net stretched around a monstrous catch. The *bělelā* ducked and weaved, trying to escape the drag of the rope. A terrible darkness dimmed Loveday's eyes. Then, like a child being born to the world, he felt sunlight warm his back. Air and sunlight burst noisily around him. He gasped and blinked, panting until the pain in his chest grew less. The rope was still tight in his hand. He looked about himself. Loveday could see the *bělelā*'s shape trembling beneath the swell; its wings moving freely. Where was Surti? He had disappeared. Drowned, surely drowned, answered the grim voice in his head. They had surfaced in the *bělelā*'s feeding ground, where the creature now grazed upon plankton. Some way behind them trailed the boat, a line of men huddling at the prow.

Honour blazed in his mind. He had to avenge Surti. Like a ravening shark he launched himself out of the water onto the head of the creature. It was the work of an instant to thrust his harpoon deep into the *bĕlelā*'s brain and kill it. He enjoyed a moment of hot satisfaction – he hated that creature, he wanted to beat it to soft pulp for taking the innocent boy.

Soon after, the crew arrived and lifted the beast up from the sucking ocean, carrying the *bĕlelā* into the airy world of men. Loveday watched as the men slit open its hollow bladder of a body and found nothing inside it but plankton. Why had the gods done this to him?

He felt weak and confused. The sun was setting and the waves were chopping fretfully. He looked out across the uneasy waters, haunted by the boy's pale face.

'We must go,' his captain Koti said, and the words brought an anguished pain to Loveday's being.

'No,' he insisted. 'Wait.' So they waited as the sun dipped into the sea in a red splash. He prayed, offering the father god, Bapa Fela, anything, any gift, any sacrifice. He had to find Surti alive. Otherwise, his happy life was over.

As if waking from a trance, he heard a commotion from behind him and a piping shout. The men were pulling something over the rail. Hope almost blinded him as he struggled through the huddling crew. Then, out of their centre staggered Surti, naked and shivering, his arm bleeding – but alive! Loveday ran to him and shook him by the shoulders. 'You stupid boy,' he said, 'you are alive, but it is no thanks to your idiocy. Thanks only to the gods.' And he embraced the boy and marvelled to feel the wriggling life inside his flesh.

After a sip of toddy, the boy told them that the *bĕlelā* had let go of him as soon as it made its descent. He had swum up towards the light, but in his giddiness had got tangled in the ropes. There he had hung, battered against the hull as the boat hurtled after its prey. 'I called to you, but no one heard,' he said.

'You are wrong,' said Koti, his wrinkled face very grave. 'The gods heard you and witnessed your brother's great courage. They have rewarded him with victory over the *bĕlelā* and over death itself.'

The *bĕlelã*'s dismembered body slid across the floor of the boat, trailing gore and slime. It was a monstrous size – it would feed the whole village. The boy was safe, and grinning as the older men cuffed him. Everyone wanted to touch Surti and his brother, to take for themselves a little magic from the boy who had survived the *bĕlelã*'s embrace and the man who had avenged it. Loveday stood firm at the prow, a man whom other men respected, and women admired.

That day the light of his Bapa, the sun, had shone inside his muscled chest. It had shone in his mind like a ball of fire. He had not known, then, that it would be his last victory. That soon the strange ship would arrive. That soon his courage would be smothered like a beacon in a storm.

Suddenly his body was tumbling through the air. He landed with a thump and found his mouth pressed hard into mud. What place was this? Rain, pain, and trouble returned. He looked about and found he was lying in the road, flung from the carriage into a rut of earth and stone. Dragging himself upright, he saw the carriage was tilting awkwardly, its back wheel hanging at a wounded angle. Could his troubles get any worse? Mr Pars and George were trying to calm the whinnying horses. Suddenly the carriage door opened and his mistress demanded to know what in the devil's name was going on. Loveday peered into the gathering twilight and groaned.

# XI

## The Great Midland Bogs

*Being Martinmas, November 1772*
*Biddy Leigh, her journal*

## ~ An English Rabbit of Cheese ~

*Toast your slices of bread then pour as much wine over as will soak in. Cut up a plate of cheese, very thin and lay it thick over the bread. Set it before the fire and brown the top with an iron shovel heated in the fire. Serve it away hot.*

*Biddy Leigh, her best way, 1772*

Our rescue was pitiful when it arrived. The only inn Mr Pars could find was a place fit only for trampers, so we must take our own food and bedding. Mr Loveday had cracked his head when the carriage tumbled, and all his fine livery was a slutching mess, poor fellow. But as I rode nervously behind George on one of the horses, the sunset gave a sudden burst of crimson glory, reflected in rain that shone like mirrors across the fields. Once the rain stopped it was a fine ride through a land of bright waters and mysterious black woods.

The inn was indeed a shattered ruin, for the landlord's wife had run off with a journeyman and left him to the drink. We had drifted four long miles off the highway, and the blackened inn was sinking in the winter bogs. Yet we had to bless our fortunes, for the roof leaked only in certain rooms, and a couple of hearths did throw out a little heat after much of a struggle with my tinderbox.

While Mr Loveday aired my lady's sheets, I set to scratching up a supper. With not even time to change from my own damp clothes I had in one half-hour some welcome tea steaming and hot brandy to mix a punch. Our bill of fare was the remnants of Mrs Garland's Yorkshire Pie, still sound and savoury, fried bacon, and a hillock of toasted rabbits that disappeared as quick as I made them. The last of the seed cake was eaten too, with a douse of brandy sprinkled over it to warm us.

'She will not eat those beggarly scraps,' said Jesmire, the spiteful old cat, when I took a tray of food to my lady's door. Yet I did see a slice of brandied cake disappear. I knew my mistress well enough by then, and she was a slave to her sugar tooth.

After supper Mr Pars got up to attend to some business with my lady. Then just as the rest of us settled down to a fire-bright doze in the parlour, we heard such a racket start up from my lady's chamber that we all jumped like startled sheep. One moment we heard Mr Pars speaking in a low rumble, and the next Her Ladyship crying out fit to burst her lungs. Wanting to get a proper earful, I made a pretence of clearing up, then loitered in the hallway. I could not hear a word of Mr Pars' speech, only that he sounded to be complaining in an unhappy manner. But my mistress's lighter voice came right through the wall, crying out, 'You will indeed,' and, 'Cannot? I will!' Mr Pars' words were again as clear as mud, then she yelled, 'Be off! Get out!' The door banged open and I scarce had time to disappear.

When I came back to the parlour, Mr Pars had returned to his deep chair by the fire and was complaining to the others. 'She says we must all lose our positions. As soon as the carriage is mended I must lead you all back home while she goes to London alone.' When I offered him his tankard he clutched it so tight his knuckles were white.

'Well, I for one should welcome it,' said George. 'She's worse than the dog's mother.' He was settled right above the fire like a great pink hog, his boots off and his wet stockings releasing clouds of steam.

'Mind your tongue before a lady, George.' Mr Pars glanced in Jesmire's direction, then took a deep draught and narrowed his eyes for a moment. I never saw him look more angry than when he wiped his bristled jowls and stared into the fire. 'And if your old place as coachman at Mawton were taken from you, too?' He spat into the flames and glared at the old coachman. George looked baffled for a moment, then a fuddled frown creased his brow.

As for me, what did I care if I lost my position? Why, me and Jem could then find work in town and soon be married. Yet what of my five guineas bonus? There was a long silence as the fire crackled.

It was Jesmire who spoke up next. Her features took on a right know-it-all simper. 'Mr Pars, pray do not be offended if I declare a little superior knowledge on this subject. May I tell you that *dismissal* is something of a refrain of hers? It is not in my nature to gossip, but she has very little grasp of genteel behaviour. Whims run through her mind like the changing weather. The facts stand that without us she would not have the slightest notion of how to proceed. By the morning she will doubtless have forgotten her hasty words.'

Mr Pars acknowledged this with a nod of his head, but he was still nearly purple with choler.

'So it's prob'ly fer't best if we forget it, Mr Pars, sir,' said old George peaceably.

Soon afterwards the others went to bed, and I began to clear the place. But our steward remained, his stout body slumped in his chair, jowls set and lower lip jutting deep in thought. As I picked up his tankard he met my glance.

'One strange matter,' he said. 'Your mistress said a very odd thing. I didn't care to share it in company.' His voice was slurred with liquor for he had drunk hard from the inn's store.

'And what's that, sir?' I said, my fingers cramping with the mass of cup handles I was trying to carry.

'That she would dismiss us all – save for you.' He blew out a plume of smoke and watched me steadily. 'Now all this evening I've been asking myself why she should make so much of our Biddy Leigh.'

I truly was too weary to mull over it.

'Sir, if I knew the answer to that I'd be the first to make summat of it.'

At that he jumped up and started to knock the ash out from the bowl of his pipe most violently against the mantel. Then he stood up straight, very large and towering above me. His expression was quite hately, as if he'd as soon see me rot as wish me good night.

'I'm watching you, Biddy Leigh. You women think you can bury your filthy secrets out of sight. But I will find you out.'

'Sir, there's nowt—'

'Shut those saucy lips of yours, girl. And get this place neat before you finish.' With that he took his wavering candle and marched off to his chamber.

It took a few days until the local blacksmith had mended the carriage and we got back on the road. Mr Loveday was shaken and his coat still stained, but no one but I cared a whit about that. As for me, I couldn't forget Mr Pars saying he was watching me.

I tried to put it from my mind once we settled into our next lodging at the Star Inn, where I was making our new quarters ready by collecting some rubbish thrown away in a basket. Once I was alone on the quiet backstairs, quite from habit I had a rifle through it, helping myself to some good sheets of paper that had clean backs. Pressed amongst those was a sheet of blotting paper that I also slid into my pocket.

That night I got out the papers to see what quality of stuff I had garnered. It was the blotter that caught my eye, for written upon it again and again in backwards writing were words that looked familiar, though I couldn't read the odd-fangled loops. Recollecting that a looking glass hung by the inn's stairs, I picked up my candle and moved very softly onto the landing, where the looking glass soon reflected my pale figure growing closer.

Slowly I lifted the candle and saw my own face peering forward in the mirror, my eyes making gleaming enquiry back at myself. Pulling out the blotter I held it to the glass and read it the right way about. It spelled again and again, as if being keenly practised:

*Sir Geoffrey Venables, Baronet*

I heard a warning creak behind me on the boards.

'Biddy Leigh. What are you doing here?'

Lord! I nearly dropped the candle and set my skirts alight. In the mirror I saw Mr Pars himself coming up behind me across the landing.

'Just wiping a smudge from me face, sir,' I said smartly, rubbing at my cheek with the edge of the blotter. 'I have no mirror, sir.'

By then he was right next to me, so I turned about, all the time praying he might not ask to see the paper clutched inside my fist.

'Mirror? A kitchen maid has no need of a mirror, girl. Give me that taper. The draught just blew my candle out.'

So then I had to fold the blotter and place the end in my candle flame. Sir Geoffrey's name seemed to stand upon it so boldly before my eyes that I thought Mr Pars would ask me where I had found it. But instead he took it and did not notice at all. I bobbed low and wished him good night and he went back to his chamber, the paper burning down fast. It was a mighty fright he had given me. Yet who was it practised Sir Geoffrey's name?

Next day, as the carriage rolled along the turnpike road and Jesmire and my mistress dozed, I listened to the *rat-a-tat-tat* of rain beating hard against the roof. Then I got to remembering Widow Trotter's old lesson:

> *It is a sin,*
> *To steal a Pin,*
> *Much more to steal a greater thing.*
> *'Tis better for me to be poor,*
> *And beg my Bread from door to door.*

Better to be poor? Even at ten years old, I reckoned it was not. When Widow Trotter left me alone to my tasks I would stroke her spotless hand-worked linen and play with her best silver spoons. I called them my pretty ladies, fancying their curling silver handles were hair and their bowls round satin skirts. Every night I had to leave that neat cottage and go home to maggots in the oat sack and a wallop across my ear. Better to be poor? Fiddlesticks.

As for those of us in service, pay a servant little and he will pay himself, they say. Nothing too grand, mind you, just the dregs of a bottle, a spare candle, or indeed, a few sheets of paper. That was quite a different matter from faking the master's name. I did not know what to think.

Mr Pars had taken a dislike to me, that was for certain. And why had my lady said she would keep me if she dismissed the rest of them? I turned these matters over in my head, but of answers none arrived.

# XII

## Stony Stratford

The Correspondence of Mr Humphrey Pars
29th November 1772

*PRIVATE CORRESPONDENCE*

*The Cock Inn*
*Stony Stratford*
*29th November 1772*

*Mr Ozias Pars*
*Marsh Cottage*
*Mawton*

*My Dear Ozias,*
*I pray you are all in good health and in better spirits than your poor brother. Tonight he sits in the Cock Inn at Stony Stratford, a den of Southern thieves, where the landlord has presented me with a bill of £3-7s-6d for one night's lodging for three persons and their servants. I do not jest! The closer we get to the great metropolis, the more boldly we are fleeced. In a mere week of travelling I have handed over more than twenty-five guineas to such vultures.*

*Little more than a day passed before our homely brick farms and soft Cheshire meadows made way for The Midlands of this country, a far less beauteous place, disfigured by wild irregularities of landscape not able to be cultivated. Indeed there is no land of such quality as Pars Fold, though I do try to put that loss from my mind.*

*Thanks only to my own diligent efforts, we made good time along the roads until my inferior map led to our losing our way around Stone, and, as a consequence, our carriage broke its axletree. I feared a fever from the soaking, but thanks to God's Mercy I am spared any consequences. After tedious repairs we found our road again and proceeded via poor inns to Lichfield, and there the jade demanded we stay only at the grandest place, namely the famous George, as she claims to need respite from the rolling carriage and low-class inns. No sooner was I settled in the excellent Newspaper Room than I was interrupted by a man with a letter that had followed me about the roads this week past. My heart quailed to see it was sent by Sir Geoffrey's man at Wicklow, written two weeks since. Brother, this was his import:*

*'It is grave news I must tell, Pars, that Sir Geoffrey arrived here in a most dreadful condition, having fallen down in a fit on the sea voyage to Dublin Bay. It seems the ship's captain had sent his servant to make enquiries after his lordship stayed so long in his cabin and found him lying on the floor in disarray. At first the question was raised as to what Sir Geoffrey had eaten, for he had been violently sick, but it was found he had taken nothing since coming on board. Now, after a full examination by Sir Geoffrey's own physician, it is found he has been stricken by an apoplexy. Pars, I must reluctantly inform you that our master can neither speak nor move his limbs and is in no condition to be moved. He is being tended as well as can be, though the softening of the brain leaves him insensible to his surroundings.'*

*My hand shook as I read it, plagued as I was by a single question: is my master close to death, and what then are the consequences?*

*I sought her out. The girl was at the card tables, disfigured by paint and sporting more blubber above her bodice than a halfpenny streetwalker.*

*'My Lady,' I said, 'I have grave news from Ireland. Sir Geoffrey is struck down by an apoplexy and may not recover.'*

*'Sir Geoffrey?' she uttered slowly. 'My poor husband.' She tried to mimic a sad face but did not fool me. 'I suppose it is of no great consequence. Old men are often sick.'*

*'He is more than usually sick, My Lady. It is a softening of the brain.'*

*She looked about herself, fearful of being heard.*

'You mean—' There was a hearkening look to her upraised face; an expression I do not care to remember. She twisted the Mawton Rose that hung upon her breast, that grew suddenly flushed with agitation.

I could not answer, for I truly did not know how low my master had sunk.

'Tell me at once if there is further news.'

'And should I alter our plans, My Lady?' I fixed upon her brazen countenance.

She returned a challenge. 'I am sure it is of little consequence. I will continue to Italy as before.'

Hark brother, at the jade's callous nature. I swore then that I would no longer be her protector. Aye, I would do my duty, I would command my little band. But she is unworthy to bear my master's name.

The next day being Sunday, I gathered my little regiment of servants and told them most gravely of their master's distress. Together we made haste to the city's ancient cathedral, where a proper Anglican service was decently performed, and we prayed most heartily for Sir Geoffrey's recovery (even the blackamoor did decently shut his eyes).

Yet as I wait here in Stony Stratford and ponder Sir Geoffrey's ailment, grave reflections plague me. Reading the letter again, I understand that my master was smitten the very day he departed from his bride. God forgive her if she has harmed my innocent old master. Have you ever heard of such a sorry tale?

I pray you do keep these true accounts of mine safe in your box, Ozias, for I mightily fear the trouble that may yet be brewing. Indeed, the account of an innocent witness may one day be called for and you must keep my correspondence safe under lock and key.

I will write once more from the great metropolis.

I remain your resolute and stoic brother,

Humphrey Pars

# XIII

## Stony Stratford to London

*Being Stir-up Sunday to Advent, 1772*
*Biddy Leigh, her journal*

## ~ Sassafras Oil ~

*Distilled from the bark of the Sassafras root it must be kept in a well-stoppered bottle away from the light of day. It is a sovereign remedy for Wens and much applied as a rub for Rheumatics and other pains. Given as a dose of five drops on sugar it has proved advantageous in cases of the pox and gleets therefrom and to ease childbed and menstrual obstruction. One teaspoonful of the oil produced vomiting, stupor and collapse in a young man.*

*A Remedy prescribed by Dr Trampleasure for which I paid 5 shillings, Lady Maria Grice, 1744*

At a place called Stony Stratford me and Mr Loveday slipped off to a fair; it was nothing to Chester Fair, but a merry gathering still. There was gilded gingerbread, a turnabout ride for the children, and buffoons crying out for all to see their counting pigs and Amazon queens and whatnots. Using a few coppers Mr Loveday found in his pocket we then took a look at a Ghost Show. It was horribly dark in the tent and the air stank of coal smoke disguised by incense. The buffoon gave us a long hogwash talk about how we must all be mighty careful not to look in the eyes of the spirits or we might fall down dead. Then at last, with a flash of light the figure of a devil came wavering out of the smoke. It was all quite cleverly done. Poor Mr Loveday buried his face in his hands and would not look at it. He was not alone, for many other people cried out in terror and some rushed pell-mell to escape. Though I told him there was a lantern contraption making shadows, Mr Loveday couldn't make sense of the trick at all.

'I very sorry think bad things,' he said with chattering teeth. 'Now devil come chase me.'

Sometimes that lad was scared of his own shadow, so I stood him a drink, and once he'd knocked back some ale he settled down. All day I'd been fretting over Mr Pars' news, that Sir Geoffrey had lost all power of speech and movement. Mighty strange that sounded to me. Naturally, George scoffed at his illness and said it was only what old men should expect if they marry young ladies. For myself, I thought it rum that my mistress spoke not a word of it and carried on just as before. As for Mr Loveday, he was sure some spirit had got inside the master, but I was having none of it. I'd read a great list of Remedies in *The Cook's Jewel* and found that apoplexy was caused by an excess of blood in the neck. Purging and bleeding were what he needed.

Then I asked Mr Loveday about when he first worked for our mistress.

'First I work as footman in Mr Quentin house. Then Lady Carinna want own footman now she married an' all that.'

'So were you there on her wedding day?'

'I go on carriage. I stand at church door.'

'On her wedding day, what did she look like?'

'What she look like? Like she look.'

Lord, it was like pulling teeth. 'I mean, was she happy?'

'Before – she look like crying. Then after she quiet face.'

'And Sir Geoffrey, was he happy?'

Loveday's face creased into a white-toothed grin. 'He drunk much liquor,' he laughed. 'Mr Quentin, he dress him, he heavy as old stone. His head hurt mighty bad.'

Just then a shower of hailstones sent us pelting back to the inn with spattered clothes and ratty hair. There I had the misfortune to walk right into my mistress and Jesmire in the hallway of the inn.

'Where have you been hiding? And what in heaven's name do you look like?'

Jesmire shook her grey head slowly. It was true my face was red raw from the icy hail.

'Your complexion will be ruined,' complained my mistress, as I shivered before her in my soaking gown. 'I thought country servants had fresh faces. That's what all the ballads say. Girl, I have some cowslip water in my travelling case, most esteemed to improve the face. I give you permission to go to my chamber and take a cupful to dowse your face. What do you say to that?'

I curtseyed and mumbled my thanks. As for Jesmire, she looked so affronted at my mistress's kindness that it cheered me up no end.

Once I was dry, I made my way to my lady's chamber while she was still downstairs at cards. The cowslip water was in my lady's travelling box, an ingenious cabinet filled with every sort of brush, powder puffer, and bottles of perfume and pomade. Admiring all her pretty things, I poured myself a cupful of the cowslip water. Then, dawdling before the lovely bright fire, I dabbed a little Cologne water on my bodice. Next, my hand fell on a little amber bottle and I lifted it to take a sniff. It was somewhat like an apothecary's bottle, tight stoppered with a label that said '*Sassafras Oil*'. Inside was a sweet heavy oil that reeked like no ordinary scent. Then suddenly a cold draught from the doorway started me sneezing, which try as I might to stop it, exploded like a flurry of gunfire. Quickly closing the portmanteau, I jumped up just in time to see a figure at the door. It was Mr Pars.

'My Lady,' he called, as I turned. I curtseyed and told him my mistress had told me to come up and dress my face. 'Very well, Biddy. That will be all,' he replied, which was kindness itself from that curmudgeon. Then I found my own closet under the eaves and had a very pleasant spell dressing my face with the complexion water.

I thought no more of the Sassafras Oil until the next night when I lay on my pallet reading *The Cook's Jewel*. I pored through the quivery old writing with my fingertip. There it was, amongst a great list of Remedies for fearful contagions: *Sassafras Oil*. I yawned, but read on and tried to guess what Lady Carinna might want with such stuff. Five to ten drops on sugar for the pox and gleets. Surely not, for I would have seen any sores if she had them. Praised for application to wens and rheumatics, it continued, and after childbed and menstrual obstruction. None of those were likely, and as for being recently at childbed, her bosom had no signs of milk. Then I read the final line. 'One teaspoon of the oil produced vomiting, stupor and collapse in a young man.'

I shut the book fast. So she did have the means if she wished it, to strike down her husband. Maybe her giddiness was all an act? After all, we all knew she was merrily spending Sir Geoffrey's money with not a shred of conscience. Was it possible that she had stirred a teaspoon of oil into the old man's drink?

Next morning I peered closely at my mistress as she dozed beside Jesmire. In the fresh light of day I could never believe she had poisoned my master. She was young and wilful, but I did not count those as crimes. Faultless is lifeless, was my opinion. And she was generous too, even if I did feel uneasy about that rose-red gown. Young and wilful and odd. Well, that made two of us amongst those canting codgers. Yet neither was she much like the noble folk we saw at inns, for she had slummery ways and was sometimes ill-tempered. When she let her airs drop I thought her a plain enough girl, being out to make her fortune certainly, but not at all wicked.

Suddenly her eyes opened so I quickly turned to stare out of the window.

'Dreaming of home?' she asked.

I nodded, for it seemed the safest way.

'My true home is far away,' she sighed, raising herself up. 'A beautiful place in Ireland, where I was born. But when I was four, my mother died. I remember her as a delicate lady, robed in white, laying on a large canopied bed. My dear father died a year later, of the drink, at Crumlin races.'

I kept my mouth shut, wondering why in hell's name she was telling me all this stuff.

Then all of a sudden she sat forward in her seat and looked at me like she could eat me alive.

'Do you have a good memory, girl? Can you repeat what I just told you? It's a little game I like to play.'

What kind of a game was that? Only to pander to her, I had a go.

'You was born in Ireland. Your lady mother is dead, now that is a sad story, for she died when you were only four. She were a beauty but delicate, like.'

'And my father?' she asked keenly, as if she did not know herself.

'Why he died of the drink at the Crumlin races.'

Just then Jesmire began to stir and wipe her hand against her dribbling mouth.

'Very good,' said my lady to herself and sat back to play with Bengo. Then the two of them began nattering, and as for me, I let myself dream awhile of Jem.

I smelt London before I saw it. It travelled on the breeze, the stink of night soil and coal smoke. As we got closer we reached a great hill and halted at the crest. Jumping down, I drank in the view so I might never forget it. Before us lay England's great capital, spread like a hundred cities tacked together from end to end, studded with spires that pierced the sooty drifts of smoke. Here, I repeated to myself, is our Capital, the seat of the Quality and of Britain's own King George and Queen Charlotte. I reckoned I would never see a finer sight, not in France nor Italy nor all the world.

It was slow work getting on the London road, what with the crush of carts, wagons, carriages and horses. Above us hung a hundred signs across the fronts of the buildings: *Foreign Liquors Sold Here* or *Tea Dealer & Grocer* or *Oilman, Italian Wares and Pickles*. Coffee houses, tavern signs, shop signs – everywhere painted words spoke of food and drink.

Old George had to perform miracles to squeeze our carriage between the loaded carts and street barrows jammed up against the roadside. At last we entered a broad road named the Strand and saw bookshops, mercers, mapmakers, milliners, and every kind of seller, all showing goods off behind glass windows like cabinets of treasure.

Lady Carinna's uncle's house was at Devereaux Court, and was nowhere near as large as Mawton, for it was only a townhouse with everything piled up in six lofty storeys. I was ordered to the kitchen by Mr Pars, and was right sorry to see Mr Loveday disappear upstairs with Her Ladyship.

The fug of old grease and blocked drains rising up the stairs told me all I needed to know about the kitchen. Being a man of fashion,

Mr Tyrone had a man cook of course, so it gave me some satisfaction to see him suffer for it. Mr Meeks was an idling, cheating blubber-guts who took whatever he could from his master. Whenever Mr Tyrone wished to entertain, the kitchen was filled with baskets and parcels of goods all delivered from pastry cooks and taverns. All he did was primp the food with his black-rinded fingers and lay it on Mr Tyrone's plates as if he'd cooked it all himself. As for the silver that passed into that rogue's palm, it was like the fellow was minting the stuff. Yet if Meeks would not cook, I at least learned what his suppliers could concoct. One night I saw a vast transparent pudding all arrayed with playing cards made of solid blancmange, a most marvellous conceit. The lad who brought it told me how it was done, and thus I obtained a fine London receipt. Meeks overheard us and waddled over to admire the prettily painted playing cards.

'Why I ain't seen that confection since the gaming night we had for that tosspot, Sir Geoffrey,' boasted Meeks, laughing to see my head shoot around at my master's name. 'We done up the salon like a right tip-top club,' he scoffed. 'The old man fell for the trick like a dead bird from a tree. You heard that story, eh, young Biddy? How your master got landed with Miss Carinna?'

I never gave him the satisfaction of a reply, but to think of my old master in that den of thieves made me ashamed, though I knew not why.

At last, one evening Mr Loveday stuck his head around the scullery door, where I was washing a heap of plates as high as a mountain.

'How you, Miss Biddy?' I wiped my hands on my apron and took his hand in mine, I was that happy to see him.

'I'm ready for the off, Mr Loveday. Why in heaven's name are we waiting here day after day? I thought we had a boat to catch at Dover.'

My friend pulled the door quietly shut behind him.

'Listen, tomorrow everyone here go to royal parade. I go shops. You come with me, you not tell?' I could have kissed him for thinking of me. And despite it being near midnight when I crept to my pallet in the kitchen boot hole, I could barely sleep for thinking of the morrow and my liberty.

'Before we go,' I pleaded next morning, when Mr Loveday came to fetch me after the others had all left, 'please let me take a quick look at the house. I have seen nothing but dark passages since I came here. If anyone comes back we can say I'm helping you around the house.'

My friend hesitated but I knew he hadn't the heart to deny me a thing. And what joy it was to climb the backstairs and find myself in Mr Tyrone's high and airy hallway, admiring the gilded stairs, great lantern, and pretty tiled floor. Though the house was old, the decoration was much finer than Mawton, the walls painted sky blue and bearing decorations like moulded sugar work in pretty patterns.

We tiptoed upstairs to the dining room. On the long mahogany table stood a vast crystal punchbowl, and silverware that flashed in the morning light. I pictured that table properly laid, the candles dancing in the mirrors, the porcelain filled with my own best food. I swore that one day I would make a fancy dinner with all the care such a table deserved.

'What room is that?' I asked, seeing a further chamber hung with velvet curtains still drawn against the day. It was scattered with padded chairs that must have felt like clouds to sit upon, set around dainty leather card tables. 'Is that the salon where Sir Geoffrey was entertained?'

My friend looked dismayed. 'You come along, Miss Biddy. We go.'

I couldn't stop myself; I passed into the room that smelt of stale tobacco and trapped dust. Lifting the heavy curtain, I saw no sign in the street below of anyone returning.

'What was it happened when Sir Geoffrey was here? Were you in attendance that night?'

Mr Loveday reluctantly followed me inside.

'We go now. Not allowed. I not remember.'

'You do. I can see it in your face.'

Miserably, he looked about himself.

'Go on, tell me,' I urged.

Then, with great reluctance, he said, 'Only because you my friend. I tell you.'

# XIV

Loveday had wanted to talk to Biddy as freely as they had done on the road, to feel her touch upon his arm and to bask in the comfort of her kindly eyes. Now he felt trapped in the airless room; his spirit smothered by the heavy woven stuffs and glassed-in windows. He scarcely ever reflected on what he had seen or heard when carrying out his work, but now Biddy's question troubled him. He blinked, remembering that the room had looked quite different when Sir Geoffrey had visited – candles had fluttered in their sconces and silver plate shone in the gloom. For many days the servants had prepared for his visit under the stern direction of the butler, Mr Tusler.

'And not a word to anyone about tonight's goings on, eh, darkie? Or you'll wish you was never born. Understand?' Mr Tusler had jabbed him hard on the chest. It had been soon after his first arrival in this chilly kingdom, when he was still waking up each morning in deep despair at finding himself to be the possession of Mr Quentin Tyrone. Loveday had not known anyone to talk to anyway, so he had nodded meekly at the butler and got on with his work. But that was before he knew Biddy. Now he wanted to please her so much that he let all his memories come tumbling out.

'Sir Geoffrey come. I show him upstair. He sit there.' He pointed to a maroon velvet armchair drawn up to the card table. 'Mr Quentin, he sit there.' The leather chair was drawn up opposite Sir Geoffrey's.

Biddy nodded. Loveday could almost taste the smoke hanging in a blue haze, and hear the *chink* of glasses.

'I serve drink. Mr Tusler say, give Sir Geoffrey from big bottle, give Mr Quentin from other bottle.' Shame warmed his face. 'I not think 'bout it, not that night. Only telling you now, I understand I got old man drunk.'

'You weren't to know,' said Biddy gently. 'It was their doing, not yours.' She nodded at him to carry on.

'They start play hazard.' Loveday pointed to the dice shaker on the table. Biddy lifted it and tossed out two ivory dice. A six and a one. 'Sir Geoffrey win and win. I keep pouring liquor from big bottle. Sir Geoffrey he got happy face. He got big winning.'

'And Mr Quentin?' Biddy asked, looking towards the smooth leather chair.

'He sad face. He lose every game, so much desperate. Sir Geoffrey win all his money. Mr Quentin say, "I ruined man. I play again. I play again, again, I stake ten thousand pound."'

'So he lost? Did he have to pay up?'

'He say not got so big money. He play last, very last game, try to win. He say if Sir Geoffrey win, he give Miss Carinna to Sir Geoffrey.'

Biddy was shaking her head slowly. 'So let me be sure of this. Mr Quentin lost so badly that he offered his niece as the prize?'

'She come that door.' Loveday nodded, pointing towards a low inner door. He remembered now, that she had looked different that night. Her usually high-pinned hair hung down past her shoulders, and she wore a plain white gown. 'I think – she make self look like young girl.'

'And how did Lady Carinna seem to you?'

'She not talk. Do what uncle say.'

'Well,' Biddy said, 'maybe she was forced to do it. But Sir Geoffrey, what did he make of it?'

'His eyes on fire. He like young girl, I think. Mr Quentin say Sir Geoffrey must marry her and he say yes. Old man so drunk he say anything. They play last game. Sir Geoffrey he keep play lucky seven. He win again.'

'Oh aye? That was very lucky.'

Biddy gave the dice shaker a good long rattle. The dice scattered in a one and six again. 'These dice always score the same.'

Loveday tried it, and it was true. He picked it up and looked closely at it. 'So this magic dice?'

'Loaded dice, more like, fixed to fall on those numbers.'

Loveday threw, and again it cast a perfect seven. Yet he remembered Mr Quentin's sorry face as he kept on losing. 'But Miss Biddy, how Mr Quentin not win seven too?'

'I bet he'd got another dice up his sleeve. Was there a candle on the table?'

Loveday closed his eyes and remembered only the sconces lit on the wall and a candelabrum on the sideboard. He shook his head. Biddy sat down in Sir Geoffrey's maroon chair and moved her head about, as if trying to get a view of her imagined opponent.

'It looks like Mr Quentin was quite in the shadows, and his hands easily hidden by the table edge and arms of his chair. They went to a lot of—'

'What that noise?'

Loveday was alert, listening to a noise in the hallway below. Silently, he motioned to Biddy and they crept back into the dining room. As the footsteps on the stairs grew louder, they both made a pretence of stacking plates.

Even with a few moments warning, Loveday gave a start as a deep male drawl asked, 'Loveday, where *is* everybody?'

His mistress's brother stood yawning at the door, dressed in a braided coat and tousled shirt. Loveday bowed very low, cringing at being caught with Biddy beside him.

'Mr Kitt, sir. No one here. All gone to royal parade.' He looked down at the floor, hoping the man would go away.

'Even Carinna?'

'Yes Mr Kitt, sir.' He motioned at Biddy to carry on stacking crockery.

'And who might you be?'

Biddy looked up, very startled. 'Me, sir?'

Mr Kitt was quite fixed in the doorway. 'Yes, you.'

'Biddy Leigh, sir. Under-cook from Mawton Hall. Here with me mistress, Lady Carinna, if you please.' She looked unnerved as she made a clumsy curtsey.

'Loveday.' Mr Kitt paused to yawn once more. 'Run down and fetch me some coffee.'

'I'll help you,' Biddy hissed, making to follow him.

But when she reached the doorway, the young gentleman let Mr Loveday pass and then stopped Biddy's exit with his outstretched arm.

Loveday ran downstairs to the butler's pantry where he slopped some lukewarm water over a spoonful of coffee. He was horribly alarmed to think of Biddy alone with his mistress's brother.

Only the previous day he had been in Lady Carinna's chamber as she nagged at Mr Kitt. She had sat at the mirror, dabbing stuff from all the pots and boxes spread about her; she had been in one of her lively, devilish moods.

'Come along, surely even you can find new friends?' she had teased Mr Kitt, who was lounging before the fire, dressed in a long black Chinese robe. He had been half-heartedly flicking crumbs into the flames.

'Oh sis, I've told you before. I don't choose to.' Loveday had thought he whined like a lazy girl. 'And it's not a case merely of friends, is it?'

She had glared at him in the mirror. 'Try, for my sake,' she had insisted, less warmly. 'There are prettier girls aplenty at the pleasure gardens.'

Loveday had glanced up from his polishing then. Prettier than whom? He wondered if they spoke of Biddy, for these last weeks he always fancied people were speaking of Biddy.

Next moment Lady Carinna had caught his eye, and he was told to take Bengo out into the yard.

As he took the squirming bundle of dog flesh into his arms, he wondered what they were going to talk about when alone. Then Bengo had nipped his hand with his sharp little teeth. The best place for Bengo, Loveday thought, as he clattered down the stairs, was roasted on a stick across a fire, though the meat would make mighty stringy eating.

Biddy was his friend, and he had to protect her from men like Mr Kitt. The tray of lukewarm coffee rattled in his hands as he ran back upstairs to the dining room. From the landing he heard murmuring voices.

'Anything else you need, sir?' Loveday challenged, brandishing the coffee tray.

Mr Kitt gave a great yawning groan. 'Only my bed. See I am not disturbed until dinner, my good fellow.'

Loveday watched him climb the stairs with resentment in his heart, still clutching the coffee tray very tight.

At last they were outside in the cold air that tasted of smut and early frost.

'Who was that?' Biddy asked.

'That Lady Carinna brother, Mr Kitt. What he say to you, Miss Biddy?'

She shook her head as if it was of no importance. 'He asked about the journey. Why Lady Carinna was taking me with her. I couldn't help him.'

Loveday suspected Mr Kitt of far more than that. All the way down the Strand Loveday hung back unhappily behind Biddy as she peered about, captivated by all the stuff in windows, her eyes glazed with wanting. Compared to rich, high-ranking Mr Kitt, Loveday felt like a no-good nobody.

'That so old and dry and shrunk,' he retorted, when Biddy praised the market sellers' fruit. He longed to tempt her with sweet-tasting mango, banana, and guava.

'But they are beautiful,' Biddy protested, admiring a great pyramid of oranges upon a stall.

'In my island we pick fruit the day it ripe.' He was straining to be heard above the yells, the wheels grinding on cobbles, and the bells ringing out at the church on the square.

At last they reached the quiet edge of the Piazza and strolled past parked sedan chairs and gentlemen gathered beneath theatre notices. She grasped his hand tightly as they approached the shop.

'Here it is at last, Mr Loveday. *The Cocoa-Nut Tree* itself.'

Once inside the confectioners, she was spellbound by sugared fruits hung in garlands and glass bottles sparkling with morsels of sugar. While Loveday spoke to the shop girl, Biddy trailed the shelves slowly, looking inside glass jars, mouthing the words on the Bill of Fare.

'Look Mr Loveday, "Macaroons – As Made In Paris",' she sighed, staring at a heap of biscuits made in every colour from blue to shiny gold.

Carefully he ordered his goods from the jars of herbs behind the counter. First, there was Mr Pars' packet of coltsfoot that he smoked to ease his chest. Then a bag of comfrey tea for his mistress's stomach. Finally, boxes of the usual violet pastilles.

Biddy came up behind him while the girl tied the parcel with ribbon.

'Begging your pardon, miss. Is it right you're selling that Royal Ice Cream?'

The girl shrugged. 'That's what it says on the board if you can read it.'

'Aye, I've been studying it all right. I've only ever read of ices before. So I'll have a try of it.'

When the girl reappeared Biddy sniffed at the little glass bowl, and then cautiously licked the ice cream from the tiny spoon.

'Why, it is orange flowers.' She looked happy enough to burst. 'And something else, some fragrant nut – do you put pistachio in it too?'

While she asked a hundred questions of the shop girl, Loveday paced up and down, fretful to get on their way. He had longed for a day out with Biddy, but something was wrong.

A sudden distinct smell stopped him as still as a stone. The air was heavy with flower syrup, but he knew that musky undertone at once. Beside him was a bowl on a tiny silver table, and inside it, unmistakeably, were lumps of the grey stone found deep inside the whales of his homeland.

'*FINEST AMBERGRIS*,' he read, but he already knew what those mottled lumps were. The high briny sweetness made him feel queasy. Back home that aroma had been one of the happiest parts of his life, the familiar backdrop to the sacred boathouse. Yet so much had happened since. That smell: it was like poison in the air, a stinking fume of death.

'We go now,' he called sharply to Biddy. When she hurried over to ask him what the matter was, he pointed at the bowl.

'Oh, fresh ambergris, that is a rarity.' She dipped her head to sniff it, her eyelids closed. 'Please Mr Loveday, just a few minutes more.'

'That why my village destroy,' he mumbled, tugging her arm. 'We go.' Then at last he was out in the cold air, breathing hard to shift the clinging scent from his head.

'Come on now,' he called out, ignoring Biddy's disappointment. 'Not allowed be late. They catch us, we punished.'

# XV

## The Kitchen, Devereaux Court

*Being Advent, December 1772*
*Biddy Leigh, her journal*

## ~ All Nations ~

*A gross composition of all the different spirits sold in a dram-shop, collected in a vessel into which the drainings of the bottles and quartern pots are emptied.*

One night someone was clattering about in the kitchen, so I lit a candle and came out of my sleeping quarters. It was that Mr Kitt, a handsome young fellow he was, so much that when he'd questioned me in the dining room I'd got in a right fluster. Now he was rummaging in the rotten baskets beside Meeks's greasy chair.

'Sir, you wanting summat?'

He looked up with a start.

'Ah, it's you, Biddy. Where does Meeks keep his liquor?'

I opened the iron doors of the range where Meeks hid the half-empty bottles kept for his own enjoyment. The young gentleman was looking at me hard, just as he had done when I first saw him. Lord, I wished I'd had time to dress my hair and put on more than my shift, which barely covered my modesty. When I'd found him a glass, he told me to get myself one, too.

'Oh, nowt for me, sir.'

'Come on, Biddy,' he pleaded, 'I've had a hellish night. Lost all my coin at the gaming table. Take a drink with me, won't you?'

His tempting worked on me, but first I went to fetch a shawl and wrapped it about my person. When I came back he'd poured me a full bumper, and motioned me to sit at the table across from him.

'It can't be pleasant for you, Biddy, down here with Meeks.'

I wondered if he were mocking me, but he looked at me quite friendly-like.

'That's true enough, sir.'

'To a change of fortune,' he said smartly, raising his glass, and I raised mine too.

'So,' he asked, after emptying his, 'you are off on this excursion to Italy with my sister. Surely that must be quite an improvement in your fortune?'

I knew he must think me a country numkin, so I said, 'I think, sir, that however grand a body's fortune, it might always be improved.'

He took a long measuring look at me. 'I'll toast that.'

He drained and refilled his glass. 'Did you know, my sister and I have spent many an hour in this kitchen? This house has been refashioned now, but when we first came here our nursery was as cold as the grave and no more cheerful. Carinna was but four years old, and I an infant. It was a fearful place.'

In the light of the candle his eyes were quite liquid and most agreeably fine. And his confiding manner gave me the curious notion he wanted to win my trust. 'Our uncle was scarcely a man of melting heart, even then. I'm sure you servants must talk of him. I swear never to be like him.' He uttered these last words so fiercely that I thought what a boy he was in spirit, much younger than me and Carinna. He had a habit of making these small trials of manliness that I thought a little sad and sweet. 'One night the rout was so loud that Carinna and I crept down and peeped through those same stair posts in our nightgowns. Down here sat a great gathering of servants supping my uncle's leavings from a pot of All Nations, singing and toasting before the fire. So you must picture me and little Carinna, eating plum cake and drinking our first heady bumpers with fingers that could barely hold a glass.' He laughed softly at the memory.

I nodded my head, quite taken by his mannerly, honeyed voice.

'It was here I learned the great games of chance with the best of teachers – Catch-dolt, Tick-tack, Hazard. We even danced for them when the table was cleared, two little creatures jigging to a penny whistle. When I bowed and Carinna curtseyed the roaring near raised the roof.'

He paused and stroked the rough-hewn table, as if he might conjure those little ghosts. Then he opened a second bottle and poured himself more, while I took only an inch. It didn't take long for the liquor to loose his tongue again as he stared into the darkness.

'We were brought here from our family's estate in Ireland. Carinna just remembers Ormond, a perfect thousand acres with a fine stone house. She used to talk of it, how grand it was. It is famous hunting country. It's where I was born and where I swear I'll take my last breath. Now my uncle, damn him, has set tenants on it. But I'll get it back.'

He fell silent, staring into the fire.

I asked, 'How's that, sir?'

He looked up quickly. 'Oh, fortunes pass from hand to hand every day. My luck at the tables will turn. And when it does, we'll have Ormond again.'

He drooped again and stared into his glass. Suddenly, from nowhere it seemed, he asked, 'Have you found out yet, why my sister is leaving England?' He peered through his falling hair then combed it back with white-knuckled fingers.

I shook my head. 'Sir, she don't confide in me.'

'You would tell me if you knew?' He smiled uncertainly.

'Beggin' your pardon, sir, but do you truly not know why your sister is heading for Italy?'

He grimaced, bemused. 'Perhaps to escape from her husband?'

'But he is laid up sick in Ireland. She has no need to travel, sir.'

He gave a little nod, then bit his lower lip. 'I thought you servants knew everything.'

'It seems not, sir.'

'But you do have the means. To listen at doors. And to search her things.'

I didn't move an inch.

'Biddy,' he said most earnestly. 'Would it be such a sin to take a little peek? To put my mind at ease?'

'What makes you think I'd do such a thing?'

'Don't you like me a little?' He patted my hand and then left his own lying upon it. 'I feel we are well met. I like you. My sister has done well to find you.'

Then he fell into another silence. I sat there quite flummoxed, his hand still on mine. I was flattered all right, but thinking of the danger, too.

'It is cold,' he said blankly, stifling a shiver as if remembering some disaster anew.

'I'll stoke the fire for you, sir.'

I rose and found the poker, and the flare of orange warmth roused him. He stood up and slipped an arm loosely about my shoulders. I stiffened with alarm. He tried to pull me closer, closing his eyes and whispering in my ear.

'Would you help me, Biddy?'

I pulled back away from him, bumping against the table. He grabbed at me from behind as I wriggled away, feeling his arm brush my jiggling breasts.

'No, sir. No!' He was as frisky as a young colt. But I was strong, and elbowed him hard in his guts. He doubled over. With another yank I was free.

'Don't be such a tease,' he gasped. 'I thought you liked me.'

I turned to face him, my shift all askew. 'I liked you better when you did not maul me.'

'Oh Biddy, do be kind. No one will punish you.' He reached for my hand. 'I swear I'll not harm you.'

'Aye, and I'm Queen Dick,' I snapped, backing into the shadows. I was faster than him, and in three steps had reached the dark doorway of my quarters. He stumbled after me, but in an instant I had the door bolted fast. As I listened to his hammerings, I couldn't help but laugh to think of him, lordly Kitt Tyrone, coming chasing after me.

# XVI

## Devereaux Court, London

*The Correspondence of Mr Humphrey Pars*
*17th December 1772*

# PRIVATE CORRESPONDENCE

*Devereaux Court*
*London*
*17th December 1772*

*Mr Ozias Pars*
*Marsh Cottage*
*Saltford*

*My dear Ozias,*
*Doubtless you will be surprised to find me still languishing in the capital. I assure you the delay is not of my making. My so-called mistress continues to dally and fritter away my master's fortune on this Frenchified lace or that fur muff – and she is not ashamed to charge bills at five, ten or even twenty guineas for such fripperies.*

*My lodgings suit me very ill. My chamber is large but thick with dust, my bed is damp, and the chimney smokes from lack of attention. Mr Quentin Tyrone may be rich, but he is a queer unwholesome creature and I avoid his company. He employs an overseer to tend his business (the importation of eastern stuffs, inherited from his late father) and spends his nights at nanny houses and those oriental hummums where I believe a bath is but a small part of the transaction. He is a rotund, bald specimen, much given to embroidered caps and a stained sort of morning gown in the Chinese style. There is something soft about his manners that a proper man can only abhor. As to the other member of the household, her brother is a shiftless youth with a hangdog expression and high taste in gold coats.*

*Of London itself, the crowds and uproar are most incredible and the coal smoke so thick that one's outpourings of phlegm are quite sooty black. To attend the theatre is to place oneself in a tumult ten times worse than Chester Fair. Oranges are sold at sixpence (each!) and these are used as missiles from one part of the theatre to the next. As to the foppish appearance of the playgoers – like the boy Tyrone, the young men outdo the ladies in glitter and musk. Why, even I was asked at the barbers if I would have my hair frowzled in hot irons!*

*Having assiduously avoided the rest of the household by taking my dinner at a respectable chop house (for the fare at Devereaux Court is worse than any Northern poorhouse) I believed I should have no new information to give you on this harlot and her schemes. However, being one day somewhat weary after walking out all morning, I chose to take my tea by the fire in the salon, believing the house to be otherwise deserted. After a rogue of a servant had served me weak tea (without even a slice of bread and butter) I settled down in my chair to draw up a memorandum of my next day's visits.*

*Not long afterwards, I heard voices belonging to Lady Carinna and her uncle from the next room. I shall endeavour to set down verbatim the conversation I had the liberty to overhear:*

*'But Carinna, are you dealing fair?' said the uncle in his low-bred wheeze. 'If you travel anywhere it should be to your husband's side.'*

*'I will not go to him. I told you, he refuses to see me.'*

*'What then is the lure of Italy? Meeting a lover, eh? If so, you must be devilish careful.'*

*To which the niece replied in a weary and sarcastic voice, 'For goodness' sake Uncle, is that all you think of? And I know to be careful.'*

*'Then why go?'*

*'I am unwell, Uncle. Have I not suffered enough in performing this pantomime to finally earn my reward? As if you care! You promised me once that as a married, titled woman I might live freely. And that is what I intend to do.'*

*'This sickness of yours,' he said slowly. 'You ain't breeding, eh?'*

'How I wish I was.'

'Because if you were—'

'I know. All would be settled.'

'You did swear to me, the marriage was consummated?'

'I told you, didn't I? It is not an event I wish to revisit.'

The old rogue chuckled. This was met by silence, then her heavy sigh.

'The truth is, Sir Geoffrey and I cannot bear sight of each other. And Uncle dear,' she said in a most pleading manner, 'I have followed what you said, to the letter. Whenever have I asked for a favour?'

'I am not easy when matters get tangled. You and your husband parted on ill terms. What if he recovers and makes enquiries?'

'Tell him I am abroad for my health.' She sighed in exasperation. 'I do not think he will even enquire. I save his face. He can write to me at the villa if he chooses.'

'Yes, the villa. If you said you needed a season in Rome or at Spa I could comprehend it. But it's a fearfully quiet place.'

'How pleasant that sounds. So, do you have the key?'

'No, it is Carlo who keeps the key. You must call on him to collect it.'

'Surely not? You must have your own key?'

'I have not. You must call upon Carlo. I will write and tell him to expect you. Don't look like that. Collect it or sleep in a ditch.'

'Well, I will not spend a minute longer in his low foreign company than is necessary.'

Tyrone laughed. 'He is a person of quite beautiful manners. I confess it will be a considerable effort for you to rise to his level.'

'He will be another filthy old man, I am sure of it.'

'Confess it, then. You have an assignation,' he accused in a jocular manner. 'Carlo will respect that.'

A sudden crash of splintered glass reached my ears, followed by Carinna's shriek. 'Damn you, look what you have made me do! I can bear no more of this.'

To my dismay, I heard the rustle of her gown moving directly towards me. Fearing discovery, I dropped my head to my chest and shut my eyes, feigning sleep. I do not believe she even saw me, for I heard her uncle call out 'Carinna!' from the drawing room in a tone of admonishment. She was so close to me I heard her huff of breath. She must have been just behind me, my figure hidden only by the large chair.

'I will do as you bid,' she cried out sourly. Then in a very low whisper, added with vicious feeling, 'Whoremonger!'

In a moment she had gone and I was alone. After some time I made mimicry of stretching, and climbed the stairs to my chamber, quite unseen and mightily pleased with this intelligence gleaned from the enemy's camp.

Now what make you of that, my tender brother? Perhaps the girl intends a rendezvous with some young buck? It is a villainous affair, so much is certain.

Alas the candle burns low and tomorrow we leave for the Kentish ports. Her so-called Ladyship has at last settled on leaving, and there is much to attend to. I shall write ere we sail for France.

Wish me strength and health for the journey ahead,

I remain always, your diligent brother,

Humphrey Pars

# XVII

## *London to Dover*

*Being Christmastide, December 1772*
*Biddy Leigh, her journal*

## ~ Christmas Pie ~

*Make a standing crust of twenty-four pounds of the finest flour, six pounds butter, half a pound rendered suet and raise in an oval with very thick walls and sturdy bottom. Bone a turkey, a goose, a fowl, a partridge and a pigeon and lay one inside the other along with mace, nutmeg, salt and pepper. Then have a hare ready stewed in joints along with its gravy, woodcocks, more game and whatsoever wild birds you can get. Lay them as close as you can and put at least four pounds of butter in the pie. Make your lid pretty thick and lay on such Christmas shapes as you wish upon it. Rub it all over with yolks of egg and bind it round with paper. It will take four hours baking in a bread oven. When it comes out melt two pounds of butter in the gravy that came from the hare and pour it hot in the pie through the hole.*

*Lady Maria Grice, from a most Ancient Receipt given to her by her Grandmama, 1742*

My heart sang to leave the city; the horses bowled at a trot all along the smooth turnpike road out of London. As for my lady's brother Kitt, what would Her Ladyship make of his chasing me? He was a mighty fine fellow in his spangled waistcoat and cambric ruffles. The very scent of the high-life clung to his honeyed voice and city pallor. Not that I'd forgotten Jem at all, it was just that I was riled at there being no news from him in any letters in London. And Kitt Tyrone was the very first man of rank to ever take notice of me. Each time I glanced at my mistress's face I saw his lordly features outlined there.

'What on earth are you staring at, girl?' my mistress snapped, breaking into a daydream that might have been written by saucy Eliza Heywood herself.

'Nowt, Me Lady.'

'Indeed. When you address me, Biddy, you must say "My Lady" correctly.'

I did my best to shape my lips, though they felt like a stiff bladder stretching around a preserve jar.

'Moi Lady.'

'Are you sure you can read?'

'Yes, a' course I can,' I said, lifting my chin up. Then I remembered and grumbled, 'Me Lady.'

'Humph. A liar too,' muttered Jesmire.

My lady rifled about the carriage seat, then suddenly thrust a paper in my hand. 'Go ahead then. Read it.'

'A hat, a coat, a shoe,' I pronounced carefully, 'deemed fit to be worn only by a great grand-sire, is no sooner put on by a dictator of fashions—' I looked up and the mistress urged me on with a flap of her long white fingers '—than it is generally adopted from the first lord of the Treasury to the apprentice in Houndsditch.'

They didn't laugh at that, for it was right well done. My mistress snatched the paper back.

'So why did you read that so nicely? It was quite comprehensible.'

I had to think about that. I didn't want to witter on about how Widow Trotter helped me mimic her own fine speaking voice. I was a natural, she used to say.

'They are not me own words, Me Lady. When I read something from a paper I can say it like a schoolmistress, all prim and proper.'

Lady Carinna leaned back, a pucker showing between her eyebrows.

'So if I wrote down your speech like the lines of a play you could recite them correctly?'

'I should expect so, Me Lady.'

And so an hour passed in a sort of game, where lines were written out for me on the back of an old almanac and I made them sound all proper. It weren't too bad a scheme, neither, for I surprised them both with my quickness. As the light failed outside, I announced in a perfect London drawl, 'Ladies and Gentlemen. Dinner will be served in the drawing room.'

Jesmire was mighty peeved to hear me read so marvellous well. Then the notion hit me – Jesmire believed my mistress was schooling me to take her place. As if I would ever give up the glories of the kitchen for a life of needles and hairpins! So all the while, as the old trot muttered into the pages of her London gazette, I crowed that my mistress was right pleased with all I ever did. I never stopped to wonder if I'd be safer keeping well out of her way.

Next thing, we all caught killing colds, so henceforth we wheezed and dripped our way to Dover. You would have thought my lady was dying from the way she complained of the potholes that jolted the carriage and the sick headaches she endured. Mr Pars was in a temper too, cursing the landlords who imposed tremendous charges on those who could take no other way to the ports. Just outside Dover we stopped at an inn and I snatched a taste of dainty fried fish named smelts, and some herrings served with their tails in their mouths. Afterwards, me and Mr Loveday went out to take a view of the ocean. The wind was blowing so strong it whistled through my teeth and the sea was horrible; a vast plain of water ceaselessly moiling like a simmering pot. At last my head cold had cleared enough to taste the sea on my tongue; it had a strange salted vegetable tang.

We both stared at the murky horizon where there was no sign at all of those famed shores of France. Then Mr Loveday nudged me and pointed to two figures fighting the wind far down at the end of the beach. I squinted, and the shapes of them were very like Mr Pars and my lady – yet that would have been a rum thing, if those two ever took a stroll together. The two of them seemed to be quarrelling like cat and dog, the lady in her flapping cloak raising her arms in a fury. Every few steps the man shook his head and halted to speak words that couldn't reach us. After a few minutes he stumped off and disappeared. The woman stood alone on the strand, watching the grey waves chase at her skirts. It was too far to be sure, but I would have wagered it was my lady, for her grey cloak was of the same shade, though she wore the hood up to cover her face.

'If it is them, why would they come out here instead of talking by the parlour fire?' I asked Mr Loveday as we hurried back to the inn.

My friend pulled his thin coat tight around his elbows, slouching low with his head down. He said something I couldn't quite hear.

'What?'

'—the wind, too hard catch—'

I followed his hunched back and thought no more of it.


Mr Pars' intention was to find an inn at Dover and from there buy passage on the packet boat to France. But every inn we called on was bursting with travellers, all holed up till the wind would change and the boats could sail. To make matters worse, we were now but two days from Christmas. I got to see the confectioners' shops, and all the iced glories of Twelfth Cakes and sugared fruits in every square of windowpane.

On each return from his enquiries Mr Pars wore a hangdog face and shook his head. At the York Hotel we took our supper not knowing where we might bed down. It was a noisy, ramshackle place, and the gale whistled through the shutters in an endless moan. Our party was upstairs in the parlour, while me and Loveday drank rotgut beer in a room below. I was sick of traipsing the earth and longed for the old Mawton range and a dish of tea with my toes up on the fender.

It was old Pars who saved us, for he made the acquaintance of a Mr Harbird, a gentleman of Dover who offered my lady lodgings at his own house until the boats should leave. So at nearly midnight we followed Mr Harbird's groom up a pitchy lane, all yawning loudly and blessing the gentleman for his Christmas spirit.

The next day we all woke up at Waldershore House, a large, grey stone manor with gabled roofs and barley twist chimneypots. There was none of the new-fangled whitework there, only oak linenfold panels and faded rugs hung on the walls against the cold. Mr Loveday told me Lady Carinna didn't care for such an old ruin as she called it, but I thought it a spanking improvement on those tumbledown inns.

Then, to my delight, Mr Harbird said I should help out with the Christmas cooking, for they were short of skilled hands. Fifty persons were invited – the largest company I had ever cooked for. Try to stop me, I swore. Oh, if Mrs Garland had only been with me, we should both have been as merry as a pair of larks.

The kitchen at Waldershore had a fireplace tall enough to walk inside, and before it three great turnspits that sprung down from the walls. It was crowded with a rag-taggle band of a dozen women and children – some ancient crones, and others young minxes who giggled and pulled daft faces. My knees shook under my skirts as I told them who I was, trying to speak plain, for my northern speech confounded them. They welcomed me kindly enough, for they needed skilled hands, the usual housekeeper being away with her sick daughter.

Thankfully, there were amongst them some women well versed in Christmas craft. A silver-haired woman named Nanny Faggeter was their leader. She made Christmas Pies, while others plucked fowls and mixed cakes and puddings. As for the children, they were set to watch fires and wash pots. I spent a joyful morning making the stuffings, fine pastries and doughs. After dinner a pair of young maidens launched into 'I Saw Three Ships', and soon the whole company joined in a chorus. I sang and hummed while I worked, all the time calculating baking times and conjuring Christmas fancies from the pages of *The Cook's Jewel*. By three o'clock we had ten great boards piled full of goods, and 'All Bells in Paradise' ringing in our ears. Five pairs of the strongest arms lifted the first two Christmas Pies from the oven, and I poured melted butter deep in their spouts, praying they might set succulent and firm.

Next we got the Plum Pudding mixed, and all the young ones crowded about the tub to make a wish. When they had finished I grasped the wooden thribble myself and walked the circle, thinking of Jem and Mawton. At least one of my wishes was answered, for soon afterward, Mr Loveday came tapping at the door.

'You been working hard, Miss Biddy.' He grinned at the boards of baked goods. 'You 'spect an army come by?'

I wiped my brow with a rag. 'Nothing is busier than English ovens at Christmas. It's the one day a year when everyone must eat their fill.'

Then he handed me a large wooden box that had been waiting at the post house in Dover for days. It was a cheese from Mrs Garland that released all the pungent richness of those sweet Cheshire meadows. There was also a letter that I only opened when alone in my room, reading every word with all attention.

*My Dearest Biddy*

*I do heartily pray this letter finds you safe in Dover and being of good cheer and that the cheese is not knocked about on the road for it*

*should make a good whet for Christmas and Mr Pars will take a slice*
*I am sure of it.*

*'Tis lonely now since you have gone and I pray you do not take our*
*parting ill for I would always wish to be at peace with you my dear,*
*for we have so long been good friends and you my stout right arm. The*
*rain and cold has been most troubling since you left and my pains*
*none the better, but I must not complain for there are worse than me*
*I be sure out there on those dirty roads. I make ready for a trifling*
*Christmas as our household is so shrunken, but I still make the pudding*
*and cakes even with no promise of great revels as so few young folk*
*remain. Teg is my only helpmate now Sukey is dismissed and she does*
*the least she can without a scolding. As for this Mr John Strutt who*
*has taken over Mr Pars' duties, we have no liking for him, he is an*
*interfering, changeabout type of fellow who sees ill in all our old ways,*
*that we know are proven best. As for what he says of Mr Pars, this*
*Mr Strutt has no proper gratitude, if you should ask my opinion.*

*Jem is the same, though I should tell you he has spent your five guin-*
*eas a hundred time on cakey schemes, so you must promise me to keep it*
*safe and spend it wisely as I know you will. Biddy, I will not tell tales*
*on any but he does still hang at the kitchen door, only now it is Teg that*
*feeds him. Being your friend I say to you as gently as I might that you*
*should not be waiting on him, my dear and that's my penn'orth said—*

Taking food from Teg? He might choke on it if he weren't poisoned
first. I saw her game. Oh Jem, had he not the wit to remember me?
Mighty vexed, I read on.

*We talk of you and my lady most nights by the fire and the letter you*
*sent me from London was much remarked upon as showing the wick-*
*edness of the capital and to my mind that Meeks fellow should be*
*flogged raw. Yet it does warm my heart to hear you have written in*
*the book and such fine receipts too. I did try the posset when I had some*
*liquor and it was most warming and was like to having you in the*
*room here cooking up a fancy as you used to in happier days, in this*

*cold season 'tis a Godsend. Biddy dear, I did forget to ask for a lock of your hair so when next you write I beg you send it. I am mighty troubled to think of you crossing the ocean someday soon and do say many prayers for your safety upon the sea.*

*Please do give my Christmas greeting to Mr Pars and also if he be with you still, to George and here is hoping you will send a letter with him minding it could not be a more safe and sure method. I have told you all for the present so must ask you to remember*

*Your Dear & Heartfelt Friend*
*Martha Garland*

It was lucky we were hundreds of miles apart for I would have had that Jem's giblets on hot coals. Cakey schemes indeed! Not for the first time I thought of that five guinea piece shining in the strongbox and how Mr Pars had stitched us up good and proper.

How to tell of Christmas Day – for a cook it's the most fat-lashing, fire-scorching, hurlying burlying day of all the year. Yet the groundwork was done and so we had only the roast beef, fowls, joints of meats, puddings, and desserts still to make. God's codlings, that kitchen was as hot as the fiery furnace once the three spits started turning. There were the usual mishaps – a girl caught her skirts in the fire, but escaped with nowt but a smoking hole in the cloth once her workmates had beaten the fire out. Worse was a spill of slippery hot fat across the flags, and a couple of folks cracked their knees before it was sanded.

By eleven we were at the sweating climax of our labours; I had the baron of beef just turning nicely and my other eye fixed on the Yule cakes lined up at the oven door.

A tap at my sleeve brought me back from this happy realm of cooking to face Mr Loveday, his face looking mighty worried. 'Lady Carinna want see you. At once.'

'Well she can go whistle,' I said, thumping my knife down. 'I am up to my eyes. No, I am up to my skull-top, and even that cannot keep in this heap of cooking.'

I glared at him, but there was no getting out of it. I did not even wipe my face or pull off my flour-stiff apron, for she must take me as I was. Breathless, I burst into Her Ladyship's chamber.

'Begging your pardon if you please, Me Lady. I have a whole Christmas to be cooked just now.'

She was lying on her bed with her shoes kicked off, staring about herself in a right dream. Jesmire was sat at a little table twiddling away with her sewing.

I tried again, moving up closer and giving her a low bob.

'I am sorry, Me Lady. All the dinner will burn to nothing.'

'Oh, shut up.' She sat up and eyed me. 'What on earth do you look like? A chimney sweep.'

I tried to rub the soot from my face, but probably made it worse.

'Please, Me Lady,' I started.

'Now Jesmire here is convinced you are too stupid to learn any foreign language – except for that northern lingo you baffle us with.'

The old shrew muttered into her sewing, 'You are wasting your time.'

'What d'you say, Jesmire?'

Raising her head she spat out words like little darts. 'This country hoyden could never speak a foreign language. She hasn't had the bringing up for it, My Lady.'

'Well I believe she can.' Then she stared at me again as I stood with my arms folded, throwing her a scowl. 'Oh, do stand up properly Biddy. You look like a scarecrow.'

I did lift my shoulders and let my fingers dangle all useless like those ladies do.

'Now repeat after me. "*Bonjour monsieur*".'

'What's that then?'

I heard Jesmire scoff, and shot her a look fit to cut her to shreds.

'It means "Hello Sir".'

'Very well. "Bonjaw miss-ewer".'

'Yes, but try to speak a little more delicately.'

I ran through the 'bonswahs' and the 'madams' and 'madmwasells' as quick as a squirrel catching nuts. There weren't that much to it, truly.

'A complete waste of time,' said Jesmire, all snappy. She was sewing like she was stabbing pins at whelks, glancing up after every prick with her beaky face. My lady yawned and thought for a moment. 'We must remember she must go marketing if we don't want to eat French stuff. Repeat after me, "*Petit déjeuner*".'

That was breakfast. 'And what sort of articles is that then?'

More bloody tittering. As if a body wouldn't want to know what was to eat?

'Well, there would be "pan".'

'What? I've got to eat an iron pan?'

Her lips twitched at that.

'Spelled p-a-i-n. Bread.' I could see I'd made her laugh. And it was driving Jesmire wild that I was tickling her. The truth was, me and Carinna were of an age to make free and jest together.

'What else?'

We went through 'caffay' and 'tay' and 'burr' and all that. If I hadn't had a Christmas dinner about to burn to cinders it would have been quite interesting. Thankfully my mistress started to fidget.

'That's enough, girl. I've proved my point.' She smirked unpleasantly at Jesmire.

'A prating parrot. That's what she is. I doubt she can remember any of it now.'

I was halfway to the door when my lady waved me away in dismissal. But I couldn't resist a little snap at Jesmire as I opened the door to leave.

'Arevwah madams,' I said, pulling a saucy grin as I curtseyed. My lady laughed out loud. But Jesmire crowed after me, 'I'm *mademoiselle* to you, you monkey mimic!'

By Christmas dinner time, I had the boar's head steaming on a plate and it had roasted a treat. All morning a stream of folk had passed the kitchen window: young families with babes swaddled up like bundles, and naughty boys who rapped at the window and drew saucy shapes in their hazy breath. Sick folk, old folk, all were lifted from carts or hefted up the lane on the backs of strong sons and grandsons. The whole roaring crowd was gathered in the long room to give my boar's head fulsome applause when it was carried aloft on a platter. And my goodness, those old folk's eyes were as round as marbles when they saw the tables piled as high as Balthazar's Feast. Plum pottage, minced pies, roast beef, turkey with sage and red wine sauce – and that were just the first course. I was mostly pleased with the second course, for alongside the tongues, brawn, collared eels, ducks and mutton I'd put some pretty snowballs made of apples iced in white sugar, all taken from a dish in Lady Maria's hand in *The Cook's Jewel*.

Afterwards, the benches were pushed back to the walls and the musicians called in from their ale-bibbing. There was dancing, and such a swinging and bumping and banging that you had to laugh as you tried to save your toes from great thundering boys' boots.

I was taking a rest with a bumper of brandy when another servant prodded me on the shoulder.

'What is it now?' I yawned. I was sick to death of sorting things out.

He told me a message had just come from the Packet Company. The wind had changed and we sailed at four o'clock. Soon enough I had my bundle tied and was taking leave of my quarters. Bless the man, Mr Harbird called me to him before I left and gave me a Christmas Box with a whole two guineas inside. Why, it were more than my own mistress, for both she and Mr Pars had not even given me a farthing, the tight-fists. I swore not to tell Jem about my two guineas neither, for that lummocks had never risen at cock-crow to slave over the fire like I had. Jem Burdett could go to the devil. The others must clean up the soot-smeared, grease-spattered kitchen. I was setting sail for France, the truest paradise for cooks.

# XVIII

Loveday stood at the prow of the boat and felt the icy rain slap him awake like an eager hunting companion. The others were all below deck, retching and groaning in the stench of the wooden cabin, but he was free, his tight boots discarded and his bare toes gripping the deck like barnacles. How long had it been since he felt this delicious vibration of a boat's wild spirit in the soles of his feet? Watching grey-green waves heave and roll around him, he felt like a bird riding the stormy heavens. And this was the right direction, he was sure of it. At last he was making his way home.

Back in Dover he had met an ancient sailor who asked where he had sailed from.

'Batavia.' He used the word the Hollanders used for the fortress of white men. 'Where that place?'

The old sailor grew excited, springing to his feet to collect something from a bundle. But when he returned, Loveday was disappointed to see it was only a paper. And when he spread it on the table there was not even proper writing on it, only jagged lines like a crazy person would draw.

'Here it is, me lad.' With a crooked finger the sailor pointed to a word in a mass of madcap patterns. And there it was, in little script:

*Batavia.* It took Loveday a long time to comprehend what the old man told him; that the knobbed fish shape on which *Batavia* was written was a tiny, tiny picture of the big island he had once walked upon.

'There are the mountains,' said the old man, pointing to some inky humps dotted about the island. Was it possible? Snatching up the paper Loveday lifted it close to his eye, squinting to find the people he remembered living there. But there were no people or trees or villages, it was only a paper drawing. He still didn't understand.

'How this Batavia?' he asked, the heartache sour in his breast.

The old man's watery eyes held his. 'It's what the captain of a ship reads to find his way around the world. So look, here's England. And this is the sea.'

England was on the far other side of the paper, but slowly Loveday began to comprehend. Back in Lamahona the huntsmen had sometimes scratched patterns in the wet sand to show a reef or a fast tide.

'So how go Batavia?' He couldn't keep a tremor from his voice.

It took him all afternoon to understand how very far from home he had sailed, after kindly Father Cornelius had died from the sickness and he had been sold at the market at Batavia. For many moons he had sailed towards this cold kingdom, and now he saw how terribly far his return journey must be. With the old man's help he found *Paris*, his mistress's next destination. Frustratingly, it was not very far at all on his great journey.

'And Italy?' he asked.

'Lookee here, son. *Italy*. It's on the right road at least.'

It was. If he stayed with his mistress he would have an easy passage part of the way back home. Finally, he asked the man, 'Where Lamahona?' But all they could find were a thousand dots and dashes in the ocean. If only it were real magic, he groaned to himself. If only he could put a spyglass to the paper and find the village and the miniature living presences of Bulan and Barut themselves. But it was not magic, and he would have to trail across those inky lands and scribbled oceans to hold them in his arms again.

Loveday clung to the rail a while longer, postponing his return down below. Peering through the spray a darker strip of land wavered before his eyes. So this was France, the first name he must cross. He mused on the letter Mr Pars had written from Dover, trying to understand what this new place would be like:

*My Dear Ozias*

*I write in haste from Dover, having this very hour received your warning and just now packing for the early boat to France. Brother, I pray do not exhibit any visible alarm before John Strutt, for such behaviour may wrongly mark you as a guilty man. There is no need to be troubled brother, you must appear easy, I do command it. The impertinent fellow is entirely dependent on myself for his position as proxy steward and I am damned surprised that he quizzed you in such an ungentlemanly fashion. Brother, you did right to say you know nothing of the matter. The bonds he seeks are no business of his and be assured they are no business of any but Her damned Ladyship. As for the jewel, it was Sir Geoffrey's wife that took it, as you well know. You do not say whether Sir Geoffrey himself or his Irish agent has prompted Strutt to make this inquiry. Tell me in your next letter what you have learned. I understood Sir Geoffrey was utterly felled by an apoplexy – so who is it gives these orders to poke about my private affairs?*

*As for me, I am right glad to say the boat leaves on the hour for France and I shall be on it with my strongbox padlocked tight. I fancy France will be my little paradise of peace till all this rigmarole is over and forgotten. Do pray for my safe passage across the ocean.*

*Your brother,*

*Humphrey Pars*

So to Mr Pars, France was a paradise. Loveday knew what Paradise was, for Father Cornelius had talked much of that other world, as different from Lamahona as this cold place. It was the kingdom of the Sun God, for the spirits there wore wings and flew above the clouds. It was where Father Cornelius was now, for the old priest had said that holy people passed inside a gate held by a man called Mr Peter. Remembering the rainbow-coloured birds of his home Loveday peered again at the heaving grey waves and hoarse-voiced scavenger birds. He saw only a flat mass of land that led to other lands that would take him many thousands of days to cross.

It was near to dusk when the wind allowed an attempt to land the passengers. Reeling and grey-faced, the others came up on deck and staggered about, as bandy-legged as new whelped puppies.

'Why did I drink like that before we set off? Oh,' Biddy raised a hand to her mouth, 'me legs will barely carry me.'

Loveday took her arm companionably and made her watch the far shore to keep her balance.

'It the waves, Biddy. You not still drunk.'

'That right? I don't like this wobbling all over't place.' She gripped his arm tightly. 'Oh Mr Loveday, p'raps I should've gone back to Mawton with George.'

'So why you not go back?' he said gently.

She screwed her face up against the wind and took a good deep breath.

'I don't know. Something. France, Italy. I don't know what, but the words make my heart skip a beat.'

He knew that skipping was a kind of dance. So, her heart danced.

'That good Biddy.' He gave her arm a fond squeeze. 'I'm glad you come with me to France and Italy. We look out for each other, for sure?'

He smiled, and then noticed a tiny rowing boat bobbing towards them, dipping every moment behind mountainous waves.

Biddy nodded her head, but then spying the nearing boat, groaned. 'Lord help us, we haven't to jump onto that bobbing cork, have we?'

Darkness was falling fast as they struggled down the rocking ladder to the boat. Miss Jesmire was in such a rigid fit of fear that she had to be carried down the ladder across the broad shoulders of a sailor. That made Loveday laugh, for the wind whipped up her skirts, showing her skinny shanks. Tying his boots around his neck, he scampered up and down the ladder on his bare feet, catching the big boxes when the sailors lowered them. By the time everything was loaded, his party were soaking wet and miserable, crammed onto narrow benches in the bucking boat. With a cry the oarsmen began to pull away from the ship towards the harbour. So this was France, Loveday said to himself, spying lantern-lit windows, and hearing jabbering voices from the quayside. He hoped very much they sold warming liquor here.

# XIX

## *Hotel d'Anjou, Paris, France*

*Being Twelfth Night, January 1773*
*Biddy Leigh, her journal*

## ~ Rôties soufflés ~

*Pound a breast of roasted chicken with some beef marrow, parmesan cheese, five yolks of eggs and then most gently add their whites whipped to frought. Prepare it on pieces of bread cut like toasts and fried in butter called in France, croutons. Garnish with bread crumbs and parmesan cheese mixed, bake in the oven and serve on a good rich bouillon.*

*A most remarkable dish for lightness and flavour, Biddy Leigh, Paris 1773*

We arrived in Paris, and everything was all the same, yet odd: the steep-roofed houses, the passion for frippery, even the taste of the ale and the rough hard bread – it was all mighty French, is the only way I can tell it. We lodged at a place called the *Hotel d'Anjou*, which was not an inn at all, but a grey house of seven storeys right in the heart of the cobbled maze of Paris. It was all very Frenchified: the furniture was all that curly-legged stuff, and the walls plastered with mirrors, and paintings of shiny fruits all heaped together that would never grow in the same season.

As soon as we got there I dumped my bundle in my chamber and threw open the window shutter. I was near overcome with the stink of French drains. My chamber overlooked a courtyard and it were strange to hear the people outside talk in a foreign tongue, shrieking and laughing. I had been thinking the Frenchies would talk slow and steady with their *bonjours* and *monsieurs*, but it was a marvel to hear them jabber like jackdaws, yarping so fast you could not make it out.

Next morning my lady sent for me. Outside her chamber sat a gaggle of seamstresses and shop girls, with armfuls of silks and samples. My mistress herself sat wrapped to her chin in cloths while a weaselish fellow prinked her hair. She had been off her food for days; even French face paint couldn't prettify her face, which had a swollen and liverish look. I watched the hairdresser teasel up a curl until it stood as tall as a soldier's hat. It must have hurt, for I could see she was all twitched up.

'Oh, it's you, is it?' she started up, scowling at me. 'It's time you did some work instead of idling all the day.'

I hung my head and tried to rub a few breakfast crumbs from the corner of my mouth.

'Yes, Me Lady.'

'Great God!' she screamed. 'Can't you say it properly?'

'Yes. My. Lady,' I snapped out very fiercely, so there was a nasty silence afterwards. I could hear the nit-squeezer make a little *tut-tut* as he reached for the curlers. There was a sudden hiss and smell of singeing hair, and my lady nearly jumped from her seat.

'Be careful you rogue. God damn, that's my scalp!'

'Madame,' he said as smooth as honey. 'Eet will be worth every little twinge, I essure you.'

'Devil roast you, French torturer.' She shut her eyes tight as he screwed another curl around his irons.

'Stop, stop,' she spat to Monsieur after a moment. 'I cannot think right with you burning my hair off at the roots.' He danced over to the corner and fretted over his pomades and whatnots, affecting a very sorry countenance.

'Tomorrow I want an English dinner,' she said to me. 'Proper English dishes, beef and so on.'

I should have seen it coming. They had all been complaining of the French kickshaws since Calais. 'So that's dinner for four. My brother will join us.'

Kitt? God's gripes. There was me thinking he was far away in London. As she spoke a hundred obstacles bubbled in my mind.

'But Me Lady,' I started up, 'where would I cook this dinner? And how would I buy the stuff? They all speak the lingo too fast.'

She glared hard at me. 'How should I know? Get along and do it.'

With a shake of my head I set off to find Mr Pars.

He was bent over his desk in his chamber, a pile of papers before him. Everyone knew his beloved System of Economy had gone all arsey-varsey.

'If it's money you are after, most of it is spent,' he growled.

I tried to read his papers upside-down and could see they were bills. One was for twenty livres for the flowery waistcoat I had seen Mr Pars himself wear, so there was something of the pot calling the kettle black. I wondered then what story all those numbers truly told. But for now I had this new task on my mind.

'Afraid it is money, sir. Lady Carinna wants me to cook an English dinner and I need French coin.'

At that he looked a little brighter. 'Well, p'raps I could find some tin for that. So what are you after, eh? Side of beef? Some chops?'

'Aye, sir. Whatever you fancy.'

He licked his lips and listed his favourite dishes: plain pudding, lemon pickle, roast beef. Then he asked for his own particulars: tobacco and coltsfoot for his pipe, and some more comfrey for Her Ladyship's tea.

'And no green oils. Get a block of dripping and cook it plain.'

It was true that the food in France had been a great hog potch of good and bad. One night on the road we were served a right mess of giblets, fishy smelling frogs' legs and mouldy old cheese. But at Chantilly the fricassee of veal was so tender I'm not sure how they softened it. I could have eaten the whole pot it was that good, but instead had to watch Jesmire scraping off the sauce, whining all the time for a little boiled ham.

'Mr Pars sir,' I protested, 'they speak the lingo too quick for me here. So many words are all different.'

'Nonsense girl.'

'So what's lemon pickle then?'

He at least gave that puzzle a moment's thought and shook his head impatiently. 'I'll speak to the landlady. For all I pay her, she should lend you a hand.' Then he gave me a right grousing look, but did drop two coins in my palm. 'I want a close copied list of all you spend, mind, every sou. None of you are to be trusted.' Then he dropped his head back into his blessed accounts again.

*       *       *

I was thrown together with Florence, or 'Florawns' as she was called, a pert girl of nineteen who worked in our kitchen and was sent out to help me. First, I followed her to a butcher where fat sausages hung from the ceiling like aldermen's chains, and I could choose the best of plump ducks, sides of beef, and chops standing guard like sentries on parade. Once the deal was done Florence paid him, gave me a wink and cast a trickle of coins into her apron pocket. So it seemed that serving girls will pay themselves the whole world over.

The size of the Paris market made Covent Garden look like a tinker's tray. And I never before saw such neatness; the cakes arranged in pinks and yellows and greens like an embroidery, and the cheeses even prettier, some as tiny as thimbles and others great solid cartwheels. As for the King Cakes the French made for Twelfth Night, the scents of almond and caramelled sugar were to me far sweeter than any perfumed waters. Our baskets loaded, I followed Florence to a yard where smoke spouted from a half-dozen chimneys. '*Mon frère*,' she started up, and I remembered from overhearing my mistress that the word meant 'brother'. Inside was a kitchen, hazy with steam from two bright fires. My first glance took in four man cooks with their heads down, hunched over their work. One was mixing forcemeat, another stirring stock, and a third preparing garnishes. I understood at once that each took a part of the dish and later all would be combined. It was the first time I ever saw cooks work that method and I was full of admiration.

'*Mon frère*, Claude,' urged Florence, leading me to a youth just like herself in broad shape and countenance. He talked rapidly with Florence, all the while tending a tiny copper saucepan. Then breaking off his talk, he reached for a teaspoon, and with all the worshipfulness of a priest at an altar, Claude tasted the shining stock, his face blank to all but his sense of taste.

'*Quintessence*,' whispered Florence, sniffing in awe at the rising steam. 'For many days the meat is reduced to create the soul of the sauce.' Then with measured care he reached for a lemon and squeezed in four steady drops.

The name of the dish was *soufflé*, as the French write it. I wrote all the particulars down, as it was a most magical dish. Who would have guessed that egg whites fraught for a long while could make a dish rise like a cloud? Once it had risen in a hot oven, Claude dressed the soufflé with a ring of honeyed quintessence. It quivered on a pretty porcelain plate like a gently steaming puffball.

My senses were so bedazzled that I scarce noticed the head cook come barging in at the door. The grizzled blubberguts made us jump out of our skins with his bellowing. He spat out the word *fam*, and pointed and waved his stuffed sausage fingers towards the door. The old slush bucket! We were women and he hated us, I could comprehend that with no need for Florence's mimes.

We skulked out of the back door, but I refused to leave until I saw who ate such stuff. The front of the house was far grander than the back, with white plasterwork walls on which were large gold letters: RESTAURANT – MAISON DE SANTÉ. The windows were very large, and by pressing up close I could see a room furnished in tip-top luxury. Yet unlike an inn there was no large table for the diners. I craned my neck and spied small round tables each with a few chairs, somewhat like a gentlemen's coffee house, yet so much more genteel. And oddest of all, there was but one diner, a middle-aged woman sitting alone in a flounced white cap and flowered gown. She was sipping from a tiny cup balanced on a painted plate.

'*Restaurant*,' whispered Florence. It was the word that would change my life.

She murmured that quintessence served in a tiny cup is called a *restaurant*, for it restores the strength with its health-giving properties; it especially restores the nerves of the weak and exhausted. I also learned how much it costs to dine at a Restaurant, or House of Health – five silver livres, more than I should earn in a fortnight.

By the church clock it was well after nine in the morning, but I no longer cared. I had lost interest in cooking plain beef, plain pudding, plain ham. I yearned to concoct a soufflé, a quintessence, a puff of whipped air. But that was not why I ruined Kitt's dinner.

Passing the post box in the hall I noticed a letter bearing my name. I snatched it up, expecting a dose of Mrs Garland's comforting words. Instead, I read a little, then felt for a chair and sank upon it.

*My dear Biddy, you must prepare yourself for bad news. Go now to your room dear, and set yourself down for I am fair sorry to write this but am left no other course. E'en before Christmas Jem and Teg were growing right friendly—*

I lay down the page and covered my eyes, squeezing them so tight that I felt the blood pounding. With grim determination I opened them again and read onwards:

*—and it seems they played false behind my back. Next Teg comes to me and says she is with child by Jem and don't know what to do. I walloped her as hard as I could, for she is a wicked lewd creature and has stolen Jem when he was bound to you. Yet A Hungry Dog will eat Dirty Pudding is all I'm saying and Teg has been kicked about the floor aplenty by my reckoning.*

*Now dear, do not be too miserable but I must tell you all now. The two were brought before Mr Pars' deputy, Mr Strutt, and he has pronounced Jem must marry her to spare the burden on the parish. He also said that as I have no other cook maid, Teg may stay on at Mawton where she will be useful. We are all astonished at this judgement but Mr Strutt is a modern man who says he lives only by practical rules and so long as Jem labours on the estate they must not take from the Parish. So you see he has no knowledge of how things are done properly here at Mawton and what high morals are held by Mr Pars. Indeed he has made such unfair judgements of Mr Pars he is in danger of being slighted by all of us loyal retainers. Now Biddy, I must tell you they was married last Friday at Mawton Chapel—*

I threw the letter down, then tore it into pieces. Florence was calling my name from the kitchen, but I wanted only to run to my chamber and sob on the floor. Yet I could not get out of cooking that scavey meal. I could have beaten Mr Kitt with a frying pan for all the trouble this dinner was causing. As for Jem Burdett, to be flayed, gutted, and spitted alive was too good for him.

So the beef was scorched black on one side and ran blood on the other. The pudding would have made a fine cannonball. Half of what I planned lay unmade. It was Florence who found me out, dripping tears into the chops. I pointed to my heart and mimed a knife stabbing hard inside it. '*Mon amie*,' Florence crooned – her calling me friend made me weep even faster. Then she picked up an apron and began to cook beside me. It was to her I owed the edible parts of that meal.

The sad fact of it was, my diners scarcely noticed. I believe Mr Pars did pass a comment next day on the blackened chops, but no one else could tell. So that was English fare, I thought. I could work my finger-ends to bare bones and none would taste the difference. I recollected the delicate timing and tasting at the *Maison de Santé* and knew that beside it our English stuff was rough indeed.

As soon as I could I left word that I was ailing, and took to my chamber for three miserable days. I threw myself down on my bed and pictured again the joy of my first meeting Jem, our first soft words, our first hard kiss. 'Oh Jem, I did love 'ee more than she ever could,' I whispered to the soggy hollows of my pillow. I saw again our bitter parting, and wished I had been sweeter to him. I pictured our marriage procession to Mawton Chapel, Reade Cottage built again as our home, the unborn babies I would never bear. I wallowed in a right pit of misery. Day after day I left my bed only to stump to the door to fetch food left by Florence and to empty my pot in the yard.

But each night I had a visitor. A knock came at my door, very soft and very secret.

'Biddy,' a gentleman's voice whispered secretly. 'Open the door.'

Each time I rolled over and faced the wall. But I could not stare at that cracked yellow wall for ever. By the third night I had cried myself dry and a young heart hammered in my breast again.

'Will you come out with me?' asked the voice. 'Paris is devilish fine by starlight.'

My love for Jem had died. You are free and in Paris and have a gentleman admirer, I told myself. I had kept him waiting and he had kept returning. Through the slats of the shutters the sky had darkened and the lamps were lit. I grinned like a vixen and called out to Kitt Tyrone to wait till I was dressed.

'No sir, you cannot come inside.' I held the door open barely an inch. He carried a candle before his face and his eyes fixed on the narrow bed behind me.

'Come now. Give a fellow a reward. It is my last night in Paris.'

'Then we should look about the city,' I said, quite fixed in my determination. 'Indeed sir, I have the very place in mind.'

I threw back the door and his glance moved from my face, and down the ruffled majesty of the rose-red gown. I knew the scarlet bodice made my waist neat and slender, topping skirts that massed in glorious frills and furbelows. I felt like a Miss from an elegant fashion plate, and Kitt's glance told me he saw the change in me too.

'As you wish,' he said, offering me his arm.

# XX

## *Maison de Santé, Paris*

*Being Plough Sunday, January 1773*
*Biddy Leigh, her journal*

## ~ Restaurant ~

*A food or remedy that has the property of restoring lost strength to a sickly or tired person; a distillation from the juices of light, flavourful meats; stimulating conserves, bouillons and other good and sweet-smelling ingredients. In the same manner, the establishment of a Restaurateur or Restauratrice: one who has the skill of making Restaurants.*

*The most remarkable method of the Restaurant Maison de Santé, Biddy Leigh, Paris 1773*

We let the crowds carry us towards the river. All about us towered the great city of Paris lit by greenish oil lanterns strung along the streets. We passed the hulks of popish churches and silhouettes of great palaces all turreted against the violet sky. On the Pont Neuf bridge we were pressed in the crush that strolled amongst crowded street stalls. At a haberdasher's stand, Mr Kitt halted to buy me a ribbon.

'You choose the colour, sir,' I said.

He smiled indulgently as he rifled through the tray of silks.

'This one matches your eyes.' It was a soft, mossy green. All evening I wound it about my fingers, stroking its shiny satin.

Then the coxcomb went and spoiled it by asking, 'Biddy, did you take a look into my sister's chamber? You did promise.'

Here we go, I thought, and said very meekly, 'I never precisely promised, sir.'

'Well, did you discover anything?'

I knew the sassafras oil was not a matter I could speak of.

'No, sir.'

He looked at me steadily, and I stared back, eyes wide.

'So why is my sister going to Italy?'

That at least needed no pretence.

'I did hear her say she were going to Italy for her health.'

He shook his head impatiently.

'She seems healthy enough to me. She was off to her perfumier or somewhere tonight. Took the carriage, too. No, there's nothing ailing my sister.'

\*     \*     \*

The thunder of firecrackers interrupted us, and we moved to the riverbank. As we lingered he slipped his arm around my waist and I made no move to stop him. With a shivering bang a shower of fireworks lit the sky, bleaching the city like a painting on a stage. We leaned on the balustrade, breathing the cold winter air that tasted of gunpowder. Then the skies lit again with silver stars dropping slowly to earth.

'I'll never forget this night in all my life,' I said, speaking softly into his ear.

From the moment the liveried doorman opened the door of the *Maison de Santé* I was in a cook's heaven. The trouble was, Mr Kitt was not right pleased when he saw where I'd led him.

'Good God, it's not one of those ridiculous health places is it?' He surveyed the powder-faced men and languishing women seated at tables. A hostess in a gown of blue silk swept us to a candlelit corner. A moment later she had left us staring at a large card written in French.

'It's the top fashion,' I told him fiercely, studying the list of refined French dishes on my card. 'And the most forward cooking you will find in Paris. Please, it will be like a dream to taste it. Thank you, sir,' I added quickly.

The lady returned and addressed Mr Kitt most genteelly. 'Monsieur, would you permit me to tell you a little about my *carte de menu*? In my profession as *restauratrice* I may be permitted to judge my clientele.' She set her powdered head on one side and assessed him with two penetrating pale blue eyes. 'I think – often, you have little appetite for anything save a restorative *eau de vie*. You are as sensitive as a duke, but those about you, ah,' at this she shrugged prettily, 'wish you to attend to coarser matters. So my prescription to you is a nourishing health supper to soothe your overtaxed physiognomy.'

In the face of this charming analysis Kitt could only agree.

'Do you honestly believe all that hogwash?' he asked, when we were alone again. I took a long look at the wealthy diners, the lavish gold clock, and heavy silver cutlery.

'I think she's a mighty clever woman, meself.'

After downing half a bottle of brandy, even Mr Kitt reluctantly admired the chandeliers of glass fruits, and wondrous mirrors that stretched from ceiling to floor. When the dishes arrived, he pronounced the delicate *Potage de Santé* to be no better than dishwater, though I could taste mushroom and thyme in the gleaming broth. To him, the delicate portions of pigeon and fish were criminally small, but I barely listened, savouring every tender mouthful.

As we tackled a restorative of orange flower cream I gazed at the other elegant diners; the ladies chattering and fluttering fans, the gentlemen making easy conversation. 'To be one of them, it would be like living in fairyland.'

'It is only money that buys them an elegant appearance, Biddy.' Mr Kitt's mouth formed a pretty sulk as he reached for the brandy. 'You are worth a dozen of any of them.'

'I fear you've pulled too hard on the bottle, sir,' I laughed. 'It's me, Biddy Leigh you are talking to. Oh sir, try these *Biscuits Palace Royal*. They are marvels.'

His dark eyes were bleary, but still sensible.

'No, Biddy. Look at you tonight.' I searched for mockery in his expression but found none. 'You are pretty, you have good sense. The damn shame is, in a better world you could rescue me.'

'Rescue you from what, sir?'

He laughed sourly. 'It doesn't matter. But truly, you are good and practical as well as pretty.'

'Come off it, sir. Soon you'll marry some rich Town-Miss and never even notice the likes of me again.'

'That's the trouble, Biddy. Everyone I know trades happiness for cash. Most people don't even know what love is.'

'And you do, sir?' I was teasing him, for I reckoned he had only the daftest schoolboy notions in his head.

He smiled a twisted smile. 'I don't know. But I'm sure my uncle has plans for me, too.'

'Can you not make your own way in life, sir?' I asked gently.

He stared mournfully into his glass. 'I've never settled to anything. Even Carinna has more learning than I. And I'm not brave, Biddy. I can't win against my uncle. Damn it, I try to put on a careless appearance, but all is confusion.' Then he laughed sadly. 'You must think me an odd sort of fellow.'

I shrugged. 'Aye well, everyone thinks I am an odd 'un too.'

'There we are then,' he said, raising his glass with a tight smile. 'To us two "odd 'uns" thrown together in this bewitching city.'

I raised my glass. I did like him too, that was the rub. He looked back at me fondly.

'Tis a sad fact,' he added. 'Forget all the flimflam. This is the best night I've had in a very long time.'

I took a sip of brandy and felt a burn behind my eyes. 'Tis for me too, sir. Best in my whole life, I reckon.'


Once we had left Paris and were rollicking along the roads of France I couldn't help but dream of handsome Kitt Tyrone. And it were not just that bonny man that haunted my dreams, but the visit to that wondrous *restaurant*. After Mr Kitt had finally slumped across the table in a drunken stew, I talked long and earnestly with that clever lady *restauratrice*. The secrets she shared were like gold to me. I learned that food was not mere food, if that makes sense. 'They pay for all of this,' she said, with a gesture of her graceful hand that jangled with cameo bracelets, towards the gilded room, the private tables, the diners who toyed with silver forks. The food had to be perfect, of course, but food might be perfect and still slip down gutter alley for a ha'penny. The *idea* of a thing is what makes it an item of fashion. I would never forget that lesson.

As for the gentleman, I knew he was a gamester and a dreamer. But in the private chambers of my heart I did like Kitt Tyrone. That moment in the restaurant often returned to me, when we had talked with no restraint. He was naught but a lonely mixed-up boy beneath all his citified manners. I believe that for a spell our two souls did chime with each other, not as servant and gentleman but as plain man and woman.

And it cheered me to know that Kitt Tyrone had chased Jem clean out of my heart. Why, Teg was welcome to the idle lummocks. And to my satisfaction I had escaped with my commodity intact. Though Lord knows there was a spell when I could have ravished my mistress's handsome brother and unbuttoned his clothes from his lily-white body. We had been all alone in the swaying darkness of the hackney and he asleep, his lashes like dark feathers and his lips just parted and wet. As I leaned across his senseless body I smelled spirits and pomade mixed with the tang of hidden flesh. His lips were full and slack and when I lowered my lips to his, he tasted of brandy and baby's sweet skin. For a terrible moment he roused himself, returning my kiss with hungry passion. Alarmed, I pulled away and happily, he slept on. Oh, I thought that kiss I stole the sweetest morsel I ever tasted.

'Daydreaming again?' My mistress's voice made me jump.

'*Non, non, ma maîtresse,*' I said quickly, for she found my speaking French less offensive than my northern talk. And besides, it rattled Jesmire to hear me speak the lingo.

'*Bon*, Biddy. Well done. And in Italian?' That was her latest notion, to teach me Italian, which even I could comprehend was not so different from French.

'*No, no, signora,*' I said smartly. She cast me a preening look and said, 'But still you know nothing of manners. Now let us fancy you were to visit a gentleman. What would you say?'

God's gripes, had she found me out with Mr Kitt? I looked into her powdered face, that was tired and swollen. Truly, she had a lumpen look to her that even the grandest silks and hoops could not disguise.

'I should never presume, Me Lady,' I gabbled.

'In the devil's name, I only ask that you fancy it,' she complained. 'Do you have no imagination, Biddy? Is it true you menials think only of kettles and pots?'

'No it is not, Me Lady,' I snapped. '*Ma maîtresse*, sorry. Give me a notion of what to say, like.'

'When you arrive in the place of a person of rank you must greet him politely. You might say, "Good afternoon, Your Excellency. I pray you are well." Dear me, I suppose we must use the old method.' She pulled out her little book and scribbled it down. I read it aloud and it sounded a great deal better.

'Now what might you say if he invited you to dine with him?'

'What's cooking?' I asked hopefully. She rolled her eyes, and Jesmire snorted.

'You are a tiresome creature,' Her Ladyship scolded. 'Say it properly.'

'Your Excellency,' I sighed in a false and lofty voice, 'that is most vastly kind of you.'

I expected my mistress to howl with cruel laughter, but she clapped her hands in delight. 'So you can do it, you minx.'

As if I couldn't if I wanted to!

'And you know you must wait to be seated?' she asked.

'I seen it every day.'

'And raise your glass to every toast with a gentle nod?'

'Yes, Me Lady.'

'And to wait until each dish is offered?'

I blew out loudly through my lower lip. 'Aye, if I've not died of hunger yet.'

'Biddy.' She wagged her finger. 'Behave yourself.' But I could see she was buttoning a splutter of laughter.

Just then Mr Pars' face suddenly loomed in at us from the window. We had both been so keen on our practice that no one had noticed the carriage come to a halt.

'My Lady. Is this girl misbehaving?' he barked.

'It's our little game,' said my mistress in a blink of an eye.

'I believe,' said he, eyeing me like it was all my wicked fault, 'the weather is good enough for Biddy to sit outside with the driver.' And he doffed his hat to my lady. 'So you needn't be bothered by her impertinence.'

'No,' said she smartly. 'Biddy stays here. She amuses me.'

Mr Pars glowered at her like a red hot coal. 'I could lend you the most interesting guide books if it's amusement you—'

'Out of my way.' My mistress was standing ready at the step. For a moment Mr Pars didn't move, only stared at her with his hately look. Then he marched away fast and we all got down at our new lodgings.

# XXI

## Lyons

*Being St Paulstide, January 1773*
*Biddy Leigh, her journal*

## ~ Burned Toast Tea ~

Take as much dry crust of bread as the top of a penny loaf and set before the fire until the crust is burned cinder black. Pour over boiling water and soak until enough then strain into a sieve and mash it down. Drink while it is hot; if the first cup does not give relief drink another.

*Biddy Leigh, a most worthy remedy for sickness of the stomach*

There was a new smell in the air at Lyons, of sun-baked southern stuffs, of strong red vinegar, and spikes of rosemary. It was a good thing too, for some of the streets were stinking warrens, and the beggars near mithered me to death. The beggary was not for want of charity, for the place was a mass of popish churches and convents, ringing out their bells every quarter-hour. Yet thank my stars, our new lodgings were mighty grand, with glass windows, and our linen scented with orange blossom.

It was good that we were comfortably lodged for my lady had begun to complain more than ever as we approached Lyons. I heard Mr Pars scoff at what he called her posturing, but I judged her from what she ate, and even the sugariest rum baba that she had once devoured no longer tempted her. One morning, when only me and my lady were alone in our lodgings, she jangled her bell so hard that I cursed Jesmire for being away and ran to her chamber door. I found her slumped in her bed and saw at once she was truly sick. Once I was right close up, the strangest sight met my eyes, for her mouth was stained such a nasty black colour I feared she'd caught some terrible French plague.

'My Lady!' I cried, helping her sit upright. Then I noticed the plate at her bedside on which stood crumbs of shining black coal.

'Let me clean you up,' I said, trying to keep the astonishment out of my voice.

She was as meek as a lamb while I changed her mucky shift, but all the while my thoughts were in a whirlwind. I knew only one reason why women had a craving to eat coal. In my guts I had known all along this journey was not straight and proper, and now

I had the proof. We were travelling for her health indeed! The whole scene was too outlandish for me to stay silent, so I spoke out boldly.

'My Lady, Burned Toast Tea is the best of remedies if you are sick in the mornings.'

She didn't answer, but she knew my meaning, for she slumped back on her bed and dropped her brow into her hand. When she raised her face, large tears welled in her eyes.

'You know?'

'I should have guessed earlier, My Lady.' She looked up at me, quite heartbroke, grasping Bengo to her chest. The dog was wearing her newest extravagance, a silver collar that bore the words *Bengo. Carinna's heart in this four-footed thing lies.* I had scoffed at that, but just then it seemed less daft than tragic.

'I will help you any way I can, My Lady. I want to tell you that, before the others come back.'

'Thank you, Biddy,' she said in a choked voice. 'I know so little of these matters, but have such a craving for black tastes. There can be no mistake can there? Look.'

She pulled back her bedcovers and I saw what I should have seen for the last month at least. There stood her belly, quite swelled beneath her fine lawn shift. She stared mournfully at it, her chin to her chest. 'It grows so fast now. And I so often feel sick, as if some strangeness flows in my blood. Is that how it should be, Biddy?'

'It can be, My Lady. The sickness, the heaviness.' I sighed, trying to comprehend it all. 'We must make haste to Italy.'

'Yes, we must travel as fast as I can bear it.' She flung her head back on the pillow and her eyes burned fiercely. 'I need you, do you understand? And Mr Loveday. You do understand I can only trust the two of you?'

Tears trickled down her cheeks, so I passed her a pocket handkerchief. Then, summoning all my pluck, I asked what I longed to know, 'Does Sir Geoffrey know, My Lady?'

She was silent for a moment, then shook her head in disgust. 'Him? It's nothing to do with that poxed old fool.' She glared at me with sudden scorn. 'What, you don't know either? They let me find out on my wedding night. How kind was that? His nightgown fell open and the scabs on his flesh were like the scars of Hell. I couldn't let that festering ghoul touch me. I thought I was the last to know, that he'd carried the pox for most of his life.'

I gaped at her. Yet it all rang true: Sir Geoffrey's raddled face, his strange temper that some called crazed. No wonder she was fleeing from him.

'But you told no one?' I exclaimed, for she had been cruelly deceived. 'My Lady, anyone would pity you.'

'What?' she cried. 'And would they pity me still, as my own child grows larger every day?' She cried a little into her twisted handkerchief. 'We parted on ill terms. He wants never to see me again. He said if I spoke of his plight he would have me divorced in parliament. So if he knew of the child as well? I needed time. And money. I needed to escape.' She was silent for a moment and I looked away.

'Do you think the others will write to Sir Geoffrey?' she asked, her voice shaking like a child begging not to be whipped.

'I can't say, My Lady.' I was truly flummoxed. I wanted to help her, but scarcely knew how. 'I'll fetch you the tea, My Lady. Now why not take some rest?'

She reached up and patted my hand. 'Thank you, Biddy. I'm so grateful you are here.'

The truth was, her kind words had left me choked up too. Fool that I was, I would have done anything for my lady, whatever she bid me in the whole world.

I got back to the kitchen, and there I re-fashioned my lady's sad story as best as I could.

To start at the beginning, she must have lain with some fellow in the summer, and when her monthly curses stopped, got a devilish fright. Then the rogue no doubt refused to stand up and give his name to the babe. It were mighty handy then, that she had the chance to marry Sir Geoffrey in October. I set a slice of bread on a toasting fork before the fire and charred it as black as the Earl of Hell's boots.

Even after finding out Sir Geoffrey was poxed, I was now sure that she had never tried to poison him. My mind ran again over the ailments *The Cook's Jewel* listed to be cured by Sassafras Oil and this time something chimed in the corner of my mind. I left the toast steeping in water and slipped back to my chamber. Leafing through *The Cook's Jewel* I found it – 'Menstrual Obstruction'. I was minded of an apothecary calling a woman's curses a 'menstres' or some such word. What was it obstructed a woman's monthly curses but a baby? God's eggs, she had bought the oil to try to get rid of the baby! So she was a desperate creature indeed. By the time I first saw her at Mawton she must have been suffering all the troublesome signs of breeding. Lord, she had played her part better than an actress on the stage. In terror of being found out she had planned this journey. And no doubt fearing foreign food would make her even sicker, she had dragged me along as well.

Now all the time I'd been bursting to tell someone of my discovery, and so after I'd seen my lady settled I called out to Mr Loveday when I heard him return. When he came to the kitchen I jumped up and grasped his hand tight.

'May I share a secret, as friends do?' I asked. When he nodded keenly, I lowered my voice and said, 'You will never believe it, my lady is to have a child. That's what is behind all this journey.'

'A child? How you know?'

I told him all I'd learned, and rambled on and on. 'But it is not Sir Geoffrey's child,' I ended, 'so who is the true father? Mr Loveday, was there ever a man she had a particular liking for, back in the summertime?'

He frowned and stared at the ceiling, then shook his head.

'Some gentlemen took her to Vauxhall Garden and all that. I think maybe one fellow, she always ask if card left at door. Mr Napier I think. He marry some other woman to get lot of money, I hear say.'

So perhaps this Napier was the rakeshame who had ruined her? I remembered the blotted letter she had been trying to write, that day I first met her in the blue chamber. I didn't speak of it, but knew now that of course she had not been writing of Sir Geoffrey. So to whom had she been writing those hot-blooded scribblings? That 'fire's heat' – why, I might have been a maid, but I knew enough of my own inner flames and desirings to know a lusty young man must have been at the heart of it. No doubt she had met this Napier at some London junket and he had convinced her that he would honour her. God's garters, it truly was the oldest of ancient tales.

After that, to marry Sir Geoffrey weren't such a bad plan at all, to turn a girl's shame into a title, and then scarper off here to foreign parts, so none would be the wiser. It was clear to me she'd kept even Mr Kitt and her uncle in the dark. And to cap it all, she was spending Sir Geoffrey's astonishing heap of money too.

'Well, I pity her for marrying poxed Sir Geoffrey, but my lady breeding – oh, I can't believe I never noticed it before,' I said, clasping my hand to my mouth.

'Nor I,' said a biting voice from the doorway. Mr Loveday and I jumped up to our feet like two jack-in-the-boxes. Jesmire was there, not five paces away, her face mighty priggish and triumphant. I wondered how long she'd been listening, for me and Mr Loveday had been gossiping so hard she could have heard every word.

'I might have known you would dig up whatever is most foul,' she snapped at me.

'It's only the truth,' I protested, folding my arms and facing her. 'At least I had the wit to discover what troubles my poor lady, which is more than you ever did!'

'Poor lady indeed,' she spat. 'Well, we shall see what Mr Pars makes of these deceits.' There was nowt I could do to stop the old sneak, who turned on her heels, leaving me mighty uneasy.

I was summoned to appear before Mr Pars that night. He sat behind the oak table in his chamber, playing the solemn judge. If he'd scolded me, it would have cleared the air, but instead old Pars was oddly calm and gentle.

'Sit a while and let me talk to you, Biddy,' he said, motioning me towards a chair. He was watching me with a soft expression; more like I was a mischievous child than anything.

'Biddy, Miss Jesmire has told me what you have discovered. It saddens me that while in my care you've been exposed to such debauchery. It must have been a great surprise to you. What did your mistress say?'

I couldn't see any harm in telling him, for my lady's condition would soon be apparent to all.

'She is most terribly heartbroke, sir. Quite overcome with it all. And fearful of you writing to Sir Geoffrey, sir.'

He took a thoughtful suck on his pipe and breathed out two mazy puffs of sweet grey smoke. 'Maybe it would be for the best if Sir Geoffrey never hears of this. He's a very sick man. Bad news could be the final blow to my dear master.' He drummed his fingers on the edge of the table top. 'And did she say any more to you, Biddy? Go on, girl. Spit the truth out. What else did she say?'

I stared at the floor and wished myself a thousand miles away.

'She said Sir Geoffrey, pardon my speaking so ill of my master, sir, was sick with the pox when she married him.' I glanced up quickly. He was studying me carefully, but didn't look at all astonished. 'So that prevented them, from like – she cannot pass the baby off as his.'

'Ah.' He nodded sagely. 'Did she say any more? Speak of anyone else?'

'No, sir. She only asked me to help her, which I will gladly do, without asking, sir.'

'You think she likes you, eh?' He shook his head, as if quite pained, then waited for my eye to meet his. 'I know she's given you all these absurd notions of your own importance. Aye, it's true, isn't it? She deceives you with her flattery and kind words. But use your wits, girl. Ask yourself, why should she care about you?'

In the silence I racked my brainbox for an answer.

'I don't know, sir.'

He was looking at me very shrewdly, his eyes quite narrow and sharp. 'I always thought you were a good honest girl. Mrs Garland reckons you are like a daughter to her.'

What with all the ups and downs of the day I couldn't bear being reminded of good Mrs Garland. I felt tears rise behind my eyes just at the mention of my dear friend. What was it she had said? To trust Mr Pars, for he was a gentleman and a God-fearing Christian besides. So my voice were choked when I answered, 'I try to be good, sir. Honest, I do try.'

'Then tell me.' He stroked the inky papers that lay in piles across his desk. 'What does your mistress mean, by favouring you?'

I wanted to answer him truly; I wanted to prove I could be good.

'That she likes me, sir?'

'Nonsense!' His knotted fist hit the table with a thump that made me jump. 'Of course she doesn't like you, you blockhead. What is going on? Tell me!'

I shook my head, brain-choked with it all.

'I wish I knew, sir.'

Suddenly I felt like a wing-battered fly in a terrible web of misunderstandings. I realised then, I had not the first notion of what Mr Pars, or Lady Carinna, truly wanted from me at all.

# XXII

## Lyons to Savoy

*Being Candlemas, February 1773*
*Biddy Leigh, her journal*

## ~ Farcement Pudding ~

*Grate a score of potatoes and let them ooze their water one hour then dry in a cloth. Render a quarter flitch of bacon chopped in pieces till golden. Line a tall pan with scollops of thin bacon hanging over the edges and meantime beat half a dozen eggs with a half pint of good milk, add a quarter pound of cornmeal, the bacon, two handfuls currants, chopped dried pears and the potatoes and salt and caraway seeds and nutmeg as you wish. Pack it tight down and lay two dozen prunes upon it and then close the bacon over the top. Boil in your pot for seven hours and serve with a ham and a shoulder of pork.*

*A dish for a wedding made from the memories of old women in the mountains of Savoy, Biddy Leigh, 1773*

From Lyons we were all stuffed into one hired carriage, for the way over the Alps mountains was too dangerous for even Mr Pars to ride outside. So our steward was squashed all vast and sweat-sour beside me, keeping his eyes half shut beneath his shaggy brows, and his thoughts as close as a coffin. Mr Loveday was brought inside too, and for that I was grateful, for he might have frozen to death against the carriage rear. I never saw him more tormented by the cold; all day he crouched in a corner of the floor with his head in his hands, suffering violently. My lady had said she would not have us all freeze for want of spending, so Mr Pars reluctantly furnished us all with bearskins. Yet even wrapped in a fur poor Mr Loveday shivered and shook, his teeth all a-chatter whenever he opened his mouth.

We now came to a new place named Savoy, a savage land of high rocks that reached right through the clouds. It was truly the most fearsome sight I ever saw in my life. We ventured up a narrow road barely six foot wide, that was on one side a steep mountain covered in curious pointed trees and the other a plummeting gorge falling down to a crashing river. Inside the carriage all our nerves were at a great stretch, for we had seen vast boulders fall from the mountaintops into the hellish chasm below. Hour after hour we were jostled and jolted, all of us queasy and fearful of our lives. Then, to make matters worse, we entered a land of blinding white snow. The carriage started to swerve and swing across the road in a fearful manner, and I cursed the day I ever left my kitchen at Mawton Hall.

\* \* \*

It was sunset before our mournful procession found the inn, perched so high on the mountain that it looked certain to slide down the snowy cliff into the valley below. Just as we drew up, the snow began to fall in a great tumble of flakes looking so pretty that I laughed to feel it tickle my face. Before us stood the remarkablest scene: the windows of the carved wooden houses peeped gold in the dusk; and the trees, the ground, and low roofs were all iced with snow like sugared cakes. Above, the welkin glowed pink and lilac, the pretty hues reflected on the glassy slopes of the mountain. I never saw a place more astonishing and strange.

The inn-folk crept out of their smothered homes like bundled moles to haul our goods indoors. It was like a gloomy cave inside, furnished with few comforts save a good fire around which we huddled and steamed. This was the parlour, where hung a great wooden cross and a mass of popish relics; pictures of every sort of Madonna, saint, and nun, like an army of poppet-dolls. The furniture was crudely carved wood and the only finery some flower-painted pots. From the backroom came the stink and ceaseless lowing of cattle, for in that desperate place a house had also to serve as a shippon. It being the feast of Candlemas, which is like our Shrovetide, our landlady fried up a supper of pancakes, first with cheese and then with honey. It was poor peasant stuff, but was all we had, for our fancy Lyons pies and cakes had all been eaten. Then there was naught else to do but fumble our way up the ladder to our straw pallets in the loft.

The next day the coachman called to say storm clouds presaged a violent blizzard. There was much griping at the news, for the inn offered little escape from each other's moping faces. For two days we waited for the weather to stop blizzarding so we might go on our way. It was an odd time, for I never felt so far from England; the quiet was so uncanny you might hear a bird drop a twig. The mountain-tops crowded the sky like jagged teeth of ice, and at night the stars glittered as hard as diamonds. I should have loved to send home a picture of that prospect, but I think no painter ever travelled there. I will never in all my life forget that curious place.

Perhaps the reason we tarried was that the coachman knew that Cécile, the landlady's daughter, was to marry that Sunday. Her betrothed was a soldier who had been much delayed in returning home for the wedding. I watched Cécile being dressed on her wedding morn, and like any spinster it brought a shine to my eye to see her plain face so wondrously beautified. Damn that Jem Burdett, thought I. My spirit shivered to think of my own bride cake mouldering to dust in the larder at Mawton, and all the ill luck that might bring me. To see Cécile's face shining when her handsome soldier called made my heart sore, to think that my bed would always be a cold one.

Cécile's bridal gown was the work of many years' needlework; her bodice embroidered with a thousand careful stitches showing all the flowers of a meadow. Her bonnet and apron were finest white lace, worked with her own bobbins. I lent Cécile my lady's large silver mirror so she could see herself all decked in her finery. She giggled into her hands and turned away, the simple creature.

Like a blessing, the snowfall stopped for the marriage procession, and a watery sun shone down as we tramped behind a crowd of villagers all in their holiday best, the women wearing those same figured clothes and lace bonnets. In truth I cared little for the Wedding Mass, for the church was a nasty place decorated with leering skulls and bones. Mr Pars made long complaints of the superstition of the Catholic people, and when I saw such horrors I took his side. Only Mr Loveday was curiously drawn to them, making me fearful that the tales of black men hunting their victims' heads might indeed be true.

When we got back to the warmth of the inn, me and Mr Loveday were ordered to help out with serving the food. The *farcement* pudding was the main fussing point of the womenfolk. It had no receipt, for it was made to old women's memories, being a sort of vast pudding wrapped tight in a steaming cartwheel of bacon.

After the wedding feast the dancing began, and it was good to watch the young folk: the boys in white stockings and girls in their lace-capped best.

'You hear that?' asked Mr Loveday, joining me and pointing up to the ceiling. I could barely hear the yapping above the screech of the fiddles.

'Bengo?'

'You want me go, Miss Biddy? Jes' I got them cups to wash.'

I looked about the room. Mr Pars was well fuddled, his head bowed over his tankard. Jesmire too, was nodding open-mouthed in a corner, but there was no sign of my lady. It was a shame to leave the warm parlour, but if the wretched creature needed the yard, someone had to take him out.

I clambered up the rough stair to the lofts and found Bengo scratching behind the door. There was no sign of my mistress. I carried him outside and let him sniff and piddle while I gazed at the delicate tracks of birds, as dainty as fork prints in the snow. Then I noticed different tracks; the mark of a lady's heel hollowed deeper than the front sole. The Savoy women wore only stout leather boots, so where had my mistress gone? I returned Bengo to the upper chamber, picked up my cloak, and set off after her into the snow.

The sun had dropped and the shadows were long and purple against the white sheets of snow. What the devil was my mistress doing? I only knew the beaten track to the village, and not this solitary way. Soon I found myself on a narrow path beside a stream, the bushes spangled with shards of ice. I didn't care to be out there at all, and wondered if I should have fetched Mr Loveday or even roused Mr Pars. Yet all the time the footprints lured me onwards, for they looked so fresh, as if I might come upon my lady just around the next corner. By now I was perished with cold, especially my fingers that were crabbed red. If she had gone off on some dangerous jaunt, what did I care if ill luck befell her? I could not forget she was breeding, that was my worry. She needed only to slip on this snow and I would never forgive myself. Then, with a sudden whip of wind, the snow began to fall again. Or I should say, it blasted straightwise into my face. It was like a plague of white bees, quite alive, and swarming so thick through the air I could scarce see a pace ahead of me. With a little scream I felt my foot slide away and I lurched to grab the high bank at my side. My heart thumping, I held tight onto a frozen tree stump and tried to blink the snow from my eyes.

The path ahead of me ended at a cliff edge that dropped over a fearsome ledge to the valley below. And there, just a few paces away, my mistress stood as still as a statue, all rimed with snow.

'My Lady.' The wind stole my words. I slithered a few steps towards her and held out my hand. 'Here I am, My Lady!'

Her face was wet, though whether with tears or snow I could not tell. Then the notion came to me like a thunderbolt, that she had come to this godforsaken place to take her own life. A gust of wind cleared the view below her feet for a moment. The chasm was so deep that trees were scattered like specks of moss, and the road was a mere thread. My heart thumped. I inched slowly towards her.

'I have news,' I shouted. 'We leave tomorrow. I heard them say it. The coachman only held back for the wedding.'

I edged my way another inch towards her and grasped her hand. It was as cold as bones, but I felt a weak grip press my fingers. Urgently I tried to chafe her hand, then pulled her towards me.

'We will be in Italy soon. A few days,' I bawled. 'Soon all will be well.'

Her hair was whipping unpinned in the air, her cloak ribbons flapping like darting snakes. Slowly, life returned to her face. With a nod she turned towards me and let me slowly lead her back.

As we reached a sheltered bank she said in a lifeless tone, 'I suffer such fits of dread.'

I knew how women suffer at their time of danger, and I put it down to that. It seemed to me, too, that she was not of the strongest mettle. She had a dropsied, swollen look, and her chest rasped as she walked. My own ma had birthed with barely a squeal, picking coal right up to the last hour before her labours. My lady was more delicate – she looked that tender, as the saying goes, that she'd break her finger in a posset curd. I supposed it was only the fear that was turning her mind, that and being alone here with no one but us for company.

We reached the inn but she wouldn't follow me inside. In the lea of the wall she said, 'I cannot face that rabble. Come with me, Biddy. Please.'

Fool that I was, I followed her, like a gormless lamb that follows the wolf from its pen. She held my arm and we took the beaten track back to the church. What with the cold and my wet feet I could have cursed her, but I thought on what she had said about not facing the wedding mob. Like me, she must have tasted bitter gall to see Cécile's happiness. My poor mistress could scarcely have felt much joy at marrying Sir Geoffrey, and now she'd got this bellyful to hide away, too. We came to the church and there she halted with a pleading look. 'I must speak with you alone, Biddy.'

Inside, the heat from the big black stove still lingered and we both huddled over it, stretching red fingers towards the embers. I glanced at her and saw she was pondering deep, picking at her flaky lips. I looked about at the church, so gaudily painted with saints, and yet flitting amongst them were all those leering bones. I shivered and thought of the merry room I had left. By now Cécile would have set off with her husband for a good night's bedding. I longed to get back amongst warm lively bodies, to sup a little leftover brandy and pick at the leavings.

At last she spoke. 'I need your help, Biddy.' She halted, then swallowed and continued. 'Fortune has dealt me a vicious blow. Will you help me?' She turned straight to face me then. What could I say? I felt right sorry for her, even though common sense told me I was probably going to be put upon something rotten.

'Yes, My Lady. I told you I would help you.'

I saw her wince.

'I mean more than what – your position obliges.'

'What then?' The babe was getting close to full size; now she had loosened her stays it showed clear enough. 'You don't mean to cast it out, do you? For I don't believe—'

'Oh, no. No, not that Biddy. Do you think I would kill my own child?' Her sharp look shamed me.

'It was only the sassafras oil, My Lady,' I mumbled.

'Sassafras?' She was truly surprised. 'That is Jesmire's, for her rheumatics. No, you are a clever girl. You know you are, of course. And given the right costume could pass for—' She dropped her chin into her hand, covering her mouth as if it might betray her. She had raised my curiosity all right. I racked my brainbox. Did she want me to dress up and fetch her something from a fancy shop?

'No. It's too stupid. I once thought you could help me.' Her head shook quickly, as if to rid herself of a fancy. 'It's too ridiculous.'

'Tell me,' I demanded. I laid my hand on her sleeve. She was sopping wet and I knew she should be back at the inn tucked up in bed. But I had to know.

'I'll help you,' I said rashly. I was thinking of her brother, of how I had passed as a better sort in Paris. If I had to go and buy some perfume or a new gown, it would at least be entertaining. 'I'll do it. If it's some sort of mimicry you're after, I'm your girl.'

'You are remarkably quick. Yes, it is mimicry I want of you, Biddy.' Then she told me my task. 'When we arrive in Italy I want you to call on a certain fellow and fetch the key to the villa. That is all. To pass yourself off as me to this Count Carlo. He never met me in his life. And we do both, of course, bear a resemblance to each other.'

'Do we?' I was flabbergasted. Me, pass myself off as her in noble company? I was trying to turn it over in my mind but all I could make out was a jumble of notions darting about just like that blizzarding snow.

'So you will do it? You did say you would do it.' There was a finger-poke of command in her tone then. The way she said it, it sounded such a slight thing, to call for a key.

'He has truly never met you?' I asked slowly.

'Never. And knows very little of me. He may ask after his friend, my uncle, so I'll school you on that.'

A queasy spasm gripped my gut. How would I sit, how would I address him, what if he laughed at my stupid attempt?

'In truth, My Lady, I don't rightly know if – if I can keep it up.'

'Listen. You have nothing to do but call on him. Then at last I can be easy.' She was watching me hard. Two patches of red glowed like fever on her cheeks. 'You did promise.'

I pressed my chilblained fingers to my lips and wished all our words had never been spoken. Yet they had been, and fool that I was, I had agreed to this pantomime.

I tried out my best, most ladylike, affected tone. 'Why if it should please you, yes my dear lady.'

'That's it Biddy. That's all you need to do. Very good.' She patted me on the arm like I was Bengo and had just performed a trick. Then she rose and left and I traipsed mournfully after her, following her snow-blurred footprints back to the inn.

# XXIII

The road ahead wound between crags splintered like broken teeth, edged by dizzying crevasses. Never in his life had Loveday imagined such a horrible place. The seasons were trapped by some kind of witchery; rain froze as white as chicken feathers, smothering crops and freezing lakes. With helpless dismay he had watched as the carriage was pulled apart, like a great carcass hacked into joints. Now he was riding a curious wooden chair carried by four strong mountain men. He dared not look about himself. In the corners of his eyes were the flicker of trees, pointed rocks, ice-crusted snow. His senses closed against the succession of horrors; it would be many hours until they stopped at the mountain-top. Commanding his limbs to be still on the narrow chair, he released his spirit to go wherever it chose.

He was standing on the beach at Lamahona. Sailing towards him was a poor sort of boat with no ritual paint or sails. Three strangers. He turned to run to the village, to bang the hollow *tong-tong* trunk in warning. But he skewed in his sandy tracks.

Behind the small rowing boat, far out at sea stood something vast and magnificent. Loveday groped for words – a tower of trees hung with banners, a palace of flags, a cage of fluttering shrouds. It was his first ever sighting of a white man's ship.

Loveday pushed his way to the front of the excited crowd and stared at the strangers. The three men standing on Lamahona beach had round, fish-like eyes and fat noses like the *juru* sea-cows. Their skin was not truly white, but pale and misshapen, seamed with scars and horrible lumps. The broadest of the white men made animal sounds. A pale jagged scar ran across his face. To Loveday he looked very old, as crumpled as the flesh-eating lizards of Komodo Island. Like the other men, he wore strange mud-coloured cloths and a headdress of flat leather. The white man lifted a string of beads that was as blue and transparent as solid ocean. After a long pause Chief Korohama snatched them and held them high. A thrill of relief passed amongst the crowd. These horrible creatures wanted to be their friends.

Later, the man he called Scarface again pulled out a bundle, but all he showed them was a grey lump of *amber* whale stones. Loveday had laughed to see it, the commonplace lump so carefully wrapped in a cloth. All in a jitter of excitement, he and his friends led the white men to the boathouse to show them how the stuff was used. The strangers had made low whispering sounds as they passed the shelf of sacred skulls, but the crowd politely ignored their disrespect. Mounds of pungent whale stones lay heaped all around the boats. One of the boat crew showed the white men how the stuff was diluted to seal the boats. It was the whales' gift to the hunters and it had always been so.

Towards dusk the white men fetched a lantern from their little boat. While the white men stood on the beach and raised and lowered a little door inside the lantern, the villagers murmured to each other in understanding. They did the same thing when the fish did not come, holding flaming candlenuts by the seashore to call the spirits of the fish. Loveday looked out to the wondrous ship still hanging on the horizon, now spangled with pinpricks of light as the sky grew dark. Only for a fleeting moment did he ponder that if he could see the lamp-lit ship, perhaps its crew could see the flashing language of their comrades' lantern, calling from the beach.

Loveday's eyes snapped open, awake. Many hours had passed since the great feast held for the strangers, but still his *manger* spirit rattled with the question: who were these white men? Gently, he freed his limbs from Bulan's warm flesh and listened as their baby son continued to breathe slowly and evenly. At the doorway to his hut he picked up his harpoon, feeling its balance and weight stiffen his courage. Creeping outside, he found his way using his bare toes and his nose. Wood smoke wafted from the fire stones at the village centre; a fug of charred dog meat hung in the direction of the chief's hall. The sea suddenly loomed, a vast lungful of briny salt. Across its plain of rocking night, the moon's rays cast a phantom path. The white men's ship could not be seen.

He turned away from the sea and sank his feet in the soft sandy path. Soon a guttural murmuring reached his ears from the clearing ahead. On the tips of his toes he edged slowly forward. The yellow beam of a lantern waved behind dark trees. His first fear was for the safety of his ancestors' skulls, but the light was nowhere near the sacred shelf. Next he feared for the boats, the living spirits that carried the villagers across the ocean. No. They were loading something into sacks. Whale stones. There were lots more white men, they must have come secretly from the tall ship. The whole scene was so unbelievably stupid that he snorted out loud.

The lantern swung suddenly towards him. A shout rose, then two men ran towards him. The shock of his discovery felt like a blow that stunned him. The first man was so close now that he could see his monstrous face. Terrorised into action, Loveday headed into the deepest thicket of trees, running at his legs' full stretch. Behind him followed the crash of heavy footsteps and shouts of pursuit. But he held the advantage; this was his land, he had played in this forest as a boy. Even in the pitchy darkness he knew where to jump high over tangled shrubs and when to stoop low below murderous branches. He headed for the brackish pool at the thicket's centre, where earth and trees sank into bog. Soon his feet slowed in sucking mud and he used his harpoon to leap like a frog across the water. Reaching the far bank he scrambled into a thicket. Breathless and frightened, he crouched against a tree trunk, his chest panting fast.

He could hear the men crashing behind him and then talking urgently. 'Kir-im', they seemed to be saying, and the words meant less to him than a gecko's bark. He waited, his back pressed hard against the tree, his ears straining for the sound of feet plunging across the water to capture him.

At that moment *fula*, the brazen moon, flooded the forest with moonbeams. In the bleached light he saw a man pointing a stick towards him, twenty paces away. It looked so stupid, for even if he threw the stick, it could never reach him across the water. Then to Loveday's amazement, a blinding spark erupted from the stick. A thunderclap sounded, rocking the earth. An invisible fist punched his chest. The next he knew, he was flat on the ground, flung on his back, all the life pressed out of him. Bitter smoke filled his nostrils; his limbs felt as dead as stone.

For a long time his thoughts spun this way and that, like a speared fish beating its tail. When he came to his senses he was clinging to a tree root as if it were his only anchor to life. An open wound in his shoulder lashed him with pain; his limbs were sore and stiff. Slowly, the sounds of the forest returned. But what he first thought were the terrified cries of birds in the distance were not birds. Muffled by distance, they were human wails and shouts. Without warning, a cry like a sacrificed pig tore the night sky apart. Loveday curled even tighter into the earth.

Just beyond the forest edge terrible things were happening. He pictured Bulan and Barut's suffering and squirmed with self-hatred. He was a hunter, a brave man, a husband, a father. Only he was not those things tonight. As he lay on the forest floor his courage flickered and died. Those white witch-men had cursed him. They had shrunk him from a man into a feeble-witted coward.

Finally, he forced himself to stand up and stagger from tree to tree. Gripping his harpoon pole, he paddled himself along like an old man with a stick. At the edge of the village he stood for a long time, his fists tight with fear. He felt shivering cold and sick.

The village banyan tree, the roofs of the huts, everything was lost in blackness. With a gasping effort he staggered crab-wise towards the chief's hall. He had barely crept a few paces when his foot bumped against something warm and solid, like a sleeping dog. Using his harpoon pole as a balance, Loveday dropped to a squat very slowly and patted the dog. It was hairless and smooth. As his fingers crept along a thick limb, they sank into something warm and sticky. As he tried to rise, a ringing metal *clack* rang out from the darkness. Then a lantern opened and Loveday blinked into the golden light of the white men's lamp.

I am a hunter, he recited to himself. I stand firm. Behind the lamplight stood the man Scarface, dragging a group of village women, all of them haltered with ropes. One of the women straining to see him was his beloved Bulan. Her lovely face was a mask of terror. 'Husband!' she called to him. 'Help me!' His frantic gaze flickered to the ground where a dozen corpses lay twisted across the village clearing. The body at his feet was Chief Korohama, his throat cut and his dead eyes staring at the stars. While he had cowered in the trees, all these honourable men had fought to save their village.

Though half blinded by the light, Loveday tried to rise with the same majestic grace as when he stood at the rushing prow of his boat. He tried to raise his harpoon straight and point it at the white man. His Bapa's words returned to him, 'Stand firm'. Though his arm trembled like a sail in a storm, he aimed the harpoon's barb precisely at the man's throat. He rejoiced as he drew back his arm to gather his power. The man would be dead before his next heartbeat.

The fire-flash punched him again, throwing him hard against the wall. To his amazement he was lying in the dirt again, slumped over Chief Korohama's corpse. His shame was such that he did not ever want to wake again and live. He gave his spirit permission to leave his body and seek his ancestors. Bulan and Barut were alive and suffering and he had not saved them. He wanted never to face another human again.

His heartfelt wish was refused by the gods. He had woken in a Damong boat, tied by knotted grasses to a wailing old man. He learned that the white men had sold all the village men to their most vicious enemies. The women and children were nowhere to be seen. He caught a glimpse of his home over the boat rail. His island was emerging in the dawn light, the cone of the volcano piercing a crown of fluffy clouds. The water was blue and glittering, the beach a curve of pearl white sand. But from the direction of his village grey smoke rose in streamers. It hung above the trees like a storm cloud, very ugly, very wrong.

Later they came to Damong island, where timber poles paraded the horned skulls of their sacrificial beasts. His insides quailed with fear. Beside him the old man whimpered and lost control of his guts in a hot stink. Courage, he discovered, was not a loyal companion who came at his bidding. It was a fair-weather friend who that day left him stranded and witless.

Loveday's mouth was pressed hard against the wooden edge of the chair. He rose to find he had reached a flat plain of snow. Pulling off his hat he felt the thin sun stroke his naked cheek. Above, a huge brown bird hovered gracefully in the sky, its pointed wings spread wide to float on a rising breeze. The great bird, so noble and sleek, its wings as wide as a devil ray, was surely an omen of good? He looked to where they would travel next. There, barely a league below, lay a shore of fertile green where the snowline ended. He had never before understood that green was such a beautiful life-giving colour.

When they set off again, Loveday watched in wonder as the nimble-footed mountaineers carried him down the looping path. He passed a cascade of water frozen like a blink in time, its crystal splashes sparkling like diamonds. Twisting off a knobbly icicle, he let it melt in his palm until all that was left was a pebble of ice enclosing a perfect leaf the size of a fingernail. Turning a corner they faced a mass of twisted ice like a frozen river, tumbling hundreds of feet into blue-green caverns. He would never see such wonders again. One day, he prayed, he might tell his children of where their Bapa had journeyed when he strayed off the edge of the world.

Finally, he saw green blades of grass sprouting bravely through lacy ice. Soon the greenness stretched ahead of him, and he motioned to the men to halt and let him dismount. Taking his last dozen steps on the snow he felt the ground soften into grass beneath his feet. Here was a valley bordered by round grassy hills, and in its midst a stone village of artful towers and red roofs. Throwing off his heavy fur he plucked a scented white blossom from a passing tree. The fragile petals smelled of life and blossoming hope.

# XXIV

## Piedmont to Montechino

*Being St Valentine's to Ash Wednesday, February 1773*
*Biddy Leigh, her journal*

# ~ *Manus Christi* ~

*First take your sugar clarified and melt it in water of roses.
Seethe these two till the water be consumed and the sugar
hard, put in four grains of crushed pearls and precious stones,
made in fine powder, then lay it in cakes on a marble stone
anointed with oil of roses and lay on your gold.*

*An unsurpassed defence against all the sickness, soreness
and wounds that do daily assault mankind, written in
The Cook's Jewel, in a very old scriven hand, 1523*

From the day I promised to help my mistress, everything felt tainted. It was like I'd baked a cake with salt instead of sugar; everything looked well enough, but no meddling in the world could ever set it right again. And the shame of it was, that now we were past those fearsome Alps, there never was a lovelier place than Piedmont. Green meadows rose before us like the land of milk and honey, the hills thick with grapevines and the sky china blue and jewel bright. I should have been as happy as a lark, being free to walk outside the carriage with the sun warming my back, but it had all turned sour to me.

'Do you think that's why she's dragged me all this way, just to use me?' I harped on to Mr Loveday. All this time I had flattered myself that my mistress maybe liked me for myself. But no, she had picked me out to play a part in some trickery. I felt as ill-used as a ten-year-old dishclout.

'You just go this fellow, fetch the key and then it done, my friend.'

Puffed out from climbing the hill I grasped his arm and stood before him, staring fiercely. 'She said we look alike. Is that true?'

He stuck out his broad lower lip and looked into my face. 'You both women, both brown hair. This man never know you not my lady.'

I had to laugh. 'That's what you think! I only need open my mouth and he'll know me for a right clodhopper.' We carried on walking and I picked a dull blackish berry from a branch, a sort of hard grape. 'It's one thing parroting the mistress, but another to talk mannerly with this count fellow.'

'When my lady meet high-ranking fellow she just talk any old thing.'

I shook my head. I was supposed to be Lady Carinna, wife to Sir Geoffrey, niece to that Mr Quentin Tyrone. I bit into the berry and it was so bitter I spat it out on the dusty road.

'She says she will write to him when we get there. What I'd give to read his reply.'

Mr Loveday was silent for a while, kicking up the dust with his boots. He turned to me and said softly, 'If I tell you secret, you not tell others?'

I looked up fast. 'What do you mean?'

In a moment I had it all out of him. That he opened the post then sealed it up again. He told me it was only to practise his reading, but I reckoned it was his way to meddle a little in the affairs of those who bullied him. I glanced back at the carriage, but it was far behind us, the horses straining to climb the twisting hill. I did my best to find out what was written in those letters, but it was like digging coal from the earth with my bare hands. Mostly it seemed, our mistress complained in her letters no differently from how she complained every day to any who would listen.

'And have you looked in any of Mr Pars' letters?' I asked breathlessly.

'Mr Pars only write his brother. Mostly I seen him write many many number, but never send in letter.'

'Aye, so have I. They are only his accounts, Mr Loveday. And what of Jesmire?'

'She only write for new position. But no reply, not one time,' he added, suddenly laughing.

'Mr Loveday,' I said, 'would you do me a very great favour and let me see any letters that pass between my lady and this Count Carlo?'

The lad blew out his cheeks and shook his head slowly. 'It not allowed, Miss Biddy. Better me my own.'

'Please,' I begged.

He looked up, his expression pained. 'You promise my friend always? You not tell them I open letter?'

'I promise never to tell. On my mother's life. We servants stick together, eh?' I touched his arm and glanced at the carriage as it reached the crest of the hill and the horses started trotting towards us. Very softly I whispered, 'When the right time comes, I'll see you get away safely.'

He still hesitated, rubbing his mouth with his fingers. Finally he nodded and grinned. 'I believe you, Miss Biddy. You only one who make promise that true. I feel my spirit free of bad thinking now. But you be careful, my friend.'

'I'll do me best. I'll just go and fetch that key. I'll have nothing to do with any of them.'

It just goes to show how wrong you can be.

We reached Turin very late, for my lady complained much about the rocking carriage and made us stop every few miles so she could dose herself and take the fresh air. When we finally got through the city gates, the roads were massed with a great procession of soldiers, all rigged out like Cécile's husband in frogged blue coats and white knee breeches. The scene was that lively it roused my lady to a giddy mood and she pulled the carriage glass down to see better. 'Wait! I heard at the inn we might see King Charles Emmanuel survey his troops. He's grandson to our own King Charles that lost his head. Stop! Damn you, I want to see,' she said, thumping on the ceiling. The view being poor from the carriage, she then got a fancy to join the crowd and called for Mr Loveday to hand her down. He and Mr Pars made way for her through the townsfolk, and soon afterwards Jesmire tottered after them with Bengo straining on his ribbon. Having the carriage quite to myself, I hung from the door, enjoying the rousing drums and the cheers of the townsfolk.

The procession had scarcely begun when a great hubbub started up and, to my astonishment, I next saw my mistress had swooned and fallen to the ground. I sprang down and soon met Mr Loveday and Mr Pars struggling to carry her. By the time they reached the carriage, thank God she had started to recover her senses. Yet still she was as pale as a sheet and shiny with sweat. Mr Pars said that it must be the heat, and told Jesmire to dab at her mistress's face with Cologne water. Only I had the gumption to loosen her stays and fan her face once we got moving again. Even when we got to the inn, my lady was right out of sorts, and had trouble walking without an arm to lean on. She had just the breath to tell Mr Pars to call a physician, which I thought very brave in such a foreign place. So a medical man was sent for, though Mr Pars all the while scoffed that my lady was affecting a fashionable ague, and would no doubt waste a vast amount of money.

I did not see the doctor when he came, but being the best with the lingo it was me who was sent to fetch my lady's medicine that evening. By then it was just before sunset, by which time all the local folk had swaggered out for a stroll. Turin was a mighty city, very modern built with fancy arcades and grand flagged squares. I let myself wander amongst the black-haired girls rolling their hips, and prim families ambling in groups, all of us watched by wrinkled crones scowling from their doorsteps. I listened hard to the chatter in the streets, for I'd been doing my best to practise my Italian with anyone who would talk to me, from our gruff driver to the maids at the inns. It was true that it was not so different from French – where good day had been *bonjor* it was *bonjorno*, and it was *parnay* for bread and *carnay* for meat.

At the doctor's house I was shown into what he called the *farmacia*. It was a dark, wood-panelled room that held a vast collection of bottles and pots all neatly labelled with queer names. While a servant mixed a concoction for my mistress, I fixed on buying rare ambergris, rosewater, and musk from my household money. Even better, as I lingered at a glass cabinet, my eye lit on an old familiar name: *Manus Christi*. The confection was not in the shape of Christ's hand at all, as me and Mrs Garland had once fancied, but a jar of transparent lozenges flecked with gold and crushed pearls. Now that confection was not cheap and I had to offer one of Mr Harbird's golden guineas to buy a small portion, but it was the greatest of pleasures to post a parcel off to Mrs Garland in England. Our journeying meant I'd not hear from her until we got to the villa, but by then I prayed the cure-all might have eased my friend.

Back at the inn I handed my lady the doctor's medicine. He had bled her beforehand, and her waxy arm was still bound with a cloth. After her first set of drops she let her head drop back on the pillow and fixed me with dull eyes.

'Lord, this is so unfair. I had so looked forward to the opera.'

I nodded but did not risk a word, for I was still in a flaming fit at her for setting me up to visit the count. I was queasy too, with fear at not being able to pull it off right.

'In a few weeks we should arrive at the villa, yet you still behave like a country hoyden,' she said, yawning so wide I could almost see her breakfast. 'You still know almost nothing of a lady's behaviour. Do try to pay more attention, Biddy. Look at me. One has to be brazen to survive. I barely had a year at a lady's academy and then I had to use my looks and my wits. In this world you must take what you need. No one else will fight your battles.'

Then she fell fast asleep and I was left alone with this task she had set me. 'A Lady's Behaviour', now that chimed like a bell with me. So for long leisurely days while she was laid up in Turin, I studied those parts of *The Cook's Jewel* that addressed 'The Behaviour of a True Lady'. There was much advice on the holding of the tongue, what they called that 'slippery member that led to vice'. That did at least make me laugh out loud, for the quaint old writer certainly knew nowt of tavern wit if that's what she called a mere tongue. Then I learned of all a lady must not do: that she must not be a wild girl and laugh out loud, or gape at a well-laden table, or make tomboy jests. Why, that was as much like me as if we were spit from the same mouth, I thought. Then I recollected that was how a gentlewoman must not be, and despaired a little.

I let my eyes wander to 'A Ladies' Guide to Love and Fancy', and was disgusted to find that our milk-sop lady must always be struck mute in the face of compliments, and stunned to stock stillness by every suitor. There was some good sense, mind, in advising her to Look Well Before She Likes, for I knew with the wisdom of hindsight that I had not looked too closely at Jem Burdett. The book said a lady should examine the compartments of a man's heart before she gave herself in marriage, for that was a great step in the Labyrinth of Life. Virtue, Kindness and Companionship in a man were much lauded, which were mighty odd notions to me. I puzzled over ever having heard of such a man in all my life.

As I read of such ladylike matters in *The Cook's Jewel*, I was reminded that St Valentine's Day had come around. On that very night, after pinning five bay leaves to my pillow and saying the chant to dream of my true love, I settled expectantly in my tiny chamber. To my astonishment, I did have a dream – that I was in a strange house and woke to find myself in the arms of a fellow I knew to be exactly that kind, virtuous and companionable paragon. I could not rightly see my bedfellow, but felt his solid arms tight around my waist as I laid my head very tenderly on his breast. And in the dream I was that happy, it was like I'd found my true home as I listened to his heart beating just beneath my ear. But when I woke and found it was only a figment, I felt so dejected, to find my true love never lived in this hard world. It was a daft thing I know, but I was near to weeping to think that sweet lover lived only in my dreams and I was doomed never to find him.

Once we set off again we were all out of sorts. The post houses delayed us with worn-out horses, the roads ran over tricky mountain passes, the hired groomsmen were sponging rogues. My mistress halted to see the famous Hanging Tower at Pisa, which was quite comical in its sinking style, but then lost her silver brush and would not return for it, so harried was she to reach her journey's end. As for Mr Pars, he was growing ever stranger in his manner. For a start, there was his brainfever over money. Every night he'd lock himself in his chamber and try to resurrect his blessed System of Economy. Then next day he'd bicker with me over a few coppers spent on a cold chicken or boiled eggs.

He summoned me one night after supper. His room was like an accompting house, filled with sheaves of bills in tottering piles, a well-thumbed abacus on his desk, and all of it smeared with pipe-ash. He glared up from his papers.

'I have had my eye on you, Biddy Leigh. And I see how familiar you are with your mistress.' His eyeballs had a yellowish cast and his breath a sour reek. I had read in *The Cook's Jewel* that the calming benefits of tobacco were wasted on those with a choleric nature. Looking at him, I feared a gut-stone or worse might be on its way.

''Tis not me provoking it, Mr Pars. I only do as I'm told.'

'Enough!' He slapped his desk so the papers shook. 'You're quick with a pert answer, aren't you girl? You must always have the last word.'

I tried to think of an answer, but all would give me the last word again. So I hung my head for a bit and waited to see what else was coming.

'It is apparent to me that you encourage your mistress's confidences with all your infantile jests.'

Infantile jests! I was getting that dishclout feeling again, feeling ever so used.

'And I will not have her schooling you to talk like your betters. You are a kitchen maid, do you understand?'

Under-cook, I thought.

'Yes, Mr Pars.'

Lord, it was like standing before a schoolmaster, pretending I was sorry.

'You are under my care and I worry ceaselessly about you – that you will be ruined by her grasping ways. Does that surprise you Biddy? That I alone can see it?'

His expression was mighty earnest, but I thought it was himself he needed to worry about.

I wanted to tell him I had to do as I was bid. That any day now, when he found out the impersonation she planned, he was going to burst with furious black bile.

'Yes, Mr Pars. Sir. But if you only—'

'There is no "but if", Biddy. Do you understand? I already know what wickedness surrounds us. I see it every day.'

I bit my lip. Sometimes I thought I'd like to tell him all about it, old Pars. But he picked up his paper and waved me towards the door.

Jesmire also guessed some scheme was afoot. We lumbered on through Tuscany, though my lady was so queasy that we moved scarcely faster, as Mrs Garland would say, than a pudding would creep. At every inn, whenever our mistress was out of sight, I found Jesmire watching me like a beady-eyed lizard. One night, as I was carrying some proper English tea up to my lady she blocked me on the stairs.

'What's that? I have already given my lady her comfrey tea,' she carped. 'I suppose you mean to drink that yourself? We all see how you are always in the tea caddy.'

'That's a lie,' I said. I was sick and tired of the woman. Small things around me were always going wrong; breakfast rolls fell in the cinder pan and new lain eggs were cracked. It was something of nothing, but I had my suspicions and they were all directed at her.

'I know what you are up to,' she hissed, standing a foot above me on the stair.

She wore that toadying I-know-all smile that so provoked me.

'What's that then?'

'You are working your way into her esteem,' she said primly. 'Me and Mr Pars both watch your every move.'

'Then you will see I am innocent.'

'You?' she hooted. 'I see your low-born tricks, how you try to be her friend. There is some plot afoot, I know it.'

Though I stared at her like she was fresh from Bedlam, what could I say? In a few weeks' time they would see for a fact that I was indeed my lady's puppet, dancing to her pantomime tune.

Finally, the dread day came and we got to Montechino, a short drive from the count's estate. My lady took one look at the busy inn beside the posting house and barked through the window that Mr Pars must find us lodging outside town. The house we found was dank and cobwebbed, and the landlady a filthy beetle-browed creature. Yet we took it, for it was private and large and no other guests were likely to call. I prayed only that this whole masquerade might be finished quickly, and was glad when my mistress told me she had written to the count without delay. I watched Mr Loveday disappear with his letter, trotting on a grey mare down the winding road between fields of corn. The sun, the blossom, the springtime, all the glories of Italy – all of it reproached me now.

It was after sunset when Mr Loveday returned. He had agreed to meet me in the yard, where he whistled me over to a tumbledown shed. He thrust the letter in my hands and I fumbled it open. To my dismay that count fellow had neither fallen in a fit nor suddenly dropped dead and did indeed await my arrival.

"'My dearest Carinna,'" I read out loud, "'I am enchanted to find you are in the environs of my humble estate. My dearest girl, I have long cherished the opportunity of our meeting, for your affectionate uncle spoke often of your charms. Carinna, dear, pray do not for one moment think to retire to your uncle's villa that has been so long neglected. At any time of day or night I will joyfully welcome you to the more luxurious comforts of my own estate. I entreat you, put me at ease and lodge here with me until my servants have made the villa more comfortable for a lady of your noble rank and title. Pray call upon me at two o'clock tomorrow. I anticipate the hour with ever increasing pleasure. Your affectionate friend, Carlo.'"

It was worse than I ever could have guessed. The man was more fluent at English than any of us, and most especially me. And flowery! God's garlands, he could string a letter together that stank of roses. My guts heaved.

'I cannot do it,' I said, clasping my hand over my mouth. Then I turned to my friend. 'Shall we make a run for the port of Leghorn, Mr Loveday? I have kept back a golden guinea for bribes.'

'But where we go?' The poor lad looked terrified. 'Maybe murdermen catch me and hang my neck.'

'Don't be daft. You can go home to your island. And I could go—' I racked my brainbox and shrugged. 'Back to Paris? Or the colonies? I could cook. If we split up they might not follow us.'

He gripped my hand tight and I looked into his open face.

'Or you get key tomorrow. Then we choose right day to get away. This fellow sound like mouth never stop talking. You just nod head and take key. You better lady than her, Biddy. You better actress than Covent Garden. I whisper your ear if you do wrong thing.'


My lady sent for me at eight the next morning, mighty early for her. I'd tossed and turned all night and only slept since the birds sang their dawn chorus. She was still in her bed, her face sleep-swelled but alert.

'Hot water, Jesmire,' she commanded. 'I want to talk to Biddy.'

I dared not even look at the old maid as she skittered out in a fury.

'I have heard from the count,' said my lady, wafting the letter, quite unaware that the seal had been slit and then mended. 'You must leave a little after one o'clock. Elegantly late would be best.'

'My Lady, should I know what he says?' It did give me some small pleasure to test her honesty.

'There is nothing of consequence.' She yawned nervously and scooped Bengo up against her milk-fat breasts. 'Now you must not let him push you about. It appears my uncle has neglected to send word and have his place made ready. But if the count wants you to stay with him, for example, tell him you are too fatigued for company.'

'Fatigued.' I tested the word.

'Because you aren't staying with him, are you?'

'Not on my soul, Mistress. He can go to hell.'

'That's the spirit. Only try it with a little more civility.'

'Your Excellency, I pray I am too fatigued—' Just then Jesmire clattered in and my lady grew distracted in giving her directions.

'What's that for, My Lady?' I asked, seeing a great jug of hot water. She told me I must have my hair and person washed. Now I was not at all happy about that, for everyone knows washing lets in contagion, especially washing of the head.

'And I need my brain working sharp,' I protested. 'And I washed it three month ago, mind.'

'You need your pretty hair distracting him from your filthy mouth,' replied my lady from her bed.

But she had not yet dealt with Jesmire, who had been wittering under her breath, and stamping her little feet as she passed back and forth to fill the tub.

'Get on with it, Jesmire. Wash the girl,' commanded Lady Carinna.

'I will do no such thing. I may catch something off her.'

'Get started, Biddy. Jesmire, stay here.'

I went off and eyed the tub in the dressing room. I didn't care to risk my health by letting miasmas into my skin so I dipped a cloth and started to rub my arms. It felt chilly and unpleasant; I was sure the distempers were passing into me. In the other room I could hear my lady telling Jesmire she might walk home to England so far as she cared. I stopped washing then, so rubbing my arm was as far as I'd got when Jesmire huffed into the room.

'You. Get in that tub,' she snapped. And she pushed me in, surprisingly hard.

Now it was my turn to complain. 'I'll bloody die,' I shrieked. Honest, it was that hot I felt like a scalded pig. Then Jesmire gave my hair a right scragging, pulling it about like a hank of knotted wool and rubbing in some oil. I felt as weak as a new-born calf when I clambered out. God only knew if I'd survive. Thank my stars, there was at least a warmed shift to pull on at once.

The hair dressing was the worst of it. I'd seen my lady being tormented often enough, but now it was me with the clay curlers hissing and my hair being tugged at the roots. Honestly, if Jesmire truly wanted hiring she could try for a position as the king's Chief Torturer. Then my head was puffed and teaseled until I thought I would cry like a baby. All the time my lady directed affairs from her bed, until at last my lips were rouged and one black patch stuck at the top of my cheek, just under my eye.

Next, she sent a flabbergasted Jesmire to fetch my rose red dress from my bundle; that mopsy's face was a picture of astonishment when she returned. But before I could put it on I had to be laced into new stays: pink whaleboned satin they were, with blue rosettes at the breast.

'Breathe in,' complained Jesmire, straining to get the laces tight. My guts were slowly compressed like brawn in a press. I was as stiff as a ramrod; my waist felt as thin as a poker, my bubbies propped like two peaches right beneath my throat. Next, two hoops on a frame of linen were tied at my waist. The dress took a devil of a time to get right, for the sleeves had to be let out to fit my muscled arms.

'There was a time when my uncle had me dress in such a pretty fashion for his friends to admire me,' my mistress said in a queer voice. 'It flatters a girl, a young girl at least.'

Then returning to her usual manner, she commanded, 'Let me look at you. Lift your sleeves.'

I did as she bid.

'That looks like a fresh scar.'

It was a livid pink weal, as shiny as taffeta, right below my elbow. 'You foolish girl, I told you to keep yourself wholesome. Must I think for everyone? Jesmire, fetch my white mitts.'

I drew on the long silk things, like fine stockings only with finger holes. I felt like a pig in a poke, but supposed it would stop me waving my hands about. My lady directed some last few adornments: a pink silk ruffle at my throat, and a bag containing an ivory fan and a pot of vermillion to repaint my lips.

Finally, I was allowed to see myself in the mirror. And the truth was that I was utterly transmogrified. Something in the needle-pricked fingers of those Lyonnaise stay-makers, something in the age-old skill of the cobblers who had stitched my ribboned shoes, something in the flounce and shine and dazzle of my costume – there was in all of that a sort of magic. I didn't know myself at all. I was some other stiff and graceful woman, cushioned in silk and fashion and money. My own ma would have ducked into a ditch to make way for me.

I looked about, all in a daze. My lady was watching me, preening herself like the cat that got the cream-pot. I only noticed Jesmire had slipped away when I heard a thunderous clatter on the stairs.

Mr Pars' boots boomed louder with every step. I backed towards the window as he knocked at the door, then thrust it open.

'My Lady, a moment please—' His face was dark with fury.

Then old Pars saw me. A number of expressions travelled his countenance: firstly apology, as he made to bow, and uttered, 'Madame, forgive me,' in a contrite tone. He did not know me. Next, he grew mute and suspicious, narrowing his eyes and staring hard at my face, trying to read my features. Finally, he knew me.

He turned to my mistress, looking like he might happily throttle her in her bed. 'My Lady. Permit me – is this some jest?'

'She is going to fetch the key,' Lady Carinna said, as cold as a cucumber.

'*She* is? Why, I could—'

My mistress's voice interrupted him, very flat and steady. 'He's expecting her. Me. A woman.'

'Perhaps, My Lady, if you told him you were indisposed?'

'He'd come and search me out.'

His colour had flooded upwards from his chin – he stiffened like a bull, nearly bursting with rage. 'Not Biddy, My Lady. Surely you can't send *her*?' And he poked his finger in my direction like I was nothing but a pile of muck.

My lady shrugged. 'She will pass scrutiny, you know.'

Mr Pars meanwhile was in a fit of outrage, yet painfully bound by the need to at least appear polite to my lady.

'Listen, he's expecting me at two,' my mistress harried. 'I tell you, Biddy is an uncanny mimic. And even you—' and at that she scoffed cruelly, 'were fooled for a full minute.'

He looked at me again very sharply and walked right around me, scrutinising every fingernail and flounce. Then he came very close and fiddled with the ruffle at my throat. 'I thought there was one I could trust,' he murmured, so low that the others could not hear it.

'But Mr Pars, sir,' I started up, wanting to explain that this shammery was nowt to do with me. But he turned back smartly to my lady, bowed low in her direction, then strode off before I could say a word. The door closed and we were all knocked back into silence.

My mistress yawned and said, 'It's nearly time, Biddy. Now fetch that key, do you understand? Don't even think of playing the fool.'

'My dear, I should never wish to disappoint you,' I said in my top-rank voice. And I didn't even bob her a curtsey, just walked down the stairs ramrod straight and had Mr Loveday hand me up into the carriage.

# XXV

## Villa Montechino

*Being Lent, March 1773*
*Biddy Leigh, her journal*

## ~ Viperine wine ~

*To make a potent brew to prolong life and promote vitality drown several vipers in your wine and drink as you require.*

*A Receipt of Count Carlo Falconieri of Montechino, 1773*

Once the villa was out of view I knocked on the ceiling and told the driver to halt. In a twinkling Mr Loveday had clambered down from his footboard and come inside to sit with me.

'I must talk to someone,' I said as the carriage moved off again. 'Now I reckon Mr Pars thinks I'm plotting against him or some such tomfoolery.'

Mr Loveday nodded and said, 'Mr Pars, he no peace inside of him.'

'Aye, he were breathing down my neck something horrible.'

I glanced out of the window and saw we were going at a fair pace. There was no stopping my fate in its tracks now, for the carriage began to climb up a smooth road, and signs of a neat farmed estate opened up on both sides of us. I started to fuss over my fancy dress and ribbons; I felt I might never be able to catch my breath again while those stays squeezed the life right out of me. All too soon we swept around a driveway and I saw a most fancified building set on the crest of a hill, the windows seeming to watch me from scores of glass panes. Falling away before the villa were layers of stairways all garnished with twisting statues and gushing fountains and other gimcrackery. It was all very rich and very fashionable and very frightening.

'Oh Mr Loveday, you must help me,' I said, but the next moment we jolted to a halt and a periwigged flunkey swung back the carriage door. I managed to follow the fellow into a vast church-like hall where the sudden gloom made me giddy. Those skirt hoops were bothering me too, for I was not used to having two bloody great baskets swinging from my waist that all the time knocked into doorways and banisters. Still, I managed to get up the stairs with some trouble, and, breathing horrid shallow breaths of fear, was shown inside the count's salon. He was waiting at the far end of the room; a lively puckered old man in a gold coat and ribboned shoes, who stood to meet me with an oily smile fixed on his face.

The footman held Mr Loveday back so I was all alone. I think those steps across that vast shining floor in that swaying gown were the worst I ever took in my life. I could see the count at the other side of the gilded room, standing with his withered arms stretched out to – what? Shake my fingers? I couldn't think straight. At last I reached him and he lifted my hand to his lips. His kiss was as wet and snuffly as a piglet. I had a great desire to wipe the tingle of spit away on my skirts, but I did resist it.

'Carinna,' said he, in a voice rich with buttery charm, 'sit, sit. Dear girl, what a joy to behold you. You will take a little refreshment?' He rang a silver bell and the flunkey approached, and then left with a bow. The count may have been old, but his face was as lively as a jay's as he feasted his beady eyes all over my person.

'Your Excellency. You are too kind.' I bowed my head a little. Lord, under his fierce gaze I was suddenly as hot as a stoked oven, and reckoned I must exactly match my scarlet dress. So I reached in my bag for my fan, but was that flustered I couldn't open the tricky catch.

'May I assist you?' He started to fiddle with it, all the while hovering very close and giving my hand a clammy squeeze.

'Oh, never mind it.' I tugged it away and then remembered to be civil. 'Why thank you, sir.'

'Not sir,' he scoffed. 'While you are here I stand in place of your beloved uncle.' He jiggled the fan and it opened, so then I had to give it a bit of a flap. 'Why, I feel I almost know you, *carissima*. Only Quentin did not tell me you were such a – an adorably unsophisticated creature. Now, I know you ladies speak a language with your fans. What is that message you are conveying so passionately?'

I brought my fan to a dead stop.

'Pleasure,' I said brightly. 'At our meeting at last.' And I dropped the fan like a hot iron and folded my hands together.

A flunkey set coffee stuff down on a little table. There was a silver pot wrapped in a white cloth and a tray of paper-thin flowered china, and I thought, God help me, is this my first test, to pour a genteel dish of coffee? Then of course the servant got on with it and I just had to sit there, as stiff as London pewter and be waited on.

'Ah, the Arabian fruit,' exclaimed the count. 'Do you not adore the reviving ambrosia?' He flothered on about the coffee for a while, so I looked about me at the gold-framed panels that covered every inch of the walls and ceiling. They were painted with naked bodies mostly, big rumped doxies and hairy men. I nodded and sipped the coffee. It was so strong it nearly flayed my mouth raw. Oh, for a proper cup of tea any day.

'You find it stimulating to the nerves?' said my host, his wrinkled little face nodding. 'Ah Carinna, it gives me such pleasure to welcome you here. I have prepared the Pink apartment for your use.'

'But sir— Your Excellency—'

'Dearest girl, call me Carlo.' He pressed my hand with his fingers and left them there, quite trapping me.

'I can't be— Carlo.' I struggled to drop my voice from fishwife panic to courtly lady. 'One of my poor serving women is ill. I cannot leave her all night.'

'A servant?' He winced. 'Do not concern yourself with servants, Carinna. Get rid of her. Get another one.'

And that truly did flummox me. So there it was, straight from the horse's mouth. We mattered as little to them as a broken cup, to be thrown out on the dust heap and replaced.

Mr Loveday was right in his judgement of the count as a flowery talker, for he wanted only simpers and smiles from me. After he'd given me a right load of whiffo-whaffo about his vastly expensive villa and how astonishingly noble he was, he started to twitch the red brocade mules on the ends of his feet and said we must take a turn around his park. So then I had to take his twiggy arm, only that meant I jostled him with my hoops, which nearly made me snort with laughter. I thought it safer to walk behind him, watching his bandy stockinged legs scurrying along, and the back of his white wig bobbing this way and that as he pointed out all his treasures. Next I had to traipse up and down the terraces and into the grotto, a sort of cave, where drips hung off the ceiling like petrified tripes. Now that at least was interesting, for inside lay squares of ice big enough to dine off.

'For ices?' I asked.

'Indeed they are. They are the *specialità* of my cook, Renzo.' Then taking advantage of my being half-stuck in the narrow cave, he suddenly slid his arm about my waist. 'I have a most delicious supper in preparation for you Carinna,' he murmured in my ear, with breath as musty as a mouldy box. 'And after that, a bed of soft silks—'

'Sir,' I said, unwinding myself so I could face him, 'if you would give me the key? I must take leave of you.'

The old fellow stood his ground, his twinkling eyes undimmed.

'You cannot live in that dreary place,' he protested, pulling his face like a spoiled child. 'I will entertain you here. And I assure you,' he said in a nasty coaxing tone, 'I have retained all the necessary powers to entertain a young lady.' And the little fellow looked straight at my up-thrust bosoms.

'I think not,' said I, shaking myself free. 'The key, if you please.'

'Ah Carinna, resistance only stiffens my resolve.' He grinned like a tiresome puppy. Then he lifted his finger to trace a saucy line straight up my ruffled bodice towards my bubbies. I slapped it straight down.

'I see you will be a cruel mistress,' he said, as if he welcomed the challenge. I swung myself away and did my best to lift my great skirts back up the grotto steps. That little count, it turned out, was a right poxy rake.

*　　*　　*

Next on our tour was the count's kitchen, a vast white dungeon under the ground. The walls glittered with rows of steel knives and hooks bearing crimson corpses. I thought it the horriblest kitchen I'd ever seen, quite counter to a homely, womanly kitchen. A dozen serving men bowed to the count and then returned to their tasks with flashy gusto. Their chief was a hulking young fellow whose conceit was such that he could barely be fagged to look up from his fancy knife work. True, his knife could scarcely be followed with the eye as he sliced and chopped like a swordsman at a fair.

'The greatest wisdom of the classical age is Pliny's treatise on the properties of viper's meat,' the count said, baring stumps of brown teeth. 'Your ailing servant would do well to drink my viperine wine. It is a most beneficial cordial. Renzo, make up a bottle for Her Ladyship.'

To my surprise the cook gave a surly nod, and I wondered if he'd understood us.

The count grinned again. 'Ah, Renzo also speaks some English. I tempted him with a vast bribe from the Duke of Clathemore. It was a favour, was it not, Renzo, to rescue you from those primitive English spits and pudding cloths?'

The cook looked up with a twisted grin; the rogues were evidently used to making sport of English fare. I took an impatient circuit about the kitchen, spying a number of ingenious machines. But before I could enquire about their purpose I heard the insufferable cook scoff in a schoolboy tone, '—English. I must recollect how to burn the meat.'

The *bombastinado*! The count then called me over to inspect a great metal vat; inside were the most horrid squirming and tangling serpents making dreadful leaps to escape their prison.

'Are you not frightened of my voluptuous beasts, dear Carinna?' the count asked with a wheezy cackle.

'Frightened? No, I am disappointed,' I said smartly, 'if that is your cook's notion of good food.'

I caught that cook ruffian giving me a bold measuring glance. I thought him the most coxscombical rogue I had ever met.

'Renzo! Tonight you will not forget to serve my vipers?' said the count as we left.

'They are foremost in my mind, Your Excellency,' the cook exclaimed with sudden energy. 'You will never have tasted them dressed more exquisitely.'

And what of me, I thought? Will I also like those slithering serpents? Yet without the key, I had no choice but to attempt them.

Our supper *intimay* as the count called it, was served in a window-less chamber all tricked out with a garden of flowers fashioned from coloured wax. To my dismay, just when Mr Loveday appeared, the count again dismissed him.

'Servants are such pests. We have no need of observation,' he said. 'Tell me, do you like my latest toy?'

He pointed at his 'dumb waiter', a sort of blind window filled with a revolving shelf. I merely simpered, for I thought it an insult to all us servants who are blessed with the power of speech. When he rang a silver bell the tray withdrew on a rope to the basement and minutes later returned laden with food.

I confess I was all in a fret at the table. Sit straight, do not mump nor mince your food, act genteel, I rehearsed to myself from *The Cook's Jewel*. The settings were lavish: gold cutlery, burning incense, and ingenious metal boxes with hidden candles to keep the food warm. God's garlands, I was just about to take a sip from a dish of water by my goblet when the count rinsed his fingers in his and dried them on some linen.

Now it did not take me long to discover the theme of our bill of fare. The first course was oysters, quite raw from their shells, with my first ever glass of nose-fizzing champagne wine. My companion made lewd observations about the chilly kisses of the oysters and their ungarnished nakedness, licking the salty juice from his lips and offering to do the same to mine. The old ninny! Next was a turtle soup from a vast tureen shaped like a naked girl, then a sturgeon fish. As any noddle would quickly have deciphered, this banquet was meant to have what is called a *provocative* effect. And what rot such notions are, for I never felt more chaste.

'At last, the viper's meat,' said the count, tucking into round pink scollops of meat.

'Vipers?' I replied, chewing happily. I should have wagered a year's pay they were some bird disguised in a powerful sauce. 'They are good,' I said, helping myself to a further portion from the salver.

'After what your uncle said of you, I am surprised to find you such a – vigorous eater. Yet how intriguing is a woman's lust for food? Your husband eh, I'll wager he has not the vigour to match you?'

I gawped up from my dinner plate. Lord, I had forgot I was supposed to be a married woman.

'I dare say he has vigour enough,' I mumbled.

He raised his brows at that. 'Ha! Then why abandon him so quickly? Have you had your first taste of the flesh – but not yet been fully satisfied?'

His brandy-clear eyes fixed upon me, and mightily unnerved me.

'I am sure these are birds of some sort,' I said, hoping to distract him. He spiked a portion, stuck it in his mouth and chewed slowly.

'Damn the wretch, you may be right. Oh, to suffer a gentleman cook so full of his own greatness.' He got up and bawled 'Renzo!' down the hatch.

'Where are my vipers?' commanded the count a few minutes later, as the cook bowed before him. 'I cannot eat this womanish stuff.' Wearily, he shoved his plate aside.

The cook stiffened, and then fixed his square-jowled head very still. I knew that look, it was the one I used when Lady Carinna or Mr Pars scolded me. But the cook had at least the pluck to protest. 'Your Excellency, I strive always to experiment, to improve your dishes. With this dish I try—'

'Try what? To disobey me? Damn you man, and your experiments. I pay you a king's ransom to put vital powers in my food. What do I care for the taste?'

Signor Renzo recomposed his face from startled affront back to rigid blankness 'There are the vipers,' he said coldly, pointing at the discs of pink meat.

I stared open-mouthed at him, for the meat had no fishy tang. I had read in *The Cook's Jewel* that snakes taste like frogs, which I remembered well from France.

'Are you certain?' I asked. 'These are breasts of doves, I think. And surely the flavour in the sauce is something else entirely. It sits on the tip of my tongue. What is it?'

Signor Renzo blinked but did not change his empty expression. 'My Lady, a cook's greatest treasure is his secrets.'

I could not believe it, the arrant knave refused to tell me his receipt.

'You forget, Renzo, a cook's secrets belong to his master,' the count barked.

While these two bickered I forked up another morsel from the count's discarded plate and let it roll about the tip of my tongue. There was a fragrant flavour to the sauce that ebbed and flowed with a hint of the sea. Then I remembered my visit to the confectioner in London with Mr Loveday. What had he said? 'All my village destroyed for that stuff.' How could I forget it?

'Sir, I believe I know it.'

The cook gave me a right affronted look. The count wasn't having it, neither.

'My dear girl, you English have many virtues, but I am afraid gastronomy is not one of them.' That curious flavour all the while blossomed on my tongue as deep and strange as a flower of the ocean. I had sniffed it again at the *farmacia* in Turin. The cook looked down on me with bottled scorn.

'Is your secret ambergris?' I asked with the sweetest of smiles.

It was a pleasure to watch the coxscomb make a crestfallen little bow.

'Your Ladyship, I surrender to your palate.'

'Ha! Don't look so furious, Renzo,' goaded the count gleefully. 'Lady Carinna is too well mannered to tease you. But she has caught you out! You will live to regret this.'

It was then that I realised the consequences of my teasing the cook. For all his puffery he was a fellow servant, and I had got him into trouble.

'Such strong ambergris,' I added, 'that it quite masked what I now detect is the flavour of the vipers.'

The cook bowed to me, with a spark of complicity in his eye.

'Humph,' the count snorted. 'I wonder. My dear Carinna has an exceedingly soft heart towards her servants.'

Dismissed, the cook left us, but after furiously quizzing a footman at the door, he looked back at me with a puzzled stare.

'Signor Renzo,' I called out to him, making him jump to attention. 'Is the vipers' brew ready? I must leave soon.'

That made the fellow scowl and trot back to his kitchen. And I had a wicked thought – that I could soon get a liking for telling others to do my bidding.

Once he had left, the count grasped my hand and started up a horrid pleading. 'Carinna, you cannot leave me.' And as he did so, he slid his arms around my waist and tried to kiss me.

I backed away. 'Do you not know the saying,' I said modestly. 'Do not make me kiss, and you will not make me sin?'

His eyelids drooped so he looked like a lovelorn sheep. 'How delicious a thought. To sin again! As for your pretty little fingers—', and he took one of my grindstone hard hands and laid it on his chicken-leg thigh.

Suddenly I could not be doing with all these false airs. 'You are a right old lecher, in't you?' I said.

That twinkle lit his eyes again. 'But so easily pleased!'

I am sorry, but I could not help myself. Daft clout that I was, I laughed out loud, forgetting all my hoity accents. What a sorry old rogue that count fellow was, no different from any arse-tickler in a country tavern.

'Carinna, name your price. I will give it,' he said in an earnest wheeze.

I batted his arm away. 'Leave me be.'

'Impossible. And I do have—'

'The key,' I butted in. 'And I am now quite fag— fatigued. And I assure you, I will not stay here with you,' I said, very steady.

'Well,' he said in a penitent tone, 'perhaps it is a little soon. The truth is, a few kisses in company will suffice. My brother arrives here next week. My proud, puffed-up younger brother.'

I sighed, finally understanding something of an old man's vanity. 'Are you saying that a little public mumbling will do the trick?'

He nodded enthusiastically.

I set my weary brainbox to work and judged the affair quite innocent.

'Very well,' I told him carefully. 'I agree to dally with you in public.' He nodded gingerly. 'Only an appearance, mind! If you give me the key at once.'

He was as good as his word. And once his footman appeared with a large iron key and a bottle of viperine wine from that bumptious cook, I thought only of reaching the villa and hoped Carinna need never be any wiser of the small price I'd paid.

# XXVI

## Villa Ombrosa

*Being Lent, March 1773*
*Biddy Leigh, her journal*

## ~ Mackeroni Pie ~

*Boil your mackeroni till it be quite tender and lay it on a sieve to drain away. Then put it in a tossing pan with a gill of cream, a lump of butter rolled in flour and let it cook about five minutes. Put in a little shred of sage leaves if you like it. Pour it on a plate and lay over with parmesan cheese and toast with a fire-hot salamander till enough. Send up on a warm plate for it soon grows cold.*

*As made by Biddy Leigh in the Italian manner, 1773*

They were all sat up waiting for me when I got back to the lodging house. What could I say, but protest that the count had kept the key from me?

'Have you been drinking spirits?' Mr Pars asked, after sniffing loudly near my face.

'Well no one told me I must drink only tea,' I grumbled.

'Save your breath, Biddy,' snapped my mistress as she made for the door. 'Pars, fetch the driver. Get on with it!'

So, still in my fancy duds, I had to stuff myself back in the carriage. Then we were off, trotting down black lanes with only the carriage lamp to spy the way.

It was three in the morning when we got to the villa, and I was near passing out with weariness. The first thing we saw was an iron gateway as tall as a house that creaked like a tormented cat when it was forced apart. Before us lay a long driveway planted either side with black shrouded trees; as we passed between them their dry leaves seemed to bend and whisper like two rows of hissing gossips. Peering out of the window I nearly jumped from my skin to see a pale body crouching on the lawn. But as the carriage lamp shone over it, I saw it was only a statue, an ugly pockmarked watcher that soon sank back into the night.

From what I could see it was a grand house, its front flat and pale in the moonlight, its windows shuttered. Then we all lumbered out onto the gravel, and the lamp was unhooked. For a long while Mr Pars struggled with the key and cursed the rusty lock. Then he forced it at last and the door swung back and we all crowded inside.

From my first sight of it I did not like the place at all. Had we come all this way for this? Candles were found and slowly the villa came into view in broken parts – a chilly front parlour, a musty dining room, a hall. The kitchen was mighty disappointing. There was a fireplace and a rickety oven, but none of the new-fangled charcoal burners I'd grown used to in France. It also had a taint of vermin; and soon enough I felt the soft leather tickle of a cockroach crawling over my thin stocking. The whole stinking pit needed scrubbing and scouring before I might ever think of cooking there. Groping in the pantry I found only two pans, and both were black with rancid grease.

Then there was naught for it but to unload everything and let the driver get off to his lodgings before we all fell asleep on our feet. I still weren't happy, even when I claimed a spanking little chamber at the back just over the kitchen garden, with white-washed walls and greying lace at the window. I slept badly; waking each hour to fret at the shadows cast by heaped trunks and draped furniture. How, I asked myself in the fuddlement of half-sleep, could Carinna have chosen this unwholesome place to bear her child?

Next morning all looked brighter, but also more filthy. There was the stink too, that my cook's nose told me was dirt that had festered in the very boards. I found a clean water pump in the kitchen yard and got a fire lit, so we at least had hot tea. After serving up a few stale rolls, me and Mr Loveday got the driver to take us marketing over in Ombrosa village, which was a queer sort of place built of ancient grey stone. To get there we must take a long white road as far as an ancient chapel with a ruined tower, and then take a cobbled road up the hillside.

At the top of the hill stood a gateway so old that the carvings in the stone were near worn away by time. Beyond we entered a maze of alleys all set about with shuttered windows and ancient double doors of rotting wood. The village seemed mighty hushed and watchful to me. We were strangers of course, and there was no hope of passing unnoticed with Mr Loveday's dark face, which got many a long stare Yet when at last we found the market in a cobbled square it was better than I feared. My fancy kept returning to all those fine dishes that puff-headed cook Signor Renzo had prepared. No, I decided, I would not stand over a roasting fire in the Italian heat to make the charred roasts so famed in England. I wanted to try dainty Italian fare, and bought spicy Bologna sausage, pink papery hams, hard white bread, and chalky cheeses. I also bought the makings of a Mackeroni Pie I had seen made at an inn, and a new sort of green stuff named *brockerly* that proved a good deal tastier than cabbage. As for the wines, they looked well enough and cost but a penny a bottle.

But come dinner time, both my mistress and Mr Pars told me they wanted to dine alone. Then Jesmire said she'd dine in her room as well. I looked with frustration at the vast table in the dining room that Mr Loveday had polished like a mirror. I had fancied practising fine dinners all in the continental style, but I wondered if our company would ever eat together again.

An hour later, as I was clearing my mistress's dinner away from her chamber, Mr Loveday ran up the stairs like a lunatic.

'Lady Carinna, a coach and six come through the gate. I think it that count fellow.'

For a moment we all stood gawping at each other in fright. Then, like a right flotherhead, Jesmire walked in, and, dropping the box she was carrying, wailed triumphantly, 'I knew it, you will both be found out!'

'Shut up! I can't think,' screamed my mistress, who was sitting bolt upright in her bed. After a moment she said to Mr Loveday, 'Can you not hold him at the door?'

He looked at me sheepishly. 'What you think, Miss Biddy?'

They all looked at me. 'My Lady,' I said, 'I have a horrible feeling he will insist on seeing me.'

'You stupid girl,' she started up. 'Have you encouraged him?'

'I have not!'

'Shush,' hissed Mr Loveday, who had gone to the window. 'He just below.'

'I haven't time to dress,' I bleated. Indeed, I had my worst gown on, with an apron of sacking pinned over it. I looked at my mistress and she looked back at me – I think we both knew the answer the very same second.

Lifting the bedclothes she heaved herself out and traipsed to the door.

'Get in,' she said, pointing at the frowsty bed.

'And Jesmire?' said I.

'Come with me Jesmire, and hold your tongue. See to the door, Loveday.' Then turning to me she narrowed her eyes and said, 'Get rid of him!'

I scarcely had a moment to cast off my apron and throw a silk morning gown over my servants' duds. Then I unpinned my hair, for I'd had it all tightly wound beneath my cap, and lay down like a corpse inside the feather bed.

In a twinkling I heard a clatter on the stairs, and the count burst through the door in a flash of satins and frills.

'My dear girl. What did I say? Did I not tell you to stay with me? This place is a hovel.' Then he sat very close on the edge of the bed and grinned like a fool. 'I have a gift for you, *carissima*.'

I tried a simper and a nod. 'You are too kind.'

'Look, look. Here, at the window.' And he reached out to lead me from my bed. Starting back, I pulled my arms right down under the sheets to hide the pink weals that scarred them. Lord, could he not leave me be?

'Carlo,' I said coyly, 'the weariness of travel is still upon me. I am not yet dressed.'

'Just a quick peep at my gift, dear one.' He gripped my arm as tightly as a blood-starved leech. There was nothing for it, if I stood up he would see my drabs right under the silks. I racked my brain as to what my lady would do, then took a deep breath. It was time to throw a lady-fit.

'How dare you!' I cried in my huffiest manner. The poor fellow's head swung around like a chimney crane. 'I am still abed, sir. You have no manners! I am not fit to be seen by a gentleman.'

'But my dear Carinna—'

'You presume too far with a married lady, Carlo. Leave me a moment, for modesty's sake.' I affected a whimper and a wipe of tears. That did the trick, for with a mumbled apology and multitude of bows he backed off to the door and I was left alone. Cursing, I skipped out of bed and peered out of the window. What was this bothersome gift that was too large to bring into the house? There before the villa stood the count's carriage, a ridiculous equipage all covered in shields and gold work, and before it six costly horses. God's gallopers, I should say there were seven horses, for beside them stood a solitary white mare held fast by a stable boy.

'Oh no,' I groaned. What the devil was I to do with that animal? I could only ride after country fashion, in other words straddle a steady farm horse – and as for all your crops and pommels I had not a notion.

Just then an even greater calamity dragged my attention from that confounded horse. A right how-row had started up outside my door, and to my horror I recognised the two voices making the racket – Count Carlo and my mistress. Sick to my stomach, I burrowed back into bed and had only just lifted the blanket to my chin when the count burst in. Behind him stood poor Carinna, who looked very shock-faced in his wake.

'Is this the slut you protect?' said he, pointing at her vast belly. 'It is quite a common sickness I should say. Was it caught from a rake in London or a tapster in Paris?' he added very spitefully.

Thank my stars Carinna stood as mute as a great fat barrel while he insulted her. She was as white as a sheet, poor thing, what with the shock of it all.

'Please Carlo,' I begged. 'Biddy –' I used the name though I cringed '– is an innocent.'

'Innocent! I caught the hussy listening at your keyhole. Carinna, it is you who are innocent. Do you not know that servants are the scourge of the earth? They will beg, steal and bleed you to death if you let them. Why, look at her. Her villainy is written all across her low-bred face.'

Behind him Carinna silently implored me.

'Leave her be, Carlo.' And so he shrugged and gave a conceited little shake to his head. But she was still in our hearing when he ran to my side and clasped my hand, saying, 'Carinna. You are too good, my darling. Too good. Your heart is too tender.'

Then, over his shoulder the count shouted, 'Girl! Fetch some English tea.' She looked mutely at me from the landing, her shoulders lifted in a bewildered shrug. That girl did not know a kettle from a crimping iron.

It was Mr Loveday who appeared ten long minutes later carrying a tea tray properly laden with milk, sugar and china cups. At the sight of him the count broke off from dandling my fingers and making sugary speeches.

'Now this youth is worth ten times your other one,' he said, eyeing Mr Loveday as my friend skilfully poured the tea. 'If you ever wish to sell him I will give you a good price.'

'I couldn't part from him.'

'Carinna, you are too fond-hearted. I suppose his dark skin flatters your own complexion. It is said that lilies look best in a blackamoor's hand. I know about these things.'

'He is more to me than a decoration,' I protested, downing my tea as fast as I could so I might be rid of him.

'Yes, yes, I understand his brain is nearly as useful as a white man's.' I could see Mr Loveday rolling his eyes behind the count's back. So stretched were my nerves that I nearly laughed.

'It is time you got off. I have had enough of you now,' I said, setting my cup down.

'Ah, that accent, I love it! Is that the Hibernian brogue of your ancestors?'

'Oh aye,' I yawned. I no longer gave a toss what the nincompoop thought of me.

Before he left, he insisted I kept my appointment to appear before his brother and play the coquette the following Saturday.

'And you will wear your husband's famous ruby? Quentin boasts of it so outrageously. I must see it upon your fair throat.'

I frowned, but I had to agree, didn't I? Though it was a strange request and even I wondered how it was the old fop knew of Lady Maria's jewel.

At last I heard the carriage roll away, and groaned out loud with relief, for I felt like I'd just performed top billing on the London stage. Yet there was pity in it too, for my poor lady had been right shown up before us all. Now that she needn't show herself in public she no longer cared to have her hair dressed neatly or keep her pretty face painted. And the look she gave me as the count slavered over me had none of her old fire in it. She was mortified, I saw that. I reckon that day was the turning point of this tale. Me and my mistress had played at changing places, and somehow our false characters had fixed and could not be reversed.

Later that afternoon the sound of a knock at the door alarmed us all again. After I gave him the nod, Mr Loveday answered and found a footman sent from the count with another gift. Mr Pars called down, and hearing it was a package, came and goggled at the string of lustrous pearls I found inside a box.

'Those must be put in my strongbox for safekeeping,' he said, feeling their weight.

I fair slammed the broom I had been sweeping with down on the floor. Mr Pars wound the shining globes through his fingers that were so tobacco-yellow he might have dipped them in turmeric. Then he stuffed them quickly in his pocket.

\*　　\*　　\*

I dare say my mistress never even saw those pearls, but she happened to be down in the parlour when the next gift arrived. It was becoming rare that she even left her bed, for she was shaky on her legs, and often leaned on my arm as she looked about herself with a startled air. This time the count sent me a riding habit of the most glorious fashion, made of forest green velvet, with buttons as shiny as sovereigns and thick gold frogging. My mistress stroked it as it lay on the sofa, and I thought she looked the most regretful I ever saw her.

We were alone together downstairs, so I said in a low voice, 'Don't fret My Lady. You will soon have your figure back to wear it.'

To tell the honest truth, it was hard to believe it. In that last cumbersome month of breeding she was in a right sorry state. Her legs had puffed up like bolsters, and her features looked lost in the swelled flesh of her face. There had been a time when she would have slapped me right down for suggesting we might share the same costume. Now, while she slummocked around in a stained shift and wrapper, it was I who kept myself neat in case visitors might arrive.

'And is he expecting you to ride out with him?'

'Lord, I hope not, My Lady. Though he sent over one of them side saddle thingumabobs with the horse.'

She picked up the jaunty tricorne hat and might have tried it on, only she caught her forlorn reflection in the mirror and flung it down again.

'I am sure you can pretend my uncle overlooked the equestrian arts in my education. Besides, you clearly have him eating from your hand.' She shot me a hard glance. 'You are lucky he is such an incorrigible idiot.'

'Yes I am, My Lady.' I cleared my throat and began to fold up the different parts of the costume: the beautiful tailored coat, wide skirts, pearly camisole, and stock.

She flopped down on a chair and began to chew her ragged nails.

'I suppose this horror will end one day?' She patted her stomach and cast me a questioning look. 'When in God's name will it be over?'

'You do not know the date?'

'I cannot calculate it.' On saying this, her face blushed hot, and I dropped my eyes. I fussed over the costume awhile, but she stayed silent.

'I should rightly say weeks, My Lady. Not a month. Should I call on a doctor? Or a midwife?'

'God, no.' She flung a strip of bleeding fingernail down on my nice polished floor. 'It's a natural enough act isn't it? Indeed, I wish to know — have you ever been present?'

'At a birthing? Aye, my own mother's, many a time. It were no trouble for her, mind. She would just take a rare day in bed and it were over in a blink. But she were no lady like you, mistress. Now don't take this wrong, but I could call on a doctor, pretending it were for my — Biddy, so to speak.'

Maybe it was the wrong thing to say, to call attention to her passing herself as me. She swept her greasy hair back off her brow and said with an echo of the old firecracker Carinna, 'I just told you, didn't I? There is no need. God, when will it be over?'

She hauled herself up and slopped back to her bed.


As for Jesmire, she pursed her vinegar lips when she saw the new riding dress.

'What on earth will you do with that? Pawn it, I suppose?'

I might have pawned it once, given half the chance. Only now I decided to try it on instead. That night when they were all asleep, I got up and did my best to tie the laces and button it up. And I must say, it was a spanking fine costume, most beautifully stitched and well-fitting once I'd got inside it. As I paraded before the glass, I saw it reflected my own green eyes and also, caught in its swaggering cut, something of my character.

But it was the count's next gift that truly put the spark in the thatch. The others cared not a jot for it, for it could not be pawned or sold. But what the count sent to me that next day, changed my life for ever.

# XXVII

Whenever the others did not need him, Loveday slipped away through the courtyard and crept through itchy, spiky trees to a mud bank beside a stream. Just upstream, hidden in the trees, was the Stone Garden. It was a humming, alive sort of place. The day he first went there, he found a green grasshopper with stick-like elbows and grass-thin feelers basking on one of the tumbled stones. All around him gnats and mosquitoes danced in flittering spirals; tiny pinpricks that he had to blink away or spit from his mouth. The grass was as high as his knees, but he could see that someone had once tended the place. The scattering of stone slabs, some upright and others fallen, reminded him of the bloodstained sacred rocks at his village. When the sun shone hard on the stones the power and thrum of it made it feel like a holy place, too.

Then, rummaging in the overgrowth, he found a stone hut. All that was left of the pointed roof was a criss-cross of struts and a few drunken tiles. Great waves of smothering greenery had grown over it, hanging inside in leafy bell cords. In a cobweb-matted corner he found a blind-eyed stone Mary, her pink cheeks flaking like a grim disease. It took a few days to make a neat shelter, to weave twigs across the roof holes, and sweep out the spiders and mouse droppings. Finally, with his lair clean and calm around him, Loveday began to prepare for the right day of leaving, when the mystical pattern of stars, winds and currents, intersected in time.

It was to this secret place that Loveday took the letters he was given, before delivering them to the post house. Jesmire was the first. As soon as she had turned her back, he had slipped off to the coolness of his shaded hut.

*'Dear Captain William Dodsley, Retd,'* he read in puzzlement.

*It is with inestimable pleasure I write in reply to your inquiry for a reliable housekeeper made of the landlady of the Albergo Duomo, Pisa. I must declare myself a sober Protestant spinster of Suffolk, England, and a most diligent and, if I might say so in my own regard, a most genteel lady in search of a position in life. My talents lie in the needle, in knotting and a little light laundry. Also hairdressing (of ladies' hair, but I might attempt a peruke) and other personal duties, as you may require. I can assure you I am ready to take up a position at the earliest opportunity. Please address your reply most speedily to,*
    *Your humble servant,*
    *Signorina Amelia Jesmire, The Post House, Ombrosa*

Loveday laughed out loud and wondered if the fellow would bother to reply. How many times had she written to obtain a position since they left England – seven, maybe eight? She had received only one answer, and that was to say that the lady she had addressed had long since departed.

Once he had returned from the post house, he had the rest of the long day to fill. His first instinct was to make an object of power; something that followed the potent designs of his ancestors. While clearing the floor he had found mouldy Jesus books and other useless stuff. Then, like a miracle, he found a wooden shaft polished dark by time. At its tip was a thin cross made of some metal that had turned grey and crusty. He recognised the shape of it from his days with Bapa Cornelius, the cross that was the favourite sign of the Catholics. But when Loveday ran his fingers over it he saw another shape. He spent many hours hammering, grinding and shaping it, until it curled into a crescent-shaped barb. When it was completed, he lifted the harpoon and felt pleasure at its weighty balance on his arm. When he threw it at a twisted tree trunk it left his palm faster than his eye could follow. It was a good harpoon; the hidden power he had worked into its being was fierce and true.

The day after Loveday finished his harpoon, Mr Pars had summoned him to take a letter. The old man's chamber had its shutters closed and smelled of stale tobacco smoke and sweaty linen. The narrow yellow look in the steward's eye as he pushed the letter across his table unsettled Loveday. He picked the letter up, trying not to touch the bad man's skin.

'Has there been any post for me?' Mr Pars shouted suddenly.

'No, sir, no post,' he said, backing away and darting quickly out of the door. Glad to be out of the steward's presence, he called in at his mistress, then slowly took the path back to the Stone Garden to read the letter in peace. He was just singing quietly under his breath as he followed the leafy path, when Mr Pars suddenly appeared right before him. The steward was standing at the edge of the Stone Garden, leaning on his stick.

'So this is where you are hiding, is it?' he bawled. 'What are you doing here when I told you to make speed to the post house?'

Loveday fixed his eyes on the ground, making sure he didn't betray his secret hideaway by glancing towards the hut hidden in the trees.

'Miss Biddy,' he said slowly, knowing she would back his lie, 'told me look fruit.' He pointed towards a clump of early lemon trees.

'Let me understand this rightly. I tell you to go to the post house. And you –' and here he jabbed the end of his stout stick towards Loveday's chest '– run about for that trull of a cook maid. I suppose she's got you sniffing after her skirts as well, you black dog. Explain yourself!'

Loveday stumbled over his reply. Then to his horror, Mr Pars grasped his sleeve, wrenched him closer and tried to give him the evil eye.

'I not know why,' Loveday gabbled, raising his palm to shield his own face from the old man's malevolence.

'You don't know why? Is that what you are trying to say, you ape? Can you not speak the King's English?'

'Yes sir, I does,' Loveday said, breaking away. Just as he backed out of reach, Mr Pars swiped out to hit him with his long wooden stick. Loveday was too agile for the blow to do any more than glance against his leg, but as he scampered away it left him shaking. The steward was certainly possessed by evil *nitu*-spirits. Even Biddy agreed that poor spirits afflicted Mr Pars, so there was no doubt about it. Loveday had heard them pace Mr Pars' chamber at night; they were blood-hungry spirits that would not let him sleep.

Once he had hurried down the white road to Ombrosa and crept into the back room of a tavern he stared at the letter, not sure whether he wanted to know Mr Pars' inner thinkings. The writing on the outside was scrawled and untidy; quite unlike the steward's usual script. Yet I must get news, Loveday told himself. So, bravely slicing through the wax, he pulled the letter open.

*Ozias,*

*Brother – if you still deserve that blood-given name – why do you not write? I ask you expressly for news and yet you withhold it. God help me man, can you not understand I am at the edge of desperation? Picture for yourself, if you have not sufficient imagination: that I am near to one thousand miles from England and quite unable to comprehend my affairs at home and want only a few words to free myself of incessant anxieties. Does Strutt still question you? Has any enquiry come from Ireland? Does Sir Geoffrey still live? For understand this: I am here in Italy in body, brother, but so troubled in my mind I scarce know where I am.*

*As for Italy, let it only be said that the heat, the stinks, the damned hubbub of it all would unsettle the soundest of natures. As for the company in this house – I have fallen in with traitors all. I alone see their duplicity. Why brother, I tremble to write of it but I know that together they plot to cheat me of all my master's money. Every day I expect some high-handed brute of a lover to join the thieving whore – and how will I keep the purse strings secure from him? How long will it be till she gathers Sir Geoffrey's fortune and is off? What then of my stewardship? What then of Sir Geoffrey's trust? Where then goes the money?*

*I had once believed that the others would stand with me against her, but even Jesmire writes secretly I know not where, for often she scratches with her quill and furtively sends letters off to the post. That heathen blackamoor is of course no more than a foul beast, no more human than a trained dog. Yet it is fair Biddy Leigh who truly hurts me. She pretends to my face to be still that simple girl of Mawton, but I have discovered she is in league with her mistress and plays a wicked game. The Jezebel has taught her to say 'Your Excellency' and practise each day before the glass and dream of greatness beyond her birth. Then she is sent out like a bawd to dupe a wealthy fop from whom they extract all manner of gowns and baubles. Extortion, Plots and Intrigues brother, that is the web that surrounds me.*

*I am fatigued now, and must lay down.*

*Pray for me brother – and write!*

*Humphrey*

Loveday threw down the letter. Mr Pars was beset by most dangerous spirits, there was no doubt of it. Back home there were ways of dealing with such matters – Mr Pars could have had the *nitu*-spirits cast out by a Spirit Man. It would have been a serious matter treated with brotherly care. A moment of sadness squeezed his heart to think of the old fellow stranded here with no help and no comfort from his family.

Then Loveday re-read Mr Pars' harsh words about himself. A foul beast. As the cruel words burned in his eyes his pity waned. Mr

Pars was an evil-thinker who spoke ill of Biddy and had tried to give him the evil eye. So, swearing to keep the steward's words secret from Biddy, he walked up to the post house and handed the letter over.

Biddy. As he walked through the golden afternoon back to the villa he knew he would soon have to leave her. He was going to feel pain, he knew it, for his liking for her had caught him like a sharp hook in his heart. Alone of everyone he had met in this strange kingdom, she had carried within her a spark of Lamahonan warmth. He would miss the way her face creased suddenly with laughter, her friendly digs in his arm with her elbow, the funny faces she pulled as she told him of her daft thinkings by the kitchen fire.

When he thought of Bulan these days, she was little more than a sun-bleached memory. No longer did he wallow in dreams in which his little family's faces were just as he had left them, a tender-eyed young mother and her helpless infant. As he worked on his harpoon he had dared to picture them as slaves of the Damong, or maybe, like him, tossed by life's tide to another unknown place. Or perhaps – he could finally think it with his potent harpoon nestled in his lap – his wife and child had gone to live with Bapa Fela in the sky. Perhaps. He did not know. Yet still he battled to keep the flame of hope alive. If any of his people had escaped from the Damong they would return to the deserted village. And once a few of them gathered, they might silently sail under night's disguise to Damong island in a raiding party. There was still a chance, whether Bulan and Barut lived or not, to return with courage and live once more with pride as a hunter of Lamahona.

When he returned to the Stone Garden that evening, the late sun bathed his body as he cradled the harpoon to his breast. 'My brother,' he said shyly, caressing its razor-sharp edge with a gentle fingertip. The harpoon was alive with all the power of its making, and urged him to test it. Clambering down into the ice-melted stream his toes gripped the weed-draped rocks like hands. Raising the harpoon, Loveday shook off all his weight of troubles. The old wound from the white man's gun had slowly been healed by sunshine and rest, his courage had conquered the snow-covered mountain: soon he would be riding the waves again on his way back home. The right day of leaving was getting closer, he could feel its spell getting stronger.

He saw a flash of brown in the fast water. He took aim and the blade shot true at the first throw. The trout, pierced through its gaping middle, instantly gave its life up to him. After offering a sprinkle of the fish's blood to the gods, Loveday gutted it and roasted it on a hot stone just outside the hut. The flesh was coral pink and as sweet as honey to his lips, and the two round eyes, as they popped deliciously between his teeth, promised far sight and fair omens for his journey.

# XXVIII

## *Villa Ombrosa*

*Being Fig Sunday, Lent, 1773*
*Biddy Leigh, her journal*

## ~ Fig Pie ~

To make a crisp pastry take one pound of fine flour with one ounce of sifted loaf sugar. Mix with a gill of boiling cream and three ounces of butter; work it well, then roll it thin. Put your figs in a pan with just enough water and stew until tender, mix in sweet spice as you like, a few currants and treacle. When you have made your pie rub over with a feather dipped in white of egg and sift your sugar over. Bake in a moderate oven for a quick oven will catch and burn.

*As made by Biddy Leigh to remember Fig Sunday, Lent, 1773*

I started to sicken for home, for that villa was no home to anyone. The kitchen never satisfied me, and even the fire was parlous. I wasted hours tempting it with morsels of kindling – while the others idled upstairs I would be down on my knees feeding it mossy twigs, getting smoke in my hair and soot on my face. My kitchen courtyard was large enough, but a bare, sweltering place, a favourite of flies and midges. As for the rest of the estate, it was a wilderness. The only good things to eat were some lemons ripening down by a ruined old graveyard. The whole place had been empty so long that it had a melancholy mildewed air, however much I scrubbed it.

So I got to thinking that it was Fig Sunday, the time folk at home went visiting their mothers. The pie I was making would have pleased even my crotchety old ma, for the figs from the market were the fragrantest globes, laced with liquorice-bursting aniseeds. I was up and away with the larks that day, scattering flour and crimping pastry, when Mr Loveday stuck his head in the door and told me there was a horseman coming up the drive.

'Lord, it's not that wretched count again, is it?' My claggy fingers went straight to my head to yank off the grubby kerchief covering my hair. Glancing down I decided my blue wincey gown would have to do. It was tatty and travel worn, but clean enough once I'd unpinned my sacking apron.

'No. It some big fellow riding alone.'

I told him to run up and tell our mistress to beware, and that I would see the visitor in the front parlour. It was a damned nuisance, for I'd just put the first of my pies in to bake, and was in no mood to talk hoity with a stranger.

But before I could make my way to the parlour a loud knock at the kitchen door made me jump out of my skin. Then bless me, none other than Signor Renzo, the count's bullish cook, strode right inside my kitchen like he owned it. When he saw me standing at the table, he stopped in his tracks and started in surprise.

'My Lady Carinna.' He made a stiff bow, and when he lifted his head he stared at me and all around the kitchen, bewildered. 'I am sorry I surprise you, My Lady. I came to the servants' door. I think to cook— I— His Excellency offers my services while your cook is ill. I am at your service.'

He was too smartly dressed for that I reckoned, for he was all buffed up in a blue frock coat and white linen. He bowed again very low and then straightened, waiting for my reply, his dark brows gathered in bafflement. He had an odd judging sort of manner; tilting his heavy head backwards a little to look at me through low-lidded eyes.

Honest to God my brainbox ground to a halt. I stared from his questioning face to the pastry cuttings on the table and back again.

'Tell your master I have no need of your services, signore.'

He tried another small bow. 'I will do so. If you would permit me a question. It is an English lady's habit to – bake?' He waved his hand at the evidence on the table. He spoke mighty good English in a rumbling bass tone, but there was an edge of impudence to the question.

I was right flustered and started to jabber any old nonsense. 'Yes, signore. The English love to bake. Have you not heard of their eccentric way? Only the best of ladies, mind you, entertain themselves so.'

He lifted his head and sniffed with his broad nose. 'I fear you burn your pastry, My Lady. I will rescue it.'

And before I could get to the oven he was there, slipping a cloth over his hands and sliding my first Fig Pie out. It had caught the fire a little around the crimped crust, but it smelled like a hot breeze from Jamaica.

'I find it not usual,' he said, placing my humble pie on the table as delicately as if it were the crown jewels, 'especially you are English?' Then he looked up fast to meet my eye. 'Why, you bake quite well. This could be sold in a village market for a few coins, certainly.'

A few coins? There he went again, the blaggart. I had forgotten what an over-puffed pumpkin he was.

'At a common market perhaps, but I could never be such a grand cook such as you, could I, signore? Did you not say the English always burn their food?'

He had at least the manners to look ashamed at that.

'Perhaps you do not understand? Such talent should – should flourish. It is just so – strange for an English to show such gifts. You must agree they have no notion of eating well. Indeed, I should be honoured if you give me the receipt.'

The sauce-box! I had not forgotten how close he was with his own receipts. I recollected his very words. 'But *signore*,' I mocked, 'a lady's best treasure is her secrets.'

This time he did redden quite powerfully, right from the black curls at his brow to where his thick neck disappeared in crisp white linen.

'My Lady.' He dropped his head and looked quite caught out. Then I did feel a shred of pity for the fellow, so apparent was it that he visited only at the count's command.

'It is only a simple plate pie that we eat at Lent with our mothers,' I said. 'But the crust I am pleased with.' I broke an inch off and put the scorching morsel in my mouth. The singeing had left it as short and crisp as a biscuit. I nodded to him and he took a little too.

'That is good. The heated sugar it is like – toffee? Is that the word? May I show you an Italian method?'

I nodded. Flinging his blue coat over a chair he began to work the pastry with fingers very graceful for a man of his size. Now what he did was this: taking a square of pastry, he slit it very fast in serried rows so that it opened to twice its size in a lacy lattice. He wrapped that around the figs so that they looked for all the world like fruit wrapped in a diamond window pane of pastry.

'Caged figs.' He smiled, and gave them an egg-wash with my feather before sliding them into the oven.

'You have a true talent,' I reluctantly admitted.

'I imagine how such things can be contrived. At home I have the little machine to cut. It is a – do you say roller, a turning barrel? With teeth to cut the openings all in line?'

'How clever,' I marvelled. 'I also often think of all the contrivances that would make cooking so much easier.'

'Tell me.'

I put my hands on my hips and began to tell only the start of my great list of notions. 'Well, look at stirring, Signor Renzo. Men use water and wind to turn great millstones, yet cooks must use feeble human arms to beat cakes hour after hour. And potters in England bake pots in furnaces at a particular heat, yet our own kitchen ovens blow hot or cold according to the dampness of our faggots.'

Signor Renzo was leaning back again, watching me keenly with those sleepy eyes. Yet they were not so sleepy at all. He was like a black stocky hound, very quiet but all the time on guard.

'And do you know why that is? It is because men do not care about what happens in their own kitchens, that is why.'

'But I care, Lady Carinna.'

Turning towards the oven, he sniffed and said, 'My caged fruits are cooked.'

The syrupy scent had increased, but he certainly had a most excellent sense of smell. It was indeed the perfect moment to rescue the figs.

'They look very good,' I said. Now that was not entirely true, for they looked like marvels – two syrupy oozing figs miraculously trapped in lace-like spheres of pastry.

I tasted them. It is a strange thing, but though the same goods were used to make both our receipts, his tasted rather better.

'Desserts are my true love,' he said warmly as he cut his fig into delicate portions.

'And mine,' I said. We got to chattering about the wonders of sugar and pastry work and how any shape or subject might be made from such stuff. Signor Renzo talked with such animation that it grew ever harder to disguise my interest in all he said.

'Yet the count does not care for desserts?' I asked.

'No.' At mention of the count his expression lost its liveliness.

'And will these caged fruits be on your bill of fare on Saturday?' He looked away and would not meet my eye.

'The bill of fare must be my master's choice,' he mumbled. Then I had the notion I must cheer this fellow up, so on a whim, I asked him to teach me the trick with the pastry.

'It would be an honour.' He came to stand beside me at the table and showed me how to score the rolled pastry. My own attempts were poor stuff beside his. I laughed as I lifted my piece that looked like a beggar's torn rag.

'Control,' said he. With a gentle touch to my wrist, he lifted my hand. 'Picture what you want. Be free.' I coloured then, as his work-roughened fingertips guided my awkward jabs. Though we touched hand to hand and stood very close it was innocent enough, that little lesson. And I scolded myself for noticing him, for he wasn't a handsome man at all, and it was not my place to get carried away with any fond notions. Indeed, he was a broad fellow with great square shoulders, and those lazy dark eyes always masked in shadow.

Before he left, he neatly wiped the table and pulled on his fine blue coat. Then he waited and looked uneasily about himself as I wished him good day. Finally, he told me what was bothering him.

'Lady Carinna, I must thank you,' he said soberly, 'for not exposing my deception. You knew I had not put vipers in that dish.'

'It took no gourmet to detect that. But why did you disobey him?'

'Because I cannot use such disgusting stuff,' he said, with an expression of such distaste that I laughed out loud in sympathy. Then seeing me laugh, he smiled too, as if we both conspired together.

'But My Lady, why did you not tell the count?'

Now I longed to tell him that we servants must protect each other, but I could not. I was all brain-knotted, so the silence seemed to grow to a full minute as Signor Renzo's low-lidded stare fixed upon me. Then the most unexpected words fizzed up from my brain, like bubbles rising from ale.

'Because I like your cooking.' That did not seem to satisfy him either, only intrigue him more, for he stared hard at the floor and rubbed the bristles on his chin. Finally, taking his leave with a bow, he said with great solemnity, 'Lady Carinna, I am honoured that you notice me. And I like your cooking also. Good day.'

I had meant to bake some more goods that day, for the oven was bright and hot, but Signor Renzo's visit set me in a jangle. I did not enjoy lying to a fellow cook at all. I felt him amiable enough towards me, but that was no doubt because he thought me rich and a rank far above him. No wonder he stared at me like an object of curiosity. The truth was, I was sick to my bones of pretending to be Lady Carinna. It grieved me that Signor Renzo might never know me, plain Biddy Leigh, at all.

Once Saturday arrived, Jesmire again dressed and laced me, taking every chance to tug my hair and stab me with pins. Then I was led to my mistress's room to show the results.

'Ah, the gold brocade with violet spangles,' my mistress said between yawns. I lifted my rustling skirts and tried to mask the thrill of wearing such a Paris picture of a gown. We are all Adam's children, goes the saying, but silk makes the difference, and so it did to me. In the looking glass I looked the very Queen of Fashion, my waist pinched tight and my skirts trailing in frills and flounces. My mistress had never even worn it; it had been hanging all the time on the wooden-faced dressing stand that stood in the centre of her chamber.

'It must be very entertaining to be forever junketing about,' she said. Junketing? Who did she reckon scrubbed the floors and cooked the meals and washed the linen she lay on? I reminded her that the count, begging her pardon, was a groping ninny and I would spend the greater part of the evening slapping him off my person. That at least raised a smile to her cracked lips.

Gathering courage, I told her the count had asked that I wear the Mawton Rose.

'The Rose? How the devil does he know of it? I suppose my uncle must boast of it.' She frowned, but could think of no objection. 'Very well. It is in my flowered box. There's not much left now Pars has taken most of my jewels for safekeeping.'

I shook my head at that. 'Can that be right, My Lady? They are yours.'

'Surely you can't suspect pettifogging Pars of getting a taste for jewels?'

'He has grown mighty strange, that is all,' I said. I found the box. There was little in it save the ruby.

'When was he not strange?' she scoffed as I lifted the jewel on its chain for her to see. At the sight of its flashing fire she looked away. With a heavy heart I clasped it around my neck where it hung as heavy as a Newgate fetter.

'Yes but My Lady, he made to beat Mr Loveday with his stick yesterday for no reason.'

'Perhaps Loveday deserves a beating,' she said. 'He often creeps off when he should be at my door.' When she spoke next I understood she had other worries.

'I believe you have been most obliging to the count. It is time you asked him a favour in return.'

Here we go, I thought. 'Like what, My Lady?'

'He knows of your having a servant in – a scrape. Well, Biddy, the truth is I need someone to take in the child till I can return for it. Someone kindly and discreet. You do understand I can't take it home? So if you were to talk of your fond feelings for – Biddy – you could ask his advice.'

She looked wretched as she waited for my answer. The damp strands sticking to her brow left me wondering when Jesmire had last bothered dressing her hair. The truth was, I would have done anything for her.

'I'll do it, My Lady.'

'The closer my time comes,' she confided, 'the harder I think it will be to leave the baby behind. Sometimes I dream of staying here, to watch the child grow. Then I wonder if a fast departure would be better. I'm in such torment.'

When she beseeched me like that I didn't know what to say.

'And then I feel too sick to face my difficulties.'

I had to get on my way, though it was hard to leave her so sad, staring into the air, chewing her red-bitten nails.

What with my lady's request and Mr Pars' odd ways, and all my other hundred chores to see to, when Mr Loveday thrust a letter in my hand, it seemed only another trouble heaped on my addled head. I ripped it open in the hall and read it in an ill temper.

> *Devereaux Court,*
> *London*
> *14th March 1773*

> *Biddy Dear,*
>
> *How goes it in Italy? I think of you all quite often and am idly tempted whenever the English wind blows to take a boat and follow you to the sun. Now Biddy, you did promise truly you would tell me of my sister, so where is your letter? I wish only for trifling information. Is she well? Who does she see? When does she return? I believe she is in a pet with me, my foolish Sis, and deliberately brief in her correspondence.*
>
> *And as for you, my pretty sweetheart, are you happy? God knows I am not. My uncle plagues me with his plans. Take pity, sweet girl, and give me news.*
>
> *Your friend,*
> *Kitt*

I barely read it before I flung it in the fire. Then believing I had one less matter to fret over, I let Mr Loveday hand me up into the carriage.

To ignore the letter was the action of a damned fool, I know that now. If only I had answered him, if I had sent him an honest account of affairs at Villa Ombrosa, might not so much have turned out better?

# XXIX

## Villa Montechino

*Being Lent, March 1773*
*Biddy Leigh, her journal*

## ~ To Make Flesh of Marzipan ~

Take blanched almonds, beat them in a mortar with a little rose water, make them into stiff paste, then beat in the yolks of twelve eggs leaving five of the whites. Put to it a pint of cream, sweeten it with sugar, put in half a pound of sweet butter melted, set it on a slow fire and keep it stirring till it is stiff enough to mould into whatever figure you desire.

For the natural effect of skin, coat with a layer of isinglass jelly which imparts a yielding softness to the touch. To tint, take a fine brush dipped in cochineal and saffron. Then dust with starch to counterfeit the bloom of a youthful complexion.

*The best way as made by Signor Renzo Cellini and eaten by Biddy Leigh, Villa Montechino, Tuscany, 1773*

The count's brother, Francesco, took one look at me and scowled like a bitten bear.

'He convinced himself you were a figment of my fancy,' Carlo whispered, as I ducked my head to let him kiss me with his mouldy lips. When I offered the brother my hand he pretended not to see it, and shouldered me aside – I think he would as soon have spit on it as kissed it. As for me, I didn't care a jot about the count's flaunting me before his brother. I merely thanked the stars that he believed I was Lady Carinna.

'And you are wearing the jewel,' said Carlo with a grotesque lift of his newly blacked eyebrows. He had painted his face and looked for all the world like a small monkey masquerading as a fresh daubed whore. He caressed the ruby that hung around my neck, then trailed his withered fingers across my breasts.

'So your husband truly is a rich man. Surely there must be tidings of widowhood soon?' I wondered if Carlo had told his brother I was to be a wealthy heiress.

'No, I am still the happy bride,' I parried.

'That is not what Quentin writes.'

I ignored him. He did talk such hogwash. I was seated between them at a table in an oval room that was draped from ceiling to floor with purple silks. I felt like a prize pig at a fair, with the two brothers both eyeing me, the one as if he worshipped me and the other as if he would do me any violence.

At least there was the food. Since Signor Renzo's visit I'd consoled myself that whatever trials the evening might bring, the eating would be good. He was so puffed up with his own talent that I was sure he would try to impress me. One good morsel, a thousand vexations, they say, and didn't he and I both know it? What did the count and his wandering fingers or his cankered brother know of all the sweat and dramas downstairs?

'My darling, you are the inspiration for this feast,' the count said loudly, as footmen silently lined up at the door, laden with dishes. 'Every morsel is in honour of you, my dear Carinna.'

At a signal from the count the servants snuffed out half the candles. Without the golden glow of the candelabra a theatrical gloom descended.

Signor Renzo did not disappoint me. The first course was a marvel, for when the flambeaux were re-lit a great spectacle of the sea stood before us, made of glittering coloured sands beside an ocean of green jelly. Standing on the sand and sporting in the waves were shrimp and lobster, all perfectly dressed, while at the table corners lay turtle soup, a terrapin in its shell, and a vast Tiber sturgeon. I smiled to myself as I ate, savouring every well-judged mouthful. Privately, I congratulated the talented Signor Renzo.

'Ah, how apt,' crowed the count as the first course was removed and the next arrangement was laid. 'My Temple of Venus.'

At the centre stood a vast painted temple peopled with figures in the robes of the ancients. Oh, it was prettier than any stone palace, for every column and ornament was made of dazzling white sugar. Our candles were again snuffed and the tiny flambeaux set in the miniature marbled walls were lit. The greatest conceit was that the dishes set about the table were an ox heart larded and stuffed, a side dish of lambs' hearts devilled, even the vegetables were artichoke hearts in melted butter.

'They are all hearts,' I laughed.

'To stand in place of my enchanted organ,' said Carlo, his wizened mouth stretching coquettishly. I heard his brother snort and slam down his glass.

Leaning towards me, Carlo crowed. 'He said Quentin's niece would despise me.'

'Indeed.' I speared a little heart-shaped tart filled with souffléd sweetbreads. He was right there, then. My snappish mistress would never have played along like this. The memory of my mistress suddenly pricked me, and I gritted my teeth to beg the favour she had asked.

'Carlo,' I said sweetly. 'I must ask your advice.'

'I am utterly at your service.' Being small as he was, he sat with his eyes quite level with my bosoms. He never even looked up to my face, the old dribbler.

'My foolish servant.' I swallowed hard. 'Biddy.' I cringed to say the name and took a rapid glug of wine. 'It is a puzzle to me what to do with the – trouble she will produce.'

Carlo's watery eyes drew themselves reluctantly upwards from my bubbies.

'Trouble?'

'The baby. I need to find someone to keep it. Good people. Biddy will return for it later.'

With a grimace of distaste the count drew out his snuff box and set a little hillock on the edge of his hand.

'I believe the usual course is to consult the Convent of Sant' Agnese. The sisters foster out such productions of sin.'

'How will she find the place?'

His reply was interrupted by a gigantic sneeze, so large that a spattering of orange-coloured spittle rained down on me.

'It is above Ombrosa. The mountain path leads to its gates.' With a gigantic handkerchief he wiped the rubbery end of his powdered nose. 'A few small coins should see the business done. But truly, my dear,' and here he clasped my hand, quite unaware I was trying to wipe orange stains from my gown, 'you must forget her. Send the slattern packing.'

'Look, here is dessert,' I said, mighty pleased to be interrupted.

Again many candles were snuffed as a flat board covered in dark cloth was carried in by four men. I mused pleasantly over its theme: we had admired the sea, and tasted the hearts of love – so what would Signor Renzo treat us to next? I confess I preened a little to think that the cook was straining his wits to impress me.

'You will adore this,' said Carlo, pulling me up to stand and so better view the unveiling. What did I expect? A pleasure park of cakes, or a paradise of sugar clouds?

The cloth was removed. I stared. A life-sized figure of a woman lay stretched before us on the table. Sleeping? No, her eyes were fixed open, as if she was dead. Then I blinked and saw as clear as day that the woman was like a waxwork, her skin supple, her hair loose. The marvel was that she was modelled all from sweetmeats: her gown finely worked from sugar paste, and her hair some sort of jellified tresses burnished with copper. Yet her face – mask-like and stiff – was remarkably flesh-like, enlivened by crimson lips and strange, half-living eyes quite glassy, green and staring. Dark lashes fringed the eyes; even the lace on her sugar gown was made from a thousand filigreed threads. I had a sudden recollection of that day when I had stood in the mirror at Mawton beside Lady Carinna. Here was that same woman – tall and chestnut-haired. It was me.

Murmuring in my ear, Carlo said, 'Do you like it?'

Then reaching out to the figure's half curled hand he snapped off a finger and sucked it between his flabby carmined lips.

I sat very still, my wine-soaked brain unpicking the puzzle. I vividly remembered Signor Renzo's penetrating glances on his visit to my kitchen. It came to me very slowly, how he had arrived unannounced and kept me talking and all the time watched me like a hawk. What I had thought was friendliness was merely loitering to fix my image in his mind.

Beside me the count saucily lifted the sugar bodice to reveal two pink-tipped breasts. With a deft tweak, he broke off one cherry-like nipple.

'Pray excuse me,' I mumbled, and hurried out of the room. My thoughts were boiling like frizzling milk; I rushed headlong away from that dining room as fast as I could, my throat tight and burning. God's gripes, I had entirely misunderstood the cook's friendliness. You fresh-air witted lump, I reproached myself. Why, he must have thought me a right soft creature to gawp and giggle for him while he impressed my features on his memory, all in return for a few base compliments. With my head sunk low I hurried past the count's footmen, in search of Mr Loveday so we might leave on the instant.

The count could go hang. My mistress too, who had sent me here, to this den of perfumed goats. It was Mr Pars' fatherly words that chimed guiltily in my ears, that I should mind my reputation and not be flattered by my mistress. Perhaps I should have listened to my old Mawton steward, as good Mrs Garland had advised. Instead, here I was playing the harlot – and for what? I had no words for the mortification I felt as I rushed about that maze of corridors.

I set off down a gilded staircase that I fancied led to the visiting servants' quarters, but my head was all stir-about, and some minutes later a dead end startled me from my temper. Now I had got myself lost and vexedly strode up and down, looking for the way back to the villa's entrance. It was then I noticed a stairway to the kitchen. I stood at the head of it and heard muffled bangs and cries from far below. After checking that no one saw me, I gathered my vast skirts and crept silently down the stairs. At the bottom a bare corridor stretched to the white kitchen from which all the hubbub came. I listened keenly and heard Signor Renzo's voice complaining, though what he said I could not rightly tell.

Some whim of curiosity made me look about the place. First, I peeped into a room that was stocked like a dry larder. Next was a scullery recently used, piled with dirty pots. Still the kitchen clatter continued, so I tried a third door. One glance proved it was what I sought, so I stepped inside and pulled the door fast behind me.

The silence was sudden and heavy with sugar dust. I was inside a small confectioner's workshop, a most curious place where the air tasted sweet as nectar. Before me stood half a dozen tables, each with a line of cord stretched above it. Flowers, jewels, and tiny creatures hung unpainted on those strings, dangling like snowy carvings as they dried. Beneath them, sugar-fangled shapes lay moulded on eggshells, and beside them the sugarmaker's tools, fairy-size blades, and forklets of brass and ivory.

At the far end of the room I found what I was seeking. Drawings of my own face hung high on a wall – my portrait modelled curiously in lines and dots both front ways and sideways. Below them, on the table, was a pair of my own hands pressed from a wooden mould in yellowish marzipan. Here was a tress of my hair made of liquorice strands, a sketch of my mouth, and a dish of waxed cotton eyelashes. A mix of wonder and disgust held me, for it was very queer to see myself so artfully dismembered. I stood and stared a long time, unable to pull myself away.

Then with a *click* I heard the door open and the bulky height of Signor Renzo blocked the way. He looked mighty surprised to find me there.

'So this is how you use me.' I jabbed my finger at the sketch of my face. 'You steal my face while pretending to help me. You should act on the stage, for you have an astonishing talent to deceive.'

He faltered and made a bow.

'I am sorry I offend you. The count told me—'

I rolled my eyes heavenwards. 'The count? The count is a nincompoop. We both know that. It is not the count, it is your play-acting that offends me.'

He swallowed and lifted his big hands helplessly. 'My Lady. I hope you might like it.' He shook his head in bewilderment. 'A compliment to your beauty.'

'Well I don't like it.' I pointed at what looked like a model for a rigid pink nipple. 'It is shameful, sir. To –' I tried to express what offended me so much '– to display me like a dish.'

Lord knows it was also a great compliment. But the nub of it was I'd mistaken his measuring stares for a manly liking of what he saw, and had got myself in a tearing great huff. 'No doubt you pretended to care for my inferior baking, too?' I said pettishly.

'No, no. I did not pretend. It is not usual to meet a woman who—'

'Yes? Who what?'

He rubbed his brow then raked his fingers through his black curls. 'Who thinks like me.'

His words silenced me. So it was true, that inkling I'd had these last few days. We did think the same. It was uncanny. A hot blush began to bloom from my bosom and neck to my face. Vexed, I stepped sideways, pretending a new fascination with the pictures.

'My Lady, you do not like it, even a little?' he asked, with a hint of insolent teasing.

'No.' But I said it without any force. What would Lady Carinna have thought of all this? Most likely she would have enjoyed the flattery. So I did my best to dampen my disappointment down.

'Very well. I like it a little. But I hate it more.' I was talking nonsense.

'It is never my wish to offend you.'

'Do not mind it.' I shook my head in irritation. 'You did all that work.'

He looked up then, his sleepy-lidded eyes flashing. 'If I could make amends? What could I do, My Lady?'

I made a move to leave. As I passed him he laid his heavy hand on my sleeve. I glanced down at it; above the fine hands I noticed curling black hairs on his arms. And then, so close as we stood, the smell of animal blood and male sweat reached me, unnerving me.

'I know you have a fine palate, Lady Carinna. If you wish to taste something remarkable—'

'To taste what?'

'Oh, it is not suitable. My words run too fast.'

'I will not be offended. Tell me.'

My eyes searched his face: exploring the shadows and bristles of his broad cheeks. Oh, he was a burly, ill-favoured fellow, but something rattled me whenever I saw him. His eyes, as dark as treacle, returned my stare. For a giddy moment our gazes locked, like groping hands in a pitchy well. Then I turned away and began to fuss at my gown.

'It is now time to hunt the first black summer truffles,' he said very fast. 'For many cooks it fulfils a lifetime's desire. It could not – make all good again, but if you wished—' Again his speech ebbed away and he stood very still in his servant's pose.

'You want to take me truffle hunting?' I laughed out loud, for I was very tight-wound.

'It is a wonder of nature,' he said in a tempting, eager tone.

I stared at him in disbelief. Lord, the fellow was as crazed about food as me. 'And the count will not know?'

He shook his head and said, 'No.' Then he looked at me with such fervour that I asked myself the question, What would I, Biddy Leigh, like to do?

'Very well,' I said cautiously. 'You may take me.'

# XXX

## La Foresta

*Being Lady Day, March 1773*
*Biddy Leigh, her journal*

## ~ *An Unrivalled Chocolate Ice Cream* ~

*Take a pint of good cream, a heaped spoonful of best chocolate scraped, put it in when the cream boils and stir them well together, add the yolks of two eggs and sweeten it to your taste, let the eggs have a boil to thicken it. When cold put it in your freezing pot of pewter and plunge into a wooden pail.*
*Pack about entirely with pounded ice and salt. When the mixture begins to firm about the sides stir it about with the spaddle so that all may be equally thick and smooth and frozen.*

*As made for Biddy Leigh, by Signor*
*Renzo Cellini, Easter 1773*

I was fretting by the window when I saw a cloud of dust moving up the road. I hurried to the glass and fussed with the tricorne pinned to my hair, and tightened the cream linen stock at my neck. Jesmire was loitering at the door, her skinny arms crossed as she eyed the flowing green of my riding costume.

'So he's not even sending his carriage these days? Seen through you, has he?'

'No, he has not,' I said, pinching my lips to give them colour. I whirled about, enjoying the lively freedom of my riding skirt. 'It's a bother, but I must make a show on that horse he gave me. Now you will behave yourself in front of the count's man, won't you?'

Her mouth dropped open, showing long yellow teeth.

'Just who do you think you are, to speak to me like—'

I had no time for this. Signor Renzo was dismounting at the front door.

'If you won't be civil, Jesmire, get out of sight,' I hissed. 'Go on, go!'

With my heart drumming fit to burst my gold-buttoned coat, I sat myself down as serenely as I could on a parlour chair while Mr Loveday answered the door.

When Signor Renzo lifted his hat and made a bow, I saw he was slick from the heat and mighty uncomfortable. And to see him so awkward and hunched in our parlour, all stuffed in a brown velvet coat and breeches – just to see him made me feel mighty awkward too.

'Signor Renzo,' I said, sounding breathless. 'Shall I call for tea?' I had baked some pretty cakes to show him my light touch, but now he was here before me I could not bear to think of us clinking plates inside that echoing room. 'Or shall we go? Yes, we should go now.' I stood and nearly tripped over my long skirt, so that he jumped toward me and caught my arm. I snatched it away, fearing Jesmire might barge in and catch us in what she would call a shameful embrace. We were both of us jittering like seeds in a tossing pan.

Outside, a bronze-coloured hound strained at a tether by the door, then rose on his hind legs to greet his master. 'This is Ugo,' Signor Renzo said, scratching the dog's ears. 'The best of hunting dogs.' It was good to have the dog nosing forward to greet me, for it gave us something other than ourselves to look at. When Mr Loveday led my white horse around from the stable my stomach quailed.

'You truly want go, my friend?' Mr Loveday whispered. He was eyeing Signor Renzo with suspicion.

'Yes,' I said firmly, and my old friend stepped back.

'I am more accustomed to a carriage than horseback,' I explained to Signor Renzo. When he looked alarmed, I protested I would do my best. The cook stroked the white mare's nose and held her very still. Then, with steady strength, he lifted me up on my side saddle and gave me instructions: to always sit at the centre of the horse's back, and to press my whip gently against her right flank to replace the leg she expected to feel upon her. Mounting his own beast, he caught up my reins and slowly walked the horses side by side with Ugo scampering before us. I did take one backward glance at the house, seeing Mr Loveday had disappeared inside. Only one window showed a figure; my lady hung back behind the lace of her chamber. Then we were away, side by side between the rows of lime trees that bowed and rustled above us.

Once we'd passed through the iron gates I grew easier. The horse walked steadily along the flat road, and in time I plucked up courage to look about. We passed between dappled hedges, beyond which rose a gentle swell of fields marked out in green and yellow patchwork. In the distance stood clumps of trees around the rust-coloured roofs of farms and barns. Far away at the horizon was a distant smudge of green-blue hills. Everything about us was very still, save for a multitude of white butterflies darting amongst the bushes, and specks of birds wheeling high in the warm blue sky.

'Is it far?'

Signor Renzo turned and said serenely. 'Not so far.' We trotted on, arriving at the ruined tower of the chapel and taking the road to the left. Soon after, the land began to rise, and we approached a great wood of oak and poplar trees. At the wood's edge we left our horses to graze, and went onwards on foot. Soon we entered a glorious glade where sunlight fell in lattices of gold and green. Ugo ran ahead of us, hind legs kicking up leaves and dirt, his nose questing on the ground. Sauntering side by side, Signor Renzo and I followed in contented silence. As we walked together I felt oddly small, for my head reached only his chin. He was a great bear of a man, striding beside me, all dressed up in a white shirt and velvet coat.

Soon the dog gave a sharp bark, calling his master to admire his find. Poking through the moss was a clump of brain-like morel mushrooms, very pale and smelling of sweet nuts.

'*Bene*. Good,' said the cook, dropping the mushrooms gently in his bag. 'But we will do better.' I looked about myself, at the mass of leaves and flowers that spread around us like a garden. As the breeze rocked the branches, a rain of speckles, dots, and flickers of light danced over my emerald costume. An idea came to me like a thunderclap: that I was too much indoors with no other view than the inside of pots and pans. All about us were birds serenading in the trees, occasionally darting earthwards to peck and flutter. The air smelled of sap, and deep, rich earth. Though it was only Lady Day, the first day of Spring, here the season was so far advanced it was like midsummer in England.

'What a beautiful place.'

He smiled shyly, with that half-mocking smile I was starting to know and like.

'I come here when I can. Collect food, listen to the music of birds. Be a man of Nature. You have read Monsieur Rousseau?'

'A little.' My mistress had a copy of *Julie*, which I had rifled through. 'He says we must live off berries and nuts. Not good for a cook,' I chided. We smiled at each other.

'Monsieur Rousseau says it is time for modern man to break with all the old ways. In every art – so why not cookery? He says that life educates us to truly live. It is a journey, an exploration. And I think – everything can change. These are exciting days. All the old rules can change because we can change.'

I thought of his words as we followed Ugo through the flickering green of the woodland. Frantically, the dog sniffed and yelped at the ground until Signor Renzo caught up.

'A beauty,' he said, and pulled out a root that looked like a lumpy potato. 'Look, the colour is good. And the smell.' He held the truffle below his nostrils, then offered it to me. 'You like it? Smell it. Like garlic and mushroom and honey. Yes? You will allow me to cook it for you?'

'Here?'

'You will see.'

As we strolled on I thought of his notion that everything was changing. Was it not also my own life he described? Since I had impersonated Carinna, I had been forced to stretch my wits to snapping point. I had been addressed with words I would once have scarcely understood, but now I strove to answer back as smartly as any high-born woman. And these gowns that at first had seemed such a hawping nuisance, did they not also make me a very fine figure? A lady who garnered respect and attention? The food, the sights, the luxury – even this walk in the woods with Signor Renzo was changing me, like the barm that turns dough into risen bread. How could I ever go back to being plain pan-tosser Biddy after this? Life was educating me, too.

'So which will you be? A man of nature or a cook?'

Rising from the earth with a fleshy amber mushroom in his

hand, he slipped a slice in his mouth and made a little murmur at the flavour.

'I am greedy, Lady Carinna. I want both. I want all I can have.' His expression was no longer humorous. He lifted a slice to my mouth and I obediently opened my lips. It was meaty and almost sweet. But it was his feeding me, his fingers brushing my lips that unsettled me. I could scarcely swallow, and had to break away and stride ahead.

You must be strong, Biddy, I scolded myself, for dangerous notions had wormed their way inside my daydreams, every day and night of that long week. And now as I walked beside the man and felt his regard, I could no longer fool myself that the danger was all in my fancies. Jem was a dandelion clock in the wind, and Kitt Tyrone a mere pretty youth. Beside them, Signor Renzo had all the attractions of a deep-thinking man with marvellous gifts. Play your part, I urged myself, for Lady Carinna would never in a thousand years have got a hankering for this fellow. But I, Biddy Leigh, could scarce take my eyes from him. As we walked on I longed to tell him, 'That is my wish, too.'

'It is time to cook,' he said when we reached a further path up the hillside, and fizzing with expectation I followed him through the trees.

Signor Renzo's lodge stood on a grassy knoll near the crest of the hill. It was a modest place, just a low stone hut, before which stretched a woven ceiling of vines. My dinner was cooked on an open fire by the table. This was no banquet, but what the cook called a *pique-nique*, a meal for hunters to take outdoors. After Renzo had chosen two fat ducklings from his larder, he spitted them over the fire. Then he made a dish of buttery rice crowned with speckled discs of truffle that tasted powerfully of God's own earth.

'Come and sit with me,' I begged, for I did not like him to wait on me. So together we sat beneath the vines as I savoured each morsel and guessed at the subtle flavourings. 'Wild garlic?' I asked, and he lifted his brows in surprise as he ate. 'And a herb,' I added, 'sage?'

'For a woman, you have excellent taste.'

For a woman, indeed! I made a play of stabbing him with my knife. It was most pleasant to eat our *pique-nique* and drink the red wine, which they make so strong in that region that they call it black or *nero*. I asked him to speak of himself, and between a trial of little dishes of wild leaves, chestnut fritters, and raisin cake, Signor Renzo told me he was born in the city and had worked at a pastry cook's shop as a boy, where he soon discovered that good foods mixed with ingenious hands made people happy and free with their purses. I told him of *The Cook's Jewel*, the constant companion on my travels. 'It is the quintessence – that is a French word I learned in Paris – of what you say. All those receipts collected for maybe one hundred years, so carefully written down. It is my greatest treasure.' We talked of new receipt books, and he praised Monsieur Gilliers' *French Confectioner*, which was like a bible to him. 'It explains so many of the mysteries of sugar. Thanks to that, I have learned to cast figures as clear as crystal.' Then suddenly he rose and reached out his hand to me. 'Enough of talk. Come with me.'

He led me along, while all the time his hand locked neatly against mine, till we reached a fast-running stream that cascaded all the way down the hillside. Pulling on a rope, Signor Renzo lifted a pewter basin that at first baffled me. Only when he produced two glass bowls did I understand that the metal casket was a *sorbetière*. Inside was a chocolate ice as rich in colour as mahogany. I tasted it, rolling it around in my mouth. The coldness numbed my tongue and then the flavour burst out, rich and satisfying, as if the thickest pot of well-milled chocolate were made of snow.

There followed many hours of delightful conversation that seemed to pass mighty quickly, for when I next glanced up, the wood was deep in shadow and the sky glowed soft purple. Beneath the table

Ugo slept, his twitching muzzle lodged across his master's boots. I shivered and felt the hush of twilight upon us. A bird sang his lonely song as a breeze riffled the vines above our heads. Signor Renzo was but a shadow at my side. We both fell silent and my mind began to racket about uncertainly. He was a food-crazed cook like me, but he was also a man, and a very strong and vigorous man at that. As the silence lengthened a new certainty grew inside me, very solid and shining and strange. Our two characters did fit together as perfectly as any face and its reflection. Next, I could not stop myself turning slowly towards him. I lifted my chin and sought the gleam of his eyes. He would never have touched me unbidden, so I reached out to him. I sought his lips and we kissed, very long and very hungrily. When his arms reached hesitantly around me I felt a homecoming warmth and slid against his wide chest. Both of us were loath to stop once we had begun. His hands cupped my head, caressed my shoulders, and stroked my throat. And I grew near senseless with longing, exciting those kisses with murmurs and caresses of my own. Many delightful minutes passed till I felt his thigh upon mine and his weight pressing at my centre. Then my conscience struck and I came to my senses. I told him we must stop. I believe we were both quite startled at how the day had turned.

'I must go,' I said with a catch in my breath. There was my mistress to see to, but how could I tell him that? He nodded and went in search of a lantern. Standing alone outside his lodge I wondered if I had ruined my impersonation, for surely Lady Carinna would never have kissed the count's cook? I pulled on my crumpled green coat against the chill. It was impossible to know if I had done some great wrong or whether instead, I had taken the best step of my life.

Then he returned and slipped his arm around my shoulders, and all was well again. We retraced our path to our horses by the light of his lantern. The forest had changed to a darkly mysterious place, alive with the cracking of twigs and cries of invisible creatures.

'What are those lights?' I asked, peering into the darkest shrubs where little fires floated and winked. For a moment he left me and clapped his fingers around a spark of fire. When he returned, a greenish glow flickered inside his hands.

'See. A firefly.'

I peered between his fingers and saw a little fly with its belly made of winking light. I never saw anything more beautiful.

'Can you keep it?'

He laughed. 'Only a short time. As a boy I catch them in a jar and read at night from their light. But keep them too long and they die.' When he released it, it was again a tongue of flame lighting up the night.

'Even a common fly is magical here,' I said. We walked on until the line of the white road stretched ahead of us back to the villa. At the sight of it my courage faltered as I remembered the old life that awaited me. I wanted to stay in Renzo's arms for ever, under cover of the forest and the firefly-spangled night.

Suddenly Renzo blocked my way. 'Carinna, I must see you again.' He placed his hands on my shoulders and lowered his face, looking full square into my eyes. 'I must see you tomorrow,' he whispered. The lantern gleamed liquid gold in his eyes.

I had no restraint left. 'Yes, tomorrow,' I said. And we kissed each other farewell beside our restless horses. All the way back down the road to the Villa Ombrosa I railed hard against the truth. That any day now Carinna would bear her child. And that any day now, I would be cast back to my old life, as put upon, pan-tossing Biddy Leigh for the rest of my loveless days.

# XXXI

## Villa Ombrosa

*Being this day, Good Friday, April 1773*
*Biddy Leigh, her journal*

## ~ Ducklings in truffle sauce ~

Kill and draw your ducklings and tie up with leaves of sage
tucked about the bodies. Spit them and dust with flour and set
them with thick slices of bread between. Baste with the pan
drippings using a feather. Your sauce is made of onion, garlic,
oil and a little ham and celery shredded fine. Add the duck
gizzards and pinions, cook till enough and add a spoonful of
flour and two fingers of sweet marsala wine. When thickened
add slices of truffle and send to your table with the ducklings.

*A very fine dish cooked for Biddy Leigh, by*
*Signor Renzo Cellini, Easter 1773*

I saw Renzo every night for two giddy weeks after we first met in the forest. I lived for the sight of him; love ran like poppy juice through my veins. Once the others were settled for the night, I slipped out and made my way to meet him, sheltering in the hedges that lined the moonlit road. Then at last the ruined tower would shine before me, looking like a ghost's lair, its ancient stones rising pale against the black tangle of undergrowth. There I waited by the broken walls, my heart like a caged bird, my skin dusted by moths' wings. I hearkened at the sounds of the night, until the hooves of his horse sent lizards and frogs scurrying through the dry grass. Then he would dismount from his horse, and a blissful moment later we clung to each other, lost to time and place. Only when the bell of Ombrosa church tolled one o'clock did we part with reluctant whispers of farewell.

Next morning I would face another endless day of half-life at the villa, of chores and drudgery, as I pictured a life of bliss with Renzo. I scarce heard what others said to me; my daydreams had the greater power. All day I listened for the sound of the messenger boy's quiet knock at the kitchen door, for Renzo had found a ragged child to run with notes between us. When we met I deliberately shared few words with Renzo, save for murmured endearments. Then one night he pulled back from my kisses and spoke.

'I have to tell you, I am leaving the count's household. I have quarrelled with my master for the last time, Carinna,' he said hoarsely. 'He has said something I will never forgive.'

'What has he said?'

He shook his head miserably. 'He wants you, Carinna.'

It seemed a ridiculous jealousy. 'Pay no attention to the ninny. But where will you go?'

'I will find work, another position.'

I gripped his hands tight. 'Where?'

We were seated on a low wall of stone, beneath a sheltering tree. I saw the gleam of his eye as he glanced away down the road. It was the first time I ever saw him impatient.

'How can I say? Anywhere I can work,' he said tightly. 'My own city, perhaps.'

'Anywhere,' I said in a heavy voice. Then he turned back to me and slid his arms around me. 'Yet I have an idea. It may be foolish—'

'Tell me.'

'To be with you I would do anything. May I not be your cook, Carinna?'

It was good that it was dark, for he could not see dismay slacken my face. The silence grew long. I scrambled for a reason, any reason, to say no.

'My cook maid, Biddy,' I said in a stumbling voice. 'She is ailing. It would not be fair.'

'She is only with child,' he said in a cold voice. 'So, after the birth? What then?'

'Maybe she will cook again. I am sorry.'

'She must be a very good cook to impress you.'

'No, she has helped me. In the past.' His arms stiffened. 'I only want to be with you,' I hissed.

'Then tell me how, Carinna. For I am trying to prove that I will do anything to be with you.'

'I wish to stay here,' I said, brimming with sincere truth.

'Then stay here at the villa. Or does your husband want you back?'

'My husband?' I felt myself under attack. 'I care nothing for my husband.'

'Yet you are mighty loyal to him.' He said this bitterly, because I would not grant him the freedom of my person. I wanted to groan aloud, that he thought me a loyal wife, and not a desperate maiden.

Soon afterwards I headed for the road, protesting I must hurry back to Biddy. Biddy indeed! And what a notion – for him to be my cook. Impossible of course, but even so, it rattled me. For the thousandth time I asked myself if he would care for me at all if he knew I was neither noble nor wealthy. He was modest enough when he spoke of his own reputation, but I knew he held high office in his Guild. He read books, owned a house, and directed dozens of men in the count's kitchen. How could he love a common kitchen servant like Biddy Leigh? Yet what did it matter? Carinna would have her child soon and we would all pack up and go home to England.

On Good Friday I sat outside the villa's kitchen door plucking a brace of ducklings, for to drown myself in hard labour was the only way I knew to ease my churning thoughts. Yet even sitting in the morning sun making a long list of chores – scrub the floors, pick lemons, make a jelly, whip a syllabub, clean my mistress's chamber, roast the ducklings, sand the pans – even all of that could not stop my misery from bubbling up like a pot of bitter aloes.

Holding the drake above my wooden pail I started the butchery that always turned my stomach. First I peeled the skin off the carcass like thick pliant silk. Then I twisted off the bird's head with a hard crack. Finally, I slung the ruby carcass in the pail, attracting a circle of buzzing flies.

What was I to do? What if I were forced to leave and never see Renzo again? A little whimper of pain escaped my lips as I pictured being alone on this earth without him. Could I bear to live?

I reached for the hen that hung from the fence by her stretched neck. The drake had been a shimmering peacock of a creature, but his little mate was drab brown. Foolishly, I stroked her brow and marvelled at its velvet smoothness. Then I tugged at the hen's neck till it came away in my hand, a torn gobbet with hanging strings like red wool. I stifled a sob. Why was love always denied me? I had thought I loved Jem once, and had him taken from me. And now I had found a worthy man, a true love whose every notion ran just like mine. A man, besides, whose art in cookery was the greatest I had seen. I could not bear to leave him.

Slitting open the dead hen, I unfurled her zigzag of guts. Then I searched for her heart, digging inside the tiny cave of her chest. There it was, naught but a lump of dead flesh. With claggy fingers I lifted the bullet-torn heart and felt my face crumple with tears. Such was my own heart. I loved Renzo so much that the pain of losing him would break me for ever. I wanted to wail my misery to the heavens, but feared being overheard. Then I damned my being a servant, condemned to eternal obedience. I wanted to punch someone hard, to break my fist on a solid wall. Instead, I rinsed my hands and marched off in a temper to pick some lemons.

At first I took Mr Loveday's path, for I knew he went to the stream and sometimes caught a trout or two. I fought my way through a tangle of bushes, cursing the briars that snarled my cap and gown. After hurrying past the grim little graveyard I smelt the refreshing scent of lemons and picked a fat crop. Perhaps it was the sight of that bountiful fruit, but I wondered if I had been too hard on old Pars and I even thought of searching for a receipt for lemon pickle in *The Cook's Jewel*. I recollected all the scoldings he had given me, and reminded myself that while he was a grousing skinflint, he maybe did have my own good at heart. I hoisted a knobbly jumble of lemons in my apron and decided it was time to make my peace with my old Mawton steward.

Before I set the ducklings to roast I knocked gently at his chamber and called his name. I thought I heard his voice, but when I opened the door I startled him at his desk. The shutters were closed and the room had a dark and festering air.

'What do you want?' The secret way he set the crook of his elbow around his scribblings made me wish I had left him alone after all. I had thought to make idle chat with him, but grew tongue-tied instead. So I made a bob and said, 'When Mr Loveday goes to town shortly, could he fetch you aught, sir?'

'Me? Let me think now.' He leaned back and stretched his elbows. I noticed the state of his clothes, that his Paris duds were all grubby and stained.

Then the hawked look returned to his eyes. ''Tis not money you're after, is it?' he added in a cratchety growl.

'It is not, sir.' A few coins would not have gone amiss, but I would not let him think I had come begging. 'Maybe a joint of beef for Easter? What do you say?'

At that he nodded and rubbed his grey bristles with his hand. 'Beef and proper English pudding. None of those mackeroni slops.'

'As you wish, sir. Anything else?'

He knocked his pipe against the desk and it pained me to see the ash scatter on the floor. 'Some twist tobacco. And an ounce of colts-foot if they have it in this infernal place. And the usual comfrey for your mistress.'

'Yes sir. While I'm here shall I give your room a tidy?'

He started and held up his hand to prevent me. I could see he'd been writing much, for his fingers had turned quite blue from the smearing of ink. There were scattered piles of paper on his desk, but I could make out nothing but rows of numbers.

There was no use to it; I took my leave and called it a peace-making, and went directly to my chamber to wash my hands clean.

I was sitting back in the garden peeling onions when Mr Loveday came back from town with my purchases. He had a letter in his hand and my spirits leaped for a moment.

'Is it for me?'

He shook his head and squatted down beside me, lifting his face to feel the warmth of the sun. Lord, it was sweltering hot by noon; the weather baked the earth like an oven.

'Jesmire not know yet, she got news. You want read it?'

I nodded, grateful for the entertainment, and we budged up close on the bench. It was a reply to one of the string of letters she was always sending off to find herself a new place.

*Captain William Dodsley, Retd,*
*Casa Il Porto*
*Leghorn*
*8th April 1773*

*My dear Miss Jesmire,*

*It was with the greatest surprise and pleasure I received your charming inquiry forwarded to me at the kind behest of the landlady of the Albergo Duomo, Pisa. My dear lady, you may scarce comprehend how timely was the arrival of your modestly expressed greetings. To explain, I am a sober, steady Gentleman who has passed the principle part of his time at sea, a Gentleman of good reputation and large profit who finds himself in a most commodious billet in the finest quarter of Leghorn town with eight bed chambers, kitchen, cellar & etc. It is now two years I have lodged here, and though the town's company is tolerable, I confess to you that rattling alone in such a large establishment leaves an old fellow somewhat in the doldrums. What I am in need of, as you so astutely observed, is a Lady of propriety, order and good sense to manage my household, and get my establishment running in a proper English style. It most especially would satisfy me if that person were a genteel English lady, a woman such as yourself, of age and experience, who would know best how matters may be accomplished. I have no taste whatsoever for these young flibbertigibbet maids—*

I turned to Mr Loveday and gawped. 'I never would have believed it.'

'Jesmire got place sound like paradise for her. Order 'bout other servants all day.'

'Maybe. But will she take it? What else does he say?' I snatched the paper from his fingers.

*—whose manners suit me not at all.*

*Pray Madam, do take the liberty of taking possession of Casa Il Porto at your soonest convenience, sending word ahead of your*

*proposed arrival. I trust I may welcome you to your new home with*
*the good speed so heartily longed for by both yourself and,*
> *Your soon to be friend and obliged servant,*
> *William Dodsley, Captain (Retired)*

'But surely she will not go,' I said. 'She will fancy herself too refined
to keep house for an unmarried gentleman.'

Mr Loveday shook his head. 'I think she want be grand lady
more than anything. And tell Lady Carinna go to devil.'

'But she cannot go before the baby comes, surely?'

'You think she care one whit for Lady Carinna baby? No, sir.
After all that shouting?'

Mr Loveday was right, of course. He had scarce delivered the letter
into Jesmire's hand before she started flapping about, packing and
unpacking her box and insisting that Mr Loveday's livery be cleaned
and patched if he were to walk behind her. She even came down to
the kitchen to boast of her good fortune, dressed like mutton as
lamb in her green silk gown. She could not stand still, she wandered
up and down, picking up pots and preening herself.

'So when are you off?'

'Tonight. I will call on Captain Dodsley at eleven in the morning.' She sniffed the cheese and pulled a disgusted face.

'You seem mighty sure you will be suited to this Captain Dodderer.'

'His name is Dodsley and well you know it. And one thing I will
tell you now before I leave—' I glanced up from scouring my pans.
'I know you think I am just some fetch-me carry-me, but I was a
person of stature once, and I will be again.'

I rolled my eyes. 'So might we all.'

'I know your schemes, jade. Do you think I don't know that you
creep about at night? Do you think I don't hear your – ridiculous
attempts to sound genteel? Just because you have men dancing at
your apron strings—' Her voice wobbled and finally choked to
nothing.

'It is not that,' I said firmly. 'You have always disliked me.'

She gave a mocking cough of a laugh. 'Dislike? I loathe you, you low creature. Just as much as I loathe her,' she said, nodding in the direction of the stairs.

'Enough to leave her just before her confinement?' I couldn't help it, my voice rose in anger. I near scraped the iron raw in that pan, I was that grieved with her.

'Oh yes. Certainly that much. I glory in this day. A prisoner with reprieve never felt such joy.'

'But you will be back tomorrow night for supper? Mr Pars wants a proper roast for Easter. And I need Mr Loveday back.'

'We shall see what Captain Dodsley's wishes are. I suppose Loveday may return when it is convenient. Captain Dodsley no doubt has a fine set of footmen of his own.'

I huffed a moment over my pans, then looked up at the old toady.

'Well, go and be happy then,' I said, with less sharpness than I intended. 'I am fagged out from all these squabbles. If this is your great chance of happiness, go and take it.'

Her jaw dropped slack for a long surprised moment. Then she lifted her skirts and marched away, leaving only a waft of her sickly Cologne waters in her wake.

Just before they left, Mr Loveday came running with a letter. Jesmire had re-laced his coat with gold, and given his old wig a new dose of powder.

'Message boy just bring this, Biddy. Waiting you answer. I go now.'

I clasped it to my bodice for I knew Renzo's hand right off.

'Mr Loveday.' He hesitated at the door. 'You will come back tomorrow, won't you?' I spoke in a low voice so no one else might hear.

He looked like a cat with his tail caught in a larder door. I knew it was a terrible temptation for him to get away and never come back.

'Please.' I touched his arm and the old shine returned to his eyes. 'Just until Her Ladyship's back on her feet.' I could tell he was thinking about it very hard. 'Please, for the sake of our friendship. I cannot manage alone. Then I'll help you on your way.' He licked his lips and grinned, the old half-worried, half-happy grin.

'I come back tomorrow, Biddy. For you. Last time, perhaps. Then go.'

'Thank you. Come at six and I'll get everything ready.'

He paused again, then nodded. 'I go now.'

'God speed,' was all I said, and patted his shoulder. Then, with a clatter and creaking of harness, they were both off into the dusk down the white road to Leghorn and the sea.

Once the silence returned I opened the letter and took in Renzo's words like the very air that kept me alive.

*My Darling,*

*My master has gone to the Easter festival in Rome after ordering me to be gone when he returns. Nothing keeps me here save you. Carissima, I must speak with you. I beg you, please meet me tonight at ten. I love you darling, I love you more than words can say. In your heart you know we were made to share our lives. Somehow we will conquer our difficulties and live as we should – in each other's arms, sharing one heart,*

*R*

I scribbled a message back to say I would see him, and hurried out to the ragged boy who waited at the gate. The urchin smiled up at me in the dusk as I handed him a coin and told him to make all speed.

The villa was mighty quiet once Jesmire and Mr Loveday had left. Slipping Renzo's precious letter in my pocket I got supper ready, lighting a lamp to see by, for the sky had turned dark for such an early hour. I escaped my worries for a while by doing my best to cook the duckling just as Renzo had, striving to possess his art if I could have nothing else of him.

At half after seven o'clock a loud knock came at the door. Another messenger stood outside; I confess I was terrified that Renzo had changed his mind. This letter, however, was addressed to Mr Pars and had come all the way from Mawton. I studied it hard, but I did not know the hand at all. When I took the duckling along with fresh peas up to Mr Pars, I brought the letter with me. But when I knocked he shouted impatiently for me to leave it at the door. I sighed and set the tray and letter down.

Then I took a dish of lemon syllabub, well sugared, to my lady. She was lying awake, weeping into her pillow.

I banged about a bit, then went to her and stroked her shoulder.

'What troubles you, My Lady?'

She rolled a tear-stained face towards me.

'I miss him,' she croaked. 'And I cannot send for him.'

I didn't know what to say to that. Then the temptation was too great and I whispered, 'Who?'

She shook her head and sniffed. No doubt it was that fortune-hunter Napier, I cursed.

'He cannot be worth it,' I said gently. She gave a sort of wild-eyed laugh at that, and raised herself up in her bed.

'So Jesmire has gone,' she said, scrubbing her tears away with the backs of her hands.

'Yes, you must put up with me till tomorrow night.' I sat down beside her and she made a go of the syllabub. I flattered myself that the food put her in a better mood.

'Having you as a maid will be no trial. I doubt you will stick pins quite so spitefully into my scalp.'

'I'll do my best not to, My Lady.'

'Do you think Jesmire will stay with this fellow?'

There was no point in sweetening the truth. 'I think she will. I've no doubt you'll find a new maid when we reach Turin or some such place.'

'And Loveday?'

'He'll come back tomorrow, My Lady. He gave me his word.'

Afterwards, not wanting to leave her, I fiddled about awhile. A battered wooden box that had once held blankets stood beside her bed. I lined it with a blanket and cloths; it was a shabby sort of cradle, but was all I could muster.

'It will be over soon,' was all I could think to say.

'Thank the stars for that. I'll pay this foster family any sum they want. Do you think they would write to me, about the baby's health? I'll pay more for that.'

I nodded. She truly was quite alone. I remembered her brother's letter and my folly in destroying it. I should have written to him, however mithered I was. The very next day, while the house was so quiet, I determined to write him a letter and tell him his sister would soon be home. I crossed to the window and pulled the shutters tight, for a wind was starting to rattle them.

'There's a break in the weather coming. At least this heat may drop.'

'Good. Oh for a spell of English rain. Come here, Biddy,' she said. I crossed to her and she held out her hand. There was a stirred-up, yearning look to her. 'You will stay with me, won't you?' I took her hand and it was hot and damp to the touch. 'I'm so frightened of the birthing.'

'I promise I will, mistress. How do you feel? Any pains yet?'

'No,' she sighed. 'All the same as ever.'

I could feel Renzo's letter stiff in my pocket. For the first time I realised just what a pretty pickle Jesmire had left me in. I would be tied to my lady every second of the day, from the moment of her first birth pangs. Renzo would never understand why I could not leave her.

She was starting to yawn again, so I fancied it a good time to ask her a favour.

'My Lady, if you settle to sleep, I should like to go out for a while at ten o'clock.'

She half opened her eyes. 'Where are you going?'

I could have made up any nonsense about the count, but the time for pretences was over. 'I have a friend. Another servant. I won't be long.'

'I suppose Mr Pars will be here if need be.'

I remembered the ill-tempered shout from behind his door, and wondered if I should tell Renzo to wait until morning. Then I reminded myself that our precious time was running out; that my chance to talk freely to him would soon disappear entirely. When I returned to collect her dirty pots she was fast asleep, her head tucked down beneath the sheet.

It was easy to lift a gown from the wooden stand. I had my pick of all the rainbow gowns hung about the room or folded in boxes. The dress I chose was the one I loved best, pale gold with spangled violets and gold lace trim. I cast my mistress's indigo cloak upon it, fearful of being seen. I waited as late as I might before leaving, then took a last peep at my mistress. She was still fast asleep and breathing steady.

She was safe when I left her. I swear it on my life.

# XXXII

## *Villa Ombrosa*

*Being this day Good Friday to Easter Saturday, April 1773*
*Biddy Leigh, her journal*

## ~ Comfrey Tea ~

*Boil one oz of comfrey leaves to one quart of water and take in wineglassful doses frequently. It is of sovereign virtue as a remedy for any internal or external troubles; for bleedings, ulcers, phlegm, lung troubles, quinsy and hooping coughs.*

*A Remedy given me by Nanny Figgis, nurse to Harriet, Countess of Tilsworth, Lady Maria Grice, 1744*

S oon after we met at the tower, Renzo pulled back from my kisses and caught my face in his hands.

'I must speak tonight,' he said. 'I have little time.'

There was no way of escaping it; his manner was very forceful and grave. Yet when he started to speak, he did not give me the lover's rebuke I expected.

'Roberto, the valet, has heard my master repeat wicked things about you, Carinna. That your husband will soon be dead. Is that true?'

'He is sick, that is true.' I did not know what else to say, so I told the truth. 'It is sad but he does not matter to me. I love you.'

'Listen, my sweet. The count thinks to marry you. All for your fortune and a famous jewel.'

I laughed at that. 'What? I would never marry that old ninny. Does he think I am simple-minded?' At least Carinna and I would agree on that.

'Carinna. You are here alone in a place in every way foreign to you. A few servants are no protection. He is powerful. He may seem a fool, but he is crafty and always gets his own way.'

I recalled all his gifts and ridiculous gallantries. Had I been walking in my sleep not to think of it?

'I suppose – if my husband were to die, I would be a free woman.' And if I was Carinna I'd be mighty rich, I thought, but I did not speak that out loud.

'Yes. And there is another danger. His brother Francesco is heir to the estate and lives for the day he inherits. He will do anything to stop his brother marrying you. I do not jest, my love. He is a desperate man.'

I gripped Renzo's hands even tighter, feeling addle-headed from all these intrigues.

'Carinna, I am leaving his service. I will play no further part in this. All those tokens of love he had me create for you. It sickens me now. That is why I quarrelled with him. And now I hear he consults his notary in Rome. It must be about marrying you.'

I reached out and clung to him, feeling the coarseness of his cheek give way to the softness of his mouth. 'What shall I do?' I whispered into his broad neck.

'You must leave this place.'

'I want to,' I said, lifting my face to his. 'But I cannot. There is Biddy. Any day her time will come.'

Impatience made his next words sound harsh. 'Can you not leave her at a lodging house? Pay for a nurse?'

In everything I longed to please him. My heart twisted in painful knots.

'Just a little longer,' I said. Yet even after the birth there would be the long lying-in to wait for. Carinna did not have the strength of a working woman, who might rise from her bed a week or so after giving birth. Carinna, I realised with an unpleasant jolt, was not the idle but strong-spirited woman I had met back at Mawton. She was a weak, feeble invalid. Her progress back to England would have to be mighty slow and careful. Now Jesmire had left, I would be her only hope of proper care. I could not abandon her.

I closed my eyes and sank my head against his broad shoulder and wished all my troubles would disappear.

'I have only a few last duties,' he said. 'Then I must leave. The count has hired a new cook.' He lifted my face very gently in his hands. I wanted to sink into his night-black eyes, but they were hard with a question he had every right to ask.

'You do understand, Carinna? I will do anything to be with you. So tell me truthfully now, do you not care for me as I do for you?'

'Yes,' I whispered. 'You know I do.'

'Then leave with me.'

I hurried back to the villa feeling even more uneasy than when I first set out. The moon was high and barely a fingernail from being full, so I clung to the shelter of the trees at the roadside, glad to be draped in my mistress's dark cloak. The night seemed to quiver with all the trapped heat of the day, heavy with midges that flew in crazy spirals. All the way back Renzo's entreaty rang in my ears. As gently as I could I drew back the screeching gates and pattered up the pale line of the drive. As I passed between the lime trees the breeze rose in hot breaths, shaking the leaves like jittering seed pods. Then at last I had a view of the house, of the pock-marked statues waiting on the terrace, and the blind windows reflecting the moonlight. No, there was one window lit with the flickering gold of a candle. My mistress was awake. I knew it was after one in the morning, for I had heard Ombrosa's bell toll the hour. I started to run across the bleached paving stones, and pushed through the front door into the pitchy darkness of the hall. From the kitchen I could hear Bengo's whimpers and was glad I had closed him inside. There was no one else about so I groped my way upstairs to my mistress's room.

Her travail had begun. My poor lady was twisting and groaning in her sheets, her damp hair stuck to her brow, her face creased with pain.

'I am here.' I took her hand and found it slippery and hot.

'Thank God, Biddy,' she wheezed. Her hunger for air was terrible to hear. 'I thought I was alone.' Her eyes were wide and black with terror.

'Where is Mr Pars?' I had seen no light at his door.

'I called him.' She had to stop speaking as the groaning pains came over her. Then, when they grew less, she panted, 'He left me comfortable with some tea. He's ridden for the doctor.'

I thanked heaven for that at least. To relieve her sweats I opened the shutters a little, for the night was as close as an oven. There was no sign of the doctor's approach. I returned to her side and learned the pains had woken her soon after I left.

'Pars was – in a fury – you being gone.'

'It cannot be helped. I am here now. Do you wish to bear down?'

She shook her head, so I knew I had time. I glanced beneath her sheets and saw the birthing had truly begun. Yet this being her first lying in, there might be hours still to wait.

'I feel sick,' she groaned. 'So poorly.'

'All is well. I am here.'

I tried to make her comfortable, and piled the bolsters so she might sit up. But in a moment she had slumped and lay writhing on her side. Her face was so white with fear and slick with sweat that I myself was suddenly frightened too.

'My Lady, I must fetch hot water for the doctor,' I said, sounding braver than I felt. 'I will be back soon.'

Her eyes twisted toward me. 'Don't leave me.'

'I promise you, the birth is some way off. I must fetch fresh linen.'

I would be lying if I did not say I was flustered when I got downstairs. The kitchen fire had nearly died away, and I cursed Jesmire for going off and taking Mr Loveday with her. I had foreseen this night of travail as one to while away the hours with a hot caudle of spiced wine and a plate of birthing cakes, but that was not to be. It took a fair while to stoke up the fire again and get the kettle boiling. Meanwhile, I found the pile of clean clouts I had set aside. Then casting around for any other useful items, I slipped Lady Maria's old silver knife in my pocket. All the time, Bengo yapped about my legs, but when I was ready I gave him a deft shove and left him whining inside the kitchen door.

'Here we are,' I said, hauling the kettle in one hand and the clouts in the other. I nearly dropped them when I saw her. She had been sick all over her bedclothes, a vivid greenish mess that had spattered all across the sheets. When I rushed to wipe her face she was as limp as a wet rag in my arms. It took me a long while to roll her this way and that and to change the bed sheets and finally set her straight against the bolsters. By then I was getting mighty agitated and listening all the time for horses. But I urged myself to be calm and steady, for I knew that many women survived the most monstrous travails. Once she was cleaned up, my mistress looked a little better. I poured hot water in her washing ewer and had the cloths all waiting. I told myself all was ready, just as if I were attempting the making of some fearsomely difficult dish.

With a sharp scream her pains began again, and this time the sound of her rasping for breath was most terrible to listen to. I stroked her wet hair, holding my own breath too, wondering if she could survive. At last the anguish seemed to ebb and she lay back, as weak as a lamb.

'Biddy? Are you there?' Her voice was a whisper.

'I am mistress. I will not leave you.'

In reply a faint squeeze pressed my hand.

'It is a judgement on me. All the journey. I have known it.' Her lips were very pale and cracked, moving slowly in her wretched, weary face.

'Don't talk nonsense. Save your breath for the child, dear.'

But she would not still herself. Her fingers dug into my arm.

'It is true. Listen. We did a bad thing. I confess it.'

'This is no time to talk—'

'Listen, Biddy. For God's sake.' For a while she halted, catching her breath. Her mouth was so drained of colour it looked tinted blue. I stared hopefully at the window, I listened for hooves on the drive, but nothing relieved my alarm.

She licked her dry lips and spoke again. 'Together we plotted against the old man. It was all a contrivance. For his money.'

I listened, not wanting to hear it at all.

'Christ forgive me,' she said. 'I am going to die. I know it.'

I could not meet her beseeching eyes. Then another forcing pain began and she curled up and bore it, pinching my hand as tight as a pincer. When it was over she stared towards me with eyes like glass. Her lips began to move again, making words from feeble breath. 'We were poor. I needed it. Money.'

'Forget that now,' I said, for such talk made me sick. All the money in the world cannot buy life, I thought grimly.

'The doctor?' She was staring dully at nothing.

'He may still come.' Yet I caught from her a mood of hopelessness.

A little later, she turned her eyes to mine and they were that sunken I could not be sure she truly saw me. 'I committed a terrible sin—'

'Hush now. You told me already.'

'No. Worse—'

The forcing pains began again and she struggled at last to lift her knees. If she could but deliver the child, I prayed, maybe all would be well. But when she tried to push she was too weak, all the pain seemed forced back inside her. It was an agony to watch her.

'The child,' she whispered in a quiet spell, so soft I could barely hear. I dipped my head and felt her breath, sour and hot against my cheek. 'Take care of it, Biddy.'

'You will live, dear,' I entreated. 'You will live to care for it yourself.'

'Give Kitt the jewel,' she said in short gasps. Then, 'Not Pars. Kitt.'

It was an odd thing to say, but then she had sworn to her dying mother to provide for her brother. Before she could say more the pains were on her again. I never saw a body suffer such as she did. She was too weak to scream out; her whole being was racked like a torture. Then a time came when she could not breathe at all, her chest made a dreadful creaking sound as she tried to take in air. I tried to lift her up, though my hands were trembling and dithering. Then I felt it, like a great shock travelling through her, as if an invisible cudgel struck her chest. The mighty power of the convulsion was so strong that she flung her arms backwards.

'My Lady, raise yourself.' I tugged her shoulders, trying to raise her. Her head fell forwards. A string of greenish spittle hung from her open mouth.

'My Lady!'

I tugged again and saw the fixed stare of her eyes. Her lips were parted and had a blue shadow about them. Her soul had departed from her body, all in a moment.

'Carinna,' I called, drawing near to her again. 'Speak to me, dear.' Her lips stayed rigid; her eyes did not move a jot. I stroked her cheek and it was warm but very still.

I knew it was over. And I was so heartbroken for my mistress that I burst out skriking like a disappointed child. My poor mistress, I sobbed. She had come all this way to die without kith or kin to comfort her. Tenderly, I wiped her sweat-rimed face. Then her arms, and her milky, blue-veined breasts. Only as my warm cloth moved across her great swelling belly did I remember the poor trapped child. For it was then that her belly-skin suddenly rippled, a flutter passing fast across the surface. I dropped the cloth and covered my mouth. The baby was still alive.

'No,' I gasped out loud. Surely it could not survive its mother's dying? My legs felt weak and I pulled a stool beneath me, trying to straighten my thoughts. A horrid memory jostled in my mind: of that little deer springing from its dead mother's carcass back in Mawton's larder. I glanced again at Carinna's face. She was as stiff and lifeless as a stone statue out on the terrace. I reached out again to her belly. It was not quite cold, and still felt yielding. Another movement trembled across the smooth skin, pushing outward like the kick of a tiny foot.

I told myself I must do it fast. That of anyone save a surgeon, I had the best skills with a knife. Shaking only a little, I laid a clean cloth over her privy parts and grasped my silver knife.

'God forgive me,' I prayed. I poked at her with my fingertips, calculating that a slice straight across her middle would probably kill the child. I decided her lower parts must be sacrificed, so the opening had to be made at the bottom edge of her belly. I tried to calm my ragged breathing. At that moment, I confess I would have known relief if the child had died. But it did not. It moved again, struggling for air, trapped in her womb like a kitten in a sack.

As gently as I could, I set the knife tip against her pale flesh. I pressed and the blade sliced through the skin. A slow ooze of blood welled up and hindered my view. I wiped some of it away and set the knife a little deeper, mumbling 'Our Father,' and scraps of prayers beneath my breath. The first cut was too shallow; all I did was make a horrid mess of blood. A faint-headedness nearly struck me down.

'It is only common butchery,' I said to myself. This time I commanded myself to slice deeper. I cut through to a layer of white fat and slid my knife deeper. Next came meaty red flesh, but I could find nothing there. My mouth was dry, my throat was tight. I began to gag and cough to see my vile handiwork. More blood was flooding over my hands now, so I paused to wipe it with the drenched cloth. I wanted to sit and get my breath back but the notion of precious time passing made me slice even deeper. I thought my blade must be close to the child now, and was terrified of killing it. So with a clutch of my heart I lifted up the cut flap of my mistress's belly and peered inside.

Something dark and matted caught my eye amongst the scarlet flesh. Sliding my hand inside the fetid warmth of her belly I felt a roundness and upon it, slippery matted hair. Then I cut in earnest, careless of the bloodbath I was making, desperate only to free the trapped child. A second time I reached inside her body and grasped the slippery skull. Then I yanked hard. All in a slithery tumble the baby came out of the gash, looking very grey and blood-smeared. It dropped on the bloody sheets, its eyes closed but its limbs weakly flailing. Behind it trailed the grey wrinkled sausage of its cord. With a slice of the blade the baby was free. I knew it must be washed, but nearly dropped it on the floor as I carried it to the ewer. I was muttering prayers of thanks as I did, so amazed was I that it lived.

Once the baby was washed of its warm lardy slime it took on a better colour. It was a little girl, with dark tufts of hair on her head and a squashed-up nubbins of a face. Her skull, mind you, was bent to one side like an apple grown askew, but I reckoned that was from the long squeezing she'd suffered. My heart swelled to see her live. I lifted her to my breast and was glad to hear her cry with a healthy bawling. Just the soft feel of her heartened me, the kicking of her thin legs and her bumpy peach of a head wobbling against my lips. Then I wrapped her in a piece of swaddling and set her down in the wooden box that was her crib. For a long while I stood over her, marvelling as she snuffled and jerked and then fell to sleep.

Before I let myself go to bed I began to tidy up my mistress. I got a fancy that if I cut strips of sheeting I could bind up her belly. I was standing over her with my knife raised to cut the cloth when I felt a prickle on my skin as if I was being watched. When I turned my head I jumped with fright, for there was Mr Pars standing in the doorway.

'Biddy!' he barked. 'What have you done to your mistress?'

I started to gabble out the tale, that she had died in her travails, my words coming all in a jumble. 'Thank God you are back,' I ended. 'I waited and waited for the doctor. But it's too late now.'

He did not move from his place in the shadow of the door. I could see him frowning at my mistress as she lay white and almost naked, slashed about like a corpse on a battlefield.

'I see that. Now put the knife down, girl.' I looked down at my hand that was bloody to the elbow. I dropped it and it clattered to the floor.

'Thank God you are back, sir,' I said, very heartily. 'When she died I knew not what to do.'

'When she died?' I could not see his face for he was far from the candles. 'No Biddy. She could not live after you had butchered her.'

'Butchered?' I cried. 'I told you she was dead and growing cold when I cut her. Look.' I motioned to the crib. 'I saved the baby.'

He took a few steps and peered towards the little scrap that now lay quiet in the cradle. 'Great god, it has a monstrous head.'

'It may mend, sir. It was a terrible birthing.'

'I see what I see, Biddy. A knife in your hand, your mistress dead. Look,' and he pointed at me in a grave manner. 'Your gown is soaked in blood. No, it is her gown is it not? Her golden gown from Paris? Girl, what have you done?'

It was then I felt a sinking like a plummeting stone in my guts.

'Your mistress was quite well when I left her.' His accusation was not hot-blooded, rather it sounded right sorry, as if he pitied me.

'Mr Pars, sir, I could never harm My Lady. I cared for her. You know that.'

'It may not come to my opinion, Biddy, in a court of law. I left her – Christ believe me, I left her well and happy. And I come back to this horror. Oh, was your head so much turned by jewels and junketing that you must murder her?'

'Mr Pars, sir! It is I, Biddy. How can you say such a thing?'

He backed away then, further from the light till he was no more than a speaking shadow. 'I did once think I knew you, Biddy. But consider how you have altered these last weeks. There are witnesses aplenty to your gadding about pretending to be her, while she was too sick to stop you. She had her part to blame, I grant you that. But I must follow my conscience. If I am called before a magistrate, I can only tell what my own eyes saw.'

'You would not. God help me, I would swing for this!'

Then, perhaps seeing the terror that struck me, he looked on me with a little more kindness.

'It has been a long, weary night. Let us sleep before we take any sudden action.' I felt such gratitude towards the man that my eyes brimmed.

'Thank you, Mr Pars, sir.'

'There may be means and ways to sort it out, if you do as I bid.'

'I would do anything, sir.' My voice shook with relief.

Then he shuffled off to his chamber and I heard his key turn in the lock. I returned to cleaning the room, which looked like a slaughterhouse. Try as I might, I could not close my lady's eyes, lacking heavy English pennies. And so it seemed to me that my mistress's staring eyes beseeched me as I bundled the bloody sheets away to be thrown in the fire. If only she could speak in my defence, I thought. And I wondered what Mr Pars would have said of my mistress's confession, that she and her uncle had indeed tricked Sir Geoffrey of his money. That he had suspected her all along, I supposed. I did my best to make all neat again, carrying the ewer, knife, and pots down to the kitchen. Bengo still yapped behind the door, but with a boot to his hind quarters I forced him back so he could not escape. Then, unable to leave Carinna's tiny daughter alone in such a chamber of death, I lifted the innocent bantling into my arms, and took her off to my own bed.

# XXXIII

## *Villa Ombrosa*

*Being Easter Saturday, 1773*
*Biddy Leigh, her journal*

## ~ *Funeral Cakes* ~

*Take a pound of sugar and a quarter pound of almonds blanched and beat them very well, then strain them with five spoonfuls of cream. Add grains of ambergris and so mix it up, and put into it three or four spoonfuls of flour. Then put into paper coffens and bake them in the oven. When dry tie each pair with white ribbons and seal with black wax. A fitting verse for the paper is set out thus:*

> *Farewell my weeping friends, farewell,*
> *My dearest friends adieu!*
> *I hope ere long in heaven to dwell*
> *And then I'll welcome you.*

*Funeral Cakes made on the death of Lord Charles Grice, 1681, writ in a fine old Secretary hand, The Cook's Jewel*

Though I was bone tired I slept uneasily that night. The baby lay beside me, and every few hours I woke to hear her whimpering. I nuzzled her close in my arms and was right glad of her little body, and I reckon she was glad of my warmth beside her. All through the small hours most awful pictures skittered through my brain: the dull china eyes of my dead mistress and the scarlet butchering of her body, and Renzo's saying that if I cared for him I would go with him. But worst of all was Mr Pars' threat to see me hang for murder. The gallows. Just the notion of the hanging tree and the final walk to that shameful death nearly made me faint with terror.

So I was cheered when dawn rose behind the shutters, and I could see the babe's grey eyes blinking trustfully into mine. By God's grace, it amazed me that from all the horrors of that night such a sweet merry-gotten girl should come from it. I dandled her awhile, singing daft songs as I pulled her tiny fingers and toes that were still crabbed up from being cramped so long. True, her head was still awry, but I rubbed it tenderly with ointment till it looked a little better. Yet it choked me too, with the pity of it, her being a motherless scrap in this foreign place.

Bengo nearly burst out of the kitchen when I released him. I could have taken a stick to him when I saw he'd been running hey-go-mad about the place, knocking crockery about and breaking Carinna's best teacup. Hurriedly, I warmed some milk, and having no bubby-pot, fed the baby drip by drip from a teaspoon. Mixed with a little wine and honey, it settled my little girl, and as soon as her lids began to droop, I bundled her into the bread basket and prayed she might stay silent. Soon after, I heard Mr Pars rise and told myself to be wary, for this man held my life in his hands. As I buttered his rolls I turned the matter over – that a judge might think like Mr Pars did, that I had harmed my own mistress. I could scarcely believe it, that he had crept up on me so quietly as the knife was raised over her body.

When I tried to argue my own innocence it was not so easy. As Mr Pars said, there were witnesses aplenty to my wearing Carinna's gowns and calling myself by her name while she lay ailing in her bed. I had only Mr Pars and Jesmire to speak for me, and Jesmire, by her own accounts, loathed my guts. And so far as I knew, Mr Loveday being a slave had no rights to speak in a court of law.

Hearing Mr Pars come down the stairs I rushed to him and served his breakfast. I tried my best to read his countenance, but he was his usual stony-faced self. Then as soon as I heard the plate-scrapings cease in the parlour I went in and curtseyed lower than I had for many a month.

'Mr Pars sir, you did say if I did your bidding today you might look kindly on me.'

He had lit his first pipe of the day and was settling back in one of the parlour armchairs. It was odd to see him downstairs, and to tell the truth he did look more comfortable than he had of late, as if he'd taken proper possession of the villa now my mistress was dead.

'So you would eat humble pie, would you?'

'Yes sir. And I'm right sorry about the mistress. She died a natural death sir. I waited and waited for you and the doctor—'

He lifted a hand to hush me. 'Enough. There are matters aplenty to see to. First, I will arrange that the poor woman is buried. And meanwhile you must dispose of the child.'

At first my heart hammered like a drum for I couldn't understand his meaning. Then I remembered Lady Carinna's notion.

'You mean ask after a foster family at the convent, sir?'

'Aye. I suppose that for form's sake you should wear your mistress's gown when you go out. It would seem too strange if the mysterious bedridden Biddy were to suddenly start gallivanting about.'

'Very well, sir. And will you write and tell her family? What terrible news for Sir Geoffrey. And her uncle and Mr Kitt.'

'I will perform all the formalities. In this heat there must be no delay. The funeral must be tomorrow.'

'Thank you, sir. And you will not summon the magistrate, sir?'

'As I said, do as you are bid and I will think on it.'

I was still mighty uneasy, but curtseyed and began to collect his pots.

'One last thing,' he said in a very steady voice. 'I must collect all her goods together. And I cannot find the jewel.'

I nearly dropped the teapot with fright. I wasn't about to forget I'd made a death bed promise not to hand it over.

'Did you not wear it recently?' His voice was heavy with suspicion.

My mouth felt like sawdust. I prayed the jewel was where I'd left it, in my chamber.

'I did sir. But I gave it back to my lady. I'll make a search for it in her boxes.'

'Her boxes? Very well. Get on with it, then.' He watched me silently from the midst of skeins of smoke. 'For if the jewel is missing, you understand it puts all these affairs in a most grave light.'

It was a hot, heavy day for the cloudburst had never come in the night. I decided to walk with the baby, for Jesmire had the carriage and I lacked the courage to ride a horse all alone. So I swaddled the poor little bantling in a shawl, and though it wasn't how a lady might do it, I bundled her onto my hip like the women of Scarth did when they set off coal-picking. Dressed in my lady's blue Paris dress, I felt a right spectacle as I lumbered up the road to Ombrosa. By the time I'd trudged past the village's stone walls I had a stitch in my side like a larding needle. I passed a few old women sitting at their doorways, and a clutch of old fellows playing greasy cards beneath some ancient arches. They stared as they always did, brazen and curious, but not breaking into speech until I'd passed them by.

Recollecting the count's directions I carried on up the track towards the peak of the hill. Slowly the brown tower and stone walls of the convent came into view far above me. By now a muzzy sun was bearing down, and I cursed the narrowness of my bodice that tightened my breath. The road moved in uncertain directions, so the buildings swung east, then north, forever out of reach. But at last, after my feet had pounded many miles of hard road, I turned a bend and found myself before a shabby gatehouse.

I knocked at the iron-studded door. For some minutes no one came. No longer rocked by my striding, the baby began to cry, a pink-gummed wailing that made my teeth ache. I knocked again, my anger growing. God damn these papists, I swore beneath my breath. Must they always be kissing the toes of stone idols and counting their beads?

Then the grille in the door creaked, and a suspicious eye looked out at me.

I said in my best Italian that I wished them to find a family for the baby, for which service I would pay good money. With no word of greeting, an ill-favoured nun unlatched the door and I followed her inside. We were in a sort of courtyard where weeds sprang through the pavings and goats tussled over kitchen scraps. I followed her hobbling figure into a dingy chamber where she set herself down behind a table. Above us hung a picture of Mother Mary, her heart pierced with swords like a living pincushion.

With a loud sigh, the nun reached for a coffer and held out the box for my money. I had my silver *lire* ready, but once I had seen the place a great reluctance stopped me from handing it over.

'*La bambina*,' I asked. I motioned her to show me where the baby would be kept until everything was sorted out. The old nun frowned and shook her box right in my face. Damn you, old witch, I thought. '*Dove la bambina?*' I struggled to think of the Italian word. '*Dorme?*' I demanded.

It was a struggle of wills, but I would not leave Carinna's child without seeing where she would sleep that night. What I did see, after a crude argument of gestures, was most pitiful. The *Bastardi* as the old nun called them, were kept by a family housed in a grim hovel with slits for windows. One babe lay kicking in his own filth on the straw. The other few children were all thin and ragged. In charge of them was a hackslavering woman with a large stick in her hand. I turned on my heels and left that hellish place. I could never in one thousand years have left that dear little girl in such a pit of misery.

Fury drove me back down to the village. The baby was crying again, doubtless hungry for her mother's milk. I found the familiar market and made enquiries of the stallholders, praying there would be someone in need of the money. An hour later I found Carla – a plump, tongue-lashed fourteen-year-old whose mother screamed oaths at her, even though the girl's own fatherless baby had died. The wet stains on her bodice told me all I needed to know. So I offered her mother half the money I had intended for the convent, and promised the girl the rest when her milk proved good. We settled on her coming the next day at supper time, after she had been shriven by a priest, and then I bought a jug of milk fresh from the cow.

I walked back up the pale road slowly, batting away the buzzing flies and trying to settle Evelina against my hip. I'd chosen her name from the cover of one of my mistress's books, and reckoned it nicely new-fangled and not like the burden I must bear of living a life of damned Obedience. The truth was I'd got a right hankering to keep the babe. Aye, I knew it was mighty stupid, but I could not part from her. The way she clung to me, the soft unformed look of her, as if she'd break as easy as an eggshell, all snared my heart-strings. Yet I couldn't settle on a plan at all, only to keep her from Mr Pars' eyes until I knew where I might take her.

I looked anxiously about as my sore feet traipsed up the long drive back to the villa. There was something going on behind the house, for a dark billow of smoke rose from the garden, and bitter ash tainted the air. Contriving to tuck the baby beneath my cloak

I slipped in by the front door and held my breath as I crept very nimbly to the kitchen. Thank the Lord Mr Pars was out at the back. From the kitchen window I could see him burning a great heap of stuff out in the garden. I warmed a little milk and Evelina took some from the spoon, until I set her down in the basket fast asleep.

That nuisance Bengo then scratched at the door, and to add to my labours, he had been disgustingly sick. The ratty creature was walking like a drunkard, it was quite comical to see it. On his snout was a crusty string of dried green sick, and there was more of it in the yard. Fearing he might betray Evelina to Mr Pars, I shut him outside the door with a dish of water.

I knew I must leave the very next day. Each time I glanced through the glass at Mr Pars I grew more and more uneasy. Though he was some distance away I could read a smug way about him; it was giving him a great deal of pleasure to destroy what looked to be my mistress's goods. I wasn't daft, I knew I had disobeyed him by bringing little Evelina back home. Thinking on his other request, I began to fret over Carinna's jewel.

Just then the clock struck four of the afternoon. Why, it is only two hours till Mr Loveday comes home, I told myself cheerily. And so, to keep my spirits up, I did what I always do when I grow fretful. I started to cook.

The joint of Easter beef was hanging in the larder, so that was easily spitted over the fire. And there was fresh stuff in the pantry, plenty to use up if I was leaving the next day. When Mr Loveday returned all would be well, I told myself. No doubt after that we would all take our different roads, and I would take Evelina with me. Tonight called for a funeral supper for Carinna, it was the least I could do to remember her. I pulled out *The Cook's Jewel* and found some fine receipts. As I laid out my cloths and spoons and bowls, all my fears seemed suddenly nonsense. First I made some pies and baked a fine white loaf. Then I started to mix some funeral cakes, and the delight of making a strange and interesting receipt worked on my nerves like balm. What with the pounding and sieving and careful cutting of the paper cases that the old receipt called *coffens*, were it not for Mr Pars and his hately threat I might have been happy. Why this is what I want, I realised with a most powerful understanding – to work in my own kitchen with little babes beside me. My very insides ached to think of my own unborn sons and daughters, and how I would fight like a she-wolf with anyone who tried to harm them. And if anyone should ever try to harm Evelina, I would kill them too.

Now 'tis a strange thing, that some folk think more clearly with a pipe clenched between their teeth, while others need a needle darting in their fingers. For me, the neat repetitions of cookery are the finest aid to cogitation. First I thought of the jewel and where to hide it from Mr Pars, and conceived a most wondrous place of concealment. It was the work of a moment to slip it safely away and to know I had carried out my mistress's dying wish. Then I got back to work, and the table in the dining room soon had a clean white cloth and my pies and beef and fruits were laid out in a most genteel geometrical display. Then, as I spooned an equal part of the funeral cake mixture into each paper case, all the separate parts of what had happened these last months began to bind together too. As I baked my first batch I thought of my lady's kindness in giving me her beautifying waters. As I washed the crocks I remembered my foolish suspicion that she had used sassafras to poison Sir Geoffrey. Why, I pondered, as I lifted the first cakes from the oven, I had been simple-minded to even think my mistress could poison anyone – it was more like she had herself been poisoned, for all her quick decline in health.

I slammed the hot board of cakes down on the table. Evelina raised a twitching hand in the air, but after a sucking motion with her lips she settled and slept once more. Poison? It had to be balderdash. Yet – Carinna's greenish vomit had been no ordinary bile. And – that was it, that was what was mithering me – Bengo had suddenly sickened too, and had also vomited green stuff.

I clasped my fingers to my mouth as if to stop myself ever uttering such a word. No, I had to be wrong, for had not all of my mistress's food been cooked and served by me? So maybe it was a contagion, I argued. For a moment I felt the balm of relief. Yet what contagion could have struck only her and Bengo? It had to be something she had eaten. Well, she had eaten syllabub, that was all, and I had concocted it. Indeed, I had sampled it and enjoyed it. Yet, Bengo had puked up greenish stuff too. What had they both eaten that no one else had touched?

My heart was racketing fast as I peered through the glass to be sure Mr Pars was still at his bonfire. He was, yet why did the very sight of him make my legs long to run and run? I closed my eyes. What had my mistress and Bengo both eaten? She had long since given up sweetmeats; there was no food up there in her chamber. Or what had she drunk? Only her comfrey tea.

An ice-cold dart of fear ran through me. This morning the remains of her comfrey tea had been spilt by Bengo, after he broke the cup the liquid had dripped all over the floor. The stupid dog had no doubt lapped it up.

But again I argued counterwise. Only me or Mr Loveday had ever bought the tea at market stalls. Yet I had a faint recollection now, like a half dream, of Carinna telling me that Mr Pars had given her a dose last night. It had to be the comfrey tea. I pictured it, standing on the table by her bedside. A walnut caddy filled with shredded leaves.

I checked the window. Mr Pars had thrown a large portmanteau in the fire and was poking it with a stick. Evelina was slumbering peacefully, her tiny eyelids fluttering. As quietly as I could I crept along the hallway and up the stairs. It would be the work of a moment to find the tea and be sure he had not exchanged it. Yet my footsteps slowed as I reached my lady's room. I had not seen her corpse since I'd laid her out last night.

Pushing open the door I found her still shrouded by the sheet, though a half-dozen flies circled her like corpse watchers. Moving quickly to the table I found the caddy, its lid down just as it should be. I opened it and looked at the pale greenish leaves. Thank God, I told myself, they are comfrey leaves. I sighed and then, from habit, picked up a couple of leaves and thrimbled them between my finger and thumb. Then I raised my fingers to my nose and sniffed.

The scent was not comfrey. Comfrey has a green smell of musty parsley. This was poppy-like and higher in the nose. I sniffed it again, dropping my nose deep into the box. It was something I knew, something I had smelled many times. Then, with my face so close, I noticed tiny hairs on the leaves. The name came to me then, a commonplace name, yet one well famed as a medicine and poison. Foxglove.

The sound of a creak on the stairs made me jump like a startled hare. I tried to drop the lid gently, but my butterfingers slipped and it banged like a crow-scarer. In a moment Mr Pars was standing at the door. He had caught me in the very act.

'I always knew you were quick, Biddy.' He was grinning like he was pleased with me, but I reckoned he was more pleased with himself. 'If anyone would find me out, it was you.'

I froze like a block of ice. Only my dead mistress lay stretched between us. Oh Lord, I thought. He killed her. I stared from her corpse lying murdered, up to her steward, so merry with himself. I opened my mouth with the notion of somehow distracting him by chattering on, but my voice was high and strangled.

'Foxglove and comfrey. Easy to mistake one for the other.'

He folded his arms and leaned on the door frame.

'So Lady Maria told me. A true scholar of herblore, she was. Trained me how to grow my coltsfoot and much more besides. Now she was a true gentlewoman, not like that filthy whore.' He nodded towards the corpse that lay between us.

I glanced at the window and saw it was tightly shuttered. There was no escape that way. Oh Lord, don't let me die, rang a silent voice in my head. I had the notion that if I kept him talking, Mr Loveday might come home at any moment.

'How long had she been taking it?'

'Since we stopped at Ashford. I first exchanged it that day I surprised you in her chamber. I should have guessed her shamming trick, for I mistook you for her then, and called out her name. She outflanked me there, bringing you along. As for the foxglove, every time I switched it none of you were wiser. Well, there was that over-indulgence at Turin, you remember? The bitch's heart near stopped. My only concern was that you would finally notice.'

I shook my head weakly.

'But you had your head turned, didn't you? She saw to that. You cannot picture my satisfaction, to think of her drinking her poison every day and night, all prepared by other hands than mine. Turin told me what I needed about the dose. Last night I merely tripled it.'

'But the doctor would have noticed.'

'What doctor? Last night I merely took a turn around the lanes.'

Again I scrabbled about for questions to keep him talking.

'But why did you – hate her?'

He laughed at me like I was an idiot. 'I forget, you still believe that brimstone bitch was an innocent. If you had seen her greedy face when she first arrived at Mawton, you would not have aped her as you did. There was nothing any of them would not do for money. I met her uncle at the law courts when I was searching for a way to get Pars Fold back, after Sir Geoffrey had bullied my father into handing it over. I fancied I might secretly transfer the land back, for who of Sir Geoffrey's heirs would know better? But the lawyer I consulted, a toad in a greasy wig, told me it could not be done in secret, and anyway, I must pay the current value. To pay a vast sum for what was rightfully ours? I couldn't let the matter lie, it grew like a canker. I took comfort in a tavern outside the courts, and found Quentin. He was up for fraud, naturally. We got to talking and found we each had a use for the other. We made an agreement, a solid agreement, to divide Sir Geoffrey's fortune between us, half for me, half for them. He said he had a fresh young niece and was on the lookout for a wealthy rook, and I – well, I had need of others to distract from my part. What was Pars Fold to me if all of Sir Geoffrey's fortune was for the taking? But I needed them, a pair of dupes to take the blame. Who would take notice of my part, after his gold-hunting wife had finished spending? It was my wits alone that devised the whole pretty trick. Quentin and Carinna landed like flies in honey.'

The silence scared me, so I stuttered out another question. 'So why not share it as you agreed?'

He pointed contemptuously at my lady. 'Because that dogess went back on her word. No sooner had she wedded Sir Geoffrey than she started up her own game. The black bitch was suddenly set upon travel, and threatened to take all the money abroad and leave me nothing. Said that if I didn't, she'd ruin me, she'd send the Letter of Credit we concocted together to Ireland, for it bore Sir Geoffrey's false signature in my hand. Ruin me! The trouble that harlot caused, making me chase all this way at her skirts just to keep her sweet. As for her spending, she did it to enrage me, you do know that? One day on Dover beach she said she would spend my share in double time in Paris. It's astonishing I didn't snuff her sooner.'

Dover beach. I recollected two figures, a greatcoated man striding fast with his hands tight in fists.

'And she's kept that jewel close. Ever since Lady Maria showed it me, when I first rode up to Yorkshire to collect that sweet lady, I've had a hankering for that jewel. So hand it over, girl.'

Please Lord, not the jewel. I had to let his boasting run on.

'So who fathered Carinna's child?'

'The devil knows which filthy rake she lay with. I only knew it couldn't be Sir Geoffrey's.'

'For sure you knew that,' I threw back. 'He was poxed half to death.'

Pars pulled a sour little smile. 'Yes, damn his soul. While he had the strength to live on like a festering corpse, the pox as good as murdered every child Lady Maria conceived and finally murdered

her. The chancre reached her heart. It was a vile sore right there.'
With eyes fiercely distant he touched his own barrel chest. 'She
kept it hidden underneath the Mawton Rose.'

I had to turn him off that jewel again. 'But you let Lady Carinna
marry him, knowing that if he bedded her, it would slowly murder
her too?'

'She deserved it. No one could replace Maria.' Then he recollected himself. 'So where's the jewel?'

I tried to blank my face like a white glazed platter. 'I don't know.'

He moved then, taking slow heavy steps into the room, so that
I backed away towards the wall, cringing like a hound. A few
inches from me he halted, panting so hard so I could smell his
sourness.

'Biddy,' he said, his head cocked sideways in a mockery of
concern. 'For some time you have worried me, girl. Carinna gave
you fancies that could only ruin you. And that fop of a count's
attentions have puffed up your head.' He pursed his thin lips, and
the red veins flushed over his cheeks like a purple brand. 'You forget
you are only a kitchen slut.'

I opened my mouth, but no words sprang to my rescue. I sized
him up and reckoned Humphrey Pars was twice my weight. I was
no match for him. We stared at one another, and I saw in his eyes
something raw and monstrous that he generally kept hooded.

'Those fools have spoiled you, Biddy. And if you will not support
your old friends, if you would play the traitor—'

He was talking very slow and sing-song, watching me and
rubbing his fingers against each other, as if rubbing away cold sweat.

'Mr Pars,' I said, and my voice came out like a whine from a
beggar. 'You can trust me, sir. You can always—'

Just then a distant sound reached my ears. At first only I could
hear it. Evelina had woken and wanted the world to know it. Then
I saw a spark of anger cross his face.

'What's that? I told you to get rid of it.'

The babe's stubborn wail rose up the empty stairs.

'That damned squeaker! I'll squeeze the air right out of its lungs—'

'You will not!'

'Only two things I asked. Get rid of that child and give me the jewel.'

Then I said it, what I had been thinking all this long day. 'And if I did. Then what?'

He showed his hately smile then and it made me shiver, for I think the old serpent himself could not have smiled wider. 'You are mighty quick tonight. It's a pity you and that slammerkin did not truly change places. She never could keep up with me.'

Evelina wailed on, still tugging at my nerves, so I opened my mouth just to cover the noise.

'So it was never her doing at all, to give Sir Geoffrey the apoplexy?'

'Her?' he scoffed. 'I sent a bottle of Sir Geoffrey's favourite Usquebaugh to London to celebrate the wedding. It had foxglove mixed into the spirit. He seemed never to drink it, but when he finally did, the day could not have been better chosen, the day he and Carinna parted with hot words. My only regret is that he survived.'

As I scrabbled for more to say, I prayed to hear Mr Loveday on the drive, but no sound came.

'But surely you will be caught?'

'Caught? They will have to find me first. And by then they will know Carinna stole the money. I am sending back to Mawton the most perfectly balanced accounts to prove she spent every penny. And letters held by my brother Ozias show I did all in my powers to restrain her. Pen and ink will prove my case.'

'I meant for her – murder.'

His mouth twisted in an acid downwards smile as if I made a great jest.

'My dear Biddy, Carinna is not dead. She was seen all about the streets only today. And even the count would testify that this swollen hulk before us was not Carinna. It helps of course, her having been a flighty piece. So none will be surprised she's run away with her mysterious lover and so thankfully, will never be seen again.'

'I don't understand. So whose is the funeral tomorrow?'

The room was suddenly airless and cold. My fingers wretchedly groped the smooth wall behind me.

'The funeral is for that poor unfortunate maid, of course. The one who came from Mawton with a bastard in her belly. The one who fancied herself so much cleverer than me.'

He fixed me with his red-rimmed eyes, but I saw his muscle twitch to raise his heavy arm. 'Obedience Leigh.'

There was no time to think on it, I dashed beneath his lifted arm and ran for the stairs. He caught at my skirts and slowed me for a moment, but I tugged and tugged and broke away free. I ran at full pelt along the landing and could see the first step of the stairs. By the time I reached it he was thundering behind me. A hand grabbed my hair, but I wriggled forward and felt the pins tug from my scalp as my empty cap came loose in his hand. Then I was clattering down the stairs as fast as I could. I could hear him, puffing his breath out just behind me. Evelina's wailing rose; every sinew in my body ached to grasp her and run away I knew not where. Then from behind me his heavy hand grasped my sleeve, but I shook it off. Evelina was screaming, and I told myself I would reach her.

With a jolt my loose hair was yanked back, and my neck savagely twisted. I stumbled and missed my footing. For what felt a long age I teetered on the stair edge, and then, with a powerful punch to my kidneys from behind me, I lost my footing and fell headlong down the stairs, racketing my way down bump after bump. Reaching the bottom, though I tried to hold out my hands to protect myself, my head walloped hard against the stone floor and I knew no more of what befell me.

# XXXIV

It was market day in Leghorn, and loud-mouthed women jostled Loveday, their squalling children staring and pointing at his unfamiliar features. At the captain's house he had waited in a dirty servants' room while Jesmire saw the master. He had dozed in the soupy heat, listening to washerwomen's voices rising and falling as they scolded their wailing broods. Then someone had opened a shutter, and barely one hundred paces away he glimpsed the turquoise sea and a harbour packed tight with tall-masted sailing ships. He asked the other manservants where the ships sailed to, but their words were hard to understand. One single word rang out like a bell. 'Kochee?' he repeated. They nodded. The word revived him like a powerful tide. Kochee. He had disembarked at that sun-gold, spice-dusty port on his passage to England. He could picture the huddle of merchants' houses, the brown-eyed sailors dressed only in knotted white cloths, the beautiful oval-faced women, their nostrils pierced with diamonds. He had to get to Kochee; it was an ache in his *manger* spirit, it stretched and strained like a sail in a wild wind.

Jesmire had scuttled back at last, twitching with triumph. 'The captain and I will suit each other very nicely,' she said. In fact, so well did she like him that she told Loveday there was no necessity to go all the way back to Ombrosa.

'But Miss Jesmire,' he protested, 'I tell Miss Biddy we back today. She 'spect us six clock.'

'Well she will just have to be disappointed, won't she?' Jesmire said, smiling sourly to herself. 'We will return to the inn tonight, and I will write henceforth to Mr Pars. The captain says my quarters will be all shipshape by noon tomorrow. The captain is a most discerning, very particular sort of—'

Loveday brooded as she squawked on. He did want to look around this city of ships, but hated breaking his word to Biddy. Yet how could he change Jesmire's mind? However fortunate he was to be here, it still felt very wrong to break his promise to Biddy.

After supper Jesmire passed him a letter and told him to find the post house. Once free of her nit-picking presence he stopped at a tavern, ordered a tankard of beer, and deftly untied the letter and read its contents:

*Dear Mr Pars,*

*I am delighted to inform you that I have secured a position at the most satisfactory establishment of Captain William Dodsley, Retd, of Casa Il Porto, Leghorn. As a consequence, I give you notice and request that you forward my outstanding remuneration to the address herewith given above.*

*I have a number of errands still to complete, for which I require the carriage, and will send it back as soon as I am able, along with the driver and footman.*

*Your servant,*
*Miss Amelia Jesmire*

Once night fell, Loveday had fallen asleep at the inn. He slept uneasily until suddenly his eyes opened wide in the darkness. A sound had burrowed into his dreams and noisily cleared a path back to wakefulness. He listened, blinking slowly. Beside him, the coachman snored softly, his dark head burrowed under his coat. The noise that had woken him started up again; the wavering yarl of a crying baby. Loveday listened closely and knew that the poor little creature was frightened. The sound grew louder and louder until it scraped the insides of his ears. Pulling his coat over his head he rolled over and shut his eyes again. It was no good. The sound seemed to be just on the other side of the room's thin wall. The baby sobbed and gasped and started up another ear-scouring wail.

Agitated, he stood up and crossed the room to pull back the shutters. Outside the air was still warm and smelled of the sea and pungent tree sap. The moon was full, a pitted globe of silver hanging low above the rooftops.

'*Mother Fula,*' he whispered to the moon. She was naked and unpitying, casting bold silver rays across the sleeping town. The baby's weeping grew quieter and sadder, sinking to a heartbreaking sob. It might be coming from anywhere; the inn was on a narrow alley with tottering buildings all about it. He trod silently on the pads of his feet towards the door, wondering if he could find its mother, the person whose love should comfort the child. But out on the landing he found only doors, and whenever he placed his ear to the rough wood, the sound of the baby disappeared. It was a puzzle, but he also knew it was something more. His *manger* was oddly excited. This sound – had he not heard it below the usual hubbub for most of the day? Amongst the market women this morning, and then echoing up from the laundry at the captain's house? Even in the ale house it had droned on just below his attention, like a mosquito buzzing in the wind. He returned to the window and looked up at the moon. *Mother Fula,* the moon, had betrayed him to the white men on that last night on Lamahona, for she was a trickster. But she was also a truth-teller, a revealer of hidden secrets.

He stared at her and thought of the tides she pulled across the earth with her magical will, the complex pattern of sea roads bringing bounty or loss to hunters and fishermen. He knew there were other dark flows of change that she wrought. The bleeding of women every month, the pains of birthing. The baby's cries rose again, beseeched him, begged him – and suddenly he had no will left to stop himself from taking fate's path. *Mother Fula* drove him to pull on his boots and scrabble his wig and coat into a saddlebag. He shook the coachman and rapidly told him he was going back to the villa so he must bring the carriage back alone. 'A message come to me,' was all he could think to say.

Down in the stables the horsemen were snoring on bales of straw. He shook the youngest boy and held out a silver coin from his pocket. *'Cavallo,'* he whispered, remembering the Italian word he heard so often. The boy rubbed his crusty eyes and rapidly plunged the silver inside his rags. With barely a chink or slap of sound he prepared a tall brown horse and led him out of the stall into the yard. Soon Loveday was astride it, gripping the horse's reins with his hands and guiding its flanks with his knees. It was a crazed sort of journey to take alone at the dead of night, yet as he rode out of the sleeping city his progress was unexpectedly easy. Above him the silvered towers and arches of the fancy stone buildings were silent save for the echoes of his horse's metal shoes. He passed the brine-smelling port with its forest of masts, and then the horse turned towards the road he had travelled the previous day. With only the gentlest of nudges, it trotted quickly from the cobbled stone streets onto the dusty road back to Ombrosa, moving as effortlessly as a fish glides to its spawning ground. Loveday's long hair fell loose from his pigtail and lifted in the warm breeze, and his chest was bare of his tiresome coat. And *Mother Fula*, shining as cold and heavy as a disc of Portuguese silver, lit the road all the way to the eastern hills.

The night was still hushed when he noticed familiar outlines. A few torches flickered at the barred wooden gates of Ombrosa up on the black hump of the hill. Then he saw the pale blur of the ruined tower at the crossroads. Leaning over the horse's neck he whispered into its twitching ears and stroked them gently, before carefully turning off the road. The iron gates of Villa Ombrosa stood black and watchful above him. Loveday dismounted and tied his horse's reins to a tree. Then he pulled off his boots and hid them beneath a bush.

His bare feet knew the way through the grounds better than his eyes. Ignoring the noisy gates he slithered under a broken fence and felt at first the hard stones of the driveway digging into his soles, then the itchy spikes of rain-parched grass. The house stood cliff-high in the darkness. *Mother Fula* was dropping low in the sky now, her fat body hanging over the villa's pointed roof. He crept as silently as a snake around to the back of the house and the kitchen door. He halted there, sniffing the unfamiliar bitterness of ash and burned cloth. It smelled wrong; it smelled of badness and destruction. Then he slipped inside and found only dying embers in the kitchen grate.

In the dim glow he saw signs of bustle and mess about the place. Cakes were scattered untidily across the table, not as Biddy usually left them, in a metal cage to protect them from insects and mice. And the air was thick with a terrible and familiar scent. Whale *amber*. The sweet strength of it reached his nostrils like a crowd of haunting ghosts made solid. He covered his nose with his palm and looked carefully around the room that was lit by only the dying fire. The bread basket was overturned, and a patterned cloth lay on the floor. He picked it up and sniffed it; it had a faintly human smell.

Footstep by footstep he moved through the rooms and listened. The downstairs was empty, so he made ready to climb the stairs. Just then, his left foot felt something wet. Crouching, he dragged his finger through the stickiness. In the moonlight it looked as dark as tar. He slid his fingertip into his mouth. The metallic flavour was the familiar taste of blood. Without a sound he rose as tall and still as a bamboo cane. He listened for a long time, striving to catch every breath and shift of the house.

The house was silent – too silent for a house of sleepers. Where were Mr Pars' rattling snores? Or Bengo's yaps and whimpers? Feeling his way toe by toe, he climbed the stairs. When he reached the top he padded silently to Biddy's chamber. The door lay open, the bed not slept in. Next he visited Mr Pars' fusty room. His door also stood ajar. The shutters were open, and *Mother Fula* showed him the room was empty. All gone were Mr Pars' tottering piles of papers, his dirty clothes, and ink wells. Only a portmanteau and his precious strongbox stood neat in the middle of the empty floor. Loveday asked himself why Mr Pars might have left the house in such a manner. Sudden news? Yet whose was the blood? And what of his mistress? She would not have left her bed so near her birthing time.

He listened hard outside his mistress's door, but heard nothing. Then, as slowly as a thief, he turned the knob and opened it. At first he thought the room was also empty. The shutters were open, and moonlight shone on the chairs, the table, the bed. The bed – his heart leaped suddenly against his ribcage. She was asleep on the bed. Leaning forward he saw the profile of his mistress lying motionless on her back, a sheet raised above her breasts. Beneath his straining toes a floorboard creaked and he flinched. His mistress did not move. Then he smelt the fug of blood – deep purple blood, like a butcher's mangled leavings. He looked into her face and recoiled in fright. His mistress's eyes were staring open, staring right at him. He touched her arm. It was as cold as stone.

He needed to know if the baby had come, for the smell of woman's blood was strong. Holding himself rigid, he grasped the sheet that covered her corpse and lifted it. Even in the colourless moonlight he could see a tar-black gash across his mistress's white belly, an opening where no woman should open. The baby had gone, that was for sure, for the belly had sunk down from its straining dome.

His mistress's spirit must still be close, but what of the baby? Was it living or dead? He crossed the room to the cradle that Biddy had fashioned from a wooden box. Inside lay a tangle of damp cloths, but none of them blood-stained. He lifted one to his nose. It still held the sharp tang of piss.

He returned to Biddy's room and pressed his hand to the bedclothes. They were cold. The open shutters drew him to look outside at the back of the villa. Only a short time now, he said to himself. Baby soon die. Not knowing what else to do, he stood at the open window and breathed very slowly, trying to follow his *manger*, trying to clutch at the threads of knowledge that his spirit-seeking mother had passed to him. He heard the creatures battling in the trees, the chirrups of warning, and muted screams of unlucky prey. And behind that he heard insects whirring and buzzing inside their tiny cities in the trunks of trees and their palace-caves deep in the ground. And, even quieter, he heard the stream by his hut, warbling and splashing across the rocks. Then, there it was, very faint and far away. A baby's wailing cry.

Noiselessly, he took the path to his hut and there he picked up his harpoon that slid so sweetly into his hand. Once outside, he followed the sound of the baby, creeping stealthily beneath the black trees. As he grew closer another sound joined the baby's hopeless wailing. A sharp crunch and thudding rumble. Someone was moving something, over by the spiky trees that circled the Stone Garden.

The faint glow of a lamp standing on the ground helped him find them. He halted twenty paces away, sheltering beneath a thick-trunked tree. Now he could hear the figure puffing and groaning. It was Mr Pars, standing in a deep hole as he shovelled earth up to the surface. The baby was in the far bushes; its wailing had quieted to a mournful hopeless mewling.

Loveday felt he had fallen into the kingdom of dreams. His right hand tightened on the shaft of his harpoon. The stink of *amber* whale stones filled his nose like rushing seawater. The white man digging the hole was square-shouldered, hard-faced, a half-seen shadow. The name he had given to the first white man he had ever seen sprang from his memory: Scarface. The white man had murdered his tribe and enslaved his beloved Bulan and Burat.

Loveday's hand began to shake. The terror of that last night on Lamahona gripped him again. When he had confronted Scarface the man had made a terrible crack of sound like thunder that had torn a hole in his shoulder. Remembering that night made his bones go as soft as seaweed. Sweat filled his palms, and his harpoon slithered in his grip.

I am a coward, he told himself. I must quickly-quickly creep off in the trees before he see me. The gods have punished me because I have no courage to act like a man. Nothing has changed. He lifted the sole of his foot and started to turn away.

Just then the moon slipped off her skirt of cloud and shone triumphantly down upon him. The hole in the earth, the baby, the white man's grimacing face – all sprang before him in vivid pearl-white detail. For the first time he noticed a bundle tossed on the grass, just a few paces from the hole. The cloth was long and crumpled and a pale face peeped from its midst. The face belonged to Biddy. She lay on the ground as still and lifeless as an old sack.

Then the white man lifted his face, and his eyes gleamed in the moonlight. The white man saw him and his evil-eyes were like sparking blades that could jag your guts out, leaving you a soulless carcass.

'Hey!' shouted the man. 'Get away from here. Get back to the house you black dog!'

Loveday froze in the act of turning to leave. White man. Black dog. The sweet reek of ambergris sizzled in every part of his skull. Instead of fear, some other pounding force rose in his veins like a whale's impatient spouting. He had lost his wife. He had lost his son. Now he would lose his only friend. Biddy. His heart thumped, his ears buzzed, his mind rumbled like a mountain erupting firestones. Evil memories chased through his mind: of every beating he had suffered from a Damong club, of every man who ever *toknogud* to him, of every devil who ever called him rubbishman – he was going to *tok* em all back now. He turned back to face the no good white man. He, Keraf, father of Burat, lifted his harpoon in his strong right arm and aimed it at the white man's ugly cry-cry face. Then with true straight aim he let go of it and it flew like a runaway bird.

The white man tried to jump away like a cowering dog. Then he was spiked through the heart and fell backwards with a thump.

I kilim, Keraf thought. Now I no afraid bilong all time.

# XXXV

Keraf had waited beside his mistress's corpse all night. He had guarded her against the evil spirits that were free to roam since the two unholy deaths had torn an opening between the living and the dead. Last night he had buried Mr Pars in the hole, and set beside him the harpoon that had taken that wicked man's life. Beside his body he had laid out a portion of bread and meat from the dining room for Mr Pars' *kewoko*, his dead spirit's lonely journey. After that he had watched and waited beside his dead mistress. The moon had sunk low, and in the long time before dawn he had roamed the land of dreams where spirits walk freely. His own Bapa and Ema had appeared to him and looked on him with a kindness as sustaining as sugar cane. Then, as soon as sunrise had reached his eyes, he had felt a great inrush of relief and quickly fallen asleep at his mistress's feet. The two *kewoko*, the two dead souls, were freed from the earth. All had been done the proper way.

With a jolt he woke up to hear someone knocking at the front door. He jumped up, and the sight of his mistress laid out in the sun-flayed room hurt his eyes like bee stings. He felt like a man awakening from a long enchantment. He remembered Mr Pars' devil face bellowing at him. And he remembered how the big man had fallen backwards, his body as heavy as a swollen sack of rice.

The knocks began again. In this place murder-men strangled your neck with a knotted rope if you killed a white man. He crept to the front window and saw a young woman sullenly staring about; a plump and fidgety girl. Scraping his hair back into a pigtail and shrugging his gold coat over his shoulders, he clattered down the stairs.

When he opened the door the girl talked very fast in Italy-talk, then sensing his lack of understanding, walked right past him. When Loveday followed her into the kitchen she was already cradling the baby. It was still safe in the basket by the fire where he had laid it last night.

Memories, like *kewoko* wraiths, flitted through his mind. He had saved the baby, and then returned to the river to carry Biddy back inside. That had been hard, straining his shoulder and making him pant and sweat. Yet he had done it and felt the joy of victory as he got her upstairs and laid her on her small white bed. Biddy had been breathing slowly, though her head bore a blood-matted egg-like lump, and her spirit wandered in the land of nothingness.

Now, stoking up the kitchen fire, he watched the girl set the baby to a breast as fat as a paw-paw fruit. He smiled to himself as he brewed a pot of tea. It was all true. He had conquered that devil Pars and saved his friend and this innocent child. He need never be frightened again.

Upstairs, Biddy stirred as he set down a dish of tea. Her eyes fluttered open and she touched her scalp with probing fingers, crying out when she found the lump.

'Thank you,' she said hoarsely.

'Girl come feed baby now. You sit up, take tea?'

'Where's Mr Pars?' she whispered.

'He not trouble you now, Biddy. He gone.'

'You are sure of that? What if he comes back?'

'He dead now,' he told her. 'I plant him in earth where he dig hole.'

She nodded her head, though her mouth hung open and her eyes stared at nothing. He got her upright, and though she was as pale as a ghostfish, she told him all about his mistress's terrible birthing and Mr Pars' fearful attack on her.

'Thank you,' she said again. 'You saved me.' This time she took his hand in hers and squeezed it.

'You my friend,' he said, and she nodded fast, though he could see she was trying to keep her heavy tears inside her, like a sea-fresh sponge. Then her round wet eyes looked straight at him.

'You must cover him with soil so no one sees. You will be in big trouble if anyone finds out. He told me he was going to fetch a priest to bury Her Ladyship today. Oh Lord, I don't know what to believe any more.' She covered her mouth as if frightened to hear her own thoughts turning to words. 'I think we should get away from here as fast as we can.'

'In harbour place ship go Kochee,' he told her. 'I go Kochee then find other ship to Batavia.'

'Thank God for that. You must go, quick as you can.' She squeezed his hand again and he was sorry to leave the goodness of her. She truly was a pearl in a jagging reef.

'I ask and many ship go Dover place. P'raps you go England, my friend?'

She shook her head and winced again. 'If I go home I don't know how to account for it all. All them questions. Mr Pars, Her Ladyship – what do I say happened to them? How could I be innocent when the likes of them are all cold in their graves?' A flash of hope drifted over her face, like sun through a heavy cloud. 'Though maybe if I changed my name. Took the baby and called myself something other than Obedience Leigh. But you, you must get away as fast as you can.'

Then he fetched some bread and cheese and wine, and once she was setting to it with a good appetite, she told him to get Mr Pars' strongbox. Inside it they found letters and a great heap of gold coins, notes, and silver.

Biddy hurriedly read the top letter. 'Listen to this. It's that letter arrived just after you left for Leghorn.'

> *Marsh Cottage*
> *Saltford*
> *Cheshire*
> *30th March 1773*

*Humphrey,*

*I write with most dreadful news and forgive me I did not write sooner only I have been all shook up aforehand. Your brother Ozias was last week arrested by the constable's men and took off to Chester gaol. Then more men come back here and turned the cottage upside down, breaking my old chest and not paying any heed to our good name. It is a disgrace, by God, for they said they were seeking papers of yours Humphrey and worse, that they bore a warrant for your arrest on account of false Letters of Credit written in Sir Geoffrey's name. They say they have evidence of letters signed and dated after that time when the apoplexy left him not able to hold a pen, but I am sure they must be making a false case, for it cannot be true. It is that slippery John Strutt's doing, I am sure of it, for he has chased admiration ever since you gave him your position. They have now took away all your letters written to Ozias and said that all your correspondence had been secretly directed to the constable's men since some months back.*

*Thanks to God yesterday your brother was restored to me, and though still weak, he will mend I pray. Now Humphrey, I beg you most urgently to come home and prove your innocence to these wrong-headed men for 'tis all a pack of the devil's lies.*

*Humphrey, do write to me this very day and tell me when you may arrive to cleanse our family's name of this injustice.*

*Your sister-in-law and friend,*

*Martha Pars*

'So he was about to be caught after all,' Biddy said. 'Maybe that's why he – took his chance last night.' She shuffled through more papers, her face creased with disgust. 'Here he writes of Lady Carinna having run off with the money. Ah, and look at this –' she picked up a sheet in a neatly scribed hand '– "that wanton Biddy Leigh has a great belly from her lewd tricks." And here, written only yesterday, "On Easter Saturday poor Biddy died in her travails." How damned obliging of me. Mr Loveday, they make me sick. Throw them in the fire if you would.'

When Loveday returned from feeding the fire she was emptying the rest of the strongbox. Just touching the metal coins seemed to revive her.

'You must take half of it,' she said forcefully, counting two vast heaps of coins. 'I'm not leaving it here. Besides, we are owed our wages and more.'

To him the great heap of metal looked like chains that would weigh him down like a ship at anchor. 'That too much danger for me,' he told her. But he did hide four gold coins in his breeches for luck, and stuffed his pockets with small silver and copper coins.

'You rest now,' he was saying to her, when the sound of footsteps on gravel made them both jump like startled hares. The footsteps disappeared around the back of the house and they heard someone rapping quietly at the back door. He crept to the window and silently peered down. The small dark head of a poorly dressed boy was in view.

'Message boy,' he said, and puffed out his cheeks in relief to see no murder-men waiting.

Down in the kitchen the baby's nurse ignored Loveday as she sat with the baby stretched across her shoulder, patting its tiny back. He took two letters from the boy and told him to wait. Then once he had spied the writing on the top one he rushed back upstairs to Biddy.

'Look, Jesmire's hand. I send it from Leghorn. Says she not coming back.'

It was addressed to Mr Pars, but Biddy opened it and read it quickly.

'She expects her wages. And she's sending the carriage back with the coachman. Now that could throw us in hot water.' She dropped the letter in her lap and stared up at the ceiling. 'Let me think.' At last she said, 'Can you fetch me some ink and paper, Mr Loveday?' Then together they concocted a letter, she hunched up in bed, writing with scowling concentration, while Loveday uttered fancy phrases from all the letters he had slit in secret. When she had wafted it back and forth to dry the ink, they both read what had been written:

> *Villa Ombrosa*
> *11th April 1771*

*Dear Miss Jesmire,*

*I do most heartily congratulate you on obtaining a most suitable position and offer you every good wish for success in the future. Enclosed is a ten guinea piece in a twist of paper, as full and final recompense for your services. As to the carriage, you are at liberty to use it as you will, for Her Ladyship, having satisfactorily delivered her burden, has taken up the offer of travelling with an English family back to Dover. Loveday having now returned at my lady's summons, and having nothing to detain us further, we shall therefore close up the villa at the soonest opportunity and make haste to join our new companions.*

*Your servant,*

*Humphrey Pars*

*(Mr Pars does give his compliments but on account of an accident his right hand is badly bruised at present and he has asked me to reply to your letter on his behalf while he does dictate it. Biddy Leigh)*

'That very smart letter,' he told Biddy. 'She never come here again, she never ask question.'

'I hope not. Can you take it down to the messenger and tell him to take special care?' She had recovered her usual pink colour at last and was moving a little more quickly.

It was only when he returned that he remembered whose hand it was had written the second letter and felt his heart gallop as Biddy broke the seal and began to read it out loud.

*7th April 1773*

*Dearest Sis,*
 *I write of a most extraordinary surprise, dear girl, namely that at this moment I wait in Marseilles for a boat to Italy—*

Biddy slapped the letter down on the bedclothes. 'Marseilles! How can that be?' Then she snatched it up again and read it out loud very fast and breathlessly.

 *—Yes, sister, I shall be with you in four days, as the captain tells me we will dock in Leghorn harbour on Sunday after noon and I shall then make all haste and reckon to see you at eventide, Easter Sunday—*

'Lord God in Heaven, Kitt Tyrone is on his way!' Biddy threw her head back upon the bolster and cringed at the pain she provoked. 'Is it not Easter Sunday today? He will be here any hour. We may well hang for this.' She began to rise from the bed, trying to move fast but was still very stiff in her limbs.

'You go now? Back to England?' he asked.

'Maybe.' Then clutching her hand to her head she floundered back down on the bed. 'God help me. I cannot think clear at all. Only do one thing for me, friend.'

He gave a little bow.

'Let me at least be easy about you.' She looked at him with those pale round eyes he had once been so fearful of. White men's eyes can pierce your soul, the elders of Lamahona had said. It was true, he thought, but instead of destruction, Biddy's gaze fixed upon him with a stern love that he had to obey. 'I beg you, go now. I will follow soon. It is better we do not travel together.'

\*    \*    \*

He found the horse still tied to the tree by the gates. He led it to the river to drink, and felt the hurry and bustle of the water agitate his being. The right time to leave had finally come, and from now on he had to be like that river, never resting, never sleeping. The sun was dropping in the sky; noon had passed, and Mr Kitt's arrival was getting ever closer. Biddy had given him some drab workmen's clothes and a low-fitting straw hat. He felt the shining luck of the four gold coins protecting him as he mounted the horse and it set off back towards the coast.

He was a few hundred paces from the villa's gates when he heard his name being called out from behind him. There was Biddy, chasing after him, waving a letter in the air. She was breathless when she caught up with him, wearing no cap over her long hair and only a grubby shift on her naked body. But her despair seemed lifted; there was the shine of anticipation in her face, as if she had made a new resolution.

'Mr Loveday, would you do me a kindness and take this letter to the post house and see it is delivered at once? Here is a piece of silver.'

He dismounted and took it, standing before her. 'My true name Keraf,' he said shyly.

'Keraf.' She spoke the word, hesitating. 'Take good care of yourself, won't you?'

'And you too.' On an impulse he touched the springy curls of her hair. 'May the good spirits guide you, my friend.'

Suddenly she threw her arms around him and squeezed him. In a moment it was over; he felt happy and blessed.

'Now get on with you,' she said, smiling back at him. 'Go and give that lovely wife and boy of yours a right rollicking surprise.'

'Perhaps.' He mounted the horse again and caught up the reins; he was free.

He rode on down the dusty road, only halting a moment on the bridge at Ombrosa. Opening his saddlebag he pulled out the stupid wig that looked like a frizzled white monkey. With grim pleasure he flung it over the parapet into the river. Next he drew the gaudy coat from the bag and dangled that for a moment, only just remembering to rescue Biddy's letter from the pocket before he dropped that too. The coat and the wig were slowly swept into a fast-running channel. Then, like a pale bladder and a small hairy creature, they were gone.

He did not bother to read Biddy's letter. Now he had begun his great journey the affairs of white people, yarping like parrots, no longer concerned him. But as he left the letter at the post house with the silver coin, he casually read the name. *Signor Renzo Cellini.* He remembered how the big man had lifted Biddy so gently onto the white horse and watched her as if she was the only living creature in the world. Then the faint scent of briny sea reached his nostrils, and he took up the reins and thought of nothing at all but the strong tide of the road pulling him home.

# XXXVI

## Villa Ombrosa

*Being this day Easter Sunday, 1773*
*Biddy Leigh, her journal*

## ~ The best way for a bruise or swelling ~

*If the bruise be very bad apply a poultice; scald a basin then put in boiling water, then your bread and elder leaves and cover with a plate. When your bread has imbibed sufficient, drain it off and spread on a flannel and put on the bruise to supple the skin.*

> *From an Ancient Remedy given to Martha Garland by a much esteemed apothecary in Chester named John Delafosse, 1747*

Not long after the dust had settled behind Mr Loveday's horse, a priest and his company pulled up at the front door in a cart. The priest himself was flint-faced and shabby; I think Mr Pars must have offered a poor sort of price for the service. Yet they knew their business, and a terrible scuffling came from my lady's chamber, and soon after, a rough-hewn coffin was scraped down the stairs. I led them to the graveyard and pressed a handkerchief to my face for most of the burial. But there came one dreadful moment when I glanced into the gaping hole and saw Mr Pars' dead finger poking through the new-dug soil. I vexed the priest by reaching down and casting a handful of earth to cover it, quite in the wrong part of the rite. Just the thought of that finger still makes me shiver; the yellow tobacco stains I knew so well, and the murderous heft of his grip on my hair.

After all the tracing of crosses in the air and maundering chantings, the priest came angling over for his tip, rabbiting on as he held out a grubby palm. I had to go inside to fetch coin from the strongbox, and that's how I missed the setting up of the headstone. When I came back they were hoisting it upright in the soil. There was no doubting Mr Pars had paid a pretty penny for that quick piece of work. I thrust a piece of silver in the priest's hand and bid him farewell, hastening back inside. But it was not fast enough to stop myself from seeing the words commissioned by that wicked man:

*OBEDIENCE LEIGH*
*a Domestic of Mawton Hall, Cheshire,*
*who died at Ombrosa, Easter Saturday, 1773,*
*aged 22 years*

I felt the spite of those words like they were cut right into my flesh and bone. But I reckoned the Bible verse he'd had engraved beneath was chosen more for my mistress's sake than mine, intending that we'd share our grave together:

*If any desire to be first, the same shall be last, and servant of all.*

Servant of all! That was mighty Christian of him. It made me giddy to see my own memorial writ out like that. No, I would not bloody oblige him by dying, I repeated again and again. Still, it gave me the shivers, to see my own given name scribed in stone, remembering my death to all who saw it.

I sat all the rest of the afternoon on the terrace thinking half-crazed thoughts. I could not rightly reckon up what had happened – my mistress dead, old Pars avenged and buried with her. The horrors flashed and flickered in my eyes, more real than the terrace standing before me, like a devilish magic lantern that could not be snuffed out. I sat and sat, struggling to decide. Which way now, Biddy Leigh?

Slowly the sun set like a peach, and night hid the rows of lime trees. The iron gates and chalky road disappeared from view. My head still ached despite the poultice cooling on my brow. I pulled on a shawl; the night-midges were starting to bite.

I knew I should go. Kitt's letter lay curled on my lap. Kitt Tyrone. Handsome Kitt, with his buttons like guineas, and his sweet plump lips. There had been a thread between the two of us, that fond look we had shared in Paris.

Trotting hooves and a creaking axle made me start. I peered into the darkness. Thank God the horses passed. Inside, Evelina whimpered, and Carla whispered murmurs of comfort. It was a good sound, like a miracle after those terrible days.

From along the valley the single toll of the Ombrosa bell rang the half-hour. I got up and batted away invisible mites. There was a ship that sailed to Dover, Mr Loveday said. I had money to buy a passage and set myself up in London or any place I fancied. Now hark at that, I thought – with the money from the strongbox I could be a lady and never lift a finger. I could spend all my days in the plush upstairs world of crystal and silks and never creep back downstairs through the boot-scuffed door. And by Christ, I wanted it now. And I had the means to have it if I played my hand cleverly. I spun myself a tale of life as Carinna, flashing my gold on fashions and routs. In time the money would disappear of course, and then the credit. Oh, but the racketing journey to ruin would be a glory.

I steeled myself to face my lady's room. It was the work of moments to turn the cradle back to an innocent wooden box. A quick search showed Mr Pars had burned all my lady's goods – all those fine silks and feathers from Paris were ash in the wind. It sickened me that, his wanting to burn her very self to a cinder. Yet he had raked the ashes, so it was surely the ruby he wanted. He had known it was hidden and no doubt believed he would find it in a heap of riddlings. Well, Mr Pars, I said to myself, you had not reckoned with my years of hiding precious things away from others' snatching fingers.

Before I left I determined to leave Kitt a message that only he could read. Not a written letter, for that might be held up by a judge and used to send me to the gallows. So I pulled out the rose red gown from my bundle and set that upon my lady's wooden clothes stand. Will he remember it, I wondered, from our night in Paris? Then down in the kitchen I found Carla nodding in a chair with the baby contentedly nuzzling her breast. Her dreamy eyes lifted and she yawned very wide. She was not a tidy servant, for nothing had been cleared since morning.

'Eat what you will, then pack. I go out first, then we all go later,' I said.

'Where we go, mistress?'

I shrugged. 'I cannot say. Carla, let no one in. *Capisci?*'

'*Si*, signora.' And the lazy kiss she set on the top of Evelina's head made me forgive her slatternly ways.

My last batch of funeral cakes were still scattered all across the kitchen table. The scent of ambergris rose from the cakes, so musky and sweet it caught like raw spirit in my throat. With my back to Carla I broke each one in half till I found the ruby where I had baked it safe from greedy eyes. With a rinse in fresh water it was none the worse for its heating in an oven. That damned stone, it had brought nothing but ill luck to those who had owned it. So back upstairs I slipped the Rose into the front of the scarlet gown, along with Kitt's own letter from Marseilles. Surely, without spelling my message in writing, he would know I wanted the ruby to be his?

It was getting late. Washing my scalp I saw the poultice had started its work and the elder leaves had soothed my bruises. I had only one last gown of Carinna's to wear, with the dark cloak I'd kept in my own room. Then I got flustered by my lateness. Yet, would he even come? Mr Loveday's note might not have reached him, or worse – he might have read it and hardened his heart to me. I hurried along the lane, mouthing little prayers that he might come. As I reached the tower my heart pounded like a racketing drum.

No one was waiting for me. I wondered at the hour, and in answer, heard the ten long strokes of the church bell. Above me bats flittered through the night, faster than my eye could follow. Leaning against the warm stone wall, I tried to make my breathing steady, though I felt a great commotion at my centre. He will not come. The words repeated in my ears like striking hammers. I swallowed down the startings of a sob. To be weak now, that will never do, I told myself. For one day more you must be strong. I strained to listen for his coming, but only heard the slither of creatures in the dry grass, and the whispery crackle of cones shifting on the black cypress trees.

He will not come, I told myself. And now I was here beside the tower the prospect was so terrible that it seemed like a great black chasm that might any moment swallow me whole. I do not know how long I stood there, as desolation weighed upon me. Then the sound of hooves reached me from the road. I lifted my head, though I reckoned it a farmer heading back from the market. The horse stopped. I held my breath tight. Then came footsteps, and still I feared it was some stranger, or even Kitt Tyrone come to search out his sister's murderer. Finally, a great dark shape approached me, and I knew the square shoulders and steady gait.

'Renzo?' My voice was thick with unspilled tears.

I remember only reaching out to him like I was drowning. Then I was deep in his arms and felt safe for the first time in many days. He caressed my hair, stroked my back, and said, 'Oh, my darling one, my dear one, do not cry.' It was like going home, but not to any place I had ever known before.

He pulled back and looked at me, and his broad face wore such a look of kindness that it made me sob again into his chest.

'My Lady, Carinna. What has happened?'

His fingers returned to my hair and found the lump on my scalp. It was time to tell him the truth. I halted my tears, took a deep breath, and jumped into that unknown place.

'My name is Obedience Leigh,' I said. 'And what has happened is – thanks to God I am still alive.'

I told him the truth in a tumble of words – that my mistress was dead and that it had always been her notion that I pretend to be her. And that any moment her brother might come and discover all.

'Mr Pars was right, they will arrest me for it, I am sure. And her being poisoned stands against me. Who else to suspect but her own cook? I have thought long about it today. I must leave this place. Take the baby and go somewhere no one knows me.'

Still he held me. There was no loosening of his grip around my middle. But neither did he speak.

'And now I have told you all of it,' I said flatly. 'I am not the great lady you fancied I was. Renzo, I cannot employ you, I have no household. I am just – an under-cook.'

I tried to read his expression; his treacle black eyes moved across my face as if he tried to decipher a letter in a foreign language.

'So much that is new.' He began to walk away. Then he turned back to face me. 'So much not expected.'

He walked to his horse, and I had to hold myself back from running after him. He fussed with the bridle and my soul held its breath to think he might leap in the saddle and leave me for ever. Instead he looked back at me and I at him. My life seemed to hang on a dark giddy edge, but I had not the strength to pull myself back. He looked at me again. He smiled and gave a little laugh. Then he strode back to me.

'You are telling the truth. I know it. I am amazed but glad you told me. Yet, a cook!' He laughed. 'No wonder I try so hard to impress you.'

He took both my hands in his and said more gravely, 'But Bibi – the name is still strange – did you also pretend to love me?'

I told him my name was Biddy.

'Bidi? Bibi is better. Bibiana is the Italian way.'

Then I showed him my answer to whether I loved him as fiercely as I could. And when our lips parted I murmured, 'I love you, Renzo. It has pained me beyond measure to lie to you. You are my true love, I swear it.'

In the moonlight I saw his hesitating smile. He touched my cheek as if it was a rare flower. 'You have a new name. But Bibi, I have a question?'

'Yes.'

'Is there a Signor Leigh?'

'Why, my father, for sure.'

'No, no. You are a married woman also?'

A flutter rose in my chest like a new-released dove.

'No. That is why,' and I laughed for the first time in days, 'you have not had your full liberty.'

'So, Bibi—'

'Mmm.' I buried my face in his neck and felt his dark curls stroke my cheek.

'You are free to wed?'

I looked up and nodded.

'So, you will marry me? And come with me to my city?'

For a while my mouth hung quite empty with surprise.

'But you do understand I am not Her Ladyship?'

'Well in that case – I can always send you out to do an honest day's work.'

I belted him for that and he laughed and grasped my hand.

'It is you that I want. Not your rank or your money. So will you marry me?'

Then I said it with never a second thought. 'Yes, I will. Yes, yes I will.'

There was no time for rejoicing, we had to set off like the wind. I hurried back to the villa with love spurring my heels. Renzo arrived with a carriage within the hour, for he had long been ready to leave the count's household. There must be no more secrets, we agreed, so when I carried the strongbox down I told him it still contained the last of my lady's fortune.

'That is good,' he said, 'for I too have saved my wages and with our capital we can start a great trade in the city.'

Trade! I kissed him for joy and hugged him so hard that he pushed me away.

'Ah, those strong arms of yours, Bibi,' he mocked. 'Now I understand why you can squeeze me like a python.'

'I shall show you more than strong arms, signore.' I batted his arm in play.

He laughed and raised his arms like a man about to fist-fight. 'Oh, I am ready for you, signorina. We shall soon see who is the strongest.' And then the rogue poked me gently in a most amusing place.

\*       \*       \*

Bengo was a nuisance to the end. When we were waiting in the carriage, and all the candles snuffed and doors locked, that eternal botheration still would not come with us. He hid in the dining room – where to my eternal shame I had not had the spirit to clear up the Easter dinner. I knelt and did my best to entice him with a morsel, but he had a madcap fit upon him and led me a merry dance. One moment he crouched with his forelegs stretched, then when I came close he ran off in circles like a scalded piglet.

'Bengo! You will be left behind,' I snapped. For my lady's sake I didn't want to abandon him in that godless house, but when I tried to snatch him up he nipped my fingers. So I marched off and left him, for Bengo had never liked me, nor had I ever cared a beggar's scrap for him.

# XXXVII

## *Florence*

*Being 1773 to 1777*
*Signora Bibiana Cellini, her journal*

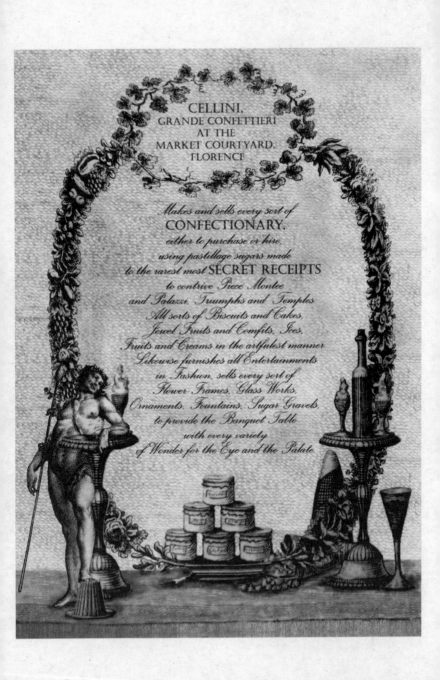

I can't say I took much heed of where we were headed. We piled into Renzo's carriage with all our belongings creaking and groaning on the roof, and Carla and the baby squeezed in a corner with Ugo at their feet. As for me and Renzo, we had eyes, hands and lips only for each other. I could have driven off the edge of the world for all I cared if I had him beside me. All through the early hours we talked in whispers of our lives, our hopes, our dreams. Never were two persons better matched, for not only was my sweetheart the most well-made and lively-witted man, but we were also well matched in ambition, in a world that had equipped us both at birth with naught but rags and moonshine. I'd waited a lifetime to meet this man and had often thought lovers' ballads the airy dreams of fools. But this man was flesh and hot blood. As dawn grew closer I was wary even of sleep, in case I woke and found I had dreamed him.

When we stopped at an inn the next morning, Renzo summoned a priest. Arm in arm we followed his shuffling figure through a shady wood; while all the time I marvelled at this great step I was taking. Had I lost my senses to find myself clinging to this man who I barely knew, in a wood I knew not where? Those advising words in *The Cook's Jewel* echoed in my ears: that the best of husbands should be a man of Virtue, Kindness and Companionship. Renzo was that man of my dream, I was sure of it, and my very best partner in what that quaint writer called the Labyrinth of Life. As he squeezed my hand I felt his strong fingers fit around mine as if we had been born twin souls.

'Do not be afraid,' he whispered. '*Carissima*, I will always love and honour you.' And in the dappled light of the wood he picked

353

me a ring of white blossom and set it on my hair.

Inside the church we took our place at the altar steps, shivering in the dank morning air. I understood only part of my wedding vows, for the priest spoke fast and the words were strange. But I repeated the phrases as Renzo prompted me, then I kneeled and bowed my head in prayer. All the while, as Renzo spoke very low and tender, I engraved the scene most carefully in my memory. I wore no bride's brocade nor even broke that blessed bride cake I had baked back at Mawton, yet to me my wedding was the great star in this story of my humble life. Feeling the hard stone beneath my knees, I recited silently, He is here, and he loves me and I love him. Then Renzo slipped the gold ring from his little finger onto mine and we were joined as man and wife.

Back at the inn we retired to our bedchamber. I stripped to my shift and waited, suddenly trembling in the cold bed. Meanwhile Renzo threw off his clothes and washed at a basin. All the while I still thought to myself – what dream have I tumbled into and when will I awake? And then I remembered the crimes of those last days, and I was suddenly as weak as a lamb, so when he came to me with flesh as hairy as a gentle beast, I clung to him all the tighter. What had I left but him? And he was all I needed, truly.

He warmed my cold body and was most tender in his caresses. So when the vital moment came, his face was above mine, watching me closely, his black hair damp and tangled over his brow.

'My love,' he whispered, his breath hot against my cheek. He kissed me lightly on my throat, my lips, my eyes. I traced his features, loving all I saw; and then we were man and wife and I was filled with joy to be a maid no more. And what appetites we had – for we had both been simmering all those weeks, and his every touch made my skin melt like gold in a fire. It took many lazy hours to satisfy our hunger, and dawn rose again before we slept.

\* \* \*

Next day it was hard to shift from the heaven of our feather bed, but Renzo said, 'We must make for the city. Tonight I will sleep at home with my bride beside me.'

By evening a vast city of glittering towers and domes lay before us.

'Look,' Renzo urged like a boy. 'Santa Maria. The Duomo.' High in the air stood a vast dome, the colour of apricot, with a globe set at its top. 'See, Bibi. The grandest church in the world.'

Once through the city gateway I gazed on houses bearing marble fronts, and every kind of magnificent carving. As for the churches, I never saw such precious stones bedded into walls, most especially that great Duomo all dressed with redstone, blue lapis and jasper, all of it so vast and lofty it cricked your neck to see the roof.

'So this is Florence,' I said, suddenly recognising the name of that place where the arts were so rich that all the world flocked to see them. Everywhere, red and white flowers decorated the wayside, as if news of our wedding had been sent before us. There were banners, too, of crimson silk unfurled from high windows, and in the vast piazza stood tented pavilions embroidered with gold.

'In Florence there is always a festival,' my husband told me. 'We have two carnival seasons, many saints' days, celebrations. At any excuse the people don a costume and open their purses, which we shall help ourselves to, for our marriage box.'

'So what do they eat, these festival folk?' I asked as my husband handed me up the steps of his house. I was very satisfied with it; for it had a neat and respectable appearance.

'Fritters, cakes, anything indulgent or exotic. They eat all they can.'

We smiled at each other in silent conspiracy. If people wished to eat, we were the pair to feed them.

Soon Renzo set up his workshop, employing workers to create his *pastillage* fancies. One night he made a great sugar paste temple for a nobleman's banquet, as vast as a shepherd's hut on its plinth. The Bill of Fare was lavish too: three courses of fifty-seven dishes assembled by four cooks, with my husband preparing the grand dessert. To help him decorate it, Renzo taught me to melt sugar and fling it back and forth on a knife tip until it formed a glassy thread. Moulded on upturned bowls it made half-spheres of sugar web as hard as crystal. Combined in pairs they formed globes of gold that we filled with bonbons and coloured flowers.

'We make the finest dainties in the city,' I murmured, 'and the orders are piling high.' I loved to tally our accounts nearly as much as I loved to make sweetmeats. Renzo was painting a sugar warrior, the tip of his tongue just pushed out as he gave it the face of the lord who commissioned the vast display.

'*Si*, but we need more room,' he grumbled. 'The sugar work needs to be kept dry so we can hire it out again.'

'Aye,' I said, doing a quick calculation, 'if we did that we could make many times more profits again.'

Then, as I passed into that happy state of contentedness as I worked, I thought, Ah, it would be like spinning gold. My heart began to race so fast I dropped a molten lump of sugar and spoiled it. A grand idea had formed inside my pushing mind. I told Renzo of how most of the travellers lodged at poor inns, or if they had deep pockets, paid rent on a *palazzo*. We knew why lodgings were few: to set up a hotel was expensive, risky, and a deal of hard work. Yet the benefits were many: we might easily give the best food to our guests, even English food should they wish it. And no one knew better than me the longing of travellers for cleanliness and neatness. In this same hotel we might also have a room for Renzo's lavish sugar displays. From a single kitchen we might serve both guests and banquets. As for bedchambers, they would be the best in the city.

My husband slapped his knee. 'We must hire a man at the city gates to guide them straight to our hotel, with a notice recommending our lodgings.'

'And write an Advertisement in those books of Grand Tours they read,' I cried. Our notions jumped as high and hot as nuts in a brazier.

Then it came to me, like a vision of heaven. 'Oh, Renzo,' I said, clutching his sleeve. 'We must have a restaurant.'

'Restaurant? What is that?'

'Remember, I told you of the superior dining rooms where the weak and moping go for a pick-me-up? The *bouillon*, the creams, all those over-priced healthful foods?'

'*Si*, and they will pay for it. As we say here, "If your mouth is full you cannot say no."'

'Yes, yes, they will pay even more for that – dandified way of dining. If we can do it, the business will succeed.'

We did it. Nothing venture, nothing have, they say, and there were never two people more hungry for success. With the coin from my strongbox and Renzo's capital, we bought a five-storey house over-looking the Arno river. We paced the high musty rooms, ignoring the coats of arms and moth-eaten velvets. Rather, we peered up the chimneys and measured the kitchen. We called it *La Regina dell'Inghilterra*, or the good old Queen of England. So I was then that elegant *Restauratrice* I had so admired in Paris. Gone were my servant's drabs; I was all busked up in French fashions to greet my guests like Lady Bountiful herself. 'Good evening, Your Excellency,' I mouthed like a perfect *magnifico*. By my stars, those at Mawton would never have known me. My hair was each morning piled high by my dresser, and pinned with flowers and jewels. My feet that never were the finest, were lifted on satin-heeled slippers. Even my poor fire-scorched arms were healed. Well, near to healed, for with fingerless mitts and a jangle of cameo bracelets, my maid said no one would ever see the scars.

The night we opened the restaurant the building near floated with light from crystal, mirrors and shimmering lamps: it was the *Maison de Santé* of all my dreams. We dazzled them with luxuries:

a golden striking clock from Switzerland, and a wine cistern filled with snow in the shape of a galleon. At the room's centre stood my husband's tour de force, a sugar paste Temple of Circe decorated with sugar globes. In a city that looks always to fashion we were at its head.

As for food, the wonder was that so many of our guests had no appetite at all. The beau monde rose late in the afternoon, taking only a cup of chocolate, and fretting that they could not lace their dainty clothes if they had eaten but one morsel of food. But from us they might take a thimbleful of *bouillon* for their health, or a dish of aspic to restore their complexion. So our guests did not fill their bellies but their noses, eyes and minds; and if they had to, they sampled the scantest peck of exquisite food.

Our English guests, those stocky, red-faced travellers, still demanded meat and pudding, beer and tea. Yet even our stout Britons had seen many wonders since first they boarded the Dover packet, so why should they not let their tongues follow?

'Honeysuckle iced petals,' scoffed one John Bull, spying my *menu.* 'I should as soon eat a bouquet of flowers. You must serve me solid belly timber, madame, nothing else.' Yet in one week I had tempted the old duffer with a restoring quintessence of veal. Then at dessert I caught him licking his spoon like a schoolboy as he scooped up a flower of my own exquisite honeysuckle ice.

After the hotel's first hey-go-mad season I fell to breeding and all slowed down. I had to loose my satin stays, and Renzo treated me like I was made of crystal. The first task of my empty hours was to write to my mother and Charity, enclosing a handful of gold coins. No reply has ever come back, but I send the money every year and pray it reaches them safely. The writing of that letter started up a right restless hankering to also write to Mrs Garland, for wouldn't she just burst to know of my being married and the hotel and all? So upstairs in our apartment, with all the racketing of our business carrying on below, I got to writing at last. I rooted about and found my old receipts stuffed into the pages of *The Cook's Jewel*. And I found Mrs Garland's best receipt for taffety tart, the very one I'd copied from her box, saucy article that I had been once. It was all in tatters, with butter blots and scabs of ancient pastry ground into the paper.

So it happened that instead of writing a letter, I scribed that receipt in my best hand and started up this journal. Receipt by receipt I conjured those dishes again. And I got to understanding that a Cook Book feeds the fancy like a dish of dreams. As I thought all this stuff, I scribbled my journal, for a letter could never contain all the news I had to tell. So I wrote of all my discoverings and adventures, and how it had all turned out in the end just like the perfect dish.

Then my time of danger came and I was delivered of a strong baby boy, named Giacomo after Renzo's father. He has Renzo's dark curls and stubborn cherry mouth, comically mixed with the mulishness of his mother. It is a delight too, to see Evelina dandle her little brother on her knee, for she is the fondest of creatures. Fond and simple, I should say, for though it pains me to write it, her wits are of the dullest. She is a lovely and a happy child, but forever slow and will never master her letters. But I would never change her, for she calls little Jack her own darling brother, and Renzo calls her his own daughter, too.

Yet each time I thought my journal near finished, some other surprise would arrive. One day as I dandled little Jack in one arm and read the Leghorn newspaper with the other, I started at a familiar name:

*At the court of sessions at Leghorn on 2nd July 1776 Mr William Dodsley was indicted for a Felony in taking to Wife Amelia Jane Jesmire on the first of September 1773, his first Wife Dorcas Bertram being then alive and living in London, England. Reverent Emanuel*

> *Trouvaine deposed that upon visiting the Mission in Leghorn he did recognise the prisoner drinking punch at the Regatta . . .*

I ran down to the kitchen and cried to Renzo, 'Goodness, listen to this for a tale.'

And I told him all the import, that this braggart Dodsley had pretended to be a retired sea captain of 400 guineas a year, and claimed to Jesmire that his hired lodgings were his rightful property worth £2,000.

'Ah, here is word of Jesmire's situation now,' I said:

> *. . . soon after their marriage he came to Amelia in want of money, which he demanded in Gold, for his Pockets disdained both Silver and Copper. Amelia, who is a lady of more than fifty years, told the court that she had lost a most genteel position to take up with Dodsley, and losing her most excellent connections in Italy had now no other way forward but to seek a domestic position; such of Dodsley's creditors having already claimed his goods against his debts. His first Marriage being fully proved by papers sent from London, the Jury found him Guilty and he was burnt in the hand with the brand of Bigamy and imprisoned for five years.*

'So that woman who scorned you has had her just reward,' Renzo said, snatching it from me and smearing it at once with veal stock. 'The world is just.'

'I am sorry for her,' I said. 'No, truly I am,' I protested, for he rolled his eyes. 'For she was one of us that left England five years past. And here am I, married to you and the happiest woman in the world,' and at that he looked as proud as punch, 'while she, the silly old trot – has been taught a sorry lesson.'

Yet always there was one of that band from whom I would never have news. How could I not remember him, when the cargoes from Batavia were unloaded at the market, drenching the air with the scent of cloves?

When I first came here I enquired which boats came from the

islands, and did any come from Lamahona? None could help me, though one jug-eared old sailor told me the Eastern Indies were made of five thousand islands and no map or chart could ever name them all. Five thousand. It is like searching for a grain of sugar in a pail of salt. Each nutmeg I grate reminds me of Keraf's island of plenty, heavy with fruits to be lifted and eaten from the branch. As I mix sweet spices I wonder where my friend is now, and whether reunited with Bulan and his son. I fancy he perches on his *prahu* boat out on the ocean, bathed in sunshine, hunting whales and rays and flying fish. I pray so, with all my heart.

Then I set down my journal and forgot it for one whole year. I was blessed with the safe delivery of a second son whom we named Renzo. He has a mop of hair with a copper glow, and was born with his first tooth cut.

Then an acquaintance arrived in Florence, and I found that my tale was not quite ended. I had pieced together my story from all the broken accounts and receipts, but like a squeeze of lemon in a rich sauce, one last sour note was missing.

# XXXVIII

## The Queen of England, Florence

*Being Advent to Christmastide, 1777*
*Signora Bibiana Cellini, her journal*

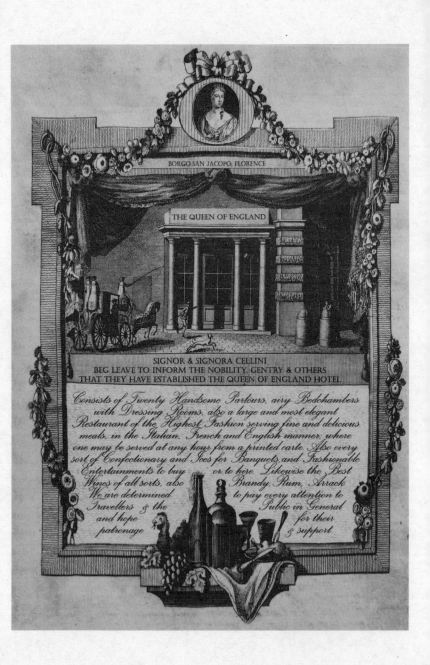

BORGO SAN JACOPO, FLORENCE

THE QUEEN OF ENGLAND

SIGNOR & SIGNORA CELLINI
BEG LEAVE TO INFORM THE NOBILITY, GENTRY & OTHERS
THAT THEY HAVE ESTABLISHED THE QUEEN OF ENGLAND HOTEL

*Consists of Twenty Handsome Parlours, airy Bedchambers
with Dressing Rooms, also a large and most elegant
Restaurant of the Highest Fashion serving fine and delicious
meals, in the Italian, French and English manner, where
one may be served at any hour from a printed carte. Also every
sort of Confectionary and Ices for Banquets, and Fashionable
Entertainments to buy ....... or to hire. Likewise the Best
Wines of all sorts, also ....... Brandy, Rum, Arrack
We are determined ....... to pay every attention to
Travellers & the ....... Public in General
and hope ....... for their
patronage ....... & support*

It began last year when the Earl of Mulreay and his mistress came back to lodge with us. The old fellow had just arrived in the city from the waters at Spa, his wrinkles powdered to the colour of decay, the outmoded patch stuck to his rouged cheeks.

'My dearest Mrs Cellini.' His touch was as dry as old hair papers as he lifted my hand to his puckered lips. At times he reminds me of old Count Carlo, but the earl would no more eat a viper than an oyster out of season. I had heard Count Carlo had snared some other heiress, poor creature.

'My Lord, have you seen our new *menu?*'

As we discussed each new dish I noticed the pretty *aventuressa* at his side appraising my costume. That was also new from Paris, a Polonaise gown in broad blue stripes, the skirts hitched up in milk-maid fashion.

'We have a Tiber sturgeon just fresh from the boat. Or a white Tuscan peacock. Or of course, if you care for something more homely, I have a taffety tart of quince and apples just baked.'

His grin showed the toffee-coloured stumps of the dedicated epicure. 'A taffety tart?' Clapping the silk-breeched spindle of his leg he smiled like an orphan promised a sugarplum. 'Bring us what you surmise your best, Mrs Cellini. And the taffety tart with – custard if you have it.'

I was standing half-hid behind a marble pillar watching my serving maid clear the earl's plates, when I heard him speak a name that knocked the breath from me like a cudgel. Without waiting to consider, I bustled over to the earl's table.

'Pray forgive me My Lord,' I said with my sweetest smile, 'but the name Tyrone just floated across the air to me. I know the man. Indeed, I owe him a debt of favour. I wonder, perhaps, if it is the same fellow?'

I donned a mask of simplicity as the earl told his tale. The English Braggadocio had arrived in Florence and reckoned himself a first-rate calculator at the gaming tables – but the local nobles had bled him dry. All I heard confirmed that this dupe was Kitt Tyrone.

'Yet to think of what I owe that gentleman,' I said, as plaintively as if I trod the boards of Drury Lane. 'Do you know how I might find him?'

A liver-spotted hand patted my arm. 'He lodges near the Coco Theatre. God will allow you to perform your good deed, only let the gambling fever abate, Mrs Cellini. He is a sick man. A little ready cash now would only agitate his brain.'

I retreated to my dressing chamber, but could not sit still. Kitt himself, and here in Florence. Unhappily, I recounted that he had followed his sister to Italy, and even more remorsefully, that his failure to discover her fate was my own doing. Yet why did the fool linger here? Oh Kitt, I beseeched out loud, catching sight of my vexed face in the looking glass. Damn him, I knew he was foolish and weak. God alone knew why, but I had to see him.

I gave myself no time to alter my course, only fretted that such an errand would enrage my husband. He might try to prevent me, might even suspect I was meeting a lover. So I will go in secret, I decided, for silence is best. Next I set on the idea of wearing an ugly black veil such as the local *donne* wear. The very next day while Renzo was out in the city I crept quickly out of a small gate at the back of the Hotel. In a black gown that matched my veil and plain leather slippers, I flattered myself I would pass for any modest Florentine lady.

The alley by the theatre was a dripping tunnel, stinking of ordure. I had to ask the whereabouts of the *Inglese* gentleman, of course.

Finally, an old woman pointed a bony finger up a set of stone stairs. I knocked at the door, got no answer, and slowly pushed it open.

Even through the lace mist of my veil I could see the room was of the poorest sort: a stained pallet flung on the cold floor, a window patched with paper. Then I saw empty bottles of raw spirit. And in their midst, as drunk as a tinker, lay the twisted body of Kitt Tyrone.

Pressing my veil to my nose I sank down on a crooked stool beside him and touched his arm. 'Signore,' I murmured. 'Wake up, Signor Tyrone.'

His eyelids rolled and finally opened.

'Who are you?' he croaked. I feared I must look like the angel of death in my pall of black lace.

'A friend,' I said, in a muffled tone.

He would not look at me, but seemed to be in a delirium, seeking points on the ceiling and walls. Then pulling the stained sheet over his shoulder, he rolled onto his side and blinked at the wall.

'I am a friend,' I urged. 'An English woman who wishes to help you.'

Still he faced the wall, where the marks of vanquished bedbugs made a grim design.

'Leave me be,' he groaned.

I sat awhile, confounded. Beneath the sweet fumes of liquor he smelled of sickness, the rotten stink of a truly ailing man. I decided I must take command.

'Signor Tyrone,' I said severely. 'You must come with me to a clean house and be nursed.'

Still he did not lift his eyes from his stupor. Vexed, I decided to surprise him by showing my face. If he knew me, I told myself, he would come to his senses. I threw back my veil, and for a moment was choked by the unwholesome air. Then I stood above him, my countenance open to his gaze.

But it was I who was destined to see how things truly were. His face was as pallid as wax in a tangle of wild hair, yet it was still Kitt's face that I knew so well. Beneath the startings of a rough beard were his cupid's lips, and though much sunk, the bones of his face still seemed handsome to me.

Then my vision shifted. It was his eyes that terrified me. I leaned over him, my face as clear as day, that face he had once called pretty. But his eyes still rolled and blinked without a sign of knowing me at all. Poor Kitt, for all my black disguise, was blind.

It was a terrible task to tell my husband about Kitt. When he returned that night from a banquet he had overseen, it was two hours past midnight. As Renzo undressed I told him of the tragic fall of my mistress's brother, and his mouth hardened into obstinate silence. Finally, he splashed his weary face with water and sat heavily on the edge of our bed.

'Are you trying to shame me?' he asked with a fast hiss of anger. 'A Florentine wife would never go to a man's house alone.'

It is true that Italian women do carry a heavy yoke of old-fangled rules. So I made myself very sorry indeed, pleading ignorance, and swearing I was merely trying to do good.

'It was an act of charity,' I urged. 'He is a stranger in the city, attacked by sharpers and somehow grown blind.'

Renzo sighed. 'It is wood alcohol that has blinded him. He should have known better.' But when I reached to throw my arms about his neck he jerked away out of reach. 'As should you,' he whispered, bitter with hurt. Suddenly I no longer knew where to place my hands. For so long they had found welcome peace around Renzo's broad shoulders.

'So tell me,' he added, his voice steely. 'When was this man your lover?'

I closed my eyes and allowed myself a silent hurrah of gratitude. Thanks to God I could tell the truth. Looking deep into Renzo's hurt gaze I said, 'He never was my lover. Think of it. You know that.'

With a grunt of agreement, he nodded. Then looking much like our little son Giacomo, Renzo scowled at the disobliging nature of the world.

'There are hospitals. If you send him there you will have done your Christian duty.'

It was true. Yet to think of poor Kitt dying alone in a foreign hospital – I could not bear it.

'No. He must come here. We have rooms. And God forgive me, but he will not be our guest for long.'

'Why, in the devil's name are you doing this?'

I scarcely understood it myself. It was a cold passion that drove me, refusing to be crossed.

'Guilt,' I said, suddenly looking away.

'In Florence we say "Guilt is a gorgeous girl but nobody wants her." Or in your case, perhaps a handsome man. Forget him. You will not be the first woman to shun her past.'

'I may never have another chance,' I said, and my voice cracked. 'He is blind. He is dying. We led him to Italy and it has cursed him. While for me it has been a blessing, for I have all this bounty, our children, and mostly you, Renzo.' I let my face fall on his shoulder. 'Let me pay a little back,' I whispered.

We sat entwined, each in our own thoughts for a long time, growing cold as dawn approached. As I pressed my eyes against my husband's solid shoulder I saw Carinna dead before me, laid on that white bed, her pale eyes as lifeless as glass. All my chasing of bustle and happiness seemed only flimsy shrouds laid over the horror of her wretched corpse. At last Renzo patted my hair.

'Come to bed. Yet I still do not see why we should have him,' he said. The fight had left his body.

'Because he is Evelina's uncle,' I said, and Renzo sighed, and I came to bed.

No one must believe that by taking in Kitt I felt any less for my husband. Renzo is my true love, the father of my beloved children. And thanks to him I run a great trade, and cook as I never could have done, back in England. Kitt is a different draught altogether. I know well enough now, that Kitt would have filled my life with despair. Yet the hours we shared in Paris do burn with a secret glamour in the calendar of my days.

Next day Kitt was moved into one of the hotel's rooms, and by dinner time he slept in a bed of fresh linen, the gauze drapes guarding his wretched eyes from the winter sun. I hired a gentle nurse, Francesca, and she sat sewing at his side. That evening I fed him myself, setting his pillows behind his back and dabbing his lips with a snow-white cloth. Alone, I studied his ravaged face.

'You need a barber,' I said. I held my fingers above the dark shadow of his cheek, but did not permit myself to touch him.

'Lady,' he said quietly, his eyes seeming to search for me but not find me, 'I need for nothing. Thank you.' His fingers suddenly grasped the bunched silk of my skirt. 'Am I in heaven?'

'No,' I laughed. 'You are in the Queen of England Hotel, Florence. With friends.' I patted his hand and loosened his pincer grip. 'Now sleep,' I murmured, standing to go.

Again he reached for my skirts but I had stepped away. 'I am afraid to sleep,' he groaned, looking about himself, but seeing nothing. 'For where will I wake?'

'You will wake here. The nurse will sleep beside you on a couch. You are quite safe.'

As I left he cried out as Renzo's dog came running to greet me at the door.

'Lady! I beg you, shut the door. Listen! Don't let it come inside.'

'It is only my husband's hound.'

Ugo scratched and whimpered at the door and poor Kitt recoiled.

'Great god has it followed me here?' he wailed.

I spoke to the nurse of his fear of the dog, and we agreed that his blindness must have given him an odd terror, for perhaps some wild dog had once found him alone. It was only a long while later that I remembered Bengo and got to wondering what Kitt had found at the villa.

He was with us only a week before he unmasked me. It was almost Christmas, and Renzo was preparing all the delicacies Florentines must eat at the festival: roast eels, goose, fancy cakes with marzipan frills, and a kind of minced pie they call *Torta di Lasagna*, stuffed with meats and raisins and nuts. As his nurse Francesca had leave to attend mass, it was I who was bathing Kitt's face one day with a cloth dipped in rosewater. By then I could look at his face without being overcome by miserable tenderness. His eyes were closed and his face was as sallow as parchment. I sighed more loudly than I should have, and pushed back a lock of his long black hair.

'That perfume. Is it you?' he asked. 'Not the nurse?'

Warily, I replied, 'It is Signora Cellini. The lady who found you.'

A wry smile tightened his lips. 'Is that the same lady who cried out last night when the loaves were burned that there "were nowt left to serve the guests"?'

My heart thumped as I listened to the movements in the house: the banging from the kitchen, the children chanting from the schoolroom.

'It is you. Isn't it, Biddy?'

His thin hand grasped mine, the veins like knotted blue string on a stretched fan of bone. For some while we continued in silence, clasping hands like innocent children. Then, in a low tone, I told him how I was sorry not to have found him sooner. 'It was good fortune you came here to Florence where I live.'

'For once in my life I was lucky.' His face grew clouded. 'For you did not wait for me at the villa, did you?' His grip was still tight around my palm. 'It was you who left me the jewel?'

'It was your sister's wish,' I whispered.

'Now tell me the truth,' he said, 'what happened to Carinna?'

I had little time left before Francesca returned, so I rapidly told him all I dared. How to hide her great belly Carinna had ordered me to act her character.

'Carinna was with child?' He looked suddenly bereft. 'Poor sis. And you Biddy, I thought you had changed much. Yet you always were sharp, I can see why Carinna used you. But what happened? I heard once that my uncle sent a man over to the villa, but there was no sign of her, or any of you. Is it true she left with a secret lover?'

'She died in childbed,' I said. 'Kitt, it was a terrible lying in. As for the child's father, he never came to claim her or the child. And to be so far from home—' But for pity's sake I did not tell the entire truth. That Mr Pars had fallen out with her as plotting thieves will, and she had died a poor suffering girl, with only us lackeys about her, and one of those her murderer. For the sake of her memory, I was too ashamed to tell him.

'Where is she buried?' Poor Kitt looked grey with pain.

'In the graveyard at Ombrosa. Oh Kitt, I am sorry to say the headstone bears my name.' I bit my lip as I saw his blind eyes move in agitation. 'To those who knew us, I was Lady Carinna. I am sorry.'

He turned his head away. 'And then you went on and prospered. Yet what does it matter?' His fingers loosed in mine. 'The dead child. Was it a girl or boy?'

At last I could cheer him. 'No, no. The child lives. It is a girl. I could not part from her. She is my daughter, Evelina.'

He turned his face back towards mine. 'What d'you say? Carinna's child is here?'

'Yes,' I whispered, for I feared his raising his voice. 'Only be quiet. My husband Renzo does not want you here. As for Evelina, she does not know you are her uncle.'

'I don't care who she thinks I am. Only bring her to me. Just once.' He clawed towards my sleeve. 'Biddy, you will do it?'

It seemed a small gift to give.

'I will bring her tomorrow.'

# XXXIX

## The Queen of England, Florence

*Being Christmastide, 1777*
*Signora Bibiana Cellini, her journal*

## ~ Minc'd Pies My Best Way ~

Mince two pounds of neat's tongues parboiled with four pounds good beef suet, a dozen fine chopped pippins and two pounds of sugar. Add spice as you will, not sparing a good pinch of salt to mingle savoury and sweetness. Stir with it four pounds of currants, dates stoned and sliced, a pint of sack, orange flower water and lemon juice and half a pound of orange and lemon candied and shred small. Mix these together well and fill your pies of diverse pretty shapes and bake until enough.

Bibiana Cellini, a receipt much favoured, Christmas 1778

To see them together was a strange thing. I told Evelina that Signor Tyrone was her uncle from England who wished her to visit him. Her nurse said it was proper to bring flowers to the sick, so together they bought a nosegay from a seller in the square. Violets, of all flowers. It seemed an unfortunate choice. I led her to his chamber and stood at the window, staring at a rare fall of snow that had settled in the night. Sunlight danced on the pink and brown *palazzi*, glittering on their crystal roofs. I pulled the gauze shut for fear of hurting Kitt's eyes, and watched from the window like a character in the wings of a stage.

Evelina was nearing five years old and losing the roundness of babyhood. In her striped muslin she looked to me the picture of a little lady, with a blue satin sash around her waist. It was only as I saw them face to face that I recognised the eggshell pallor of her skin and satin weight of her hair. Yet there was more than that: seeing her with her uncle I noticed she possessed a careless charm quite different from my two rapscallion boys. She looked at Kitt with bold curiosity and answered his questions as well as she might. He wanted to know how she spent her days, whether she was happy. In a faltering concoction of Italian and English she chattered of her brothers and her dolls and the snow she had touched for the very first time. I think I never saw a man's face burn more fiercely with feeling.

'Evelina,' he asked finally, 'would you indulge me?'

She giggled and looked over her shoulder at me.

'May I feel your face? For then I can tell how you look, even with my eyes not rightly working.'

Again, the little girl looked over her shoulder, and I signalled my agreement. She sat very still, her spine as straight as a rod from her new stays just arrived from Paris. Kitt's fingertips traced the brushed silk of her hair, her narrow brow, short nose and blinking long-lashed eyes. As he touched her mouth she giggled again, and he traced the smile that lifted two rosy cheeks. His fingers halted at the ruffle of blue ribbon tied about her neck. Strong feelings worked across his face, though whether pain or joy, it was hard to say.

'Come along, Evelina,' I said, reaching for her hand. I feared the meeting had overpowered him.

'Signora Cellini.' Kitt's voice was thick. 'Would you do me the courtesy of returning alone?'

I delivered Evelina to her tutor and dropped a kiss on the scented softness of her head. Then I returned with a choking heart to that gauzy white room. The little nosegay had tumbled on the sheet and he scrabbled for it. He could not settle till he held it tight.

'You should sleep now,' I murmured. Discomforting passions roiled within me: terrible pity, anguish, tenderness. 'I must get to the kitchen. Your nurse will be back soon.'

'A moment,' he croaked, pain creasing his brow. 'I want you to know. I am ready now to join Carinna.'

For a moment I could think of no reply. My conscience told me to comfort him, but what are hollow words in the face of death itself?

'You will meet again in God's presence,' I said.

Tears welled and overbrimmed his lids, running down his sunken cheek. 'No, we will not meet in heaven, Biddy dear.' His mouth twisted and he struggled to speak steady. 'This house was my only taste of heaven. I will be reunited with Carinna in a far worse place.'

'You have not been such a bad man.' I pitied him for believing himself beyond redemption. 'Christ will forgive those foolish sins.'

'Sometimes I think it is you who are blind,' he said with a grim attempt at laughter. He lifted the little posy to his nostrils and I too smelled cloying violets for just one moment. They were crushed in his hand, their lilac faces wilting around each yellow eye. The smell of them made bile rise in my throat.

'The girl, Evelina,' he said, as if he stared into his own open grave. 'When I leave this world, there is a pawnbroker's ticket in my saddlebag. Redeem it. It is for her.'

'That is kind of you. To think of your niece.' The violets cast their scent very strong then, and all at once I was back again, in the blue chamber at Mawton watching Carinna's tear-stained face as she chewed on violet pastilles. There had been a letter on the bed. From London, from Sir Geoffrey, we had all imagined. Yet looking backwards over all that time, remembering her tears, it must have been from her lover. She had tried to reply to that letter, she had hunted for words to confess their love – 'fire's heat', 'reckless taint', 'life's blight' – and then scratched at and blotted them, so that no other soul might ever read that unspeakable confession.

'Not my niece.' Grimacing with pain, Kitt turned away from me towards the wall. I heard him say it, though I wished I never had. 'My daughter.'

Christmas is different here. The Catholic way is to have a crib and characters all carved in wood lit up by ranks of candles. My husband embellishes it with sweetmeats, spun sugar and bonbons. It may be very pretty, but this year I miss the dancing and carousing I knew in England, the sweet oblivion of kissing and forfeits and all those harum scarum revels. Here on Christmas Eve we gather for prayers, and my husband serves plates of dainty fish, and gingerbread *panforte*. It is all very tasty, but it is not and cannot be Christmas.

So on Christmas morning I was up at five o'clock, making the fire as bright as a furnace, baking minc'd pies and boiling plum puddings the size of Medici cannonballs, and setting three sides of roast beef to turn on the spits. Soon I breathed again that steam that tells the soul it is Christmas, and all the year's work done, and time for feasting; the smell of oranges, sugarplums and cloves, all mingled with roasting meats. So eager were the English in Florence to eat their usual Christmas fare we might have filled another twenty tables. I even found mistletoe, and with Evelina made a kissing bough.

It was near ten o'clock on Christmas night when Renzo and I sat down in our dining room. The day had been a success, and even Renzo was quizzing me about my receipt for minc'd pies. The children were long abed, and we were toasting the year with the best Malvasia wine. I took deep draughts that night, for I longed to forget Kitt's words, whether in liquor or in hard work, either salve would do.

'So what is this kissing bough for?' Renzo said, affecting puzzlement. He led me to the crown of greenery where candles burned low and barely half a dozen berries stood unpicked.

My Renzo. He took me in his strong arms and kissed me as if he might eat me alive. I know I do rattle him, but in truth he is my entire life. What I have recollected this last season, daft article that I am, is what a good man he is. Virtuous, Strong, Companionable: the perfect husband.

'What say you to making more babies tonight?' he murmured as we stripped the bough of its last berries, one for every kiss. I smiled and pressed myself to him, feeling the fiery spell catch between us. It was a pleasure indeed to leave all the clearing to the servants.

It was not yet dawn when the nurse woke me. Leaving Renzo naked in our tangled sheets I slipped a shawl around my shift.

'Signor Tyrone is leaving us,' she whispered as I followed her candle down the stairs.

'Have you sent for the physician?'

'More likely a priest, Signora Cellini.'

I sat by the window as Kitt was given his last rites by a minister of the English Church. Outside the window the moon hung like a curved knife, shining silently amongst the stars. I shivered as I stared at the great snow-rimed palaces rising from the river. I believe Kitt may have been sensible when he took the last sacrament, and I know the papists would say he was shriven. But I do not know if he was, we shall none of us know till our final hour has come. Later I sat with him, but he did not know me; the rattle was shaking him by the throat. 'He is only five and twenty,' I sobbed into my clasped hand. As a heavy grey dawn approached I saw it was not sleep that blessed him with stillness. His face was more skull than flesh. Uncaring of what the priest or nurse might say, I kissed his lips and they were dead.

He was buried on a new plot set apart for the English of Florence. Every few months Evelina and I throw on our lace veils and take a carriage across the city. We take violets for remembrance, for the scent is not like any other flower. There is something of burned blackened sugar, of overcooked sweetness in their pulsing fragrance. Now I believe that by being abandoned together, brother and sister were trapped in a terrible love. A strange love it must have been, as unsettling as that charred scent of violets. What good fortune it is, that so many of us are spared such unholy love.

Evelina arranges the nodding purple flowers on Kitt's grave and I watch her, admiring her grace as she turns to smile at me. She will always know me as her mother, and is her papa's darling too. The secret of her birth is bound strong within the iron bands of my will. Not another soul will ever know it.

The pawnbroker's ticket led me to a dark wooden shop near the marketplace. The broker shot me a shrewd glance as he read it, then calculated a price based on my gown and jewels.

'Five hundred gold *lire*,' he spat out, and pulled his dark beard. I paid without hesitation, for the Hotel is a veritable money mill now. It did not surprise me when that vast sum was redeemed for a dusty leather bag no larger than my fist.

I waited until my return to open it, and sat with Renzo at the long table in our dining room. I dangled it from my fingers, and the

Mawton Rose spun and sparkled on its gold chain in the bright winter light.

'Oh, it is beautiful,' Renzo cried, trying to catch it as it turned by its own weight. It felt heavier than ever, as heavy as a convict's ball and chain.

'We don't need it,' I said. 'It is not a lucky stone.'

Renzo grasped it in his large fist and held it up to the sunlit window. Flashes of scarlet lit the room, like blood splashes spoiling our frescoed walls. 'You say he wanted Evelina to have it?'

'That was his wish.'

They are strange these commands from the dead. We feel they watch us from above, observing as we carry out their wishes. I could see my husband was bewitched, staring into the jewel's fiery core.

'Then Evelina must have it. She will marry exceeding well with a fortune like this. It was very good of her uncle to think of her. And you are rewarded for your charity.' I turned away. Of course Carinna's daughter should marry well. However slow her wits, with a dowry like the Rose she will join the highest rank of society.

'Very well,' I agreed, sliding the jewel back into the darkness of its pouch. 'Only we must lock it away in a bank vault. I want no one tempted by that stone again.'

# XXXX

## The Queen of England, Florence

*Being The Feast of San Lorenzo, 1778*
*Signora Bibiana Cellini, her journal*

# ~ To Make A Globe Spun With Sugar ~

Beat your sugar till well refined and sift through a hair sieve.
Put on a silver salver and set it aslant before a moderate fire.
Set close by two china dishes in shape like half globes with the
mouths set downwards. When the sugar runs clear like water,
take a clean knife and take up as much syrup as you can and a
fine thread will come from the point which you must draw
backward and forward as quick as possible and spin around
your china mould. Then dip your knife again and take up
more syrup, keeping spinning your web until it is done. Put
inside your web sprigs of small flowers, turn one web on the
other to form a globe, and spin a little more to bind the two
together.

> *A most remarkable dessert for a grand table,*
> *Bibiana Cellini, Florence 1777*

And now there is not so much paper left in my book for my ramblings. The letter from England arrived last week and it did not surprise me, only skewered my heart as I read it. How long it had been passed from hand to hand I do not know, for it was travel-stained and crumpled from many weeks stuffed in the post boy's bag. It came from the Montechino post house, bearing a message scribed by our former message boy, who now styled himself the Post House Clerk. He must have remembered our little coins and kindnesses, and directed it to Renzo's Florence address. I stared a long time at the writing; it was an awkward secretive hand, I thought, and not one used to corresponding:

> *To Biddy Leigh*
> *Villa Ombrosa*
> *Italy*
>
> *I know not if this should find you Biddy but 'tis sad news I write. Must be two year back, after a sad decline Mrs Garland died in her bed at Mawton Hall. There having been no news of you all so long we have given up I am sure. When Sir Geoffrey died at the end of '73 the parson did tell us we must wait on Lady Carinna coming home but you never did come back did you so now the magistrate has taken charge. He said that with her brother also gone away, it were a right mess as the uncle also claimed the right to Mawton. So all Sir Geoffrey's affairs be snarled up in the courts of London and not much hope of sorting them for years.*
>
> *One black day the whole place were stripped by the bailiffs and all Sir Geoffrey's fine old stuff loaded up on carts to be sold. After that me and Jem were sent off packing, which was a scandal and disgrace. As*

dwelling place we have called squatters rights over Reade Cottage down at Pars Fold. It is a leaky rattling place but Jem is trying to mend the roof, for we have no money spare now I am delivered of four naughty bairns forever mithering at my skirts.

Some say Mawton Hall has turned bad and will not wander there, but me and Jem go over the fence betimes to fetch them sweet fruits from the garden that's all grown to riot. 'Tis not a place to linger, the kitchen windows being all broke and the floors turned mouldy from a flooding. 'Tis all rack and ruin, even that old stillroom blows empty for all the fancy glass were took out and sold. A blessing it were Mrs Garland never saw the sorry end of it.

If this should find you, 'tis to tell you Mrs Garland did leave a testament which is here enfolded as all was carried out proper for we saw her buried with a headstone all paid up in Mawton churchyard. I am sending the Testament for she writes of you but spite us all looking there was no book as she talks of. We have done our duty Jem and me and we have no obligation to you that be the end of this business.

Mrs Teg Burdett

Within the letter lay a paper wrapped in oilskin, raggedly written in my old friend's well-remembered hand.

*Martha Garland of Mawton in the county of Cheshire who departed her life makes her last Will in the manner following that is to say that her Will is that she be decently and handsomely buried at Mawton Churchyard and to each of her fellow servants she gives a pair of white mourning gloves and when her funeral expenses be satisfied and paid her Will be that the remainder should be distributed to the poor of the parish of Mawton aforesaid, only save one thing being her Cookery Book that she wrote in be given to her Friend Biddy Leigh as a remembrance of her happiest years of industry shared.*

*All these matters aforesaid witnessed here unto my hand this 2nd day of January 1775.*

*Martha Garland*

I said this news was long expected. For a while I have wondered who *The Cook's Jewel* is for. I sit at my ivory desk and gaze out of clear glass windows, watching our riverman steer his cargo of lemons into our watergate. I hear Evelina chatter to her tutor in the next room, his bass rumble murmuring in reply. Jack is jumping up and down the stairs in a noisy clatter, and baby Renzo shrieking joyfully as Ugo barks. All about me the house chunners and hums. I grasp at the question again, for it is a hard one. Who did I write all this down for, I ask myself? To say I wrote for Mrs Garland, that is the simplest answer. Yet she was never likely to read these pages. When I kissed her soft cheek I knew it was the last time. Sighing, I wipe my eyes, for I will never kiss that cheek again.

I leaf through the older parts of the book. All those receipts and remedies, caudles and possets. Why collect them at all? That band of women stretching back in time, each giving their best pleasures scratched in precious ink. Men, they say, make wars, but women are more generous. Lifting that butter-stained scrap that bears Mrs Garland's taffety tart, she is conjured right before my eyes. When I hold the cinnamon smears to my nose I am back in that sunny kitchen at Mawton, lining up blue-glazed pots on the knife-scarred table. I could eat that paper, so much do I long to be there again.

I think of Mrs Garland's box of scraps, scribbled down like beacons against the coming darkness. Those women made their perfect dishes, then wrote them in forget-me-not words so we might taste them. My understanding glows, like the hollowed fruits Renzo fills with candles at his midnight feasts. What are receipts but messages from the dead, saying 'Taste me'. I am minded that when we eat, we eat a dish of love.

So did I write this great journal all for me? I have long suspected Mrs Garland gave me this task to help me on my way. What better method to help me forget my cares than to call up each day as it passed and write it down by rushlight. Yet as I tuck my handkerchief back in my flowered pocket and watch the light grow dim on the river I have an odd thought. Who am I now? Am I still that

Biddy Leigh who set off six years past? Am I still that raw-tongued clod-hopping chit with a brain bursting with old receipts? No, I am Signora Bibiana Cellini. I would scarcely know myself, for my jewelled fingers are pale and neat from my dresser's attentions, my face powdered, and my waist grows thick as another childbed approaches. I search for a thread that leads from that day when I crimped those taffety tarts at Mawton, to today as I tuck my diamond-buckled shoes beneath my desk. The thread is as thin and brittle as spun sugar. For now I am loved, I am as whole as two half sugar globes spun back together as one. I have made life in my dear little children. I have tasted life. And I have touched the rotting chill of death.

So Mawton stands empty; our kitchen invaded by wind and rain, the tall windows shattered, its brick carcass rotting. Even Sir Geoffrey's ancient paintings and furnishings are sold and scattered like the wind. I wonder if that tale has come to pass, of a white lady who walks the dark plantation path to her ruined stillroom. I understand more of Lady Maria's tragic history now, her husband poxed near to madness, the numberless babes conceived and lost, her passion for herblore hiding a darker quest. Here in *The Cook's Jewel* I've found pages of Remedies against Contagion: the sassafras oil, the cordials of henbane and wormwood. Pitiful Lady Maria, the curse she carried to Mawton was surely the love and avarice she stirred in young Humphrey Pars.

How far away I feel from rain-washed England, from Mawton and its mossy churchyard. 'Tis a pity I cannot visit my dear friend's grave, though I fear if I did I might fall sobbing on the ground. It reminds me of another graveyard too, back at Ombrosa. Outside, the sun has dropped below the roofs and brings the golden hour of sunset. The sky blazes like polished copper and our riverman is but a silhouette of black in the gloom.

The sun must be setting there too, on that lonely headstone at Ombrosa. It must be setting on the long white road to the villa, and on the faces of the statues that watch on the lawn with unseeing stony eyes. The sun must be leaching too, from the cypress trees, casting black spikes against the violet sky. The inscription may have faded, grown mossy in the barren ground. 'Obedience Leigh', it says. Obedience Leigh is dead, I think. Yet not so dead as the poor bones that lie there, coupled by greed, unvisited by any.

The boatman is a mere smudge in the dirty gold of the waters now, setting out toward the further bank. The house has quieted. The last shaft of sun escapes in a beam and quickly dies. And I am glad of this book I have written for you, my curious reader, this memorial of love that celebrates the dishes of the dead.

# Acknowledgements

This story was originally inspired by the wonderful kitchen at Erddig Hall, near Wrexham, and its collection of handwritten recipes. I then set off on a thrilling journey, both geographic and gastronomic, from Cheshire to Florence in the company of Biddy Leigh. My greatest debt is naturally to those shadowy figures who wrote down their recipes in Household Books or in early printed books. In addition, the following books and people deserve a special mention:

Elizabeth Raffald, *The Experienced English Housekeeper*, (Southover Press, 1996)

Gilly Lehmann, *The British Housewife: Cookery Books, Cooking and Society in 18th Century Britain*, (Prospect Books, 1999)

Hannah Glasse, *First Catch Your Hare (1747) The Art of Cookery Made Plain and Easy*, (Prospect Books, 2012)

Rebecca Spang, *The Invention of the Restaurant: Paris and Modern Gastronomic Culture*, (Harvard University Press, 2000)

Robin Weir, Caroline Liddell, and Peter Brears, *Recipes from the Dairy*, (The National Trust, 1999)

Laura Mason (Ed.), *Food and the Rites of Passage*, (Prospect Books, 2002)

Janet Theophano, *Eat My Words: Reading Women's Lives Through the Cookbooks They Wrote*, (Palgrave Macmillan, 2003)

Stephen Mennell, *All Manners of Food: Eating and Taste in England and France from the Middle Ages to the Present*, (University of Illinois Press, 1995)

Barbara Ketcham Wheaton, *Savouring the Past: The French Kitchen and Table from 1300 to 1789*, (Simon & Schuster, 1996)

Laura Mason, *Sugar-plums and Sherbet: The Prehistory of Sweets*, (Prospect Books, 2003)

Piero Camporesi, *Exotic Brew: Art of Living in the Age of Enlightenment*, (Polity Press, 1998)

R. H. Barnes, *Sea Hunters of Indonesia: Fishers and Weavers of Lamalera*, (Clarendon Press, 1996)

Journals and letters of eighteenth-century travellers are my particular delight, especially John Byng and Tobias Smollett's acerbic opinions of inns and their outspoken views of foreigners. I also owe debts to Samuel Sharp, Hugh Walpole, and James Boswell for their accounts of European travel, and to Hester Lynch Piozzi for details of dress and social nuance often missed by her male contemporaries. Servants' diaries are uncommon, but John Macdonald's *Memoirs of an Eighteenth-century Footman: Travels 1754–1779*, (Routledge, 2004) is a gem, describing a servant's world of good eating, merrymaking, and opportunities for travel and romance at his master's expense. In Macdonald's own words 'I thought my life was heaven upon earth.'

The guide book followed throughout is Thomas Nugent's *Grand Tour*, (Ganesha Publishing) originally published in 1756.

Biddy speaks a Lancashire dialect in part remembered from my late granddad Alfred Redvers Hilton's reminiscences, bolstered by the glossary of John Collier ('Tim Bobbin' or 'The Lancashire Hogarth') in *A View of the Lancashire Dialect*, (Lightening Source UK).

I would especially like to thank the following people for their help and inspiration: Ivan Day for a last-minute place on his Georgian Cookery Course, and the freedom to discover Taffety Tart in his library, and also for the treasure trove that is www.historic-food.com. Thanks also to the Lace Wars re-enactment group for the chance to discover what a skilled task cooking over a fire is. Philippa Plock and Rachel Jacobs of The National Trust were also kind enough to allow my husband and me access to Baron Rothschild's Tradecard collection at Waddesdon Manor, Buckinghamshire.

## Acknowledgements

My fascination with Indonesia stems from the childhood memories of my late mother Mary Witsenburg, whose family lived in the former Dutch East Indies from the 1750s. Thanks also to Mr Piter, of Floressa tours, for insights into magic and ritual on the fascinating island of Flores, and to my sister and brother-in-law, Marijke and David Snell, who braved that trip with me.

Two writer friends, Elaine Walker and Alison Layland, provided priceless feedback and inspiration at our monthly meetings. Yvonne Hodkinson and Lucienne Boyce also provided timely feedback and support. In New Zealand, thanks go to Philippa Branthwaite and Anne Cullen, while Nancy King generously provided a perfectly timed Creative Arts Scholarship at Muriwai Earthskin. My sister, Lorraine Howell, sparked my interest in eighteenth-century costume, and this book is in some part a product of our shared childhood obsessions. Similarly, my former teacher, Stuart Horsfall, reminded me that I was already writing this story at the age of ten, and needed to get it finished. My late father, Derek Hilton, who sent me enthusiastically scribbled recipes, was often in my thoughts. For their crucial encouragement and belief in the novel, thanks to Ella Kahn and Sarah Nundy at Andrew Nurnberg Associates, and Laura Macdougall at Hodder and Stoughton. And for ceaseless encouragement over the years, thanks to my son Chris, and my husband Martin, the latter for also tirelessly reading my manuscripts.

# HISTORY LIVES
## at Hodder

From Anya Seton and Mary Stewart to Thomas Keneally and Robyn Young, Hodder & Stoughton has an illustrious tradition of publishing bestselling and prize-winning authors whose novels span the centuries, from ancient Rome to the Tudor Court, revolutionary Paris to the Second World War.

———

Want to learn how an author researches battle scenes?

Discover history from a female perspective?

Find out what it's like to walk Hadrian's Wall in full Roman dress?

Visit us today at **HISTORY LIVES** for exclusive author features, first chapter previews, book trailers, author videos, event listings and competitions.

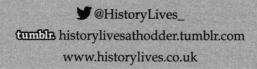

@HistoryLives_

historylivesathodder.tumblr.com

www.historylives.co.uk